A. Moody Stuart

Life and Letters of Elizabeth Last Duchess of Gordon

A. Moody Stuart

Life and Letters of Elizabeth Last Duchess of Gordon

ISBN/EAN: 9783337016562

Printed in Europe, USA, Canada, Australia, Japan

Cover: Foto ©Raphael Reischuk / pixelio.de

More available books at **www.hansebooks.com**

LIFE AND LETTERS

OF

ELISABETH LAST DUCHESS OF GORDON.

ELIZABETH, LAST DUCHESS OF GORDON.

W H Mote sculp.

LIFE AND LETTERS

OF

ELISABETH

LAST DUCHESS OF GORDON

BY

REV. A. MOODY STUART

AUTHOR OF 'THE THREE MARYS,' 'CAPERNAUM,' ETC.

THIRD EDITION.

LONDON

JAMES NISBET AND CO., BERNERS STREET.

1865.

CONTENTS.

VI.—HUNTLY LODGE.

VII.—STRATHBOGIE.

VIII.—THE CONTINENT.

IX.—THE CASTLE PARK.

X.—THE END.

CHAPTER I.

THE GOOD LORD BRODIE.

" As sometimes in a dead man's face,
 To those that watch it more and more
 A likeness hardly seen before
Comes out to some one of his race :

So . . . now thy brows are cold,
 I see thee what thou art and know
 Thy likeness to the wise . . .
Thy kindred with the GREAT OF OLD.

But there is more than I can see,
 And what I see I leave unsaid
 Nor speak it, knowing death has made
His darkness beautiful with thee."

      IN MEMORIAM.

A

IN the troublous times of the unhappy Charles I., and within four years of his lamentable death, there lived at Brodie, in the county of Moray, a Scottish laird of ancient family in the prime of manly youth; a man singularly attractive and loveable, whose one woe seemed to be that "all men spoke well of him." He was himself twenty-eight years of age, his son James a boy of eight, and his daughter Grissel a girl of nine. The children had been bereft of their mother when only three and four years old; their father had been widowed at twenty-three, and he took upon himself the responsible charge of their training. For his own loss, being convinced in the depth of his sorrow that no earthly joy could ever repair it, he earnestly besought the Lord to give Himself as a portion instead; and having been assured that he had heard the prayer and sealed the exchange, he walked with God in a not uncheerful widowhood for forty years; remembering every year the anniversary of his bereavement, till death recalled him to the fellowship of the sainted wife of his youth.

THE LAIRD OF BRODIE passed his quiet days in bringing up his children in the nurture and admonition of the Lord, praying in his family, catechizing his servants, counselling afflicted souls, warning the unholy, suppressing vice, promoting schools, and feeding the poor. Indoors he read many books in theology and history, and spent much of his time in secret prayer and meditation; out of doors he was occupied with building farm-houses, and planting, grafting, and pruning trees; in sunshine with securing the stacks of corn for winter food and the stacks of peat for winter fuel, and in rain with the oversight of his workmen hewing stones in the quarry and fetching them home for his various buildings. He enjoyed the esteem and affection of all his neighbours for his justice and his charity, hospitably entertained strangers, honoured all that feared God, but avowedly contemned the vile, and consistently testified for the faith once delivered to the saints. The Most High had set a hedge about him and all that he had; the candle of the Lord shone upon his tabernacle, and the dew lay all night upon his branch.

From the Castle of Strathbogie, the ancient seat and fortress of the Earls of Huntly, there often sallied forth at that time the youthful and bold marauder

LORD LEWIS GORDON, whose wayward mood seems to have been a trouble to his family, as his arms were a terror to the neighbourhood. Though lauded by his friends as fearless in fight, he had the character of attaching his followers by shunning the foe in the field and plundering the peaceful and defenceless home. They rejoiced in victories that enriched them with booty at little cost of blood, and extolled his attractions in the rhyme:

"If you with Lord Lewis go,
    You'll get reif and prey enow;
If you with Montrose go,
    You'll get grief and wae enow."

Descending from his rocky stronghold, Lord Lewis made a winter raid upon the fruitful plains of Moray; where he fell first and suddenly on the fair lands of the Laird of Brodie, with their quiet mansion, pleasant trees, and thriving home-farm. Rifling the house of what was precious for a spoil, he destroyed or carried off the ancient charters of the family; whilst his followers ravaged the farm-yard, with its well-cared for stacks of corn, and loosed the cattle from the stalls, or drove them from the fields for a booty. The stores of peat prepared for the household hearth lent a ready fuel to the aggressor, and he burned to the ground mansion-house and mains, barn, stable, and dovecot, till of all that was pleasant to the eye of the man of God, in his own and his forefathers' cherished home, there was left only a black and smouldering waste.

The good man murmured not, but bore all with
submission, meekness, and hope. He fled with his
boy and girl, and took refuge in the house of his
cousin at Lethen; which they fortified first with such
outward defence as they could command, and then
with earnest supplication and the dedication of themselves anew in solemn personal covenant to God in
Christ. The Lord accepted the sacrifice, and the foe
withdrew from the unavailing siege. The father and
children came forth from their hiding-place, but only
to visit the desolation of many a cherished remembrance and many a budding hope, and to find themselves shut up to the Lord alone as their refuge, their
one help in the time of need.

Winter passed into summer, the marauding foray
gave place to the bloody field of battle, and there the
restless Lewis was not to be found. But his eldest
brother, George Lord Gordon, who was much beloved
by his kinsmen and vassals, drew around him under
Montrose the well-mounted gentlemen of his powerful clan, and with a valour worthy of a better cause
led them into battle against the Covenanters at
Alford. After a successful onset on one part of their
army, he dashed forward against another in a final
and triumphant charge; but in the crisis of victory

he was pierced by a ball from the retiring foe, and fell dead from his horse into the arms of his comrades. The triumph passed in a moment into the bitter weeping and loud sobbing of the brave over their fallen chief. They embalmed the body and conveyed it with a strong escort to Aberdeen, where they buried it with military honours in an aisle of the old cathedral; his next brother, Lord Aboyne, died in exile; and now the roving and impetuous Lewis was Lord Gordon, and at his father's death became third MARQUIS OF HUNTLY.

A hundred and seventy years passed away; a cycle of seven generations had run its course at Brodie since the darkly memorable day of the Gordon Raid; and George, afterward fifth Duke of Gordon, was then the gay and handsome MARQUIS OF HUNTLY. Inheriting the military zeal of the family, he had served in the army under the Duke of York while quite a youth, and had fought in various sieges and battles abroad. In the alarm throughout Britain that followed the French Revolution, his father, Duke Alexander, undertook to raise a regiment in the north of Scotland, and the offer was gladly accepted by the Government. By his active personal exertions, chiefly amongst his numerous tenantry or his own and the neighbouring clans, backed by the flattering smiles of the Duchess in enlisting the recruits, he formed in

little more than three months the noble regiment of
the 92d Gordon Highlanders, of which the young
Marquis was appointed colonel. By him the regiment was nine years later led into a bloody conflict
with the French in Holland, in which the Gordon
men fighting hand to hand put their foes to flight;
but only after their young chief had been disabled
by a gunshot wound in the shoulder, and obliged to
retire from the field. The ball was soon removed, but
it took years for the red wad of the charge to work
itself out through the flesh and leave the wound to
heal. After this battle the Marquis returned home;
and although employed in the army both in Ireland
and Scotland, and advancing to higher military
honours, he took little further part in foreign warfare.

In Scotland Lord Huntly's lot had not fallen, like
that of Lord Lewis, amidst the civil commotions of
the reign of Charles I., but in the peaceful times of
George III.; and unlike his wayward ancestor he ran
no warlike raid through the plains of Moray, and
brought back no forceful prey to replenish his Castle
at Huntly. But the gallant soldier made a better
conquest. In the ever strange circling of events, he
sought and won the hand of the young and beautiful
ELIZABETH BRODIE, the subject of the present Memoir,
and conducted his bride with festive rejoicings to his
ancestral home in Strathbogie. There she shone a

far nobler treasure than the ancient spoil of her father's house; for in due time she was called to inherit the untold riches of that father's grace, and so to shed a brighter lustre on the coronet of Gordon than it had ever worn before, illuminating it with a heavenly radiance ere it was buried in her tomb.

LORD BRODIE'S DIARIES.

In a memoir of the Duchess of Gordon, some notice is due to the family of Brodie; for Brodie House, though not her own, was her father's birthplace, and having herself no children her cousin of Brodie was her heir as next of kin. Her grandfather, Alexander Brodie, held the distinction of Lord Lyon of Scotland for many years, towards the middle of last century; and the name of her aunt, Lady Margaret Brodie, wears a memorable badge of mourning through the melancholy fact of her having been burned to death in a second but accidental conflagration which consumed the family mansion eighty years ago.

But the most noted in all the family was her ancestor Alexander already referred to, who lived in the time of the Charleses and of Cromwell. He was commonly called LORD BRODIE, as one of the Judges in the Court of Session, although he did not serve long in that capacity, and had no opportunity of becoming distinguished in it.   But he was much respected as a man of talent and high character ; was a ruling elder in the Kirk of Scotland, a Member of Parliament, one of the Scotch cited to London by Cromwell to attempt a union of the two kingdoms, though he declined the call, and one of the Commissioners sent abroad for the recalling of Charles II.   His great distinction, however, was by grace; for the memory of the just is always blessed, and the fragrance of their character gives them a memorial through all generations, even in the cold annals of the world. In his case that memory has been specially preserved by means of his Diaries, which were partially published in a small volume in the last century, and much more fully last year in a quarto of six hundred pages printed by the Spalding Club.   As this book may be in the hands of few of our readers, we are induced to present some extracts from its pages ; both because the Duchess of Gordon was deeply interested in the Diary, and earnestly desired its publication twenty-five years ago ; and because there were closely resembling features between her own and her ancestor's character, as well as between the religious histories of the periods in which they lived.

After the dangers and immediate privations attending the burning of his house were past, Lord Brodie's losses were more than repaired by a watchful providence, as he thus records: "My estate was made desolate, and no place left me, nor means to subsist; and my dear friends and Christian brethren were besieged and blocked up, and in fear of their lives by Huntly. But when we and our race and family were in other men's appearance ruined and undone, then did the Lord begin in mercy to blink and raise up, and lifted up our head. He made every affliction to me a rosebud for smell and sweetness; and withal was adding to my outward estate sometimes one thing, sometimes another." His most permanent grievance was in the family charters and all his papers having fallen into the hands of his foe. But any direct inconvenience from that source was remedied by Act of Parliament; and the chief loss to his successors was of documents that might have thrown light on the history of their ancestors, who are supposed to have received the lands of Brodie from Malcolm IV., about the year 1160. Notwithstanding, the family tree descends from the reign of Alexander III. through the long period of six hundred years; and the present Brodie is the twenty-third in direct descent from Malcolm, Thane of Brodie in 1249.

In the heritage which a good man leaves to his children, a moral resemblance may often be traced even through intervening generations. One of the

most marked features of character alike in Lord
Brodie and the Duchess of Gordon, with an interval
of two hundred years between them, was extreme
kindness of disposition which led them both to do
good to all men as they had opportunity, striving in
every way they could to be of use to any. The temptation attending that kindliness was often lamented
by the Duchess, as her besetting sin of trying " to
please everybody ;" and is expressed by Lord Brodie,
as if they had been brother and sister, in what he
calls " the facileness and plausibleness of his nature
by which he laboured to please men more than God,"
and against which he thus earnestly prays :

" Oh remember the prayers at Clatt and since, that
Thou wouldst set my heart against, edge the affections
against complying with any evil or appearance of evil.
Fill with discerning and zeal that I may not care for
men, nor self, nor safety, but may offer up all for and
to the Lord. Oh for light, conviction, strength, encouragement in Jesus Christ. O Lord, my heart has
to do with this devil : All men speak well of him :
Woe unto you then, saith the Lord. I have made this
my aim, at least it has been a strong, dreadful temptation ; I have been loath to incur the ill report and
opinion of men, or to displease them, but have been
for pleasing all men, complying with all men. Oh
for strength and uprightness to be emptied of secret

self! ... These, these are the sins, the lusts, the idols which I desire to slay before the Lord. Where is the knife; where is the fire to burn them? They are readier to burn me and kill me, than I to kill them. Lord, these or my soul must be presently killed and undone; break in therefore forcibly and effectually. Let me be hated, persecuted, torn in pieces by the world and wicked men ere I sinfully keep silence at, consent unto, approve or comply with any wickedness.

Persuasions, as—	*Answer to them all.*
1. Yield a little to the time.	
2. Save thyself and thine.	' Get thee behind me, Satan.' "
3. Art thou wiser than such and such ?	

There are a hundred similar struggles recorded by Lord Brodie against his " facile and complying" disposition; but there is another element frequently mingled, as in the following confession: " I found my niggardly and saving nature encroaching, and I feared to be overcome with it, and made my supplication to God for grace to escape." Partly from difference of natural disposition, and partly from diversity of providential circumstances, it was quite otherwise in this respect with the Duchess of Gordon; and if she had likewise filled a large quarto volume with diaries, there would probably not have been found in them all one of those complaints of niggardliness which flow by scores from Lord Brodie's pen ; for her temptation was always rather to a generous disregard of money. But whatever he had to strive against within, it must not be inferred that he was not liberal by grace, as well as most conscientious both toward the Lord and toward the poor. " I was counting with tenants of this bounds. Lord, help me to sobriety, moderation, charity, compassion, tenderness in dealing with poor tenants, and to do to others as I would have them do with me, if I were in their room and place." This is taken from his son's diary, but quite agrees with various remarks about poor tenants in his own. When in London he makes the following entry : " My heart did challenge me that I could so freely lay forth money for books, plenishing, clothes to myself, and the like, and was so straitened and loath to lay out for the Lord. Oh ! what does this presage and witness, but that I am of the earth and believe not ! . . . Moved with (Lord) L.'s want, I gave him the lend of some money ; I desire to do it to the Lord."

Lord Brodie never lost a lesson of contentedness, whether from children in the parish-school or from Red Indians across the Atlantic : " The storm of water detained me in Forres ; I saw the children of the school act and personate the two great vices of pro- digality and covetousness, and saw something of the evils and nature both of these and other deficiencies.

. . . An Englishman came to me this night. By him I heard much of the Lord's providences in New England, the richness of his goodness, the variety of his wisdom; also the misery of the poor infidels, that by all they enjoy do not know nor acknowledge the Lord, but worship the devil that is frequent among them; yet is their land for outward things better than ours, although they make small use of it. Oh that, as these infidels are easily contented with food and a little clothing, desire not land, care not for it, that I were so also, and could learn something from them!"

He had great delight in his grounds, and when in London was fond of inquiring after new plants: "At noon, I saw beyond Bishopgate a variety of trees, plants, flowers, and seeds, that I had some desire to have." But having sown acorns and planted birches at Brodie, and having watched the young trees growing into beauty, he thus records their sudden desolation: "This day came Captain Deal and his troop, and quartered on my land in their march. They destroyed the young oak and birch, which I had sown and planted in the little park. Now this was in my estimation a very great loss: but by it the Lord reproved my too much care of my planting and young tender trees, and my too little care of the desolation of his Church, ordinances, and people, which are his delight; my taking too much pleasure in these outward comforts, and he would have that mortified; my not trying to cherish the cause of his vineyard, which was far more beautiful and delightsome than my perishing plants."

His diaries are full of touching examples of the most sensitive tenderness of conscience: "It was put in my thought to go and visit a sick woman, that I might have that occasion to speak a word for the Lord; but I did not obey, for which my heart was smitten. Oh so fearful a thing as it is to refuse or disobey the Lord's Spirit in a motion to any duty! I desired to be cast down under this, and to go back next day. . . . I prayed in (Lord) Warriston's family yesternight, but oh so little solid grace; for there is much difference betwixt that and a gift of prayer that passes like water through a spout. . . . Hervie gave out an ill report of me, and in this I acknowledge the Lord; for I had earnestly flattered and commended him, and used carnal policy that he might not report ill of me, and now he thus requites. . . . I called (Archbishop) Sharp Lord; I desire to examine if I sinned in it. . . . I read something of the romance of Cassandra, and was so impotent that my affections were wrought on more by these inventions and fictions than by truth. I desire to be instructed and know what the importance of this is; Lord, teach me what is lawful, and what sin is in it." When in London he bought many books; and on one occasion he examines himself afterwards with self-distrust, because he found the books he had bought that day were almost all in history or literature, and few in theology, which seemed to him to indicate a declining of soul.

Not the least of the employments in the life of the Duchess of Gordon was taking and transcribing notes of sermons, of which she has left a very large number. This strongly developed taste was quite hereditary, for Lord Brodie left not fewer than four volumes of sermons, many of them by the most eminent ministers of the time. Amongst these are sermons by Rutherford, Gillespie, Henderson, Hutchison, Leighton, Blair, Dickson, M'Kail, Guthrie, and about fifty other ministers. They are all, however, written in a short-hand that has not been deciphered. After hearing the celebrated Andrew Gray of Glasgow, on the occasion of the baptism of Lord Warriston's son, he makes one out of many notes on renewing his covenant with God: "This day I did again enter in covenant solemnly, and gave in my name, consent, subscription, and acceptance of the Lord Jesus to be my Head, Lord, Husband, Guide, my All in all. Being required by Mr. Andrew Gray in the Lord's name to declare if I would refuse him or not, I said before the Lord I could not refuse, but with my heart gave over myself, poor, miserable, sinful, weak, ignorant as I am, to God

in Christ to be his. Little use can he make of me ;
but if he can, His I am, and shall be, totally, perpetu-
ally, thoroughly, if he will be at the charge to maintain,
confirm, make good and perfect his work in me."

At that time Lord Brodie was honoured with the
freedom of the city of Glasgow, and entertained by its
burgesses with an abundance of good things in eating
and drinking, such as he had not found at the tables of
the noblemen and gentlemen whom he visited by the
way. This profusion, in which that city still rejoices,
he describes in the following homely fashion : " This
day I was made a burgess of Glasgow, and saw some
plenty of God's creatures, and the finest, and the
strongest, and the sweetest. Oh so little as meat pro-
fits ! The meat for the belly, and the belly for meat,
and both for destruction." A seasonable memorandum for the rapidly increasing luxury of our own day.

In the course of his journey from the north, there
is one notice which subsequent events have invested
with a very peculiar interest : " We came to Moulin
in Athole. There did we acknowledge the Lord's protection in bringing us over these hills ; and we prayed
for that place, where we saw much ignorance of God,
and unkindness and inhumanity to ourselves. Oh the
gospel's coming in and being received, would reform
and change their nature !" The good man was moved
to pray for the people, because they were so ignorant

toward God and so inhospitable to himself; and that not in a hopeless unbelief, but under a lively impression of the glorious change that would be wrought in men so barbarous by the entrance of the blessed gospel. A hundred and fifty years later the minister of that parish, who married one of Lord Brodie's own descendants, was the Rev. Dr. Stewart, afterwards of Edinburgh, and father-in-law of Sir John Herschel, of whose closing days this characteristic anecdote is told : Being unwell, he sent for Dr. Gregory, who announced, with much expression of sorrow, that his case was one of danger, to which he made the memorable reply, " But, doctor, is there any danger in going to heaven ?" Dr. Stewart, when first settled at Moulin towards the end of last century, was a high type of what is called in Scotland a moderate minister. But the prayer offered of old was heard in the Lord's own time. The minister had been awakened to earnest desire ; and the glad tidings of salvation came home to his soul in connexion with a visit of Simeon of Cambridge and James Haldane, whom he called " messengers of grace." The gospel came with saving power to the pastor and then to the people ; and so changed and refined them, that they became more noted for grace and the beauty of love and holiness, than they had ever been for ungodliness and inhumanity.

Lord Brodie's deep sense of the deadness of his own

and the surrounding parishes, and his setting apart special time to pray for power from on high to descend upon them, were all literally renewed again in the Duchess of Gordon : " I purposed on the day following to set myself apart to seek for this, that He would cause the gospel to have a full and free course, as in those lands where it is not received, so particularly in this poor country. Oh! my soul cannot tell the fearful judgment of a dead, ineffectual ministry. I found much corruption, unsoundness, and darkness ; the case of Auldearn and Dyke was my sole burthen ; that the Lord would shine in on this dark place, and breathe on these dead bones, is one of the great desires of my heart. . . . This evening I prayed for the setting up of the Lord's work in the dead North-country. I desire to be affected with the withered, cold, dry state of Dyke and Auldearn : Oh! does there fall any rain upon them ?"

There is more introspection in these diaries, and less of a simple looking to Jesus than believers now seek to cultivate, in which we have run into the opposite extreme to our great loss. But they are full of Christ, though in a rather different form. The following sentences represent, as exactly as words can describe, the thoughts of the Duchess of Gordon at one period of her life, alike in the darkness and longing, and in the subsequent rejoicing : " The Lord Jesus is hid from me, and I cannot stand or be established out of him ; if he be hid, my soul may give over and renounce salvation, safety, and defence. And is he not hid from thee, O my soul ? Is he not unapplied ? Is he unbeautiful, unmade use of, lying by ? Once the Lord Jesus was known to be the All in all ; that I may never unknow, forget, nor unlearn that, is my soul's desire this day. Therefore will my soul wait, breathe, look, pant, and desire to believe ; and in the meantime renounce all confidence, hope, or comfort out of him, and shall desire never to be at rest until he appear. . . . Oh, good news ! my soul shall bless thy name for ever and ever. I dare not question but thou wilt forgive and hear. Ere I come to glory and my journey's end, I will spend much of thy free grace ; what in pardoning, what in preventing, what in convincing, what in enlightening, what in strengthening and confirming and upholding ; what in watering and making me to grow ; what in growth of sanctification, knowledge, faith, experience, patience, mortification, uprightness, steadfastness, watchfulness, humiliation, fruitfulness, resolution, self-denial, discerning of snares and avoiding them ; what for the public, what for the private, what for the family ; what against snares on the right hand and on the left. O Lord, I can conceive thy grace to be above and beyond my need and wants : Lord, let me see the sufficiency of it."

HIS SON AND DAUGHTER.

The care that Lord Brodie took 'of his own soul was extended to his children and grandchildren, which makes us wonder the less at finding the same grace appearing in his family even in our days. " I spoke a word this night to the children, and inquired at them if they desired to serve a good master, and were willing to give up themselves, soul and body, to God, to take him to be their Father, their Master, their God, and to engage themselves to be his children, to do his will, that he may serve himself of them whilst they lived in this world. They professed that they desired it and were willing. . . . This night I did before the Lord admonish, examine, reprove, and exhort my daughter ; and that it may the more deeply sink in her heart, I caused her to write down her confession and purpose and promise with her own hands. 'This day I desired to give up myself again to God ; it is my heart that I desire to give him, and not my tongue only. I desire not only that the Lord would be witness, but that he would be cautioner and surety in this covenant, that by grace I may overcome. This Lord's day I have taken new resolutions upon me to be the Lord's wholly, and not to live any more to sin. And in sign and token of my unfeigned desire and purpose, I have in the sight of God subscribed this confession and covenant with my heart and hand.—GRISSEL BRODIE.'"

As with his daughter, so there are many records of
his dealings with his son James. "My son's first
covenant and my offering him up to God was registered in my first diary book. But my first oblation
was as soon as he was born, even before his baptism;
and then at the Lord's solemn ordinance of baptism,
where he received his mark and seal upon him to
be his. Having yesternight put the family in mind
of their duty, and stirred them up to prepare for a
solemn fast against this day, we acknowledged our
sins and made supplication to God for forgiveness.
My son acknowledged his sins were more than all, for
none had such means of knowledge, nor had been so
often and solemnly engaged to the Lord. This is not
his first vow to God, and he therefore took shame to
himself for his forgetfulness and slackness, and promised himself anew to be the Lord's, and to walk
more closely with God than ever." In the same
manner his son's wife, a daughter of the Earl of
Lothian, subscribed her covenant to God on the
third day after their marriage : "28 *July* 1659.—My
son was married with Lady Mary, and on the 31st
she did subscribe her covenant to and with God, and
became his and gave up herself to him."

Lord Brodie frequently laments the want of the

fruit of holiness in his family, but much of that regret is probably of the same character as his grief for his own defects. " I was told of my son's irreverence and incogitancy in time of prayer and divine worship," is one of the earlier records of this kind; but he afterwards grew up to be a man singularly devout. His daughter Grissel having been married to a neighbouring proprietor, James and his wife Lady Mary with their children lived under his father's roof. The arrangement was not always agreeable to the young people, and at one time they asked for a separate establishment of their own. Lord Brodie, while willing to grant this if necessary, felt it most deeply, because he had given his whole life to his children; and they lived on happily without any change. After the restoration of Charles II., in which he was actively instrumental, and to whom he was ever intensely loyal, he was in constant fear of fines and even forfeiture on the charge of favouring conventicles; so that he once thought of resigning the estate to his son, but he was not called to make the sacrifice. He died in 1680, in his sixty-third year, seeing his children's children walking in the way of the Lord, and through his instruction entering into covenant with their God. His last words to his son were, " My son, be strong in the Lord and the power of his might; my son, to the law and to the testimony."

James Brodie took up the broken thread of his father's diary on the very day of his death, and carried it on with similar watchfulness and spirituality. The son honoured his father with an intense affection, and embalmed his body as " the cask which kept a noble jewel; the body still united to Christ, and therefore to be taken care for, to rise again in glory though sown in corruption."

The controversy regarding the exclusive headship of Christ over his Church in matters spiritual, which issued in the Disruption of the Church of Scotland in our own day, was carried on, not perhaps more earnestly, but in the midst of more violent measures in those early times. In substance it was the same question, whether in things purely spiritual Christ or Cæsar was to rule in the Church; but then the State went a step further, not only controlling the appointment of ministers and the ordering of worship, but compelling the people to attend on the ministry and worship appointed by the civil authority. In the case of the Duchess of Gordon, and many in later times, there was no trial except the reproach of the cross, but for the Laird of Brodie and his lady there was the addition of pains and penalties. He did sometimes go to hear ministers in whom he had no comfort, and from whom he derived no profit. " I staid this day at Elgin, and heard Mr. James Straquhan and Mr. Turnbull of Inverness. Alas! are not such given in wrath? Are these the Lord's ministers, servants?" But his partial conformity did not save either himself or his lady from citation before the Court as " delinquents." Lady Mary's deposition is the briefer of the two, and is in these terms :

" *Elgin*, 3 *February* 1685.—In presence of the Earls of Errol, Kintore, and Sir George Munro, Lady Mary Ker, Lady Brodie, being examined upon the libel, declares she abstained from the church till September last, and that Mr. Alexander Dunbar was a servant in their family, and has prayed and read the Scriptures there when the Laird of Brodie has been from home. Depones he was a servant to the Lord Brodie, and was recommended by him to the Laird, and that the Laird used to exercise in his own family himself when at home. Depones she has had no children baptized irregularly since the Indemnity, nor been at nor heard conventicles, nor entertained any vagrant preachers since that time. The Lady Brodie, being examined upon oath, depones to the truth of the above written declaration in all points. MARIE KER."

James Brodie having also been examined, the following judgment was delivered : " The Lords of the Committee of His Majesty's Privy Council having considered the deposition of the Laird of Brodie, whereby he confesses half a year's withdrawing, and the keeping of an unlicensed chaplain, and the Lady

Brodie's deposition, whereby she confesses three years' withdrawing and more after Lord Brodie's death, at which time they became heritors and masters of their own family: They therefore fine and amerciate him, for his own and his Lady's delinquencies, disorders, and irregularities, in the sum of £24,000 Scots money."

In the Diary the record of this severe fine, for his own and his Lady's delinquencies, is made by Mr. Brodie in these submissive terms: "One of these days I was fined in two thousand pounds sterling, or £24,000 Scots. The world has been my idol, and covetousness the root of much evil, and the Lord justly may punish in this." Walking together in the fear of the Lord, and suffering together for the sake of Christ, they died in peace together nearly twenty-five years after these events, presenting in this respect a great contrast to the long widowhood of the elder Brodie. Lady Mary died only a few days before her husband, and they were interred together according to his dying request, his last words of direction being that he might be buried with his Lady on the same day. "They were lovely and pleasant in their lives, and in death they were not divided."

From so truly noble an ancestry sprung ELISABETH BRODIE, the last DUCHESS OF GORDON; and when we recall it we marvel the less, yet rejoice all the more at the grace that was so conspicuous in her. Her greatest ancestor recorded that he would not be detained "one hour from glory, to see those come of him in chief honour and place in the world." But how his soul would have rejoiced, could he have foreseen one "come of him" so highly honoured and useful in the Church of God; and how he would have marvelled could he have anticipated her using all for the Lord, yet advanced to "a chief place in the world" through her marriage to "Huntly," a name so memorable in his Diary as the source of his heaviest calamity, and prayed for only as numbered among his enemies.

In connexion with this genealogy, there is another element of interest worth noting. The wife of Dr. Stewart of Moulin was Emilia Calder, whose mother, Margaret Brodie, was aunt to the Duchess of Gordon. This relation moved that man of God to bear his youthful cousin as a special burden before the Lord, and to engage others to pray for her salvation, especially after she was called to occupy the high position of Marchioness of Huntly. And so the prayers of the minister of Moulin formed a link in the conversion of the Duchess of Gordon, even as the prayers of her forefather, Lord Brodie, had been made a link in the conversion of the minister of Moulin. "This also cometh forth from the Lord of hosts, who is wonderful in counsel and excellent in working."

CHAPTER II.

ELISABETH BRODIE.

1794–1813.

" And what if there be those,
   Who in the cabinet
Of memory hold enshrined
   A livelier portraiture :
And see in thought, as in their dreams,
   Her actual image verily produced :
Yet shall this MEMORIAL convey
   To strangers, and preserve for after time,
   All that else had passed away ;
For she hath taken with the Living Dead
   Her honourable place,
Yea, with the Saints of God
   Her holy habitation."

                       SOUTHEY.

ELISABETH, last Duchess of Gordon, was born in London on the 20th of June 1794. Her father was Alexander Brodie, a younger son of Brodie of that Ilk; who returned home after acquiring a large fortune in India, purchased the estates of Arnhall and the Burn in Kincardineshire, and was elected member of Parliament for Elgin. Her mother was Miss Elisabeth Wemyss of Wemyss Castle, a grand-daughter of the Earl of Wemyss; and her grandmother, Lady Betty Wemyss, was one of the Sutherland family.

Her early life, though possessing little notable in itself and bearing no mark of grace, may help along with some later incidents to bring out the features of natural character by which grace is so modified in every child of God. The first six years were passed at Leslie house in Fife, and were rendered memorable to her by the early loss of her mother. A sun-dial in the garden, with its flight of broad steps, presented to Mrs. Brodie's eye a fair and tempting seat; and she availed herself of the pleasant rest, not dreaming of the cold death that lurked for her beneath the surface-warmth and brightness. The fatal stone struck disease into her frame, for which she was taken to Wales, not to return again but to die. The child was only six years old when thus left motherless in the world. Her solitude was the greater, because she had already lost an only brother in his infancy, and her father now remained to her alone. Of a parent removed so early, it was impossible that she should retain a very defined or lively remembrance ; yet she never forgot her, and kept to the last what she called "her mother's box," in which were found after her death little reminiscences of her mother, and of her own infant days.

Leslie House is not far from Melville, the residence of the Earls of Leven ; and Lady Leven took a warm interest in the motherless girl, and maintained it till after her marriage. But before her mother's death, the three young Ladies Melville had Eliza Brodie for their companion, one of them having been born in the same year with herself. After their respective marriages their lots were cast far apart, and they seldom or never met, but they were dear to each other as the children of one heavenly Father ; for the four companions of childhood were all made partakers of a grace that was " exceeding abundant with faith and love that is in Christ Jesus." They were all of the seed of the righteous, for Lord Leven had married one of the Thornton family, so noted in the Church of Christ in England, and the Countess, his mother, was one of the most eminent among Scottish Christians.

One of their remembrances of those early years in Fife was of a poor man seeking alms who, before eating the food that was given him, asked a blessing in these weighty words, which were found after the Duchess's death written on a small slip of paper in her own hand : " Lord, give me grace to feel my need of grace ; give me grace to ask for grace ; give me grace to receive grace ; and, O Lord, when grace is given, give me grace to use it.—Amen."

After her mother's death Miss Brodie stayed for some time with her maiden aunts at Elgin, a happy mirthful child, robust in frame and vigorous in mind, extremely amiable, but possessed of a strong and resolute will ; wanting less than most girls a mother's arm to lean on, however much she needed a mother's eye to guide. She was not strictly fettered by her kind old aunts, but allowed to run about in a liberty healthful both to body and mind. Elgin, therefore, she always remembered with affection as the home of her early years : little thinking then, while she played in a merry childhood under the shadow of the broad and lofty pile of its august Cathedral, that she was to

c

sleep within its ancient aisles as the last Duchess of Gordon; and little caring now that she was ever called in providence to be a Duchess, but for ever grateful that she was called by grace into the number of the children of God.

When about eight years old she was sent to a boarding-school in London, where there were some twenty-five young ladies all motherless like herself, or fatherless, or orphans. Here first of all, the broad Scotch of Fife and Elgin was to be eradicated by every means, alike from lip and thought. While, therefore, she was thoroughly educated in all other respects, her memory was allowed to lie waste; because the Scotch was so engrained in her thoughts, that after the solitary exercise of learning poetry by heart, it all came out Scotch instead of English. The rigid discipline was thoroughly effectual, and she spoke, as she did most things else, remarkably well. The penalty for acquiring English was a defect of verbal memory, which she often regretted; yet her natural power in this respect must have been good, for in her latter years she learned and repeated a large number of hymns, in which she greatly delighted as in the songs of her pilgrimage. The proscribed Scotch, also, she reacquired, and spoke it well both in its northern and western dialects. She would not have stumbled for a moment at the question, "A' ae 'oo ?"

put by the Duchess Jane to the hosier in Aberdeen for the trial of an English friend ; nor at his assuring reply, which so puzzled the southern ear with its string of vowels, " Ou ay, a' ae 'oo."

Along with a world-wide benevolence the Duchess had a strong feeling of nationality and a great love for everything Scotch, including Scotch reels in the days of her gaiety. She had great musical talent, and this likewise took the direction of our national music, for which she had quite a genius, both playing it with exquisite skill and adding variations of her own. She never quite lost the taste, or laid the practice aside ; but in later years her great pleasure was in the songs of Zion, and the utterance of her heart was that of Israel's captives : " If I forget thee, O Jerusalem, let my right hand forget her cunning."

Her education was thorough in all the ordinary branches, as in French, which she wrote and spoke with fluency. It also included some mathematics, which she thought of use to her afterwards in think-ing out subjects and in business ; but irrespective of such aid her Grace decidedly excelled both in faculty for business and in powers of reasoning. She could sketch well ; and tradesmen were surprised at the quickness of her eye for proportions, inherited perhaps from Lord Brodie's love for building. The instant she saw the alterations at Huntly Lodge after her widowhood, she told the gardeners that they had sloped the ground at the entrance toward the house instead of from it. They had done so as the only way of saving the trees which she cherished, but so slightly as to make sure that it would escape notice, and were pleasantly surprised when she directed them very simply how to spare the trees and yet rectify the slope. So with the Duke's monument at Kinrara, at the first distant glimpse she remarked that it was not straight ; and on inspection there was found a slight deviation from the perpendicular at the centre of the column.

Her early dispositions are described by those who knew her as remarkably amiable and attractive. Amongst her school-fellows was a young lady who became afterwards the Princess de Polignac, and who ever retained the highest regard for the Duchess. Her account of those school-days is that Miss Brodie "made herself liked by all the world, small and great," exceedingly beloved both by teachers and companions. This attractiveness of her childhood increased with years and with grace, and she wielded through life a singular power of winning the devoted attachment of all around her ; we cannot say quite unconsciously, for she saw it, but with a deep feeling of its being undeserved on her part, and of wonder why she was so beloved.

In partial contrast to her amiableness, the friends

of her youth all agree in ascribing to her an innate
and strong independence of character.   "She had
a very independent spirit," was the deepest impression regarding her left in the memory of the young
Ladies Melville.   This moral element characterized her
throughout life, and, when she had become the subject
of divine grace, stood her in good stead in many a
severe trial of principle.   Those who had seen only
her kindly and yielding disposition were often taken
with surprise by her immovable firmness; for while
she would give way to others in things indifferent, and
yield even too easily in points where she had not
made up her mind, no opposition had the slightest
effect in moving her from the position she had once
deliberately taken.   The Baroness de Cetto, at whose
mother's house she visited whilst at school in London, writes of her: "She was amiable, affectionate,
and upright as a child.   I have heard from my
mother all through life of dear 'Eliza Brodie's'
visits to her, and of her excellent and endearing
qualities that seemed innate; and the strong moral
courage that led her steadily to follow her sense of
right-doing on occasions where others of her age, and
left as she was much to her own guidance, might have
failed."

Along with independence of mind, and helping to
sustain it, physical courage was strongly marked in

her character from childhood upward, till after her
severe illness three years before her death, so that in
travelling or otherwise she rather enjoyed that kind
of risk for which her friends required to brace their
nerves. She was at the same time most thoughtfully
considerate for the feelings of others, that is to say, of
other ladies; for she had little patience for timidity or
nervousness in men, or making much of little difficulties, which either annoyed or amused her as the case
might be. "The Duchess was a woman of remarkable
courage," said her grey-headed groom, who had served
her forty years. "When the bridge over the Spey
was carried down by the floods in '29, I took her
Grace across in a pony-chaise on a boat, along with
Lady Madalina Palmer (the Duke's sister). The horse's
hoofs were within two inches of the water in front,
and the wheels within two inches of the water behind,
and I was myself rather uneasy. Lady Madelina
became alarmed and asked, 'Isn't this dangerous,
Duchess?' 'I never see danger,' she replied; and
with this quiet remark we crossed the river."

As with Elgin, so with London; her early days were
ever fresh in her remembrance, her walks into the
Regent's Park and to Primrose Hill, then quite in
the country, her youthful joy at a great illumination
for some Peninsular victory, and her sorrow in
witnessing Lord Nelson's funeral.

But in the midst of many natural attractions for the present, and germs of promise for the future, there was then no seed of grace in Elisabeth Brodie, and she enjoyed no teaching fitted to enlighten her in the way of salvation. The moral training was excellent, as well as the intellectual; but there was nothing specially religious, still less any light shed on the peculiarities of the gospel; while in the church she was taken to attend, all was formal and lifeless. Still, some awakenings of conscience would gleam across her mind, as they do with most children, but only to vanish away. One day at school the truth of that special providence, in which she so trusted afterwards, having been called in question, and the doctrine turned into ridicule, she had the courage not to join in the laughter but was silent, feeling the necessity of an ever-watchful eye to preserve her from accident every moment. On another occasion, her father sought to instil humility of mind regarding her own efforts and attainments. "It made," she said, "a great impression upon me, when he told me that if I did all I ought to do, I should still only be an unprofitable servant." The words sank deeper than she knew herself, or than her father ever imagined; for when afterwards she really did all as few others have done, there is not one saint in a thousand who has so thoroughly or so constantly felt the worthlessness of their whole service in the Lord's vineyard. This text, dropped on the soil of her still unbroken heart, expresses the deepest and most habitual of all her future thoughts, " I am an unprofitable servant ; " or, translated into her own words, "a useless log" was her written estimate of herself.

HER YOUTH.

At fifteen or sixteen years of age Miss Brodie left school, and spent her summer months at the Burn, and her winters at Bath with her father; taking with him summer tours through England and Wales, which she enjoyed all the more, as they had riding horses with them as well as their carriage. Her governess now was an eccentric and clever woman, who taught her geometry, and whom she described as a sort of Dominie Sampson in petticoats. But the completing of her education came now to be very much under the charge of men, wise and intelligent friends of her father, who cared for his motherless child with a deep and painstaking interest. Amongst these she derived most benefit and pleasure from the teaching and counsel of Colonel Imray, her father's most intimate friend, and her rides and walks with him she always remembered with gratitude. His conversation imbued her with a taste for intellectual and scientific

pursuits, and implanted in her the seeds of a knowledge of minerals, shells, and geology, which enabled
her to read books on natural history with intelligence
and lively pleasure ; and though she ceased to pursue
those studies, she never lost her interest in them.
This manly superintendence must have done much to
cultivate that masculine vigour of mind, which the
Lord so used for enabling her to discover the truth
of great doctrines to which even the good men whom
she first knew were not alive, and to take her own
decided course through all conflicting elements.

While not yet seventeen, Miss Brodie " came out "
into society at the Fife Hunt in Cupar with her cousin
Miss Wemyss, afterwards the Countess of Rosslyn, who
drew every eye toward her by her beauty ; while none
more sincerely joined in the admiration than Miss
Brodie, for she was singularly free from jealousy, and
beauty was always a great attraction to her. For
herself, the Duchess of Gordon had a fine face with a
smile of peculiar sweetness. Singularly attractive in
manner, her expression, which in later years was quite
heavenly, so lighted up all her features as to convey
the impression that she had been beautiful in youth.
But she appears to have been then admired, not so
much for handsome features, as for her tall and grace-
ful form, with a countenance beautified by intelligence
and life and winning gentleness.

She was introduced into the world under the protection of Mrs. Rigg of Tarvet, her father's asthmatic
habit keeping him at home. That young entrance
into gaiety was a step which the knowledge of a
higher and more joyful freedom caused her to retrace
without a sigh for the fancied loss : with the clear
conviction that all such assemblies, whether public or
private, are "not of the Father, but of the world ;"
and with deep sorrow for the present mingling of the
Church with the world, as working manifold death.
But kindness in any form she never forgot, and always
remembered with gratitude the kind friend under
whose roof she then dwelt, and beneath whose shield
she had launched into life "falsely so called." After
the festivities were over, so far as we know, they
never met on earth again ; but in her own widowhood
the Duchess heard with peculiar pleasure of that lady's
daughter and granddaughter dying in the Lord, and
of herself becoming a partaker of the same grace in
her old age, though with more doubt and fear. How
many who began life together in a common thoughtlessness, have been led by widely separate paths to
rejoice in the common salvation ; like those two
entering that glittering ball-room as mother and
daughter, not to meet again till they should welcome
each other in the light of the Lamb above.

About this time, when on a visit to a family in

England, there was a beautiful child staying in the house, who was greatly attracted to Miss Brodie, and pleased to be noticed by her; and her own love of beauty and of children made the little one's fondness highly gratifying. On Sabbath she had joined the company in playing cards. Next day the child kept aloof from her, giving no heed to her overtures of kindness, and when invited to sit on her knee flatly refused, saying, "No, you are bad; you play cards on Sunday." Her Scotch training told her that the child was right, and she replied, "I was wrong, I will not do it again;" and she kept her resolution, for even then she was remarkable for the decision with which she gave up any sin of which she was once convinced. In her gradual reception of grace afterwards we know of some, and there must have been many, successive steps like this, as her conscience became enlightened; and in due time she obtained the gracious fulfilment of the promise, "If any man will do his will, he shall know of the doctrine whether it be of God."

While accepting reproof from a child, she did not refuse it from older monitors. As a young lady she was on one occasion warned with some severity, by her faithful friend Colonel Imray, against the sin of trifling with the feelings of any one whose affections she did not intend to reciprocate. She took the counsel meekly, scrupulously obeyed it ever after, and transmitted it as a valued lesson to her young friends in the generation following.

But the interval was brief till she left her father's home for her husband's. The burning of the house of Brodie by Lord Lewis Gordon had not so estranged the two families, as to prevent all renewal of social intercourse between them even in the same generation ; for after many years we find Lord Brodie lamenting in the conduct of one of his relatives the hurtful influence of Lord Huntly's society. In later times Mr. Brodie used to be honoured at the Burn with a visit, on her way from Gordon Castle to London, by Jane Duchess of Gordon ; so celebrated for her gaiety, her unchastened but exuberant wit, and her successful ambition in having three Dukes and a Marquis for her sons-in-law. On one of those occasions, observing the great care he bestowed on the education of his daughter just entering into society, she said to him, " You are surely training her for a wife to Huntly," to whom she was ardently attached. With all her famed sagacity, how little at that moment did she foresee the future ! With her skill in contriving, and her tact in securing matrimonial alliances to perpetuate the greatness of her family, how little did she suspect that the wealthy union she was now forecasting would far more than neutralize the greatness of all the rest, by leaving her cherished son childless, the noble name and title of Gordon extinct. Doubtless she fancied that she saw in the open countenance and buoyant spirits of the young heiress, in her noble figure and hale and blooming youth, at once a wife who would make her son happy, and a fit and likely mother for the future Dukes of Gordon. But "the Lord knoweth the thoughts of the wise that they are vain."

The marriage which the Duchess thus initiated took place only after her own death; and that death presented a striking contrast to her life, of which the following account is given in an article on the Seaforth Papers in the *North British Review*. The romantic story of her early sorrow has been represented as unfounded; but if true, it is alike honourable to her feelings, and explanatory of her subsequent course, about which there is no question. "Early in life Alexander, the fourth Duke of Gordon, married Jane Maxwell, 'The Flower of Galloway,' and a handsomer couple has rarely been seen. As a girl she was strongly attached to a young officer, who reciprocated her passion. The soldier, however, was ordered abroad with his regiment, and shortly afterwards was reported dead. After the first burst of grief had spent itself, she sank into a state of listlessness and apathy that seemed immovable. But the Duke of Gordon appeared as a suitor, and partly from family pressure,

partly from indifference, Jane accepted his hand. On
their marriage tour the young pair visited Ayton
House, in Berwickshire, and there the Duchess received a letter addressed to her in her maiden name,
and written in the well-known hand of her early
lover. He was, he said, on his way home to complete
their happiness by marriage. The wretched bride
fled from the house, and, according to the local tradi-
tion, was found, after long search, stretched by the side
of a burn, nearly crazed. When she had recovered
from this terrible blow and re-entered society, Jane
presented an entirely new phase of character. She
plunged into all sorts of gaiety and excitement; she
became famous for her wild frolics, and for her vanity
and ardour as a leader of fashion; her routs and
assemblies were the most brilliant of the capital,
attracting wits, orators, and statesmen."

In most cases the death is only too like the life, and
a course of thoughtless pleasure commonly conducts to
an unthinking and callous end; yet not with all, and
not with the last but one of the Duchesses of Gordon.
In the dark and earthly day in which her lot was cast,
"the lust of the flesh, the lust of the eye, and the pride
of life" rose like a swollen flood, before whose proud
waves the Cross and all its fastenings seemed to be
swept irresistibly away. She had all the pleasures of
the world at her command, and she freely drank the

poisoned cup. But the cold hand of death arrested her gay career. Her years indeed had not been few, for Lord Huntly was now more than forty years old ; but she was at the moment saying, " To-morrow shall be as this day, and much more abundant." Having been summoned to Carlton House to visit the Prince Regent, she procured a magnificent dress ; and, willing to make the most of it, she arrayed herself in the splendid attire to receive her own friends in her apartments at the Pulteney Hotel. A few weeks intervened, and those gay rooms were thrown open a second time ; but it was now for the reception of her friends, amidst the pomp and pageantry of death, to admire the gorgeous coffin of crimson velvet in which she lay in state.

Three or four years before this event the Duchess had a severe affliction in the death of her son, Lord Alexander Gordon, a young nobleman whose life had been "immersed in the sins and vices of the day."[1] Being taken ill at Edinburgh, as soon as he was made aware of his danger he cried aloud with heart-rending complaints, often started up and called to God for mercy, and then declared that there was no hope for him and his soul was lost. The nurse who waited on him was a pious and well-instructed woman, selected

[1] This account of Lord Alexander is abridged from a little volume entitled *Plain Truth*, by the Rev. Dr. Thorpe of Belgrave Chapel.

for him by his physician, Dr. Stuart of Dunearn. She told him kindly of Jesus Christ, as the Saviour of the chief of sinners; while she spoke he raised himself on his elbow, gazed intently on her till she ceased, and falling back on his pillow clasped his hands and exclaimed, "Oh, if that were true!" She then read the Bible to him to prove the truth of her statements, prayed with him at his urgent request, and brought her minister to converse more fully on the great salvation. In his few dying days Lord Alexander appeared to receive the truth as it is in Jesus.

Meanwhile the Duchess had arrived, and the day before his death he solemnly addressed her: "I remember all your kindness with love and gratitude; but you omitted the most important thing of all, religion,—my sinfulness before God, the judgment to come, and the love and compassion of our Saviour. Look at this poor old woman: she has been to me more than a parent: my merciful God has made her the instrument to raise me from despair. Death is at hand, but I am at peace." Returning to England, the Duchess overtook on the road one of the itinerant missionaries sent out by the noble-hearted Robert Haldane, and with her usual kindness stopped the carriage to take him up. By and by the coachman, alarmed by his disclosures of the world to come, insisted on his alighting; but the Duchess, taking him

into the carriage beside herself, was surprised and
affected by hearing from his lips the same awakening
and saving truths that had been uttered by her dying
son, and cordially thanked him for his faithfulness.

These lessons, though not lost altogether, did not
lead at the time to repentance unto life; and there
was a painful awaking of the soul at the last. On
being seized with sudden and fatal illness, the Duchess
sent for the daughters of Lord Reay, who were related
to her by marriage; and the last survivor of the two,
the Honourable Miss Mackay, often spoke with interest of the closing scene, and expressed her full conviction that the repentance was genuine and spiritual.
A penitence so unproved must remain doubtful; but
it was at least a testimony by one of the worldliest in
the world to the bitter end of a thoughtless life to an
awakened conscience. The dying Duchess, seeking in
death the counsel which she had slighted in life, earnestly asked one of those two sisters to be with her
every day to the last, for she had found them faithful
before, and knew that she could rely on their sincerity
now. The Sabbath had been the day for her most
select assemblies, because she could then secure the
coveted presence of the graceless Prince Regent; and
the highest compliment she could think of for her
friends was to invite them to the distinguished parties
which he honoured as a guest. The two ladies were

missed by her in the gay scene, and in answer to her
kind inquiries they gave a full statement of their views
on the sacredness of the day of holy rest. "You are
perfectly right, my dear cousins," her Grace replied;
"and I mean soon to do so likewise."

The passing purpose of repentance appears to have
taken little effect, till the strong hand of the last
enemy had seized her with a grasp from which there
was no release. Her ungodly life now returned to her
memory in its real character; for the past there was
an awakened conscience with its terrible sting, and for
the future a fearful looking for of judgment. The salvation of her soul was the great subject of conversation with her two friends day by day during those
anxious weeks. Through them she sent for the Rev.
Dr. Nichol, of the Scotch Church, Swallow Street; and
before her death she bequeathed a service of commu-
nion-plate to his church. She narrated to him at
large her son's last words, and the traveller's repetition
of the message, which seemed now to have sunk into
her heart. The faithful minister dealt honestly with
her conscience as a dying sinner, and was persuaded
that she had been moved to look on Him whom she
had pierced, and enabled to trust in his salvation.
She then earnestly desired the communion of the
Lord's Supper, which he hesitated to grant contrary to
the use of the Church of Scotland. But he consented

in the peculiar circumstances of the case; assembled
a few friends, her own kind counsellors and others,
to constitute a little church in her house ; and, after
a very faithful admonition addressed more specially to
her, gave the Holy Supper to them all, to the living
as well as the dying, in remembrance of the Saviour's
death for our eternal life. The Lord alone knoweth
them that are his, yet we are warranted to hope
that her awakened soul may also have been saved,
although so as by fire. We are permitted to take
the consolation that if Jane Maxwell rushed in the
wildness of an early grief to the false refuge of the
world's gaiety, she may have been drawn by grace on
her dying pillow to that Saviour who invited her,
" Come unto me all ye that labour and are heavy
laden, and I will give you rest." But in that case, as
in Manasseh's late repentance, the good was personal
to herself alone : while a long and brilliant life without holiness or the fear of the Lord had exerted its
baneful influence through a wide circle.

The two last Duchesses of Gordon were both widely
known, with a fame far beyond the lot that is wont
to fall to woman even in the highest ranks of life.
Which was the more noted of the two it were hard to
decide ; the one in the world, and the other in the
Church, yet both before the eyes of the whole community. The first was imbued with the world, in-

tense and undiluted; the second imbued with grace in all its heavenly power. Each proved for herself the inmost happiness of the life she had chosen, and both spread their principles to the uttermost of their respective circles. The first lived for self, and time, and sense; the second lived for God, for eternity, and for the profit of many that they might be saved. The one exhausted life to its dregs, and then at the summons of death looked back upon the past with sorrow, and forward to the future with fear. The other counted the reproach of Christ greater riches than the treasures of Egypt, forsook the world when it was all in her grasp, with youth, and health, and every element of earth-born joy; fought the good fight, kept the faith, and finished her course, thankful for all the way by which the Lord had led her, joyful in the hope of the future, resting from her labours, and her works following her. Yet all is of God's grace alone; and it might be, we trust it hath been, that having called that thoughtless idler, even at the eleventh hour, the Lord of the vineyard hath decreed concern-these two, "I will give to this last even as unto thee;" and that casting their crowns together before the Lamb in the midst of the Throne, they are now both praising the grace that aboundeth to the chief of sinners, and both loving Him much by whom to both "much hath been forgiven."

CHAPTER III.

THE MARCHIONESS OF HUNTLY.

¦ 1813–1827.

" A good that never satisfies the mind,
  A beauty fading like the April flowers,
  A sweet with floods of gall that runs combined,
  A pleasure passing ere in thought made ours,—
  To me *this* world did once seem sweet and fair :
  Now, like imagined landscape in the air
  And weeping rainbows, her best joys I find.

" Therefore, as doth the pilgrim whom the night
  Hastes darkly to imprison on his way,
  Think on thy HOME, my soul, and think aright
  Of what's yet left thee of life's wasting day.
  The wary mariner so fast not flies
  An howling tempest, harbour to attain ;
  Nor shepherd hastes, when frays of wolves arise,
  So fast to fold his bleating train,
  As I   .   .   .   .   .
  Now fly the world and what it most doth prize,
  And sanctuary seek, free to remain.

DRUMMOND OF HAWTHORNDEN.

THE Marquis of Huntly was possessed of many attractions. He was tall, and handsome in form and feature ; was amiable, affectionate, generous ; and was endowed with excellent natural talents, though they had been little cultivated either in boyhood or in his youthful service in the army abroad. A great favourite in his own circle, he was likewise highly popular with all classes of the community. But he was a thorough man of the world, and made no conscience of keeping himself from its follies and its sins. Miss Brodie herself was still only of the world, and in that sense the yoke was not unequal, while the marriage was both approved of and desired by her father. But the reasonable prospect of its yielding true happiness was slender ; the step was a hazardous one for a simple-minded girl to take ; and her old friend Lady Leven affectionately warned her of the risk she was about to run. The marriage, however, turned out on the whole a happy one to them both during the twenty-three

years of its duration ; and in the end she believed that
they were made both one in Christ.   Her love to him
was ardent, and there were few relative claims to divide
her affection.   Her mother she had lost in infancy ;
she had a strong attachment to her father, and a re-
verential respect for his memory ; but there was no
brother or sister to draw out her affections before her
marriage, no son or daughter to share them afterwards.
The difference of twenty-five years between her husband and herself only made her regard such a disparity as trivial ; and if disparity of age in a proposed
marriage was spoken of as an objection, she would
remark, "You forget how much older the Duke was
than myself."   After his death her love continued
unabated, and grew in strength to the close of her
life ; extending itself to every person and every object
associated with his memory.   On the part of the world,
the marriage was regarded as one of interest on both
sides ; his high rank on the one hand, and her large
fortune to repair his extravagance, being the supposed
inducements.   But whatever it may have been in its
origin, it was afterwards a union of mutual affection.
As in her toward him, so likewise on his part toward
her there was not only the highest esteem, but sincere
and growing attachment.

Fifteen years after their marriage, the famous
Morayshire flood made great devastation on the Duke's

property, carrying down the fine bridge over the Spey, while one of the wings of Gordon Castle had shortly before been consumed by fire. On the occurrence of this second calamity it seemed to him as if all were going to wreck; the flood destroying what the fire had left, with both evils coming upon him soon after his accession to the estates, and these found to be heavily burdened. In the sorrow of the moment the thought of his heart broke forth in the exclamation : " All things are against me : I've been unfortunate in everything except a good wife."

Still she had undoubtedly much to try her; in the past many things to forget, for the present much to overlook ; and after her conversion there were added the strongly conflicting elements of the world and the Spirit. From the first she conducted herself with singular discretion. Her position was beset with difficulties, both from its great elevation, and other elements of trial which must have burdened her.

> " But she strove against her weakness,
>   Though at times her spirit sank ;
> Shaped her course with woman's meekness
>   To all duties of her rank.

> " And a gentle consort made he ;
>   And her gentle mind was such
> That she grew a noble lady,
>   And the people loved her much."

The marriage took place at Bath, where Mr. Brodie usually passed the winter, on the 11th of December

1813. After living a few months at Southampton they went up to London in spring, and the MARCHIONESS was introduced into the gay circle of rank and fashion in which her husband was so popular. There, as everywhere else, her lively and amiable disposition made her liked by all, and her skill in Scotch music rendered her a favourite. But, while she never possessed the brilliancy that would make her shine above others in such a circle, the change must have been great from her previous pursuits and studies; and little trials were frequent for the first few years. The ladies of the Gordon family were at home in society in a way to which she was a stranger, and which she found it hard at first to acquire. They captivated every one by their fascinating manners, and by their manifold attention to all that was going on around them; so that, after being engaged in conversation with one friend, they delighted others with the cordial and intelligent interest which they showed at once in whatever was occupying them. The acquisition of this courtly art, of attending to several things at the same time, the Duchess afterwards regretted when her mind became more earnest, for she found that she had thus impaired the power she formerly possessed of concentrating her mind on one subject of thought.

In the course of the year they went to Geneva, where they remained for the winter. Lord Huntly had been partly brought up there under a Genevese tutor, and was always fond of the society, the scenery, and the sports of Switzerland. Lady Huntly was extremely popular in the town, and greatly liked by the families with which she associated, forming also more intimate friendships which she retained ever after. In the spring of 1815 they made a tour through the most interesting towns of Holland, the Marquis desiring to recall the memory of his early campaign in the Low Countries. The Duke and Duchess of Richmond had passed the winter at Brussels with their family, and it was arranged that they should visit that city before returning to England. Their tour brought them into that neighbourhood in the midst of the exciting events which signalized the middle of June; but they approached within two or three stages of Brussels in entire ignorance of all that was occurring so near them. The Duchess of Richmond had already given, on the night of the 15th, her famous ball to the officers of the Guards,

> "And Belgium's capital had gathered then
> Her beauty and her chivalry. . . .
> But then and there was hurrying to and fro,
> And gathering tears and tremblings of distress,
> And cheeks all pale,—and choking sighs
> That upon night so sweet such awful morn should rise."

They were too late for that night of mirth and morning of alarm; but the day following they found themselves unexpectedly in the midst of a scene of fear and distress. On the road to Brussels on the Saturday, there was nothing but tokens of apparent disaster and defeat amongst our allies. As they drove forward they passed carts of wounded men, or were themselves overtaken by foreign soldiers flying past them in the haste of panic. In the confusion they could learn nothing of what had occurred, till at last a Hessian officer came up whom Lord Huntly knew, and his removal of their doubts was only to inform them that all was lost. " Mon Général," inquired Lord Huntly, " où est votre regiment ?" " Je ne sais pas," was his reply; "tout est perdu, je m'enfuis." As they were on their way to England at any rate, the Marquis asked Lady Huntly if she would like to make for the coast; and few young ladies would have had the nerve to refuse so reasonable a proposal in circumstances of such alarm. But she declined it instantly, and insisted on going forward to Brussels, because his presence would be a great comfort to his sister, the Duchess of Richmond; as she would be in great anxiety both for her daughters, who were with her, and for her son, Lord March, who was in the army. Their progress, however, was not so easy now, as there was a scramble for horses at every stage, but they reached Brussels in the evening, and found rooms at a hotel.

Next morning Lord Huntly, with a soldier's interest in the army, could not rest in the city, but rode out to see what was going on at the scene of action, leaving his young wife with the Duchess of Richmond, whose son was meanwhile wounded in the battle. It was a day of dreadful suspense for them all. The rooms which three nights before had shone so brilliantly, while all "went merry as a marriage-bell," were now a scene of harrowing distress; with the incessant roar of cannon within ten miles, the conflicting and distracting reports from the field of battle that reached them continually, and the numbers of English, as well as others, hastening to escape from the town. There were many proposals at their hotel for packing and taking to flight. But Lady Huntly had with her an English maid called Cossens, often mentioned in her letters under the kindly contraction of "Cuzzie;" who had been selected for her, in her own youth and inexperience, by old Lady William Gordon on account of her age and character; and who remained with her for more than forty years, first rendering service, and afterwards receiving it as an object of kindly interest. In the confusion Cossens remained imperturbably cool, and by her resolute attitude helped to keep the whole party quiet. She had perfect confidence in the kindness and care of the Marquis, was sure that he would make every arrangement for their safety, and, in the midst of tumult and fears from hour to hour of the long day, steadily refused to put forth her hands for any preparation to depart. Their remaining still where they were enabled them to hear the glad news of victory the earlier, with the unspeakable relief it brought them after tasting the bitter cup so often. That night those rooms were lighted up with a quieter joy than the exciting whirl of the dance, and we trust there was mingled with it praise to the Lord of Hosts from some hearts and lips now prepared to exclaim, " Thanks be to God who giveth us the victory through our Lord Jesus Christ."

Next day they left for Ghent, where they dined with Louis XVIII., exulting in the fresh joy of a great deliverance. While sitting at breakfast that morning, the King had received by a special messenger the news of Napoleon's defeat; and the windows of the room where the royal party sat coming down to the ground, the embraces and ejaculations of the little court on the joyful tidings were said to have been observed by a spy of the Rothschilds, watching for the issue and so contriving to convey the first news of the victory to London. On the 20th they sailed for Dover in a vessel which Lord Huntly chartered at Ostend, where with his usual frank kindness he had taken on board many people who were anxious to get home. Their passage was unexpectedly prolonged;

and the little stock of provisions laid in for themselves, being all they had in the ship for the whole
company, fell so far short of their wants that they all
suffered great hunger before reaching England.

In the autumn of 1815 they came to Scotland for
the first time after their marriage, first to the Duke of
Gordon's Highland Lodge of Kinrara, then to Gordon
Castle, and finally to their home at Huntly Lodge.
Finding here all that belonged to her at the Burn, her
books and various youthful remembrances which she
had not seen since her marriage, Lady Huntly felt at
once that she had "come home;" little surmising how
many years she was to spend in it, but drawn to the
place from the first with an attachment that was never
weakened till it had received her dying breath. They
passed a quiet winter, slightly diversified except by
the marriage of the Marquis of Tweeddale to their
niece, Lady Susan Montagu, who was living with them.
But Lord Huntly desired to give his bride a festive
reception by the people on her coming home to Strathbogie; and because the winter was not suitable, he
deferred it till her birthday in June. That day was
celebrated by a large assembly with feasting and
dancing. The place of meeting, though not on the
same spot, was in the same Castle Park where the
silver trumpet of the gospel sounded the year of
jubilee to assembled thousands after the lapse of more

than forty years. Some who were present at the last could remember the first rejoicings, when the people danced on the green sward, and Lady Huntly distributed small silver coins to the children, with that large-hearted love for the young which so marked all her future course. A year later is the date of her first note in our possession. It accompanied a little present to one of her earliest friends, and tells too plainly that to our only true talisman, the "peace of God keeping the heart and mind through Christ Jesus," she was quite a stranger :

" Accept, dearest, with kindest wishes for your welfare, this little Thistle. May it act up to its motto, and become a talisman ever to preserve your Heart or Happiness from being 'touched with impunity.' —Your very affectionate

" E. HUNTLY.

"GORDON CASTLE, *Oct. 29th*, 1817."

The first public 'rejoicing was limited to the neighbourhood of Huntly ; but a few years later it was followed by a festive Highland tour in which she took far greater pleasure, the mountain scenery delighting her taste, while the cordial welcome touched her heart. On this occasion the spirit of the old Highland clanship was revived ; fiery crosses were lighted from hill to hill ; and Lady Huntly made a progress in Celtic style over all the Gordon estates in the Highlands, receiving the homage of her vassals as she passed from place to place.

In the year 1819 they had the honour of a visit from Prince Leopold, the present King of the Belgians, who had been a friend of the Marquis, and always showed great kindness both to him, and to the Duchess after his death. It was arranged that the visit should be received, not at Huntly, but at the beautiful Highland Lodge of Kinrara, that the Prince might enjoy himself among the red-deer and all sorts of game, which were there so abundant; and Lord Huntly thought to give his royal guest a Highland welcome worthy of his rank. He possessed the energy and munificence to accomplish such a design; whilst his singular power of fancy and imitation, by which he could personate different characters so as to deceive his most intimate friends, lent its aid to create a picturesque scene and to carry it through without mistrust or mishap. He circulated far and wide amongst his vassals and retainers, and the surrounding clans, a summons to meet the Prince at Kinrara. His great personal popularity went far of itself to secure a cordial response to the call; but with the ardent loyalty of the Highlands, the husband of the Princess Charlotte was sure of an enthusiastic welcome, and the kilted clansmen held themselves ready

E

to honour their own chief and to welcome his royal
guest.

The time of the Prince's arrival being still early in
the day, and the weather being extremely fine, his
host invited him to ascend the Hill of Tor Alvie ;
which was in the neighbourhood of the Lodge, and
commanded a fine view of the lofty mountains and
magnificent scenery around, with the noble Spey
carrying the breadth of a river along with the rush of
a mountain-torrent. With his Highland bonnet and
eagle's feather, and kilted in the dark tartan of his
clan, he quietly conducted the stranger to the summit,
where they found the Marchioness and her party
waiting to receive them. But the host of tartaned
Highlanders, for whom the Prince was not looking
but whom Huntly had summoned to greet him, was
nowhere within the wide range of vision. With his
tall, handsome form, graced by his free and picturesque
garb,—

> "Their Chieftain stood with eagle plume;
> But they with mantles folded round
> Were couched to rest upon the ground,
> Scarce to be known by curious eye
> From the deep heather where they lie ;
> So well was matched the tartan screen
> With heath-bell dark, and brackens green.
> The Mountaineer then whistled shrill,
> And he was answered from the hill ;
> Instant through copse and heath arose
> Bonnets, and spears, and bended bows,

And every tuft of broom gave life
To plaided warrior armed for strife ;
Watching their Leader's beck and will,
All silent there they stood, and still.
Short space he stood, then raised his hand
To his brave clansman's eager band ;
Then SHOUT OF WELCOME, shrill and wide,
Shook the steep mountain's steady side;
Thrice it arose, and brake and fell
Three times gave back the martial yell."

"Ah," exclaimed the Prince, surprised and highly pleased, "we've got Roderick Dhu here!"

In the course of the following year, 1820, Lady Huntly made the acquaintance of Sir Walter Scott, who was captivated with her Scotch music, to which he thus refers in one of his letters :—"Lady Huntly plays Scotch tunes like a Highland angel. She ran a set of variations on 'Kenmore's on and awa',' which I told her were enough to raise a whole country side. I never in my life heard such fire thrown into that sort of music."[1]

[1] Two years later Sir Walter published the tragedy of "Halidon Hill," in which he introduces one of the early chiefs of the Gordon family, soon after their transference from the Borders to the North, who, in conversation with Swinton, a Border chief, speaks of "his Elizabeth" as the "fairest grace and honour" of "an ancient northern house," and so extols her musical gifts as to leave no doubt that the description is that of Elisabeth Brodie :—

> "*Gordon.*—And if I live and see my halls again,
> Each hardy follower shall have his field,
> His household hearth and sod-built home,—
> And my Elizabeth shall smile to see it !
> "*Swinton.*—Hath thy Elizabeth no other name ?
> "*Gordon.*—Nay, then, her name is—hark—(*whispers.*)

HER CONVERSION.

The slow and successive steps of Lady Huntly's entrance into the narrow way, we cannot undertake to trace either minutely or clearly, because the materials for such a narrative have partly been destroyed and partly been withheld. But if the source be hid in mist, all men saw the flowing of the broad river. Her own letters, on which we depend chiefly afterwards, are of no service here ; because her friends with one exception were not then like-minded, and she did not

---

" *Swinton.*—I know it well, that ancient northern house.
" *Gordon.*—O, thou shalt see its fairest grace and honour
In my Elizabeth ; and if music touch thee—
O, her notes
Shall hush each sad remembrance to oblivion,
Or melt them to such gentleness of feeling
That grief shall have its sweetness. Who but she
Knows the wild harpings of our native land ?
Whether they lull the shepherd on his hill,
Or wake the knight to battle ; rouse to merriment,
Or soothe to sadness ; she can touch each mood.
Princes and statesmen, chiefs renowned in arms,
And grey-haired bards, contend which shall the first
And choicest homage render to the enchantress.
     Swinton.—You speak her talent bravely.
                    Gordon.—Though you smile,
I do not speak it half. The gift creative
New meaning adds to every air she wakes ;
Varying and gracing it with liquid sweetness,
Like the wild modulation of the lark,
Now leaving now returning to the strain !
To listen to her, is to seem to wander
In some enchanted labyrinth of romance,
Whence nothing but the lovely fairy's will,
Who wove the spell, can extricate the wanderer.
Methinks I hear her now !"

open her heart to them on the subject. That one spiritual friend was Miss Home, and the letters to her are more than we have had patience to number, though we have read them with deep interest. The kind contribution of another early correspondent embraces two hundred, but the correspondence with Miss Home is vastly more copious. These letters, however, are all from the Duchess of Gordon, and none from the Marchioness of Huntly; the earlier ones having doubtless been destroyed at her Grace's own desire, or by her own hand, just as on a large parcel of Miss Home's letters to her she had left the direction, "To be burned without being read."

While Marchioness, her winters were for many years spent at Huntly Lodge, her springs in London, her autumns at Kinrara, and all in a life both unprofitable and idle. The gaieties at the annual county meetings in Aberdeen, and at the Highland gatherings in Inverness, made a break in the routine; and in going and returning, the evenings of her little travelling party were enlivened with overflowing mirth by the buoyancy of her spirits. A reproof by a cousin of her own for the way in which she spent the Lord's day, going to church in the morning and passing the rest of the time in novel-reading and other frivolities, entered so far into her heart; but it did not turn her to God, and her whole life continued idle and useless.

One of her oldest friends has stated that a Highland servant whom the Duchess Jane had left at Kinrara, while glad to see her young lady so happy in this life, was deeply grieved with her entire thoughtlessness about eternity. The little maid waiting on Naaman's wife has often dropped a word that has issued in healing the leprosy of the soul; and the clanswoman, with all her reverence for her Chieftain's lady, ventured to utter a quiet remark, a word of the wise heard in secret, which clung to the hard soil of her unbroken spirit till the softening rain quickened it into life.

In the year 1821 another, and less likely incident, was the first hammer of the Lord's hand for the real breaking of her heart. "God can make use of poison to expel poison," writes the old Lord Brodie. "In London I saw much vanity, lightness, and wantonness. Oh that the seeing of it in others may cure and mortify the seeds of it in myself." And in his ennobled daughter it was the very same deadly poison, met in the high places of England, which the Lord first used to kill the seed of all sin in her soul. Her own training, though not religious, had been in the principles of the highest morality; and ere this the gay sphere in which she now moved must sometimes have tried her nobler sentiments; but at length, unconsciously to herself, her heart had been secretly prepared by

the Lord for his own work. And now the unavoidable
sight of revolting vice, that did not care to veil itself,
gave a shock to her moral sensibility that reached her
inmost soul. To escape from her distress she sought
refuge in reading the Bible; and became at once so
deeply interested in its unfamiliar pages that, instead
of finding there a mere soothing balm for an hour's
relief, she could not refrain from searching the hidden
treasure daily.

One day, unhappily at the moment but happily in
the issue, one of her friends found her engaged in this
new and strange employment. To the brilliant circle
around her, the leaders of aristocratic gaiety, life at
best was only a lengthened holiday; and the young
Lady Huntly discovered in the act of Bible-reading
was a fresher incident to jest upon than most of the
table-talk that beguiled their idle hours. As for any
graver results they could have no fear; because a
little clever quizzing, in which they were so thoroughly
at home, would soon make her glad to return to her
old ways. They were goading a young spirit keenly
sensible to the loss of their good-will, as they well
knew; but they little suspected that beneath her
placid temper lay a deep heart-courage, which they
were rousing to stand at bay against all odds of
numbers; and far less did they imagine that the Lord
Most High was using their sharpened words as his

own keen arrows to drive her to the Rock that was higher than her, whence they could never more cast her down.

They called her "Methodist," and the taunt sounded strange to her ear, for she had done nothing to earn so peculiar a title. But she said within herself, "If for so little I am to be called a Methodist, let me have something more worthy of the name;" and instead of desisting on account of the reproach, she set herself to read the Bible all the more earnestly. While left thus alone among her equals, she could not even fall back for help on "old Cuzzie," who had been of such service in the tumult of Waterloo. This new battle with the world, the flesh, and the devil, was both contrary to her tastes and above her comprehension; and ere very long her vexation broke out in the same complaint, "My lady has turned Methodist."

Hitherto Lady Huntly had lived thoughtless of God and disobedient; yet conceiving of him as a Father who loved her, and had crowned her with many mercies, and liking always to look at everything as done for the best. She was sadly ignorant of scriptural truth, having no solid conviction even of the divinity of Christ, much less any knowledge of his redemption; and even now she had no deep conviction of sin or fear of an offended God. But in her

new course of Bible reading she had not advanced far
till she came upon the promise, "If ye being evil
know how to give good gifts unto your children, how
much more shall your heavenly Father give the Holy
Spirit to them that ask him?" The words arrested
her, "and from that time," she said, "I began to
pray for the Holy Spirit." Always slow in receiving
any lesson, she held it firmly when once apprehended.
She prayed for the Spirit to lead her into the truth;
and when she had learned that truth as it is in Jesus,
in the fulness of its length and breadth, she never let
go her first teaching, but magnified the Person of the
Spirit, his work, and the constant necessity of his
teaching, more and more unto the end.

Lord Huntly could not sympathize with this change
of tastes, but he was not offended. He had seen so
much of the world and its hollowness that he did not
object to his wife becoming more retired, and beginning to withdraw from it; while the change in her
own views on conformity to the world was singularly
slow. Meanwhile her attachment to him, along with
her great discretion, imparted a growing strength to
the hold she had on his affections, notwithstanding
this element of division in the want of religious sympathy. He both permitted her to pursue the course
which she chose for herself, and did all he could to
gratify her desires, even when it took him out of his

own line of things. Such an occasion occurred a few
years after this, when she set up a school in one of
the parishes of Strathbogie in which she was specially
interested. The parents and children had assembled
for its opening; and the parish minister having been
requested by the Marchioness to pray for a blessing,
and having declined on the ground of not being prepared, she turned to her husband, and said, "Huntly,
will you do it?" He complied at once, and offered a
brief prayer, to the great delight of the people.

The year following her commencement of Bible
reading in England, she was led to spend some time
along with Lord Huntly in Geneva; not with the
design of finding friends who would show her the way
of salvation, yet secretly prepared to follow those who
knew the road and could direct her into it. Such a
guide she found in Madame Vernet, who spoke to her
with affection and faithfulness on her lost condition,
showed her her need of conversion, and opened clearly
the plan of redemption by Jesus Christ. Through her
teaching Lady Huntly appears to have apprehended
the truth as it is in Jesus to the enlightenment of her
mind, although she had not fully embraced him with
the heart unto salvation. "If any one is to be called
my spiritual mother," she said, "it is Madame Vernet
of Geneva."

From Geneva they went to Paris, where Lady Olivia

Sparrow was residing, accompanied in the journey by their nephew, Lord Mandeville, who was engaged to be married to Lady Olivia's daughter. While travelling, she read in the carriage Erskine's *Internal Evidences*, which she found very profitable to her soul; and wrote soon after to a friend, "If you have not read Erskine's *Internal Evidences of Christianity*, or his *Essay on Faith*, pray get them."

In Paris she made the acquaintance of Lady Olivia, and through her of other religious people, both there and in England after their return. She had not yet abandoned the gaieties of the world, probably imagining a certain necessity for their continuance; but as her heart was now turning to the Lord, so it was also turning toward the excellent of the earth. For several years she visited much at Lady Olivia's, got religious books from her, mingled with religious society at her house, and always looked back to that period as of great advantage in her Christian course. Another family, to whom she was much indebted at this time for the Christian fellowship she found in their guests, parted with her by and by on the road; for while Lady Huntly threw off the remaining trammels of earth, and firmly chose the narrow path with all its steepness, they returned again to the world and the smooth descent of its alluring way.

After leaving Paris Lord and Lady Huntly passed

the winter at Kimbolton Castle, the residence of his brother-in-law, the Duke of Manchester. There first "she hoped she was brought to believe savingly on the Lord Jesus," and enabled to commit her soul to Him to be kept till the Great Day. She afterwards said, "I knew Christ first, if I really know him, at Kimbolton; I spent hours there in my dressing-room in prayer, and in reading the Bible, and in happy communion with him." And as her eyes now saw the King in his beauty, so also they beheld the land that is very far off. "Oh! where is that verse," she inquired at one of the maids in the house who was likely to know it, "'In my Father's house are many mansions?' it is so beautiful;" for love to her heavenly Father had now begun to transfer her affections from things on earth to things in heaven, though the transference manifested itself slowly by outward tokens. The change was deep and everlasting in her soul, and must have been great in all her tastes and feelings; but for a while it was very partially made known to others. Some of them knew that she had sympathies now into which they could not enter; but she saw afterwards, that she was not dealing fairly by them in bearing so faint a testimony against the way that was leading them down into the chambers of the dead. But the slowness of her own withdrawal from the world made her always tender in judging the state of others who remained in too much conformity with it, while she decidedly condemned their inconsistent walk.

To this first period of her Christian life the Duchess referred three months before her death. An observation having been made to the effect that deep conviction of sin is almost invariably the beginning of the work of God in the soul, she remarked: "I did not quite agree with that statement, and do not think it is by any means always the case. In my own case I believe that for two years I was a saved sinner, a believer in Jesus Christ, and yet that during all that time I did not see the exceeding sinfulness of sin. I believed in a general way that I was a sinner, who deserved the punishment of a righteous God; I believed that whosoever came to Jesus Christ should be saved; but I had no deep sense of sin, of my sin. Since then, I believe I have passed through almost every phase of Christian experience that I have ever read or heard of; and now I have such a sight of my own utter vileness and unworthiness, that I feel that the great and holy God might well set his heel on me, so to speak, and crush me into nothing."

Lady Huntly's next step was the renewal of a youthful acquaintance with Miss Helen Home, daughter of Sir George Home, Bart., of Blackadder; and finding now that they loved one Saviour, she was knit to her with a strong attachment which continued through

life. Miss Home, without the calmness and deliberation of the Marchioness, had quickness of perception,
clearness of doctrinal knowledge, singleness of eye,
energy and decision of character, and was of great use
to Lady Huntly both by her counsels and her prayers.
Lady Huntly had other religious acquaintances, but
few personal friends of her own age who were taking
up the cross. She was therefore drawn to her, as by
a great attraction, out of the weary circle of the world,
and consulted her in the varied trials and difficulties
of her path. In calling on her young friend in London, she sometimes alarmed her a little by joyfully
saying that she had ordered the carriage to return in
three hours. In her own hunger for the bread of life
no time seemed long enough, while her companion
doubted how she might be able to entertain her so
long. But while Lady Huntly unburdened her mind
of its cares, first to her friend and then along with
her before the Lord, and while they searched the
Scriptures together, the hours passed rapidly as well
as profitably away. Those Bible readings were often
referred to by Lady Huntly, as of great service in
leading her to more decided views on separation from
the world. Through them she first learned that the
converts, addressed as "adulterers" in James iv. 4,
were not open sinners; but followers of the Lamb
with divided hearts, retaining the world's friendship

which is enmity against God. About this time she
began to have morning prayers with her maids at
Huntly Lodge, and with such of the lady visitors as
could appreciate the privilege. Such a commencement of the day was a novelty in the house; and had
to encounter various difficulties in the household for
a time. But they were all overcome by decision
and steady perseverance in the path of duty; and
thus a good beginning was made in the way of that
family devotion which was afterwards to embrace the
whole establishment, and to endure for nearly forty
years to come.

After Lady Huntly's conversion, there was no
change more remarkable to her friends and household
than the diligence with which she began to redeem
time, in contrast with her previous idleness and
frivolity; yet we must in faithfulness present the
following extracts from her letters. They are dated
from Kimbolton, where she first tasted that the Lord
is gracious, but two or three years later, when first
impressions are often weakened; and the worldliness
indicated in the outward walk is probably not so
much retrograde, as the remnant of old habits that
had not yet been broken off. The absence of religion
in them is doubtless owing to the circumstance of its
being a theme little known to her correspondent, who
was afterwards, however, instructed in the truth by

Lady Huntly herself. But while there is nothing higher throughout the two letters, the extracts we give seem rather to indicate a heart carried away with other things :

"KIMBOLTON CASTLE, *New-Year's-Day*, 1826.

"I must begin the year by offering you and your family party the most cordial good wishes of Huntly and myself. We have had the merriest Christmas party I ever remember. May the new year bring you all good things. *February 6th.*—I have been obliged to delay answering your letter for some days by extreme fatigue, having had the house full of people for a ball at Colonel L.'s. This is a very bad excuse, but the true one. Huntly joins me in thanks to you and your kinsfolk for your kind wishes on his birthday. I tired myself on that day, and the ball next night put a finishing stroke, so that I am not yet recovered. I have been writing many letters for Huntly this morning, and also been busy looking over accounts and business with poor Wagstaff, who is almost out of his senses with grief about his wife. They have really been cruel in not writing to him oftener, after saying she was ill, and we have allowed him to go home. Old Cuzzy cries with him to his heart's content, which cannot improve his spirits. The fête at Wollaston was magnificent.—Ever your truly affectionate

"E. HUNTLY."

Later in the same year Lord and Lady Huntly went abroad on account of the health of their niece, Lady Emily Montagu, who was living with them as their daughter, along with her sister Lady Caroline ; taking Switzerland first, and going to Naples for the winter. Lady E. is one of the young ladies who send remembrances in the following letter, written to Miss Margaret Gordon of Wardhouse, one of Lady Huntly's earliest and dearest friends, to whom we are indebted for many subsequent letters and extracts :

"NAPLES, *January* 21*st*, 1827.

" MY DEAREST MARGARET,—A few days ago I had the pleasure to receive your letter of the 10th December, and to learn by it that you were all well at Gordon Hall, notwithstanding the severe storm. From all I hear of the accounts of the weather in Britain after November, it has been much worse here than with you. We have not seen above three days which would do credit to Italy ; and at this moment the ground is covered with snow, though a bright sun has been melting it till near four o'clock. It was full three inches deep this morning, and even the rocks which overhang the Strada Nuova di Posilipo, opposite my windows, appear quite white across the bay. We all like Naples very much, indeed too well I think, as there is very much to disapprove of in the most essen-

F

tial points. No one seems to live here for anything but pleasure, or to think of anything but the amuse-ment of the hour. But yet every one is so kind and good-humoured, so anxious to please, that one must be strong-minded indeed to resist the attraction of a society where nothing outwardly offends, and where truly I have not been able to discover any of the improprieties which are supposed to exist.

"Huntly made a flight after his own heart on Friday, setting off at four o'clock in the morning—thermometer 48° in the room—to join the King's shoot-ing-party thirty-five miles off. He returned in time to accompany us to a party at Lady Drummond's, bringing intelligence that the day before his Majesty had killed 43 wild boars, the Queen 14, and the Prin-cess Christina 11. The whole party killed about 120.

"Huntly goes to-morrow to Venafro to stay a week with their Majesties ; and as we are assured there will be fine weather after the snow, we mean to go to Vesuvius one day during his absence. He has hitherto neither had riding nor shooting, but was in the highest possible health and spirits till he heard of the loss we have all sustained in the dear Duke of York. It is a sensible affliction to us.

"Prince Leopold is here now, very unwell. The sickness here this winter has been general and fatal. We have entirely escaped, thank God, and intend remaining here as long as we can to admit of seeing Rome before the Holy Week. The English of this winter here, besides Prince Leopold and sundry bachelors of no note and numbers of unknown travellers, are the Lambtons, Sir G. Talbot and daughters, Dowager Lady Warwick and three daughters, Lord and Lady Cork; Mr. and Lady Julia Lockwood, just come from Rome to take apartments for Lady Abercorn; Sir Grenville, Lady, and Miss Temple, and—I am not acquainted with any more. These, with Sir William Drummond, *ci-devant* ambassador, and his Lady, the Actons, the Russian, Austrian, Prussian ministers, some Poles higher in birth than in reputation, and the Austrian troops, form our society, with a very few extras and still fewer Italians. I write, as usual, in haste in this idle place. The weather has prevented our excursions though we are all well enough to undertake any exertion. Huntly joins me in kindest regards to all your kin, and the girls desire best love to you.—Ever your truly affectionate

" E. HUNTLY."

Lady Emily Montagu died suddenly of an inflammatory attack, ten days after the date of this letter. The chastening seems to have been needed at the time. The Marchioness felt the bereavement severely, and it appears to have been blessed in a special manner to the quickening of her soul. About the same time she read Leighton on Peter, to which she attributed a great deepening of the Lord's work within her; and she wrote of it afterwards to the same friend : " Pray keep Leighton for my sake, as I have a particular value for that copy. I truly rejoice to find you can read Leighton with pleasure. I know by experience it is a test of the state of the mind."

Of this season the Duchess of Gordon used to talk as almost a kind of second conversion, and the previous and subsequent correspondence amply confirms that conclusion. The difference, indeed, is so great between the letters of the Marchioness and the Duchess, so far as they are preserved, that judging by these alone we should infer that this was not a second, but her first conversion. From her own testimony, as well as that of others, we know that she had been drawn to Jesus Christ two or three years earlier ; but this season of chastening and teaching was the Lord's accepted time both for deepening his work in her own soul, and bringing out her Christian character quite differently before the world. Six months after Lady Emily's death the Marquis of Huntly succeeded to the Dukedom ; and the Marchioness had meanwhile been graciously prepared to take up the cross more lovingly, and to unfurl its standard more boldly.

CHAPTER IV.

THE DUCHESS OF GORDON.

1827.

" Near the town are the ruins of the once magnificent fabric of Huntly Castle. On the avenue that leads to it are two large square towers which had defended the gateway, adorned with the arms of the family, cut out in stone. Great part of the Castle seems to be very old, and is nearly demolished ; but there is a massy building of a more modern date, bearing the names of ' George Gordoun first Marquis and Henriette Stewart Marquise of Huntly.'[1] A spacious turnpike stair leads to what has been a very grand hall, sixteen feet in height, and which still bears the marks of splendour and magnificence. There is another grand apartment immediately over this ; the chimneys of both are highly ornamented with curious sculpture of various figures.

" Some of the apartments, and in particular their curious ceilings, are still preserved pretty entire. They are painted with a great variety of subjects in small divisions : a few lines of poetry underneath each describe the subjects of the piece. In these the virtues, vices, trades, and pursuits of mankind, are characterized by emblematical figures. In the chamber which was appointed for a chapel, or place of worship, the Parables and other subjects are represented in the same style. The whole opens a field of various reflection and entertainment, well enough adapted to amuse a leisure hour."—*Old Statistical Account ; and* Cordiner's *Antiquities of the North of Scotland*, 1776.

---

[1] This inscription is in large letters outside the Castle ; and the reader will find its seven initial letters in the monogram in the centre of the interior wall, which is shown in the Vignette on the title-page.

THE next great event in our narrative is the death of the old Duke of Gordon, which occurred in the summer of 1827, when he was at the advanced age of eighty-four. Lord and Lady Huntly were still abroad and were in Geneva at the time, but they immediately returned to England and soon after to Huntly Lodge. When Miss Brodie had become Marchioness of Huntly at the age of nineteen, it was in all the ardour and hope and gaiety of youth; without the least serious thought of the responsible position on which she entered, and for which toward God she was so unfit. Now when she became Duchess of Gordon, she was thirty-three years of age, had seen much of the world and its attractions, had tasted something of its bitterness, had tried and known its emptiness, and above all had tasted that the Lord is gracious. In all respects she was now better fitted to occupy the position of Duchess, than she had been at first to fill the place of Marchioness; but this very fitness made her

feel the responsibility very differently in the second
instance from the first.

Her husband had now succeeded to a title, than
which there were few higher or more illustrious in the
kingdom; to estates which were still of vast dimensions, and had once stretched from sea to sea, winding
across the entire breadth of the country between the
Atlantic and the German Oceans; and to an hereditary influence which in other days was scarcely short
of regal in the North of Scotland, and even then
retained the strong element of clanship added to those
of wealth and rank. In the last century a learned,
though servile historian of the Gordon family dedi-
cates the first of his two volumes in these high-
sounding terms:

"To the high, puissant, and noble Prince Alexander,
Duke of Gordon, Marquis of Huntly, Earl of Huntly
and Enzie, Viscount of Inverness, Lord Gordon of
Badenoch, Lochaber, Strathavin, Balmore, Auchin-
doun, Gartly, and Kincardine: May it please your
Grace."

To this high rank of DUCHESS OF GORDON, Lady
Huntly had succeeded by her father-in-law's death;
but it was only after she returned to Huntly Lodge
and was about to leave it for Gordon Castle, that
she fully realized the greatness of the change and
the weight of responsibility that was now to rest upon

her. There was a double trial at the moment. She had already felt that she must confess Christ more boldly than she had yet done, that she must become more devoted for herself and bear the cross more openly before others, irrespectively of any altered circumstances; and now in her higher rank she must be not only as decided, but more decided for the Lord than before, and in circumstances where such decision would be more trying, the worldly influence and temptations more powerful, and the singularity and offence of the cross more marked. Along with this providential weight on the spirit there mingled a natural sadness. With her intense attachment to old remembrances, she felt at removing to a new home; and at leaving Huntly where she had lived happily so many years, where she had learned to walk with God through its green woods and by its rushing river, and where so many pleasing associations of various kinds were to be left behind.

One of the chief of those associations, and by far the finest object in the neighbourhood, was the OLD CASTLE OF HUNTLY, standing on a rising ground on the banks of the Deveron, occupying the angle formed by that river and the Bogie above their junction, and commanding a wide view of the surrounding country. Its dilapidation was not such as to destroy or even greatly to mar its imposing appearance; but it remained, as it still does, a noble building extremely picturesque in its ruins. Its present name of Huntly is comparatively modern, as well as the chief part of the existing ruin, which is built on the site of the demolished and very ancient Castle of Strathbogie.

The family of Gordon is of Norman origin, and is supposed to have removed from England into Scotland in the time of Malcolm Canmore. They were originally settled at Gordon and Huntly in Berwickshire, and took a prominent part in Border warfare. But in 1376 John de Gordon obtained from Robert II. a grant of the lands of Strathbogie, forfeited by the Earl of Athole, and transplanted his martial clan from the Borders to the Highlands. The Earldom of Huntly was created in 1449, and the Castle of Strathbogie was afterwards called Huntly, though it long retained its more ancient name. But in 1594 the Earl of Argyle having been sent by James VI. against the Popish Earls of Angus, Huntly, and Errol, and having been defeated by Huntly at the battle of Glenlivet, the king marched north in person with an army and reduced the Castle of Strathbogie to ruins. It was soon rebuilt, however, for the present ruin bears the date of 1606 ; the Earl of Huntly having been restored to royal favour and created Marquis in the interval (1599) ; a title which was again exchanged for that of Duke of Gordon in 1684.

Just before leaving Huntly for her new home there was a party of friends, including the Marchioness Cornwallis and her daughters, staying with the Duchess at the Lodge, among whom it was proposed to visit the Old Castle. The curiously painted ceilings, described at the commencement of this chapter, no longer remained "to open a field of various reflection and entertainment," with their emblematic figures and quaint rhymes portraying "the virtues and vices, trades and pursuits of mankind." But the words of the antiquarian of last century still held good, that "the whole was well enough adapted to amuse a leisure hour;" and the party at the Lodge agreed so to occupy the leisure of that forenoon. Some of them were going probably to examine the ruins for the first time with a fresh curiosity, and others to survey them with a parting glance; but all full of hope and glee in the prospect of quitting the quiet Lodge and upland neighbourhood of Huntly, and accompanying their loved hostess to her new home in the spacious ducal residence of Gordon Castle, with its large and beautiful domain.

The Duchess went along with them, thoughtful at one generation having gone that another might come, saddened at leaving scenes she had loved so well, and deeply burdened with the vast responsibility of which the princely palace was to be the index and the centre.

The other ladies, with lighter heart and nimbler foot that day than hers, were climbing the broken stairs and exploring the ancient stronghold from its dungeon beneath to its battlements above ; and with quicker eyes, for she was not long-sighted, were trying to trace the sculptures and decipher the legends of the olden time. She alone found nothing to attract or interest.

A century ago there was still "the grand hall sixteen feet in height, with another grand apartment immediately over it, and the chimneys of both highly ornamented with curious sculpture." But the ceiling of the one, along with the floor of the other, was already gone, and the interior of the northern wall of the Castle remained very much as at the present day ; with the stag-hounds of the Gordon arms and other sculptures, as shown in the photographic Vignette of our title-page, surrounding the desolate hearth of the oldest home of the now extinct family. The carved figures on the fine old chimney-piece are still well preserved. The inscriptions are at a great height above the eye from the present floor, but they are fresh and entire ; the longest of them running along the whole breadth of the lintel, with others briefer chiselled upon scrolls on the right and left. The ladies looked at them, but failed to make them out ; they asked the Duchess if she knew what they were, but she had to confess her ignorance; and as she made no effort in a vain attempt to help them at the moment, they all passed on in search of anything else that might present itself to their curiosity. But— .

" Place in stony hands that pray for ever,
    Tender words of peace ; and strive to wind
  Round the leafy scrolls, and fretted niches,
    Some true loving message to your kind.

.   .   .   .   .

And think when years have floated onward,
    And the stone is grey, and dim, and old,
  And the hand forgotten that has carved it,
    And the heart that dreamt it still and cold ;

There may come some weary soul o'erladen,
    With perplexed struggle in his brain,
  Or it may be fretted with life's turmoil,
    Or made sore with some perpetual pain :

Then I think those stony hands will open,
  · And the gentle lilies overflow
With the blessing and the loving token,
    That you hid there many years ago."

Left alone the young Duchess stood pensive and burdened, absorbed in the past and the future, while gazing vacantly on the cold and voiceless stones on the other side of the old saloon. Just then the sun burst suddenly from behind a cloud through the broken window mullions over her head, his beams shone bright upon the opposite wall, and in their light she read these words taken nearly from our old Bibles :

TO · THAES · THAT · LOVE · GOD · AL · THINGIS · VIRKIS · TO · THE · BEST ·

The letter written and engraven on stones was glorious to the outward eye; but its glory was dimmed by the glory that excelled in the light of the Spirit, which shone in that moment on the word written with the finger of God upon her heart. The burden was lifted in an instant from her spirit; and she went forward relieved and gladdened. "It was," she often said, "a message from the Lord to my soul, and came to me with such power that I went on my way rejoicing."

Ever after, Romans viii. 28 was one of the pillars that upheld the temple of God in her heart; one of the elements that leavened her spiritual life. Usually her memory was not precise, nor her recollection quick for chapter and verse of Scripture; but if Romans viii. 28 was ever wanted, she would joyfully repeat it; or if any one sought to find "All things work together for good to them that love God," her countenance brightened, and she would answer, "Oh, I know very well where *that* is."

This text pertains to support and consolation rather than to guidance, yet it serves to bring out a deep element in the inner life of the Duchess of Gordon; and to illustrate the combined leading of providence and grace through all her life. The word of God shone upon by the Spirit was the light to her path during all her pilgrimage, and imparted to her whole

walk a singular decision, consistency, and perseverance. "My web of life he wove" was in later years
a favourite expression often on her lips, and her eyes
were ever toward Him for the ordering of all her
footsteps. In this view she read with interest, but
with sorrow, the life of the *Earnest Student*, and its
touching account of one now entered into the rest of
his Lord; remarking that she looked upon the course
of young Mackintosh as an affecting example of a
talented and devoted youth who, with all his qualifications literary and spiritual, seemed to have missed
his providential path by delaying so long to enter the
ministry, and had died at nearly the same age as
Robert M'Cheyne without having begun the great
work of his life. Special providential leading after
the manner of Newton and Boston, with application
of the Word to the soul and then to the way, lay very
near to her heart; and entered largely into the firmness with which she took her steps, always more difficult, as well as more momentous in so conspicuous
a position as hers.

Such guiding, in its combination of quietness with
decision, is probably more characteristic of a bygone
generation than the present. It was deeply marked
in her old friend, the widow of the Rev. Dr. Buchanan
of the Canongate, and the friend and correspondent of
Simeon, who was amongst the few that had prayed

for her in youth, and who closely resembled her both in large-hearted bounty and in steadfastness of course. That old lady, reserved and silent on subjects of spiritual experience generally, on taking some very important step after thought and secret prayer, would, rarely yet very significantly, make such a remark as this: "The word of the Lord came to his servants of old, and it is the same still."

In such leadings the Duchess knew well that the soul is never safe without severe self-discipline, and that acting on special guidance is always safest in time of trial; and along with this lesson she had learned also the command, "Hast thou faith? have it to thyself before God." Yet she had been taught that "the secret of the Lord is with them that fear him," and that "the sons of God are led by the Spirit of God;" and she firmly believed in the promise, "I will teach thee in the way which thou shalt go, I will guide thee with mine eye."

On the day following her visit to the old Castle, or the next day after, she was to set out for her new home; and she read that morning, as her daily habit then was, a portion of Bogatsky's *Golden Treasury*. She had missed the proper passage the day before, from two leaves of the book having accidentally stuck together; and this morning the omitted portion presented these words to her earnest eye: "Have not I

commanded thee? Be strong and of a good courage;
be not afraid, neither be thou dismayed : for the Lord
thy God is with thee whithersoever thou goest."
(Joshua i. 9.) "That was another message from the
Lord," she used to say, "that put strength into me;"
and the verse was greatly loved by her to the end
of life.

Several years after her widowed return to Huntly
Lodge, she writes from it on 16th August 1843 : "It
was this day sixteen years that the text in Bogatsky
was given to me from Joshua i. 9, and truly I have
found the goodness of the Lord with me, and every
thing temporal that I committed to him he has indeed
kept. It is really most wonderful when I see trials
and troubles all around me, to see how everything I
prayed for regarding my own home has been accomplished; and shall I not trust him for my soul, and
for all that guidance I so greatly need in all that
he would have me to do? Surely he will guide
me in spiritual as well as in temporal things; and
the more I cease from man, and from any child of
man, the more I shall be enabled to live simply to
his glory."

After the lapse of another sixteen years, and within
a fortnight of her death, hearing that a young man in
whom she was interested was burdened about his way
in preparation for the ministry, she said : "He looks

to difficulties; give him for a New-Year's message from me, Joshua i. 9 : 'Have not I commanded thee ? Be strong and of a good courage ; neither be thou dismayed.' These words were given to me after Duke Alexander's death, and from that day onward they have been a help to me."

Strengthened thus once and again by the word of the Lord given through providence as well as by grace, she left Huntly Lodge for Gordon Castle ; and trusting in it she was not put to shame, for "the Lord her God was with her whithersoever she went." Transferred to a more trying sphere, the Duchess of Gordon took up her cross more boldly than the Marchioness of Huntly, made a more open profession of her faith in Christ, kept a wider separation from the world and its vanities, and amidst all the allurements of earth set her affections more firmly on "things above, where Christ sitteth at the right hand of God."

CHAPTER V.

GORDON CASTLE.

1827–1836.

" Fame, honour, beauty, state, train, blood, and birth,
Are but the fading blossoms of the earth.
Would the World now adopt me for its heir,
Would beauty's queen entitle me the fair ;
Could I be, more than any one that lives,
Great, fair, rich, wise, all in superlatives :
Yet I more freely would those gifts resign,
Than ever fortune would have made them mine ;
And hold one minute of this HOLY LEISURE
Beyond the riches of that empty pleasure ;
And if contentment be a stranger then,
I'll ne'er look for it but in heaven again."

SIR HENRY WOTTON.

AFTER the memorable visit to the Old Ruin, Huntly Lodge was left by the Duke and Duchess for GORDON CASTLE. The Marquis had been well known and extremely popular amongst the tenantry on the Gordon estates, not through any efforts for obtaining applause, but from his own noble and most generous nature, aided by genuine frankness and affability ; and they were not disappointed in their confident hopes of finding in him a kind and liberal landlord. Amongst many tokens of his popularity in a wider sphere there are handsome monuments erected to his memory in various places ; and there was a magnificent silver candelabrum presented to him by the County, as Lord Lieutenant ofAberdeenshire, which was a heavy burden for several men to carry. It was left by him to the Duchess, by whom it was bequeathed as an heirloom.

On their arrival at Fochabers the tenantry met them with the demonstrations of kindly feeling that are usual on such occasions; and in this case with the warm expressions of an affection most sincerely felt. But while the Duchess quite enjoyed such tokens of attachment as the fiery cross blazing on the Highland mountains, it was no pleasure to her, but a pain to see the tenants unyoke the horses and draw the carriage down to the Castle. The customariness of this mode of showing respect made it little thought of by others, but she felt it to be a degradation for men to humble themselves before their fellow-creatures by taking the place of beasts of draught. Such a homage was repulsive to all her feelings both as a woman and as a Christian, and she never mentioned it but with pain and aversion.

Her Grace's letters in our possession are for the first few years at Gordon Castle merely brief notes, but the change in the tone of her correspondence is marked and immediate. Whoever the correspondent may be, or whatever the subject, there is always some reference to that which chiefly engaged her heart. In her shortest notes she qualifies a report of unfavourable weather with the brightening ray "but it is good;" her disappointment at not meeting a friend with the consolation "but it is better not, or it would be;" and so in everything else.

The morning prayers with her servants and lady visitors, which she had begun at Huntly Lodge, were maintained from her entrance into Gordon Castle. In the following year, while she was thus engaged one morning, the Duke unexpectedly entered the room. She rose, laid her hand upon his shoulder, and whispered some remark in his ear, when he gave a good-natured shrug and withdrew. Immediately after she procured the assistance of a catechist to conduct worship in the family till his place was more adequately supplied by the Rev. David Dewar, a licentiate of the Church of Scotland. The Duke became a regular attendant at the morning devotions, and afterwards in case of necessity he read the family prayers.

The Duchess appears never to have kept any continuous account of her life, although she was in the habit of jotting down her thoughts in pocket almanacs; but among some other papers we find a Diary for a single week at Gordon Castle, in the year following her husband's accession to the dukedom. This journal, which is marked by her own sterling honesty, is so brief that we transcribe it entire.

Novr. 16*th*, 1828 (*Sabbath*).—Rose at 8. After dressing offered up my prayers for the grace and assistance of God's Holy Spirit to strengthen my faith. My heart is harder than stone, with a mind convinced of the truth of the Divine word. I find my love and gratitude to Jesus so cold, so dead, that

I cannot even command my thoughts while offering up my short prayers.

"I desired to have resolution to commence and continue a journal, that I might obtain a clearer view of my own heart, which I know, alas! to be deceitful above all things and desperately wicked. Well may I say with Job, I abhor myself and repent in dust and ashes.

"9 *o'clock.*—Decided with Mrs. R. that I should continue to choose prayers myself, and not to follow the morning form of the Church. Looked out prayers, lesson, and sermon : prayers, Cotteril ; Lesson iii. John ; sermon, Simeon, Romans vi. 8-11.

"*Ten.*—Breakfast : joined in the conversation about horse-racing, for which I am sorry ; as, though but a few words, it might seem to approve, and I dreaded lest unpleasant discussion should be the consequence.

"Went to the English chapel ; cold and indifferent in the prayers. I listened to the sermon more with hope to find fault than to profit. It was, however, good : a comparison between the righteous and the wicked, here and hereafter. Text, Proverbs.

"At home, returned to look over prayers and sermon.

"At 3 went up to Cossens ; began Anne Murdoch with 'Shorter Catechism,' which she seemed to understand.

"3½.—Prayers : enabled to pray with less wan-

dering and more fervour, but afterwards found poor
Cossens very ill; indeed, she asked me to pray but
I could only join her, and felt bitterly the hardness
of my heart and want of grace. But God hath promised that where any two are agreed their prayer
shall be granted, and he will have, he has had mercy
on her soul for Christ's sake.

"*Six.*—Dinner. At 8 returned to her, found her
better, with much hope in the Saviour; and although
she has not yet the clear view of Jesus we desire, she
feels an assured hope that she shall see him as he is,
and she knows that he who cannot lie has said that
all those who come unto him shall not be cast out.
Sermon, Noel's; Prov. i. 33; good.

"How wretched is this review of the Lord's day!
'Lord, take away this heart of stone and give me a
heart of flesh. Lord, I believe, help thou mine unbelief.' Let me count all but loss for the glory of the
Cross of Christ, and let me have no other desire but to
accomplish thy will. And now, O Lord, I commend
myself to thee this night, body and soul; guard my
dear husband from all evil, and teach us both that
the peace of God passeth all understanding, and is
of more value than anything this world can give.

"17*th, Monday.*—A day lost though well begun :
more peace, more clear belief, but alas! not less indifference, not less hardness of heart; great idleness;

after breakfast little or nothing done. O Lord, deliver me from pride and vanity, and make me a humble and devoted follower of the meek and lowly Jesus. He indeed is our peace.

"18*th, Tuesday.*—Another unprofitable day, but when, alas! is any day otherwise with me? In the morning continued 'Samuel;' may I be always ready to say, 'Speak, Lord, for thy servant heareth;' and let me constantly lean on Jesus as the Rock of Ages.

"19*th.*—I had some little time for reflection while sitting for my picture, but still the actions are like Martha, 'cumbered about many things.' But blessed be God who has given me more hope and joy in believing. May he keep me from presumptuous sins, and enable me to look with a single eye to God.

"20*th.*—Before breakfast as usual studied 'Henry's Bible;' 6th Samuel. How apt indeed is the natural man to seek and *find* excuses for all that is wrong! How apt am I in my idleness, coldness, lukewarmness, to say to myself, Oh, I cannot do otherwise, circumstances will not permit, etc.; and on the contrary, when trusting simply on the word of God, how wonderfully are 'the valleys exalted and the high places made low.' Still an unprofitable day; will it ever be otherwise? Yet I must acknowledge mercies innumerable even this day and every day of my existence. O Lord, make me truly thankful, and take away, I beseech thee, this heart of stone ; and let me love, as he ought to be loved, that Jesus who saved us from our sins, who is the Lord God blessed for ever. 'Hide not thy face from me ; be thou my salvation.'

"*Novr.* 21.—O Lord God, deliver me, I beseech thee, from lukewarm indifference to the blessed tidings of salvation. Thanks be to thee that I can now feel that Jesus is my Saviour ; but alas ! alas ! what does this profit ! All that belongs to me is only evil continually ; each day is as unprofitable as the last. Still this unprofitableness may be because I am still disposed to look to my own works which are worse than nothing, like Martha troubled about many things. I cannot wait humbly on the Lord. But thy grace is sufficient, and I know that the desires of my heart offered up in prayer shall be accomplished, and that if I commit my way unto the Lord he will surely bring it to pass. 'Wait, I say, on the Lord.'

"22*d, Saturday.*—On a review of the past week, what have I to observe but unprofitableness and indifference ! In the beginning of the week positive unbelief, because I would not look simply with a single eye to Christ, but wished reason and argumentative proofs to convince me of what can only be taught of the Spirit. O that I could pour out my soul in thankfulness to God for the blessed revelation.

"Bless my dear husband, and make him taste that

peace which the world can neither give nor take
away. Bless all that belongs to us ; purify my heart
more immediately, that I may know him who is of
purer eyes than to behold iniquity. Enable me to
support all the trials, great or small, which in thy
good providence thou seest fit for me. Give me
strength and courage to be useful, but oh let me not
trust in anything that I do.

"Sins of the week : unbelief proceeding from pride
of reason, selfishness, carelessness, hardness of heart,
vanity, evil speaking. Against thee, thee only, have
I sinned! The blood of Christ washes away all sin.
Lord, I believe, help thou mine unbelief."

Her self-accusation for the sin of evil-speaking is
noteworthy ; because it was impossible for any one
acquainted with her not to remark in her conversation a remarkable freedom from that vice, which so
easily besets us all, and also from its kindred habit
of taking pleasure in idle gossip.

From this journal it appears that the Duchess was
at this date conducting prayers herself, but that she
did not use her own words. Her maid Cossens, suffering under sickness, did not now despise the Bible-
reading Methodism of her Grace, but sought the same
consolation for herself ; yet it seems that the Duchess
felt unable to pray by her sick-bed. Afterwards, in
her widowhood, she always prayed in the family

without a form; and her prayers were characterized by unction, fluency, and power.

LONDON IN 1830-1832.

The vigilance of the Duchess over her own heart now extended itself to all that was under her control. In Gordon Castle "the world and the fashion thereof" were disowned by her from the first; as one distinctive token, there were no balls there during the nine years of her residence; and she set herself, according to the wisdom given her, to seek the spiritual good of her guests. There was much of course that did not fall under her own sphere, and which she could not regulate after her own mind, but as far as in her lay the house was now ruled in the fear of the Lord.

Her zeal was at the same time so tempered with the meekness of wisdom, and in her secret sorrow for slighted mercy she so remembered the precept to "anoint the head in fasting," that the affections of the Duke were not estranged, but strengthened by her heavenly grace. The year following the date of the Diary which we have already quoted was 1829, so memorable at Gordon Castle by its great flood, preceded by the burning of one of the wings of the house; and it was then, after making full proof of the unbending steadfastness and daily progress of her reli-

'gious course, that the Duke said, " I am unfortunate in everything except a good wife."

Next year, in May 1830, the accession of William IV. to the throne brought the Duchess of Gordon into terms of great intimacy with the Court. Queen Adelaide selected her as Mistress of the Robes at the Coronation, and honoured her ever after with her special friendship. Too often in the Christian life, every addition to the cares and allurements of the world tends to deaden the higher affections for a season, and we should now have feared some arrest of spiritual progress in the midst of the highest honours and strongest attractions of earth. But just as in her own personal elevation to the rank of Duchess, so now in her being called to share largely in the royal favour, we come upon deeper tokens of earnestness of spirit, and further footsteps in the narrow way.

The ministers whom she had been accustomed to hear in Scotland, either parochial or Scotch Episcopal, had not been men in whose services she could find much either to instruct or to edify. But her awakened spiritual instincts now discovered in the Rev. Mr. Howels of Longacre a pastor who presented living bread to her hungering soul. She was deeply interested in his preaching, as in that also of Mr. Harington Evans, and of Mr. Blunt of Chelsea. But Mr. Howels came first, and his teaching both greatly

furthered her spiritual progress at the time, and left
the deepest and most lasting impression on her mind.

Long after his death she used often to quote his
pithy sayings, such as—" If a Christian is only a shoe-
black, he should be the best shoe-black in the parish ;"
his striking illustration of the complete corruption of
fallen man : " When the tiger saw his own image in
the glass, he sprang upon it and broke it into a hundred pieces, but every piece reflected the image of the
tiger ;" and his picture of the remembrance of sin in
heaven : " God puts his people's sins behind his back,
that he may never see them any more, but that they
may see them as a dark cloud behind Him, causing
the brightness of his glory to shine forth the more
transcendently."

Mr. Howels was invited by her Grace to Gordon
Castle, as Mr. Blunt and others were afterwards, as
an honoured servant of the Lord Jesus Christ, whose
fellowship in the gospel would be a privilege and joy
to herself, while his presence in the house might further
the highest welfare of her friends, and his preaching
be blessed to the profit of many. In her widowhood
there was no house in the land more open than hers
to every minister of Christ for his Master's sake ; but
Mr. Howels was probably the first who was invited on
this footing of spiritual friendship. He accepted the
invitation on the condition, most acceptable to her,

that they should have daily Bible-readings together ;
but he did not accomplish the visit the first year, and
when two years were passed his Lord called him home,
to her deep grief and the great loss of the Church of
Christ.

It is under his ministry, in May 1830 and the
following months, that we find the first notes of sermons taken by the Duchess, just when the highest
honours of the Court were enjoyed by her through the
accession of Queen Adelaide.   She then commenced
that course of note-taking, in which she persevered
with singular diligence for thirty years to come.   This
exercise formed ever after quite an important part of
the occupation and enjoyment of her life ; for the notes
were taken very fully in pencil at the time, and carefully copied out during the week.   They embraced
two sermons every Sabbath, and often included the
less elaborate remarks of a week-day service.   The
manual effort did not appear to interrupt in the least
the emotions of her heart ; the preacher's words had
evidently the same effect in convincing, comforting,
and instructing her, as if she had been only engaged
in hearing them.   The same freedom, however, could
not always be affirmed on the part of the minister,
especially in less formal services ; for her seat was
never distant from the pulpit, and the sound of the
rapid running of her pencil over the page would some-

times suggest the thought, that what he was uttering was not worthy of being so recorded.

The Duchess always enjoyed a sermon preached greatly more than a sermon read, of which she also found the notes more hard to take ; and the ministers of her choice, as Mr. Howels in London, and Dr. Rainy and Mr. Williamson at Huntly, prepared their sermons carefully, but did not read them. Yet she could not endure mere talking in the pulpit, or the slovenly discharge of its high and holy work ; and even at the hands of good men, it was a severe deprivation when her spiritual food for the week was spoiled by remissness in preparing it for use. But if the light of the Spirit was absent in the ministry, and the bread of life was not broken, no gifts, however great, were of any account to her ; the painted stone was no food for her hunger ; the flickering sparks of mere natural eloquence left to her only a dark blot, for what was ever looked to by her waiting eye as the central light in the week.

For the last quarter of a century, the large stores of her manuscript sermons are chiefly taken from Scotch ministers ; we are therefore the happier in being enabled to present a specimen of her notes from an English divine. Amongst her manuscripts there are between twenty and thirty sermons by Mr. Howels ; the notes are very copious, as they usually were when she was deeply interested; but instead of giving a single sermon entire, we have extracted a number of detached sentences from nearly as many sermons. These thoughts, so valuable in themselves, will serve to show the truths that were arresting the mind of the Duchess, and feeding her soul at this period; and also to indicate her own sentiments, because she would occasionally mark her expression of dissent from particular statements.

"Professors of the present day want to keep both worlds; but we must determine to press into the kingdom so earnestly, that the loss of what is dear to us as a right arm may not deter us."

"Come to the Saviour as you are; yes, but come to be what you are not.—If faith is the fountain, obedience will be the stream flowing from it; delightful filial obedience is always the consequence of justification through Christ."

"When God's children under chastisement learn that the rod is in the hand of a tender Father, it becomes endeared to them.—God is good in giving, but is better in taking away, for then he leaves himself in all his goodness.—God loves his family as well upon earth as he will do in heaven; the soldier is as much esteemed in the field as at home."

"To make sin offensive to the sinner is a mightier work of God than the creation of the world."

"The defect in the profession of the day is that it makes not God its object; all finite being is infinitely unworthy of the whole human heart.—Spirituality is that virtue which embraces God as the supreme good of creation.—Woe to that man or woman who intermeddles with anything without having intercourse with God."

" Election is absolutely necessary, even on the supposition of one sinner being saved.—God gives his Son as fully to each one of us as if he had only one child to redeem ; God only can do this.—The whole earth proves that God is merciful."

" Thank God unceasingly, and be diligent; do not rest satisfied : while you work for others, begin with God and end with God, and with yourselves ; but ever be ashamed of yourselves and give God all the glory."

" The obedience of the Church during the millennial period is the obedience of faith, differing only in degree, not in kind, from what it now is. When man is so full of love to God that his cup runneth over, then he will know the millennium."

"The humanity of Christ was as free from sin as his deity, else they could not have been united."

" Heaven cannot contain all the love of God, nor hell all his hatred of sin ; but the covenant contains both in the sacrifice of his Son."

" It is not surprising that the shepherds could not

remain silent, but surprised the people by telling the
wondrous tale of Bethlehem ; but Mary kept all these
things and pondered them in her heart, for her faith
could even tame the tongue."

"The best reasoner who ever spoke disarmed Satan
by the word of God, saying, 'Thus it is written.'—In
Christ we have a speaker, from whose lips flowed the
universe in more than its present beauty, and we will
not listen to him.—He alone has an ear for music, who
has an ear to the will of God."

"Punishment is not an arbitrary act of Deity ;
the law without a penalty would be nothing.—If
God has not passions, he has principles in the highest
degree."

"Sin must die many deaths : one is famine ; give
it nothing contrary to God's word.—There is now a
general profession of Christianity, but very slight conviction of sin, which prevents the reception of the
truth. We cannot know too much of our weakness
and depravity ; the danger is knowing too little. May
God convince us of the evil and desert of sin, and
hold us in his hand while he does so, that we may not
sink under the load of such horror. We cannot see
the deformity of sin till we contrast it with the mercy
of God, neither can we appreciate the mercy of God
till we know in some degree the evil from which we
are saved."

" All finite beings are destitute of more life than they are possessed of.—Everything in Deity is incomprehensible and must be so for ever; but we shall know much more than we do, especially of the moral perfections of Jehovah."

" All the beauty of colour proceeds from light. The diamond is the brightest emblem of the child of God ; buried in the depth of its parent earth, when brought forth to the light of day it receives all its beauty and lustre from the sun ; and so does the believer from Christ, the Sun of Righteousness."

" A preacher has but one voice ; example has ten thousand tongues."

" It is more to Daniel's honour that he continued in his distress to pray three times a day than if he had prayed four times ; for it showed the efficacy of his prayer, and that he was unmoved : ' He that believeth shall not make haste.'—A conscience at peace with God gives a man invincible fortitude."

" Consider the intimate union between Father, Son, and Holy Ghost, closer even than that between the deity and humanity of Christ; the Son, Father, and Spirit in infinite love and fellowship with each other, and this including the love and fellowship to fallen man. God, Father, Son, and Spirit our delightful theme morning, noon, and night ; the angels also filled with the love of God, bending towards each other, cry,

' Holy, holy, holy, Lord God Almighty,' to whom be glory, honour, and power, for ever and ever."

OUTWARD AND INWARD LIFE IN 1833.

Gordon Castle was visited in 1833, to which our narrative now brings us, by an American gentleman, who portrays the surface of the scene with the pen of a clever and lively writer. In several circumstances, which we omit, his description is inaccurate ; it always tends to exaggeration, and is highly coloured through-out. When most faithful, it is the account of a foreigner detailing nothing that was peculiar to Gor-don Castle, but only what he would have found in the mansions of other noblemen and gentlemen. The Duchess was annoyed with it in various respects, as well as by its publicity ; and, to a friend who playfully inquired for some particular features that had amused her, she replied that she had never seen them.

But the writer, after travelling through various lands, had been in other noblemen's houses in our own ; and there must have been something extremely fascinating in the one which he designates by the title of a "Castle of Felicity ;" and to its attrac-tions the accomplishments, affability, and good sense of the Duchess largely contributed. Some extracts from his glowing pages will serve to show the allurements through which she was threading the narrow path to life and walking humbly with her God ; while it is not a little instructive, that the ten days which he most sentimentally " set apart in his memory as a bright ellipse in the usual procession of joys and sorrows, a little world walled in from rudeness and vexation in which he had lived a life," were spent under the roof of a lady who at that very moment was counting all her wealth and rank only loss for the excellency of Jesus Christ.

" The immense iron gate surmounted by the Gordon arms, the handsome and spacious stone lodges on either side, the canonically fat porter in white stockings and gay livery lifting his hat as he swung open the massive portal, all bespoke the entrance to a noble residence. The road within was edged with velvet sward, and rolled to the smoothness of a terrace walk ; the winding avenue lengthened away before, with trees of every variety of foliage ; light carriages passed me, driven by ladies or gentlemen bound on their afternoon airing ; keepers with hounds and terriers, gentlemen on foot idling along the walks, and servants in different liveries hurrying to and fro, betokened a scene of busy gaiety before me. I had hardly noted these various circumstances before a sudden curve in the road brought the castle into view, a vast stone pile with castellated wings ; and in another moment I was at the door,

where a dozen powdered footmen were waiting on a
party of ladies and gentlemen to their several carriages.   I passed the time till the sunset looking out
on the Park.   Hill and valley lay between my eye
and the horizon ; sheep fed in picturesque flocks, and
small fallow deer grazed near them ; the trees were
planted, and the distant forest shaped by the hand of
taste ; and broad and beautiful as was the expanse
taken in by the eye, it was evidently one princely
possession.   A mile from the Castle wall, the shaven
sward extended in a carpet of velvet softness as bright
as emerald, studded by clumps of shrubbery like
flowers wrought elegantly on tapestry, and across it
bounded occasionally a hare, and the pheasants fed
undisturbed near the thickets.   This little world of
enjoyment, luxury, and beauty lay in the hand of
one man, and was created by his wealth in these
northern wilds of Scotland.   I never realized so forcibly the splendid results of wealth and primogeniture.

" . . . I was sitting by the fire when there was a
knock at the door, and a tall, white-haired gentleman,
of noble physiognomy, but singularly cordial address,
entered, with a broad red ribbon across his breast,
and welcomed me most heartily to the Castle. . . .
The Duchess, a tall and very handsome woman, with
a smile of the most winning sweetness, received me at
the drawing-room door, and I was presented to every

person present. Dinner was announced immediately, and the difficult question of precedence being sooner settled than I had ever seen it before in so large a party, we passed through files of servants to the dining-room. It was a large and very lofty hall, supported at the end by marble columns. The walls were lined with full-length family pictures, from old knights in armour to the modern dukes in kilt of the Gordon plaid ; and on the sideboard stood services of gold plate, the most gorgeously massive and the most beautiful in workmanship I have ever seen. There were among the vases several large coursing cups, won by the Duke's hounds, of exquisite shape and ornament. . . . The Jacobite songs, with their half-warlike, half-melancholy music, were favourites of the Duchess of Gordon, who sang them in their original Scotch with great enthusiasm and sweetness.

"The aim of Scotch hospitality seems to be to convince you that the house and all that is in it is your own, and you are at liberty to enjoy it as if you were, in the French sense of the French phrase, *chez vous*. The routine of Gordon Castle was what each one chose to make it. The second afternoon of my arrival I took a seat in the carriage with Lord A., and we followed the Duchess, who drove herself in a pony-chaise, to visit a school in the grounds. There were a hundred and thirty little creatures, from two to

five or six, and it was an interesting and affecting
sight.   They went through their evolutions, and
answered their questions with an intelligence and
cheerfulness that were quite delightful ; and I was
sorry to leave them, even for a drive in the loveliest
sunset of a lingering day of summer. . . . The
number at dinner was seldom less than thirty, but
the company was continually varied by departures
and arrivals.   No sensation was made by either one
or the other.   A carriage drove to the door, was dis-
burdened of its load, drove round to the stables, and
the question was seldom asked, 'Who is arrived?'
You are sure to see at dinner; and an addition of
half a dozen to the party made no perceptible difference in anything."[1]

So the outer picture smiles to the eye of the stranger,
and such we find it transferred to his printed page :
" A castle of felicity, where the *gêne* of life seemed
weeded out, and into which, if unhappiness or *ennui*
found its way, it was introduced in the sufferer's own
bosom."   But the inner side of the canvas presents a
very different scene, when we turn to our manuscript
for what was passing meanwhile within the breast of
his noble hosts.   Duke Alexander had left the estates
heavily burdened, and it had been found neces-

---

[1] *Pencillings by the Way*, by H. P. WILLIS, Esq.   Date of the visit not
given, but the public events referred to appear to make it 1833.

sary to place them under trust, for the sale of large portions in order to relieve the rest, and for confining the yearly expenditure to a limited portion of the entire income. Before the Duke's death these measures were becoming effectual to allow him a free use of his revenues, but meanwhile there was a fixed sum allotted by the trustees for the expenses of his establishment. This included all that befitted his ducal rank; but the allowance for charities would scarcely be on a generous scale, and would not include extraordinary efforts that demanded a large amount. The Duchess, who was always anxious for infant-schools, was now also set on building and endowing a chapel in connexion with the Church of England, that both she and the people might enjoy the pure preaching of the gospel, which she could not find in the neighbourhood. The Duke entered cordially into her views, and having an ample allowance for horses, proposed of his own accord to sell some of these to assist.

Meanwhile the state of his feelings is described in the following letter, written to a friend in the south, and · evidently referring to a grant of £300, which the Duchess mentions as having been made by the Trustees to assist in the erection of the school. The letter is highly honourable to the feelings of the Duke, and although it is dated about ten months earlier than

the visit of the American traveller, there had been no
alteration of circumstances in the interval :—-

" GORDON CASTLE, *November* 10*th*, 1832.

"MY DEAR SIR,—I really cannot express how
much I feel obliged by your ready attention to my
request, for I certainly was most anxious to do what
I knew would be agreeable to the Duchess, the more
so as it was in a good and useful cause, and there
is no saying but the schoolroom may rise up to be
a small chapel.   Had I the means, the work would be
accomplished, but there never was in my life the
power of doing so little. . . . My situation vexes me,
but I bear up as well as I can ; for did my excellent
wife know my feelings she would be miserable.   You,
who know the world well, may easily believe that it
annoys one with a generous heart not to be able to
meet the constant applications made to me.   You
will excuse this long story, for I am convinced you
take a warm and friendly interest in everything concerning me.—Believe me, my dear Sir, yours very
sincerely,   GORDON."

A greater contrast cannot well be conceived than
between the stranger's surface picture and the Duke's
confidential account of his own feelings.   The tourist's
memorandum made in Gordon Castle : " A season
of unalloyed happiness, a bright ellipse in the usual

procession of joys and sorrows; no unhappiness finding its way into the Castle, but what was introduced in the sufferer's own bosom." The Duke of Gordon's private record : "My situation vexes me, but I bear up as well as I can ; for did my excellent wife know my feelings she would be miserable."

Let us now turn to the "excellent wife," from whom her husband was so careful to conceal his own sorrow lest it should burden her, " the tall and very handsome Duchess with her smile of most winning sweetness," the bright centre of the charming circle. The traveller's eye is attracted by the splendid sideboard laden with services of gold plate, the most gorgeously massive, and the most beautiful in workmanship he had ever seen, and vases of exquisite shape and ornament. The eye of the Duchess rests upon it also; not thinking however on the golden vases that now glitter there, but on one, doubtless the finest of them all for it cost £1200, which she has left in London to be sold for the chapel, and wondering if it has yet found a purchaser.

The traveller came down to breakfast, and found the guests already seated round the table. But there had been long before this time a room fitted up in the Castle expressly as a little chapel for morning family prayers. Hence the voice of psalms had

already risen, aided by the tones of an organ ; which
the Duchess had introduced for the special purpose of
playing and singing hymns on the Sabbath evenings,
and so rendering them profitable to the mixed society
with which the house was often filled.   The Duke
was always present at these morning devotions ; and
about this time had begun occasionally to conduct
them himself,. when called upon by the absence of
the chaplain and the Duchess.   The family had thus
assembled elsewhere half an hour earlier than their
guest found them in the dining-room : and while he
was enjoying and noting the fascinating ease of the
breakfast-table, the Duchess had already written, " I
get but little time to myself ; but not being so lazy as
I used to be, find from 8½ to 10 the most profitable
hours of the day."

He describes her infant-school as very delightful,
part of an entire scene of life of which the Duchess
was the sunny centre ; but at a somewhat earlier
period, the pen of the noble hostess in his paradise of
"unalloyed happiness" wrote other thoughts in these
simple terms : " I have got a little infant-school, but
am *wofully alone* here."   Even the " phaeton and
four," and the " beautiful blood-horses prancing along"
which so charmed the stranger's eye, were not without
the " gêne" that seemed to him so thoroughly "weeded
out."   The Duke left her Grace four Flemish mares,

which she drove for some years after his death till
they were unfit for work. They were very handsome creatures, excelled in speed of pace as well as
symmetry of form, and were great favourites with the
Duchess for his sake. But about this time the glossy
beauty of their jet-black coats sometimes rendered
them useless when their services were most needed ;
for we find her writing in London to one of her
intimate friends, " I could send for you on Tuesday
evening, but my own mares are rather delicate, and
appear to me rather useless, since there is such a fuss
made about their coats, that I dare not promise to
send them *if it rains.*"

But, a few months later in the year than the traveller's rose-coloured autumn, we find the contrast
between the seeming and the real marked in all its
breadth in the following winter scene at the Castle.
It is the Sabbath evening, the eve also of the coming
year, and the ducal party in the dining-room are not
to separate till the old year has given place to the
new. For the Duchess, there is not one there that
night like-minded with herself, and the kindness of
the Duke cannot reach the inner sympathies of her
soul. Hour passes on after hour, chattily, gaily,
quickly with all the rest, but for her dragging slowly
over a crushed and weary spirit. Not a word is
uttered fit either for the sacredness of the Sabbath

or the solemnity of the dying year, while she has not
power either to quiet the babbling of the ceaseless
talk, or to cast any seasoning salt into its insipid froth.
At last the iron pierces her soul ; she can endure it
no more, and rising suddenly she rushes into her own
room to weep the tears she can no longer restrain.
The fair world so "walled in from vexation," had
brought to her nothing but a rankling sting, because
the Lord was not in it all; but sitting alone by the
fire with her face buried in her hands, she finds support and relief in Him who receives the heavy laden
into his bosom for rest.   " Here I heard these words,
as if a voice had spoken them audibly to myself :
' Will he plead against me with his great power ?   No,
but he will put strength in me.' "

One extract more, from a letter at the commencement of this year, will conclude the section, with an
outpouring of heart which cannot fail to touch the
hearts of others.   Many who earn their bread by the
sweat of their brow plead their occupation in this life,
as an excuse for not labouring for the life everlasting.
But there is a wonderful balancing of opportunity in
all positions ; and almost every letter of the Duchess
during the Duke's life complains of excessive distraction, and is full of longing for time and quiet.   Yet
in the midst of every allurement that the world could
offer, and in the throng of an unceasing bustle, though

so quietly conducted as to look to the stranger like a
perpetual calm, the longings of her heart are ever
toward the Lord, and the remembrance of his holiness :

"Seven days of this year are passed over my head,
and I have not yet written to my dearest friend. Your
complaints, my Helen, are mine, especially that hardness of heart and insensibility both to the love and
commands of God ; and oh, how much greater is my
sin than yours ; for I fear the evil with me is not only
apparent to myself but to others, for I am evidently
less disagreeable to worldly people and feel them less
so to me. Sometimes I think it is because, knowing
my own sin better, I am more indulgent ; but then
I should be more zealous to warn and carry on the
gospel message. I am quite worn out in mind by the
constant succession of company we have had, and to
how few, if any, have I been faithful as I ought!
Oh! my dearest Helen, I cannot see how I can do
otherwise than I have done; I cannot see how to
redeem the time, and yet my health is good. I can
only cry, Woe is me, unprofitable! and we have
mounted another step of the ladder towards eternity.
One thing is clearer every day, this is not our rest :
'O that I had wings like a dove!' Jane left us on
the third; we have not been as much together as we
might have been, but then I have so little time to

myself that I cannot give a part of that little every day even for Christian communion. You know it is a relief to me to pour out my heart to you; and is not this permitted, is it not indeed one of the greatest comforts which the Giver of all good has bestowed?"

PROPHECY—EDWARD IRVING—BOOKS—HOUSEHOLD.

As in most other questions of the day, so with the subject of prophecy, then so largely discussed, the Duchess made herself well acquainted; meeting also with many of its ardent, if not excited students. During these years she sought for a time to interest some of her visitors at Gordon Castle in the subject of religion, by presenting one of its more attractive aspects in the shape of books on prophecy to engage the intellect and the imagination. The bait was successful in some cases, and eagerly swallowed; but she was by and by mortified to find that it concealed no barbed hook beneath, and that the soul, though allured, was not taken and brought safe to the shore. "I saw," she said, "that people would take the crown without coming to the cross, and that cannot be." She therefore gave over the expedient for other more reliable efforts. This subject is referred to in the following letter of this year (1833): "Have you heard of Captain Gambier fasting nine days, and walking twenty-five miles at the end of the time without fatigue? The Duchess of Beaufort is a good deal troubled about it. I do not feel so, perhaps from the deadness that overwhelms me almost, but I think rather from the conviction that believers have nothing to do with miracles, as all that is necessary is in the Bible. We need no further proof. I don't know what this was intended to prove; for if it be a proof of 'the redemption of the body,' which is said to be what he sought, why did our blessed Lord eat after his resurrection? Captain G. has given everything he possessed in charity, except 7s. a week, which he shares with the *Jew* (Mr. Simons), with whom he lives; and he has reduced himself to the poorest fare in ordinary.—How sorry I am for dear old Mr. Tait; I cannot understand it; it seems to me *some* positive disbelief of the Word, which teaches us to expect no other manifestation. This is what old Bridge told me long ago, but I feel it now.

"I had a most delightful letter from Lady Dalhousie, with an account of Lord Ramsay's death. But the greatest triumph of faith I have ever read of in our day was the death of Mrs. Boswell; she really went forward as seeing Him who is, and those things which are invisible.

" I sent Lady Grace's *Boston's Christian's Walk* by Mr. Gordon; I am very much obliged by it; it ought to be reprinted. Lady Denbigh is going to reprint some sermons of Boston ; she is very fond of him. I have a folio volume of his works belonging to her ; I am reading ' On the Covenant' when I can find a quiet half hour. Is it not to be found in a smaller shape ? I think I should quite agree with you now in *all* points of doctrine ; not sure, however, about prophecy. You were beginning to study it, and I have quite left off, being satisfied that my former view of the personal reign was inconsistent with the holiness of that glorious God in Christ Jesus, who shall appear the second time without sin unto salvation. But this is not doctrine, for we both love and wait for his appearing; and oh, what comfort is there in those words of Paul, ' of whom I am chief,' when he spake of the fulness of salvation through the crucified and glorified Redeemer and Mediator. I do need your prayers, and may the Spirit of grace and truth be to us effectually the Comforter promised to lead us into all truth, and to keep us from the evil that is in the world."

The fanatic feat of Captain Gambier leads us to a portion of another letter, referring to the views of the lamented Edward Irving, so richly endowed with many gifts, but so sadly misled by his wayward fancy in his latter days. "Mandeville pointed out a very strong thing to me in consequence of the expressions used by those who speak in 'tongues,' and of Irving himself; see 1 Cor. xii. 3. Is not everything 'sinful' *accursed?* It is most painfully satisfactory to have the matter made so plain. Have you heard that Mr. Percival, Irving, some other man, and one of the gifted sisters, believe that they have raised a child of Mr. P.'s, who had been in a state of lethargy for fourteen days? I can believe it without being much impressed, when I have heard of a lady that believes in these views who sent for Mr. Blunt's curate to pray with her, and declined his ministration because he refused to pray *unconditionally,* that is, in subjection to the divine will. She said she *knew* that it would be for the glory of God that she should recover, and therefore he must pray for her recovery unconditionally. Can there be any doubt that answers to such prayers would be in anger? It is very awful."

The secret of her being kept through so long a life in the narrow path of doctrinal truth, as well as practical holiness, is found in the sentiments expressed at this time to another friend: "We must, indeed, in these times, most earnestly pray to be kept by His mighty power, that we may discern truth from error, devotion from enthusiasm, and caution from coldness; for oh how cold, how dead are some, how *ready* to be cautious, instead of being truly so through the Spirit of love and of power and of a sound mind, and the wisdom which is from above, promised to those who ask it. When we pray to be kept from error, let it be from what God knows to be error, not always what we think so, and this will keep us from prejudice. I did not intend this when I began, but I have told you what I need, and therefore I desire for you what I do for myself."

In several of these letters there is reference to books that she had been reading, and there are few subjects more frequently referred to in all her letters. With the Duke's confidential agent, William Paul, Esq., the Duchess had much correspondence, not as the Duke's amanuensis, but writing for him in her own rapid manner, yet with a precision and clearness which a man of business might envy. The entire spirit in which the letters are written is admirable : " I, confess it grieves me to think of these poor children in Bencroy, and that quarter, more than of any other particular respecting the sales of Lochaber. Can nothing be done for them ? I know you will let me know when you hear."

While the business of the letters is conducted in such a tone, there is also a frequent allusion to the nobler subjects that were nearest her own heart. After giving instruction or asking advice on the sale of large portions of the vast Gordon estates, and the entailing of others, she will add a postscript of a very different tenor. The following is one of these additions to a letter of pure business : " I continue reading Boston on the Covenant, and I do most strongly recommend it for perusal when you have time, as the book of all others which shows the fitness with which the difficult doctrines of the gospel mystery are all brought together for the salvation of the redeemed. I would, however, recommend to those who do not like to dwell on the doctrine of election, to read the head which treats of the administration of the covenant in that part which is open to the world, before they study the deeper mysteries. I wish the Glasgow reprinters would give us this most valuable work." A month later she writes again from London : " There is so much difficulty in London in procuring a copy of Boston on the Covenant, that I am induced to ask you if you could get me one, however old, as the object is to get it reprinted. I do think it most valuable and useful. I find the loss of my old friend Mr. Howels a sad blank."

In her later days she looked back with interest and profit to the views of "the everlasting covenant, well-ordered in all things and sure," which she received at this time from Boston and similar writers. Owen and Durham were also favourite authors; but perhaps the one to whom she referred oftenest, was " her old friend Bridge" of Yarmouth, in whose works, full of " the

great things faith can do, and the great things faith
can suffer," she found much good for her soul. Amongst
later writers, she took great delight in O'Brien's Sermons on Justification by Faith, his well-weighed views
commending themselves to her clear judgment. The
following notes are to different friends : " I know
Newton's works very well. Did you ever see his ob-
servations on the Oratorio of ' The Messiah ?'—I have
been much pleased lately with Brougham's Sermons
(an Irish clergyman), a small volume, and short, but
very full and strong ; truths most plainly stated in
beautiful language.—Have you ever seen *Christ our
Example* by Caroline Fry ? It is one of the most
useful modern books I have read, and so practical."

The following letters of the same year will help to
show both her diligent examination of doctrine and
her earnest striving after holiness : " I have had but
little of religious society this year, but that has been
sweet, and on the whole I think the season has given
many practical lessons, from which I hope to profit.
I have much to be thankful for. My dear husband
has not been well sometimes, but every now and then
there is such a bright gleam of sunshine to nourish
hope, that the idea of sickness and sorrow flees away.
I was a day and a half with Lady Olivia ; Mr. Dods-
worth there. It was very pleasant, and we had none
of that sort of unprofitable disquisition which I have

too often met with. Perhaps her having the house full of young people made the subjects discussed more simple, and that suits me best : the sincere milk of the Word that we may grow thereby. I have thought much of that promise, 'If ye do his will ye shall know of the doctrine whether it be of God.'

"There was a young clergyman at Brampton, who was as decided against the doctrine of general redemption as Mr. D. is for it. They said little in public about it to each other, and every word that passed was truly Christian ; but each spoke to me separately, and I own I find myself completely convinced that Mr. D.'s view is unsatisfactory and almost contradictory. So that I do think we are quite of one mind as to doctrine, and also I am sure in desiring for ourselves and each other more love, more zeal, more light and life and strength, to do all to the glory of God. May the grace of God abound in you richly with love and knowledge."

"I must tell you how much I have been delighted with an exposition of Phil. iii. from the 3d verse. St. Paul proves that the Christian can have no confidence in the flesh, that all the righteousness wherewith to appear before God must be in Christ, and that even walking according to the law blameless he counts but as dung for the excellency of the knowledge of Jesus Christ our Lord ; yet his object here is, 'if by any means he might attain unto the resurrection of the dead.' What then is this? The verses which follow show that it cannot allude to that which is to come at the great day. It means therefore that *all* things are possible to him that believeth ; that he who is in Christ can do all things through Christ which strengtheneth him, and therefore that we *must* press forward toward the mark for the prize of our high calling in Christ Jesus, if so by any means we may attain to that likeness unto him here which we shall bear when we shall see him as he is. Even now we may, by looking unto Jesus, be changed more and more into the same image as by the Spirit of the Lord.

"I have really more to do than I can accomplish, which has too often this year ended in my doing almost nothing at all that can be called doing. O that we could have, as a dear friend of mine expresses it, Mary's head and Martha's hand, never cumbered about many things, never slothful, but always doing right things at right times, and *all* to the glory of God, looking up, pressing forward, and waiting patiently, redeeming the time."

The subject of doing good to others *directly* was one of great difficulty with the Duchess to the end of her life. There was no complaint oftener on her lips than that "she was of no use, she did good to nobody ;" with a special reference to her sense of inaptitude for speaking directly to others on the subject of religion. With those who were like-minded with herself she had no difficulty whatever, but delighted in their fellowship, and took her full part in the conversation. Nor did she ever rest satisfied without more aggressive effort for souls; and while she was still Marchioness of Huntly, one of her earliest friends was led to Christ through her faithful conversation. But she ever remembered that she was a woman, and exercised great wisdom in all her walk, and could not bear its being thought that she presumed upon her rank to press her sentiments on others. The following letter is in reply to one from Miss Home, who had evidently urged her to personal dealing with her servants :

"GORDON CASTLE, *July* 27.

"You do not know how much good your letters do me, my beloved Helen; we do need in this world to help one another. St. Paul, who had been thrice told by the Lord, 'My grace is sufficient for thee,' yet complained mournfully of the absence of his fellow-labourers. True it is, I am not called to labour like St. Paul, but Wisdom hath said, 'It is not good for man to be alone.' And I am not alone in one sense ; there are, blessed be God, some Christians amongst us ; but they are not such (except Wilson, who is just now much engaged, having two houses on his hands and a gate to watch alone,

besides his usual avocations, so that I have only
seen him once for a conversation) as would speak a
word in season.

"My bustle is so different from yours, that nothing
but the fortnight's quiet we had on our first arrival
could have shown me what it is. But, dearest, I
grieve to say I do not feel as you do about my interruptions; I grieve because I am too ready to yield
to them, too ready to let that pass as an excuse
which on reflection seems a very bad one ; too ready
to say in my heart, 'The Lord requires it not,'
when he hath commanded us to do whatsoever our
hand findeth to do with all our might. I should
prefer, it is true, to sit down quietly to read or
make extracts according to my own taste; but I
feel, even when a headache or some other excuse
makes writing or business unpleasant, it is not doing
what I ought to do, because the others are things
that ought to be done. If my heart were right,
full of love and truth, I think I should have time
for all and no bustle. It is that speaking, of which
you complain, which is often my bane.

"Alas! I cannot answer your questions as I should
wish about my household, altogether, at least. I
think my housekeeper well disposed, anxious to do
right, and without prejudice, though very ignorant
of the truth. She is a bustling little woman, and

seems to know her worldly business. The Duke's servant I have many opportunities of speaking to. He is much prejudiced, and a strange Irishman ; but extremely attached to the Duke, and attentive to him, and honest, I do think, in every sense of the word, for even in his prejudice he means to be honest. The butler is very attentive indeed at family prayers, a quiet unobtrusive creature, and very stupid in many things. Mr. Dewar sees him often when we are away ; I have never spoken to him *directly*, but have given him books and tracts.

" But, dearest Helen, you do not know the difficulty I have in speaking to any one who does not meet me half way. I think if I could see my way clearly, I might get over this painful shyness, which I know would then be want of faith. But I cannot see that, situated as I am, it is my duty ; and moreover, I *fancy* I have not the talent, and it is not one which I have to account for ; for I have so often done more harm than good, even when I have prayed to be directed ; indeed, I trust I have not often had to speak without that prayer. Again, in family prayer, and in a simple word without more than the general desire for the glory of God, I have been greatly blessed in more instances than one. So I trust that, continuing earnestly to pray for that mind which was in Christ Jesus, for living faith and the power of the Spirit, I may in time be fitted for a more active station in my Master's service : 'for he that is greatest among you let him minister.'

"We have got a most excellent coachman in the place of poor B. (who had died of apoplexy on the coach-box). He was one I had some opportunities of speaking to, who discouraged me the most; it was very awful! Dixon comes to prayers regularly, and was never known to swear. I have not had anything like an opportunity (to my mind) of speaking to him yet; but I daresay, dearest, you would have found one. Oh! I do pray for more zeal for souls, more true sense of their infinite value ; for I think if I felt it as *I see* it, I should do more. Oh that we may both be filled with that love which filleth him in whom dwelleth all the fulness of the Godhead bodily; may we in every dispensation be enabled to feel that He is love. Yet I would pray, my beloved Helen, that your prayers may be heard, and that you may unite your voice in this world, with those of your dear brother and sister, in praise and thanksgiving ; and that it may not still be the ear of faith alone which heareth those praises in a beloved voice, which shall be poured forth throughout eternity. I have not ceased to read the chapter with you daily. May we learn obedience through the sufferings of our great High Priest, and be enabled

by his spirit to discern good and evil. A Dieu.
Yours most affectionately,

"E. GORDON."

LETTERS—CAPTAIN J. E. GORDON—JEWEL-STONES IN CHAPEL WALLS.

In reading these letters, it is to be borne in mind
that they are all written with a very swift pen ; not
thoughtlessly, yet in the free and rapid outpouring of
the thoughts without premeditation, and in the midst
of interruptions. The most earnest parts of them are
often broken with a parenthesis like this : "Lord
Arbuthnot waits," which we have omitted as interfering with the sense ; and to several of her correspondents she speaks of the letter she is writing as
the ninth she had written that morning. At Gordon
Castle she mentions six or seven letters daily as
part of her occupations ; but after the abolition of
franks and the introduction of the penny postage
had abridged all correspondence, the number was
sometimes doubled. There is never an attempt at
elaborate writing ; and more than once she closes
abruptly with such a remark as this, "But I think
I have said this well, and it is therefore time for
me to stop." The letters dated from London are
briefer than those at Gordon Castle, yet full of the
same spirit.

"MY DEAREST HELEN,— ... My friend had a most providential escape on her return from Windsor. The axle-tree of her carriage broke, her maid and two little girls were thrown out over her, and two men on the box, the carriage falling flat on its side ; not one hurt. It is singular that her pencil-case in her pocket was bent, yet she not bruised. I feel very much for this dear friend and her family. Their situation is a slippery one, but by grace she sees her danger in some respects ; yet she likewise sees her place to be *there* ; and many things which she could not avoid without an *éclât,* she thinks will have no bad effect if taken as matters of course. She was much pleased with the last visit to Windsor, inasmuch as, being a juvenile party, she was the only one of her Majesty's *friends* there, and therefore she had more quiet and serious conversation with her.

"Oh, how thankful ought I to be that I am kept out of the way of those who talk much without practice ! I am thankful that I have been very quiet ; have only dined out once since I came, a family-dinner at Lady Cornwallis's. I am never asked (I *don't* mean I have no invitations) to go out of an evening. The Duke does not object to my going to Mr. Evans's. Did I tell you he read prayers to the servants without my asking him, the morning I was too ill to get up ?"

" 1st May.—If I could have time to write without interruption I could now do so with much more comfort than when I last addressed you, for I was then almost in despair at my utter helplessness even to ask for strength. Mine was much of physical as well as moral debility. The former, I am thankful to say, is greatly relieved ; and the latter, though seen (and felt) even more strongly, is seen in something of the light of the Sun of Righteousness, who has arisen with healing under his wings. I think I *may* seek for strength to *bear* these interruptions, rather than to have them removed. Indeed, all along this has been clearly my duty, but my heart has been very impatient under it ; but it may be a means of helping the attainment of one great desire of my soul. I am now hardly ever alone, and as seldom have anything that interests me, though now and then there are precious morsels to cheer and encourage. Have you read Miss Graham's Memoirs ? I have only looked at them, but am told that though Mr. Bridges is disappointing, Miss G.'s *own* is most excellent and useful. Tell me if I can do anything for you here. I think we mutually do the best thing we can for each other— pray ; and I am most thankful I can again feel that I do pray. Oh for a quickening Spirit of grace and love."

. K

Toward the close of this year the letters from Gordon Castle have frequent reference to a meeting for religious objects, held apparently in the adjoining town of Fochabers. " I have unspeakable reason to be thankful for the manner in which the truth seems steadily progressing in this country, or rather corner ; and in which I have been upheld and kept in my difficulties, which seem to force me closer to the only source of strength, or comfort, or peace, or hope. He hath promised and he will perform : ' As thy day is so shall thy strength be ; in thy weakness my strength shall be found.' I have very great reason to be thankful for much that is doing here. Our little meeting is to take place, *D. V.*, on Tuesday next, when I trust some progress will be reported. Mr. S. Mackenzie of Seaforth, I hear, is to attend the meeting ; Lord Saltoun is going on purpose. How many kind friends we have ! Lord Gray, too, offered to go." And again : " Mr. Stewart Mackenzie and J. E. Gordon did wonders at our little meeting yesterday."

James Edward was Captain Gordon, then M.P. for Dundalk ; he was noted for his zealous efforts against Popery ; and, though really of a thoughtful and tender spirit, was apt to be looked upon by strangers chiefly as a Protestant champion. He was a man of sterling Christian principle, undaunted courage, and great logical powers ; and set himself so assiduously to his one great subject of the antichristian character and stealthy encroachments of Popery, that he was irresistible in argument, till shattered health compelled him to retire from public life. He was a religious friend of the Duchess before her own sentiments had become so decided, and the Duchess cherished his friendship to the end, and called upon him very frequently during the last winter she was in London. The strong man of a quarter of a century before was sadly altered now, and tottered most feebly under sickness and age ; but his intellect was clear, his memory fresh, and his spiritual affections lively. To those who knew him before, it was intensely interesting to mark how the soul of the keen and sometimes fiery disputant had become like a weaned child, and the root of grace had so grown as quite to overshadow all besides. He was longing for a sense of the Lord's presence, like those who watch for the morning, yet giving thanks for "glimpses of sunshine" in his heart. All the severity of earlier years was gone, and the fruit of the Spirit in him was singularly ripe and sweet : "bringing forth fruit in old age, to show that the Lord is upright." When so many blossoms go up like dust, such a case confirms faith, brightens hope, and kindles love. He soon followed the Duchess to the better country.

Another event of the year still remains, in the pecuniary sacrifices which the Duchess now began to

make in the Lord's service; we say *began*, not referring to the past on which we have no evidence, but to
her future course, in which a most liberal giving became a continual habit. Sacrifice of her own will and
her natural feelings she had made from the outset of
her Christian course; and every other sacrifice followed,
not always easily yet ever successfully, as the call and
the trial came. As already stated, her heart was set
both on the education of the children and the spiritual
good of the parents in the neighbourhood of Gordon
Castle, and on the erection of a school and a chapel
for these great objects. But one of her own letters
will best show how this good design was effected;
and that, like every other work of love, it became the
fruitful seed-corn of similar good works; the Duchess
of Gordon's gold vase, destined for a chapel in Morayshire, leading to the consecration of the Duchess of
Beaufort's diamond ear-rings for a chapel in Wales:

"GORDON CASTLE, *July 6th,* 1833.

"I have had so many letters to write less agreable
to me than it is to address my very dear Helen, that
more than a week has elapsed since we came home,
without my having done what I so much wished,
because I always long for the letter in return. I wrote
to Mrs. Macpherson yesterday, but was prevented
doing more according to my mind; and now I have

been talking of business first with Wagstaff, and since with the housekeeper who is about to leave me, till my head is bothered. For both their subjects are interesting; the former about our chapel and school, which led on to the objects of them; the latter about all the poor bodies, and the ways and means of being of use, and of setting the new housekeeper to the same work. She seems likely to give me more trouble than Mrs. Delbuge, but that is good for me. She has not, I should think, either the education or decision of character of Mrs. D., who certainly was the model of housekeeper to a house of this kind, and is, I do hope and trust, a Christian.

"I think our good Mr. Dewar has been of much use there. He, I am sorry to say, is very far from well; but he is such a good man, truly a Nathanael, and it is what everybody calls him. It sometimes surprises me that he should be so universal a favourite, but I know the loving-kindness of our God. There are so few here to fight for him that he, the Captain of our salvation who can soothe even his enemies, will cause them to be at peace with him and restrain the opposition, so that it should not be too much for that tender frame and tender heart.

"I was interrupted by a visit from friends, and went on with Mr. Dewar instead of the new housekeeper. She is, I think, one of those voices which

our Lord hath sent me, to cry, 'Awake thou that
sleepest!' Oh how I have slept; how awfully de-
ficient in diligence ; how much lost time ! Maria gave
me one lesson : Blessed be the promise which follows
the call, 'Christ *shall give you life.*' It is all his
work, but I have not had, because I have not asked
aright. Prayer, as well as walking, has been without
diligence. It is this *life* I want most of all ; and shall
the temple of the Holy Ghost be deserted ? Shall that
not contain a living spirit, which is destined for the
Spirit of Life ? It is want of faith to think so. It is
want of faith which makes us strive (but oh what poor
striving !) to do that for ourselves which Christ hath
promised to do in us ; and we waste time in seeking
to acquire power, instead of using that power in faith
that we have it in Christ. In him are not *all* things
ours ? More faith would make the way so much more
plain ; and how often do we find, if we do what we
can in faith, God will do more than we could either
ask or think even here. It is in temporal things, as in
spiritual doctrine, 'If ye do the will of God, ye shall
know the doctrine whether it be of him.'

"I think I told you about my wish to have an
Episcopal Chapel here (together with an infant school-
house), as the most apparent way of opposing the
increase of Popery, if we can procure a gospel minister,
which I look in faith that God will provide. I took

up to London a gold vase that cost about £1200, in
hopes of selling it, but could not find a purchaser even
at half price, and I do not like a raffle.   I have still
left it to be disposed of; but in the meantime the
chapel was begun with £300 from the trustees for
the school, and £100 of Mrs. Drummond's, which she
would subscribe.   I could not leave it unfinished, and
see how Christians help one another.   The Duchess of
Beaufort, hearing of my vase, thought of her diamond
ear-rings, which she got me to dispose of for a chapel
in Wales, and her diamonds made me think of my
jewels; and as the Duke has always been most
anxious for the chapel, he agreed with me that stones
were much prettier in a chapel wall than round one's
neck, and so he allowed me to sell £600's worth, or
rather what brought that, for they cost more than
double.   The chapel is going on nicely, and I have
still enough jewels left to help to endow it, if no other
way should open.   I do think I may with confidence
hope for a blessing on this.   It is no sacrifice to me
whatever, except as it is one to the Duke, who is very
fond of seeing me fine, and was brought up to think
it right.

  "This is not at all the letter I wanted to write to
you, but then I like you to know all I am about.   I
could say much more, but the interruptions I am now
expecting prevent me, and this is a thing I cannot

pray to get rid of. I find it one of the greatest draw-
backs to redeeming the time; and as the interruptions must needs be in my situation, why should I
not believe that God can so dispose my mind that I
should seize every moment to devote to him, or to
meditating on his word, his law, and above all, his
love? Hitherto I have fancied it impossible to give
the mind unreservedly when interruptions are expected;
but it ought not so to be, for with the temptation God
will make a way to escape, that we may be able to
bear it. Nevertheless these interruptions are a very
heavy burthen; but will not Christ bear all our bur-
thens if we lean on him? I have been thinking
much of his love lately; of the inseparable connexion
between love and sanctification; see 3d and 4th chapter
of 1st Thessalonians : love and holy obedience increasing *more* and *more,* the one helping on the other *more*
and *more,* increasing and abounding. Oh may we,
dearest, increase and abound more and more in love
and holiness, being in Christ, and Christ in us. I
trust your fears for your dear brother will be swallowed up in love; but this I know, whatever happens,
it will be in love to the children of God. May the
God of love and peace be with you."

The sums mentioned in the letter make £1000,
which was to have covered the whole expense; but
this chapel, like every other, cost another £100 before

it was finished; and the Duke, following his wife's example, offered of his own accord to sell some of his horses to make up the deficiency. There were also "jewels enough left to help to endow it," while the sacrifice of these was nothing to the Duchess; and the Duke had now come to think with her, that "stones looked prettier in a chapel wall" than on his lady's neck, so that there was no obstacle to their disposal. But a bountiful providence is ever ready to interpose on behalf of those, whether high or low, who deny themselves for the Lord's sake. Duke Alexander had given a property near Huntly to Andrew Gordon, Esq., with the power of willing it as he pleased, but with the condition that if he died intestate it should fall to the Marquis of Huntly at the time being. Duke George, when Marquis, had often reminded Mr. Gordon of his father's arrangement, and urged him to make a will in favour of some of his own relatives. This advice, however, he had neglected; and he died soon after the chapel was finished, leaving no testament, so that the Duke of Gordon, being now the only Marquis of Huntly, became his heir. The lately finished church had cost £1100, and the property thus unexpectedly falling in was worth £1100 a year. Be it Duke and Duchess, or "the maid-servant behind the mill," the Master has announced, and he keeps his promise, "Give, and it shall be given to you; good measure, heaped up and running over, shall men give into your bosom."

GORDON CASTLE IN THE SEVENTEENTH AND NINETEENTH CENTURIES—THE TEN COMMANDMENTS—1834.

In the summer of 1834 the Duchess writes: "The Duke has planned to have the two schoolrooms opened on the 20th of June, as a celebration of my birthday." When ready on that day to repair to the schools, she was surprised, on coming down to the door, to find six horses in her carriage by the Duke's orders; for he was so pleased with this desire of her heart being accomplished, that he wished to add a little state to the ceremony. The chapel was opened in the autumn by the Rev. Mr. Blunt, whose letters from her Grace would probably have thrown some interesting light on her spiritual history after the death of Mr. Howels, when she began to attend his ministry. It is so desirable in a memoir of the Duchess to preserve, as far as possible, her own breadth and catholicity of view, that we regret we have none of these to present to our readers. But the following extract is sufficient to show her enjoyment of Mr. Blunt's lectures: "*Belgrave Square, April* 1834.—London is, as usual, much ado about nothing, for though I am always in a bustle, and constantly interrupted, it does not seem to me to any end; for I have nothing to show, or even to tell for all this busy-ness, not business. During Lent I enjoyed myself very much, not missing one of Mr. Blunt's lectures, and since I came to town, I have only been at two dinner parties, besides dining once or twice at the Tweeddales and Denbigh's *en famille*. To-morrow we are going to Windsor, where we are to stay till Wednesday. I am glad that the weather seems to be greatly improved, for I rather dread His Majesty's open carriages."

In the next month, we find a reply written by the Duchess to a letter from her deceased father's parish minister on behalf of one of his poor parishioners. Her Christian course from its commencement to its close was marked by a prompt and bountiful attention to the case of the poor or distressed, and her liberality was quite as great in deeds of benevolence as in promoting the cause of the gospel: " *London,* 18*th April* 1834.—The expressions your letter contained of regard for my dear father, and consequent feelings toward myself, were more gratifying than any other testimony of esteem that you could have offered. I perfectly remember Robert Ley, and am obliged to you for letting me know that I can be of use to him. I shall be happy to allow him £4 per annum, which I should hope will be sufficient. I thank you also for mentioning other old friends,

none of whom I forget; my own maid was born at
the Burn.

"It is most melancholy to think of the state of
things connected with the Burn. Mrs. S.'s trials
have indeed been great. I trust she is enabled to
cast her care on Him who afflicteth not willingly, and
who has taught you with so much tenderness the
truth of the words of the prophet, 'Even to hoar
hairs will I carry you.' May you find that He who
enables you to tend your flock in pleasant pastures,
will bring you nearer and nearer to the good Shepherd,
until you have through grace attained to his image
and his presence for ever.

"I am happy to say that the Duke and I are quite
well. We purpose soon returning to Scotland, as
the Duke must be in his place in the General
Assembly as a ruling elder. In these times it is
absolutely necessary that those who wish well to the
Church should not remain idle."

Except for the privilege of a spiritual ministry,
London with its many distractions appears to have
brought little good to her own soul, and to have given
her little opportunity of being useful to others; and
she always contemplated with pleasure the prospect
of returning to Scotland. She writes of the Duke
being at the General Assembly of the Church of
Scotland in May; and speaks of the times being such

as require him to be in his place as an elder, although
his own sentiments appear to have been Episcopalian.
Outside the Church, the Voluntary controversy was
keenly agitated for the abolition of its endowments;
while within it Dr. Chalmers, with the other ablest
and most earnest advocates for Church Establishments,
were putting forth their utmost efforts against the
evils of lay patronage ; some seeking its entire removal,
but the majority aiming at so limiting its exercise as
to make it consistent with the spiritual well-being of
the people. With these the Duchess agreed, and wrote
at this time to a gentleman who held these views :
"You may believe that I cordially agree with what
I understand to be your views on the subject of
Church patronage. My simple politics are from
that Word which you also desire to be the rule of
your life."

The Duke's opinions were different ; and she used
to relate a conversation that occurred at this time,
not indeed on the lawfulness of patronage, but on
the manner of its exercise. The Rev. Mr. Carment
of Rosskeen, one of the most talented and respected
of the Evangelical ministers, and a veteran soldier of
the Cross, paid a visit to Gordon Castle at the close
of the Assembly ; for the Duchess earnestly embraced
every opportunity of inviting good men to the house.
Conversing on the subject with his Grace, Mr. Carment

said in his quaint Scotch style: "Ay, ay, my Lord
Duke, you and I are on opposite sides of the house;
but an' ye were seeking a shepherd you wouldna tak'
him just because he was this or that man's son, or
a man o' gude moral character, but because he kent
weel about the sheep; and my Lord Duke, in choosing a minister, you shouldna just tak' your friend's
tutor, but a man that can care for the souls of the
people."

Meanwhile the Duchess was finding great and
growing delight in her infant-school, about which at
first she seemed less hopeful. The teacher was one
after her own heart; and not a few of the children
gave her great satisfaction. Some died in infancy,
but delighting to "go to God," and departing with
the words, "Praise Father, Son, and Holy Spirit;"
others lived to comfort her by their good report in
later years.

Two hundred years ago, Gordon Castle, then called
the Bog of Gicht, presented a very different scene.
The Farquharsons of Deeside having slain a Gordon
of note, the Marquis of Huntly, along with the Laird
of Grant, prepared to take a bloody vengeance for his
death. That none of the guilty tribe might escape,
Grant occupied the upper end of the vale of Dee
with his clan, while the Gordons ascended the river
from beneath; each party killing, burning, and de-

stroying without mercy all they found before them.
The men and women of the race were nearly all
slain; and when the day was done, Huntly found
himself encumbered with about two hundred orphan
children. About a year after this foray, the Laird of
Grant chanced to dine at the Marquis's castle, and
was of course entertained with magnificence. After
dinner Huntly conducted Grant to a balcony which
overlooked the kitchen, where he saw the remains of
the abundant feast of the numerous household flung
at random into a large trough. The master-cook
gave a signal with his silver whistle; on which a
hatch like that of a dog-kennel was raised, and there
rushed into the kitchen, shrieking, shouting, yelling,
a huge mob of children, half-naked, and totally wild,
who threw themselves on the contents of the trough ;
and fought, struggled, and clamoured for the largest
share. Grant was a man of humanity, and asked,
" In the name of Heaven, who are these ?"   " They
are the children of those Farquharsons whom we slew
last year on Dee-side," answered Huntly. The Laird
felt more shocked than it would have been prudent
or polite to express.   " My Lord," he said, " my
sword helped to make these poor children orphans,
and it is not fair that your Lordship should be burdened with all the expense of maintaining them.
You have supported them for a year and day, allow

me now to take them to Castle Grant, and keep them for the same time at my cost."[1]

Such was the savage sport of the lord of Gordon Castle two hundred years ago ; and when his lady looked over that balcony, it was only to enjoy the spectacle, and not to rescue any of the wretched children from their revolting degradation. The Castle itself had been greatly altered now, retaining its ancient central tower, but surrounded with modern additions of princely dimensions, more commodious but far less picturesque. But the building was not so changed as the thoughts and habits of its noble occupiers, when the Duchess was opening schools for the children of the people and the Duke sending her in a carriage of state as if for a royal pageant. One of these days the Duchess visited her infant-school, where between one and two hundred children were gathered beneath her wing. In the happy throng her benevolent and discriminating eye singled out a little boy ; and like her great Master on earth she took the child in her arms, and placed him on her knee with all a mother's kindness. "What does Jesus mean," she inquired at them all, "when he says, 'Except ye become as little children, ye shall not enter the kingdom of heaven ?'" But they stumbled unsuccessfully in their attempted answers, which were more prompt than

---

[1] Abridged from Sir Walter Scott.

intelligent. She then turned to the child on her knee, and put the question to him. "A little child kens that it can do naething its lane," the boy replied. She was greatly taken with the simple solution of the mystery, and received and retained it as a lesson for herself; and nothing could more accord with that constant sense of insufficiency to think a good thought, and that childlike dependence on the Lord for help, which lay so deep at the root of all her character.

In the earlier part of her Grace's residence at Gordon Castle, we presented our readers with a brief Diary found among some other papers. But such a journal appears to have been discontinued, partly perhaps from want of perseverance and partly, we believe, from a change of mind regarding this mode of recording her thoughts. But we now find her again, after an interval of six years, adopting a different mode of recollection and self-examination, by transcribing passages of Scripture with her own reflections interspersed. "*Gordon Castle, Aug.* 10, 1834.—Isa. lix. 1, 2, 3 : ' Behold, the Lord's hand is not shortened, that it cannot save ; neither his ear heavy, that it cannot hear: but your iniquities have separated between you and your God ; your lips have spoken lies, your tongue muttered perverseness' (if not lies, things I do not know to be truth, and oh what perverseness !) 'None calleth for justice, nor any pleadeth for truth' (alas! it is so). 'Therefore we wait for light' (we wait, O Lord, let us not wait in vain). 'For our transgressions are multiplied before thee, and our sins testify against us' (if we know them not fully, it is because we seek not to know them; for oh! how much do I depart away from our God).

"Blessed be his name, 'His own arm brought salvation; he came to give repentance, as well as remission of sins; to fulfil his covenant, as he said, My Spirit that is upon thee, and my words which I have put in thy mouth, shall not depart out of thy mouth.' Oh may it also be in our heart, in my heart. Lord, thou hast promised to take away the heart of stone; melt it speedily, crush it, break it, as thou wilt, but do it, O my God. For thy truth's sake, for the sake of Him who hath fulfilled our part of the covenant for us, give us the new heart which thou hast promised through our Surety, our Redeemer.

"2 Tim. iii. 2, 5.—'Lovers of their own selves, covetous, boasters, proud; unthankful, unholy, without natural affection, high-minded; having a form of godliness, but (by the conduct) denying the power thereof' (O Lord! all these things are against me; turn me, O Lord, and I shall be turned).

"Rev. xxi. 8.—'The fearful and unbelieving' (fearing and believing the devil or man, rather than God)."

These meditations she follows up with a more

laborious writing, showing in a marked manner how painstaking and thorough and practical she was in the whole work of God. This consists of an exposition of the Ten Commandments, taken from the "Larger" Catechism of the Westminster Assembly; yet not exactly copied, but with the requirements and prohibitions mingled and condensed. The following portions will give an idea of the whole; and while the reader will easily see that the greater part is a transcription of the words of old divines, he will recognise occasionally some expressions of her own, proving her self-application of the whole. In the prohibitions of the eighth commandment, "making what is called a good bargain, and not acting in all things as God's stewards," are examples of her own additions; and under the ninth, "thinking evil of any without very sufficient grounds, and knowing all the circumstances."

"*Larger Catechism,* 1*st Commd.*—Omission or neglect of anything due to God; self-love, self-seeking; taking off our mind, will, or affections from God, in whole or in part; unbelief, misbelief, distrust; incorrigibleness, insensibleness under judgments; hardness of heart; pride, presumption, carnal security; trusting in lawful means; lukewarmness and deadness in the things of God; slighting and despising God and his commands; resisting and grieving his Spirit." "O Lord! help me to search and see; do thou try my

reins and my heart; wash me throughly; without thee
I cannot be clean, but thou canst take away all my
sin. O Lord, make me loathe and detest it."

" 2*d.*—Neglect of prayer and thanksgiving, or
anything instituted in God's word; of reading and
hearing the word; of church government and discipline; of the ministry and maintenance thereof; of
religious fasting; all neglect hindering in any way
others or ourselves."

" 8*th.*—Not acting in all things as God's stewards;
want of frugality, any waste; making what is called
a good bargain, overreaching in the least degree;
seeking and prizing worldly goods above what is
necessary; not enjoying what God has given us."

" 9*th.*—Not attending strictly to truth in every
way; thinking evil of any without very sufficient
grounds and knowing all the circumstances; detracting from the merit of any; repeating evil reports;
concealing the truth; holding our peace when iniquity
calleth either for reproof from ourselves or complaint
to others; speaking the truth unseasonably, or to a
wrong end, or so as to lead others to draw a different
view from it; slandering, detracting, tale-bearing;
rash, harsh, and partial construing, or misconstruing
intentions, words, and actions; flattering, thinking,
or speaking too highly of ourselves and too meanly
of others; denying the gifts and graces of God;

aggravating smaller faults; hiding, excusing, and extenuating sins when called on to a free confession; unnecessary discovering of infirmities; raising false reports; receiving, countenancing, or repeating evil reports; rejoicing in the disgrace or even disappointment of others; neglecting such things as are of good report."

She had long before this time attained that clear and glorious view of the righteousness of Christ, which by grace she never let go through life, and which increased in brightness till her dying hour. But this careful study of the holy law shows how practical her faith was; how clearly she perceived that the New Testament in no way absolves us from the law as a rule of life; and how far she was from supposing that our Lord's summary in the two great commandments was designed to release the believer from the entire tables of the law. The good Duchess adhered most firmly to all the ten, and earnestly sought to come under the power of each, both in heart and life. The whole is concluded with these meditations: "It is a great aggravation to sin when our sin causes others to stumble; when our station, knowledge, and character lead others to watch for our halting, either as an excuse for themselves, or that they may cast reproach on our Christian profession. O Lord, open thou our eyes that we may behold all that thou wouldest have us to do, that we may see all that Jesus did who was given for our example ; and . knowing that thou hast provided strength for us, give us grace to use it in following the Lord fully. Oh that we may see sin in the light of Christ's example, and loathe and detest and flee from it in every degree."

One of the events of this year, and one of the mile-stones marking the progress of life to the Duchess, was the death of Miss Bell Brodie, the last survivor of the two maiden aunts with whom she had lived in her childhood at Elgin, and for whom she always retained a warm affection. The following extract refers to this bereavement : *"Gordon Castle, Sept.* 13.—I got a frank this morning in the hope of writing you a long letter, but the carriage is gone up to fetch some friends, and I am prevented. I have much to say to you of my dear aunt, and of the great comfort I derived from our last interview. The thought of her Redeemer's sufferings seemed to swallow up that of her own, and to keep her in perfect peace. Mr. Blunt is here, and I get a little quiet talk every morning, with reading and prayer ; but as it is the only time I can see him and Mrs. B. alone, I am selfish in not writing for an addition to our party, because there are many subjects which I could not then so properly bring forward."

At the end of this year the Duchess had a visit

from the Rev. Mr. Stewart of Cromarty, for whom she cherished the highest esteem. On the Sabbath, he preached in the parish church a sermon of great power from the words, "Turn ye to the strong hold, ye prisoners of hope." While Mr. Stewart stayed at the Castle, he told an anecdote which the Duchess often repeated with great animation : Hector Munro was a half-witted man ; but like so many of the weak in this world, he was strong in the grace that is in Christ Jesus. Mr. S. having invited him to pay him a visit at Cromarty Manse, he came most inopportunely on the Saturday afternoon, with the design of remaining all night, when the minister was busily engaged with his work for the Sabbath. Mr. Stewart was a man of genius as well as grace ; his sermons were often the product of a high effort of intellect; and he was not constitutionally free from the sensitiveness, which might be ruffled at and resent such an interruption. But he overcame his discomposure, received and kindly entertained his guest, and found his reward in an intercourse more precious to him and more memorable than the interrupted sermon. Hector having come in his best clothes, the minister addressed him, " Weel, Hector, ye've made yoursel' braw the day." " Hout ay, folk mak's thamesel's braw to gang to thae vain markets ; but I'se warrant the Sabbath's the best market, for it's there we get

without money and without price. An', Maister
Stewart, I'm thinkin' the Saturday's just like the
Christian's deathbed; he's dune his wark, an he's
washed, an' he's clean, an' he lies doon, an' he
waukens—an' it's the Sabbath! An' He was braw
Himsel' that day."[1]

JEWELS STOLEN IN LONDON—THE CONTINENT.—1835.

In the spring of 1835, while the Duke and Duchess
lived in Belgrave Square, a great sensation was excited
in London by the theft of her jewel-chest from her
dressing-room, when the Duke was out at dinner. The
great value of the stolen property, the rank and popularity of the sufferers by the theft, the extreme quietness of the robbery, and the impenetrable mystery
covering the thieves, all combined to excite the live-
liest interest in all classes of the community from the
throne downwards. In token of her sympathy and
regard, the Queen sent next day a handsome present
of some of her own favourite jewels, which the Duchess
highly valued. Her letters written at the time will
show the spirit in which she bore the loss:

[1] W. P. Kennedy, Edinburgh, has just published a volume from Mr.
Stewart's manuscripts, under the title of *The Tree of Promise;* marked
throughout by quick apprehension of the meaning of Scripture, deep
insight into the grand truths of the gospel, and singular power in
stating those truths with point and self-demonstration.

" *Belgrave Square, March* 1835.—We have every reason to believe that no one we are in the least degree connected with is implicated in the robbery. The annoyance it occasions to the feelings of many, and the quantities of advice and suspicions, give me far more trouble than the loss of the things; for that has only served to give me more perfect assurance that 'my treasure is where thieves do not, cannot, break through and steal.' I am also quite certain that it would not have been permitted but for some wise purpose; and if I could satisfy the Duke of the folly of buying more if my own are never recovered, I should be perfectly satisfied to be relieved from the care of the jewels; though to be sure it would have been pleasanter to have had money for them. I have my mother's, father's, and Emily's hair; the little old curb-chain bracelet I always wore; and my watch and glass with the chain. Three other brooches were on the pincushion, which were always there; and *every* thing else was taken except a box of jet. . . . . The Lord has been very gracious to me in not allowing me to feel one moment's pain or alarm on the subject. I believe there is no doubt as to the perpetrators of the robbery being three notorious London thieves, but the proof is wanting."

The progress of the divine life in her soul is brought out in the following letter to Mr. Paul, on receipt of a

little book which he had published on the Believer's
Union to Christ: "*April* 1835.—I received your
very kind letter more than a week ago, and the deed
and book a day or two after. The latter I am reading
with the greatest interest. I have come to nothing
but what strengthens the belief and hope which by
Divine grace I hold as 'my life.' The view of the
everlasting covenant is that on which my soul rests,
and in which it could have no part but through 'union
with Christ.' I trust through his Spirit I may grow
with all other members into the fulness of the stature
of Christ, and when I shall see him I shall be like him!
It is this resemblance I pine for; oh, how unlike still!
Worn and tired with things of no profit, I cannot go
about doing good; I cannot do whatsoever my hand
findeth to do with all my might. Oh for more of the
Spirit of Christ, even now and daily increasing; may
He who hath done great things for us, yet do more;
and as he has put it in your heart to see clearly the
blessedness of union with Christ, enable you to walk
so that all may take knowledge that you are one
with him."

In the course of the summer, the Duke and Duchess
made a tour on the Continent, which is thus referred
to in prospect: "I have the usual consequence of
bustle, a very bad headache; although I had not, as
the newspapers announce, a large party of *haut ton*.

But the drawing-room, a dinner-party, and about as many more in the evening, are enough to show how little either body or mind can benefit by that sort of society ; and I am most thankful that this is the case, and acknowledge it as one of the most valuable proofs of the love of my heavenly Father. We propose leaving England within three weeks, for a tour of four or five months." Of the tour itself, one of the most memorable notes is the fact of their commencing their daily journeys with family prayers, which never hinder progress. This sanctifying of the journey we find noticed in the following letter to Miss Gordon of Wardhouse, written a few days after her Grace's birthday. The tumbling sea between Dover and Calais made this birthday a contrast to the last, which had been signalized by the opening of the schools at Gordon Castle; yet being alone with her husband, the quiet of the one pleased her more than the excitement of the other :

" BRUSSELS, *June* 25, 1835.

" I was sure you needed no assurance from me to prove how much I enter into your feelings regarding your dear niece, now gone home, and the strange but very profitable lessons we so constantly receive together : a bond of union leading us towards that better country, where we shall be no more strangers and pilgrims, but fellow-citizens of the household of

Christ. May we more and more be taught to feel, not only the absolute necessity of the infinitely precious blessings which are treasured up in Christ, but the no less great necessity of asking for them ; that living by faith on the Son of God, we may show forth that faith by the fruits of the Spirit working in us, and making us conformable to the image of our great Example.

"I have, since I began to write this, been interrupted so often that I see I must seize every moment, here as much as elsewhere ; the Duke and I being alone, he wants me oftener even than usual. Think, dearest, what great reason I have to be thankful, that after one-and-twenty years' journey through life, we both rejoice to declare that the last five days, in which we have been *quite* alone together for I believe the first time since our first journey, have been among the happiest we ever spent. I cannot say that I enjoyed the excitement of my birthday in 1834, as I did the quiet *tête-à-tête*, even with the discomfort of passing from Dover to Calais, on the 20th. What pleases me more than all is the Duke's frequent expressions of thankfulness, and the serious cheerfulness which has not admitted of a single check since we left England. We have also family prayers every morning before starting ; and I trust, from the great comfort we all seem to have in meeting, that we shall find no interruption to this privilege necessary, but daily ask God's blessing as a family to prosper our journey, and to preserve and bless those whom we have left behind."

On this tour the efforts of the Duchess were unceasing on behalf of her husband's soul; she was thankful for the opportunities she had of reading the Bible with him; and he said to his old friend, Colonel Tronchin, at Geneva, "Tronchin, I am a very changed man to what you once knew me, and I owe it all to my dear wife." At the same time she afterwards feared that her own soul was suffering loss, because as the Duke advanced in life his affection to her increased; in travelling, he endeavoured to secure for her every attention and respect; and she was much made of by the society in which they mingled, which was of the most elevated and attractive kind. From Geneva she writes: "9th July 1835.—Our journey has been very prosperous; everything seems favourable; and we have been able to continue our morning family prayers every day, except when we started very early indeed. This is a great comfort in a foreign land. I have also reason to pour out my heart in thankfulness that my dear husband seems to enjoy our tête-à-tête, and says constantly what a blessing it is, that after twenty-one years' marriage we like the company of each other better than any other. He has done and said many things since he came here, which almost give me hope that the Spirit of God is really at work, and that he begins to experience something of the blessedness of those who fear the Lord.

"This, however, is rather a dangerous place, as the very simplicity of the society makes one forget that it is still the world ; and we know everybody, and must drink tea with almost everybody. I have been reading Owen *On Temptation*. My hard heart did not feel the force of that work so much as of others I have read ; especially the treatise on the *Mortification of Sin*, which I am now reading, and I really trust God is sending it home to my heart.

"We have just heard of a most wonderfully providential escape of Lord and Lady Munster and their two children, who were thrown over a precipice in an open carriage, and fell thirteen perpendicular feet besides rolling. None of them are seriously hurt ; the maid on the dicky was rather more so ; the courier, who was much crushed, is recovering. It happened in the Val *Münster*, or Moutier, coming from Bâle.

"Mr. Malan's substitute made a very good distinction between those that obey the word of Christ, 'He that *eateth* me shall live by me ;' and those who have only *tasted* of the heavenly gift, that food which cannot nourish if not taken into the heart, as natural food only tasted cannot do good to the body. May we eat and live for ever."

The following letter is further on in their tour :

"*Neumarkt in Silesia, Sept.* 1835.—The Duke dined yesterday with the King of Prussia, and all the great people assembled ; and the Emperor of Russia and Empress were so exceedingly civil to him, that we are almost sure of going to Kalisch. If the Emperor were not going afterwards to Töplitz, I should not be surprised to find myself on the road to St. Petersburg instead of Vienna, after the great reviews of the Prussian troops, which are now going on here in Silesia. . . .

" We were stopped at a little inn here on Saturday, by advice of the postmaster, as being much nearer the troops ; and I am very thankful for the three most quiet days I have spent in peace of mind and body, except so far as I have a still greater cause of thankfulness in an increased and increasing sense of sin, as a burthen indeed which even hides from me the shining of God's countenance. But he is faithful, and enables me to say, 'Though I walk in darkness and see no light, yet will I stay myself upon my God.' Yes, he is faithful ; he never said, Seek ye my face in vain. It is for such as me, even for the chief of sinners, that he gave his well-beloved Son. Lord ! I believe, help thou my unbelief, and let me once more see the Son in his beauty, the sun of righteousness arising to shine on my soul with healing under his wings. I know it is in answer to prayer that I am thus ; I have earnestly

prayed for a deeper sense of sin, and now I see nothing
but sin. I have known that I could not so much as
think a good thought; at least my reason has known
it; but now I think my heart feels it, and sees a
depth of iniquity which nothing but the depth of that
fountain of love filled with the Saviour's blood could
wash away. I have been enabled to see that in nothing but greater knowledge have I differed from the
world; in nothing have I been more willing to take
up my cross than they. Every moment I could say,
What do I more than others? how have I laid out
the talents intrusted to me? and therefore I can also
see, that my sin is greater than that of those who
have not light. Oh! may I henceforward strive as I
have never yet done; may I stand fast; and if it be
needful, amid the smiles and allurements of the great
ones of the earth, may I witness a good confession for
the sake of Him who so witnessed before Pilate. May
I be able in his strength to do as well as say with
David, ' I will speak of thy testimonies before Kings,
and will not be ashamed.' Oh how much do I find
my experience or my desires expressed in the 119th
Psalm."

DEATH OF GEORGE DUKE OF GORDON.—1836.

The great bereavement in the life of the Duchess
was now fast approaching, though not anticipated by

herself as at all so near. On her yearly journey to London in spring she had been in the habit of passing a few days in Edinburgh, where she spent the Sabbaths with Miss Home, and attended the ministry of Dr. Gordon. Her last visit of this kind was in the spring of 1836, when the Duke was already very unwell, though she was not yet fully aware of the fatal character of his malady. Miss Home herself was dangerously ill, and in great grief from the death of her brother, Sir James Home. These varied afflictions affected her deeply, and she proceeded on her way south with her spirit bowed down under great heaviness. But her sorrow was turned into the joy of the Lord even under the continuance and progress of the Duke's illness, and her mouth was filled with the high praises of her God :

"LONDON, *April 21st*, 1836.

"Among the other mercies which you have to enumerate, my dearest Helen, and which I know you will not consider the least, is that through you and your house the power and love and faithfulness of our blessed Jehovah Jesus, whose earthly name I must employ to express his tenderness, have been shown to me as they never were before. And how shall we sufficiently praise Him who can make us feel, when we can neither see nor hear, his presence ; and give us a foretaste, not perhaps of that glory which is to be revealed at his coming, but of that rest and peace in Him in which he will keep those whom the Father has given him until the great day! But then there will be no pain, no oppression, no weight of the body of death to recall our souls to worldly things.

"I have also to praise God for the opportunity afforded through you of saying more to my dear husband, and seeing more interest apparent in listening than I have ever yet done. I read part of your precious memorial of the Lord's goodness to him yesterday, while Mr. Farquhar (a truly Christian man) was putting on leeches for his eyes; and he said, 'Is not that a good letter to hear from a person who has been so near death?' In short, dearest, we must just praise the Lord together in our hearts, till we can praise him together for ever, with those who are already called to rest in his love, and those who would now join our praises or need our prayers. Margaret Drummond gives the same testimony in kind, though not in degree; and having been one whole year deprived of public ordinances, is able to make the anniversaries of date and day times of thanksgiving and praise, and says she knows far more of the love and mercy of God than when she could, as she thought, make herself more useful in his service. I desire also to join you in thanksgiving for your dear sister, only do not let her think of me as I do not deserve; for, oh, how cold is my heart, how dumb my mouth, to feel and speak of goodness and mercy and truth! My kindest love to Lady Home, with thanks for her letter. I don't want more hair at present, unless it is all coming off ; if so, pray let me have a large portion."

In writing in this strain of unusual joy, the Duchess was not anticipating the sad event that awaited her before the end of the next month. The sorrow that was soon to darken her sky was as yet only a little " cloud like a man's hand," and the abundant joy vouchsafed to her was in the Lord's faithfulness preparing her for the evil day. On the 27th of May the doctors informed her that the Duke had only a short time to live. The dark tidings were more than she had expected ; the sequel we give in her own expressions : " I had not realized till then the hopelessness of his case. I retired to another room and fell on my knees ; and as if they had been audibly uttered, these words were impressed upon my heart, 'Thy Maker is thy husband ; the Lord of Hosts is his name ; and thy Redeemer the Holy One of Israel ; the God of the whole earth shall he be called ;' and I rose up to meet the trial in his strength." The Duke died on the following day ; and a letter dated two days thereafter will show how fully the strength of the Lord was made hers : " I must tell you of the blessed consolation I have in thinking of the perfect peace which my beloved husband enjoyed uninterruptedly, and the presence of the Comforter from the Father and the Son to my own soul. Pray for me. Although I feel indeed in the wilderness, yet like her [who was led there, I would desire to lean on the arm of the beloved One, who has truly given to me 'the valley of Achor for a door of hope,' and who is my very present help in time of trouble. The comfort I have is at present almost without alloy. It is only when earthly things pull me from my resting-place that I see the desolation of all earthly joys; and yet I am not excited, but as the Lord has enabled me to 'stay my mind on him, he has kept me in perfect peace.—Kind regards to them around you."

When she left Gordon Castle a few months before, the Duchess had so little apprehension of the fatal issue, that she contemplated a little pleasant surprise for the Duke in the hope of his returning home in restored health. There was a large quarry within a mile of the Castle, long out of use, and screened from the view as an unsightly object amid the varied beauties of the princely grounds. Her eye had rested on the hollow as capable of attractive beauty. Its rugged sides and its heaps of rubbish she had shaped into green banks and grassy knolls, relieved with winding walks, and planted with ornamental trees and beautiful evergreens; and pleased herself with the bright hope that in another summer she would drive the Duke to the spot, and give him a happy surprise with her little paradise blooming out of the desert. But the fond dream was sadly reversed in the issue ; for one of the King's ships was ordered to convey the body to Scotland by sea in honour of the deceased ; and as the Quarry Garden lay between the shore and the Castle, the corpse was carried close past it on the way, while the gay flush of summer all around only made the coldness of death look darker by the contrast.

The Duchess herself travelled by land with her niece, Lady Sophia Lennox, and arrived at the Castle a little after midnight, that she might not be disturbed by any one meeting her. " *Gordon Castle.*—The dear Duchess has borne the journey well ; she arrived here a little after twelve o'clock at night on Tuesday, so that no person should meet her. Her mind is astonishingly composed and calm. That heavenly source to which she has so long applied does not now forsake her ; and she feels that inward peace and wonderful support He has promised to all in trouble who trust in him. She has determined on attending the funeral to-morrow ; Lady Sophia Lennox and I will of course accompany her. Her command of feeling is so great that I do not doubt her firmness during the trying ceremony, but cannot help fearing for her health after all this exertion." Attended by Lady Sophia and a cousin of her own, she accompanied the remains to their resting-place in an aisle of Elgin Cathedral; and standing over them as they were moved into the vault, she dedicated herself to the Lord : "When the coffin was lowered into that vault, I felt as if God had shoved under my feet all that was most dear to me, the only one on earth to whose love I was entitled, and that now I must live to himself alone." In connexion with this event she would often at Huntly Lodge express herself in prayer : " Lord, thou art the Master in this house ; I have given it all to thee."

She was calm throughout the whole ceremony, and only gave way to her feelings after entering the carriage to return to Gordon Castle. "*June* 23*d.*—I left Gordon Castle on the 16th, and the dear Duchess has from that time been quite alone ; you may be sure it was at her own earnest desire that I left her alone at such a time. None of the visitors who had been collected for the mournful ceremony remained after the 16th; and then the Duchess said she must be alone with her God, that she might know her own mind under the severe affliction he had sent her, for she had been in a constant state of over-exertion and excitement. On Saturday she has written to Lady Georgiana Baillie to come to her, and after that she will attend to business and see a few of her friends.

It is fortunate she has so much to arrange ; it keeps her mind from dwelling too much on her grief. I never saw her more composed than on the evening of that trying ceremony. She was much agitated as we came near Elgin ; but when we were in the Cathedral she was quite calm, and said she had never before felt the full force of these words in the Service, ' When this corruptible shall have put on incorruption, and this mortal shall have put on immortality, then shall be brought to pass the saying that is written, Death is swallowed up in victory :' they had given her such blessed hopes. She remained alone some time after we returned to the Castle, and when we met again showed that she indeed knew in whom she trusted, and that she possessed that inward peace which our Heavenly Father alone can give."

Her own letters continue to breathe the same spirit of elevation above the world : " *Gordon Castle, 1st July* 1836.—I have to give my testimony to the love and faithfulness of our reconciled Father, revealed in and through his Son Jesus Christ, and by his Holy Spirit the Comforter. Truly his love passeth knowledge, and his peace all understanding. I long to tell you something of all he has done for my soul, and especially the unspeakable comfort afforded me by the peace vouchsafed to my beloved husband, which was manifested in the very spirit of the Lamb of God.

July 16*th.*—I have still cause to bless the faithfulness of my God, though I do and must daily feel more and more what I have lost. But when I look around, and see nothing in the wide world like a natural tie to bind me to it, then I must flee and hide me in the ' Rock of Ages cleft for me.' And I am left without excuse if I do not give my heart to that tender reconciled Father who has asked it, and who fulfils the assurance of the prophet in keeping me in perfect peace ; a peace which passeth all understanding, which the world may disturb but cannot destroy. I yesterday had the great comfort of settling in my Chapel a minister whom I do think every way qualified to be useful here."

After leaving Gordon Castle her natural and very earnest desire was to return to Huntly Lodge, the home of her married youth, and now also of her widowhood by her marriage settlement. But her spirit was severely tried by its having been let for a further term of years a little before the Duke's death, and by the tenant's insisting on entering upon the new lease, although the circumstances were so altered. She therefore determined to go abroad for a year or two, and from Gordon Castle she wrote to her agent in Edinburgh : " I will not claim Huntly Lodge at law, as I think I see the finger of God pointing another way in these disappointments ; but I felt it very bitter to leave my own country without a home in it, till I was reminded of Him who had not where to lay his head. . . . Many and bitter are the trials of which my Almighty Father sees that I have need. I feel more and more the misery of my utter bereavement as touching this world; but I see in the acute sense of affliction, which was not at first so keenly felt, a means of learning more of what our blessed Redeemer felt and suffered for us. May this heating of the furnace effect more truly the work of purification."

But her soul soon returned to its quiet rest: "*Corfe Castle, Sept.* 1836.—The quiet of this family has through mercy enabled me to see my sin and danger, and once more to *feel*, as well as to acknowledge (which I have always been able to do), that 'He doeth all things well.' I was very much harassed in London; but though I know that it was my own sin that made my desolation so bitter, yet I am thankful I have felt it; and the power of him who has delivered me shows me yet more and more of his infinite love. I trust henceforward to remember that it is the tenderness of my heavenly Father who, asking my whole heart, leaves me without excuse for unwillingness to give it, by taking away all that might seem given to rest it upon. . . . I see how very easily sin rises up as a thick cloud between our souls and the blessing of

God's countenance, and how *very* guilty I have been in murmuring, fancying all the while that—but I can hardly say what I fancied. Through infinite mercy and love the cloud is removed, and the love of God shed abroad in the heart enables me to go to the fountain opened for sin and for uncleanness."

> " Some murmur, when their sky is clear,
> And wholly bright to view,
> If one small speck of dark appear
> In their great heaven of blue.

> " And some with thankful love are filled,
> If but one streak of light,
> One ray of God's good mercy, gild
> The darkness of their night."

CHAPTER VI.

HUNTLY LODGE.

1837–1847.

> "IF ye would know
> How visitations of CALAMITY
> Affect the soul,—
> Look yonder at that cloud which through the sky,
> Sailing alone, doth cross in her career
> The rolling moon.   I watched it as it came,
> And deemed the deep opaque would blot her beams ;
> But, melting like a wreath of snow, it hangs
> In folds of wavy silver round, and clothes
> The orb with richer beauties than her own,
> Then passing leaves her in her light serene."
>
> SOUTHEY's *Roderick.*

> " HERS was a gracious and a gentle house ;
> Rich in obliging, nice observances ;
> And famed ancestral hospitality.
> A cool repose lay grateful through the place ;
> And pleasant duties,—promptly, truly done,
> And every service touched by hidden springs,
> Oiled with intelligence—moved smoothly round."
>
> WOOLNER.

DURING the winter of 1836 the widowed Duchess lived at Pau, whence in spring she wrote in her own thankful spirit to one of her old friends in Aberdeen-shire : "*Pau, 20th Febry.* 1837.—I have little to say but of the continued goodness and mercy of my God ; who, while he leads me further and further into the wilderness and into an increasing sense of desolation as regards this world, shows me more of his unspeak-able love in so doing, and in taking away all else says only the more loudly, 'Thou art mine :' purchased with his own blood, comforted by his own Spirit, and enabled to rest on him as an all-sufficient portion, Saviour, God, and Father."

Four months later she wrote again on her journey homeward, and in the painful prospect of returning to her now desolate home : "*Brive, 21st June* 1837.—I have seen during the last winter more of the hidden depths of iniquity, than I could have any idea of without the help of that light which is promised to those who seek it. But we must be brought very low, before anything more than a general idea of sin can be attained; and while we have any lurking notion that we are better than those we live amongst, this is impossible. We must indeed see with St. Paul that you or I *is* the chief of sinners; we must be convinced that, according to the light given us, we have done less for Christ than any one around us. The Lord alone *can* know how far each of us acts up to the light we have. But of this I am sure, no other human eye can be aware how little we avail ourselves of the strength and help which Christ has purchased, how far short we come of the high calling with which Christ calleth his people, never calling them without giving them strength to come. There is no way but in following him closely, first to the cross to see what he suffered for our sin, and then daily carrying the cross, which he has laid on us, looking for his footsteps in our walk through life. O what a blessed Saviour! what a compassionate High Priest! tempted in all points like as we are, yet without sin.

"See Him, as Rutherford says, ever ready to bear the heaviest end of our cross, and if we are weary, to take it all and leave us nothing but his peace. Must we not love such a Master with an undivided love? Must we not strive with every faculty to walk as he walked, and to imitate his sympathy who was made in all points like unto his brethren, that he might be able to succour them that are tempted ; not that he needed to try for himself our trials, but that we might know that he had tried them, and might therefore come boldly to him for help. Oh, keep close to him and learn of him who was meek and lowly of heart, and you shall find rest unto your soul. We are here on the road to Lyons, whence I purpose to return straight to England. As the time approaches, though you know how dearly I love quiet and home, I cannot tell you how much I dread returning to Huntly."

The sorrow, however, of the dreaded return was graciously relieved beyond all her expectation : " *Huntly Lodge, 31st August* 1837.— The Lord has been better to me than all my fears. Wagstaff (the Duke's factor), accompanied by both Mr. Bigsby (of the English Chapel at Gordon Castle) and Mr. Dewar (minister of Fochabers) received me. My heart was so full of the Lord's goodness that there was no room for bitterness ; and after a few moments alone, I could not rest till we had thanked our tender Father ; Mr. Bigsby was the organ of our thanksgiving. The three gentlemen, Annie (Sinclair), and I joined in prayer then, and at night with all the people of house, stable, and farm ; this morning Mr. Dewar's prayer was very much what I needed. My blessed Lord Jesus is very present, and I know I cannot come to my Father without him. Oh, pray that I may be more and more awakened and never fall asleep again. Oh for the quickening grace of the Holy Spirit to realize continually that blessed presence. *4th Sept.*—My heart is full of thankfulness and wonder as to myself. I dreaded above all things the bitterness of desolation on my return here ; and behold the Lord made his presence so manifest that I am now, as in times past, rejoicing in his unmerited love."

But a few days later she tasted again the bitterness of that conflict with things around which never ceases on earth, but which she found at this moment peculiarly trying : " *8th Sept.* 1837.—I have already told you of the wonderful love of my Father, who really made me feel his arms about me on my first arrival here ; but now my battle is beginning. I still feel, and trust I shall feel, that every trial and disappointment sends me closer to Jesus. Oh, I am a poor, weak creature, acknowledging always that there is nothing solid but what is founded on the rock Christ. Still I am ready to sink when I am shown that I must not put my trust in man. I keep repeating, 'I am not surprised ;' and yet the wounds in my mind show that I thought things were otherwise. Truth, truth, is the only thing needed ; even He who is truth, and without him truly we can do nothing. The Lord will do his own work in his own time ; and he will have me

kept constantly in mind, as he sees I need it, that I
have no helper but him who is the Mighty One. Oh
that I could say at all times, The Lord is my helper;
I will *not fear* what man can do unto me." "12*th
Sept.*—Oh yes, it is desolate to be in an earthly home
all alone; but I do trust my Father is showing me
that it is all to make me look to my own country, to
the city of habitation, which, if Christ be mine, is
mine in him. I think I am getting better, I mean
in mind, for the body is well enough; but I am an
ungrateful creature, seeing it is all to keep me closer
to my God, and he will give me strength to do what
he would have me to do, though I be alone. My
prayer is, that the Spirit of grace may be abundantly
given to me; that the delight of my life may be communion with the Father, and with his Son Jesus
Christ; that God may dwell in me, and walk in me;
and that we, being indeed the daughters of the Lord
Almighty, may serve him in every thought, and word,
and deed, and may never look even to the arrangements of an earthly home with more anxiety than if
it were a house taken for a month."

The house into which she desired to enter, as if one
"taken for a month," was now to be her home for
more than a quarter of a century, as it had been
already for twelve years while she was Marchioness.
A widow's sorrow is often aggravated by her removal

from the scenes of married happiness; but the jointure-house of the Duchess with a suitable extent of land around it was Huntly Lodge, where she had lived more years with her husband than at Gordon Castle, with which she had so many pleasing associations, and whose scenery she not only loved but admired. This circumstance, so soothing in itself, mingled for the time both joy and sorrow in her cup: "The Lord has ever proved himself to me a very present help and most tender Father in Christ Jesus our Lord; yet on my return to this place, where I have been so happy, I do feel that constant and more than human aid is needful to support me."

The district round Huntly on approaching from Aberdeen is not attractive to the eye of a stranger; it seems to want alike the grassy slopes and undulating hills of the south of Scotland, and the bold mountains of the Highlands. Yet like nature everywhere it possesses a charm of its own, chiefly in the open and wide-lying nature of the country, with a free air in summer, and a clear and bracing winter. The cold is three degrees severer than at Gordon Castle, and the snow is apt to fall deeply and to lie long. The letters of the Duchess sometimes contain such remarks as these: "The roads are impassable for wheel-carriages; we have been blocked up with snow for six weeks.—Almost every day last week I consulted whether the sledge could go for you, but was told of some reason or other to hinder." The sledge at Huntly Lodge with its handsome furs, its tingling bells, and horses running tandem, had rather the air of a picturesque and pleasant variety of driving, even. when there was no other way of moving about; but the sleighs of the medical practitioners seemed to indicate a liability to such a depth and continuance of snow, as to make this mode of travelling a real convenience, if not an occasional necessity.

The grounds of Huntly Lodge are marked by a good deal of variety and beauty, with their woods, parks, and gardens, the impetuous river spanned by its narrow bridge, the old Castle on its banks, and the wide circle of mountains in the distance. All these the Duchess admired and enjoyed. Where the hand of man could aid, she loved to enrich nature by art, and delighted to make improvements in buildings, gardens, and walks. The fine situation and noble edifice of the old Castle had great attractions for her, and after her marriage she deeply regretted to find that it could not be restored as a residence. The Marquises of Huntly had transferred their home to Gordon Castle, and under the Dukes of Gordon the old Castle of Huntly was left in charge of their factors, who so dismantled it for their own ends as to render it for ever useless as a habitation. In the last

century, on the marriage of the Dowager Duchess
Katherine to General States Ley Morris, Huntly
Lodge was hastily extended with little regard to
architectural beauty; and it was further enlarged
and greatly improved for the Duchess Elisabeth, when
she was Marchioness. This house was now to be
her home for twenty-seven years, during which it
became well known and endeared to a larger circle
of the Lord's servants than any other house in Scotland.

Among the lesser relics transferred from Gordon
Castle to the Lodge were some old pets of the Duke's
and her own, to which there is a passing reference in
her letters. " Your poor bullfinch! how true that
we must not set our affections on these things.
Vicky was so happy to see me ; Sall, an immense
lady of the Talbot family, is a daily visitor in the
dining-room. I wish you could see us all, and scold
me sometimes." To a stranger the most remarkable
of the Duke's old favourites was Kaiser, an Hungarian
wolf-dog with a snow-white fleece, and most sheep-
like aspect in the distance, but at whose appearance
out of doors, man, woman, and child fled as from a
wolf. The Duchess called him " The wolf in sheep's
clothing." Her husband's tastes having brought her
much into contact with all sorts of dogs, she had
learned to pat them confidently at their first intro-

duction, when a large space between their eyes betokened a kindly temper. This open breadth of forehead was strongly marked in Sall, a fine old mastiff that used at this time to walk round the dining-room after breakfast, with her noble head reaching the level of the table. But the Duke had chosen Kaiser for other qualities. Two of those wolf-dogs had been brought to him for sale when travelling on the Continent; the other was the larger and handsomer animal; but Kaiser's eyes sunk deep in the head, and all but meeting under the shaggy hair, at once fixed his choice on him as "likest his work." That work was to defend the sheep from the wolves, and one mode of defence was by laying a strange trap for the enemy. The dog was remarkably like a sheep, his hair white without a dark speck, and he carried a great load of it, long and fleecy like wool. In the Hungarian steppes four or five of those dogs would lay themselves down on the grass in the evening, like so many harmless lambs sleeping there with their faces inward for the heat of each other's breath. The keen eye of the wolf was soon attracted by the white fleeces, with no shepherd near to guard them. Eager for blood, he careered swiftly over the plain, and sprang unsuspecting into the midst of the flock, only to find himself clinched in the relentless jaws of Kaiser and his comrades, wolves more terrible than himself under the clothing of timid sheep.

A conversation once took place at the Lodge on the character ascribed to dogs in Scripture. It slightly vexed the good Duchess that they were so often mentioned in the Bible, but only as emblems of what is foul and fierce, except in a single instance, and that not of commendation but neutrality. This exception, she said, occurred in the Book of Proverbs, where the greyhound is named along with the lion and the goat as "comely in going," yet merely in praise of his external beauty. But her difficulty was relieved by the reply, that in Isaiah lvi. 10, the "dog" is really used in a good sense as applied to the spiritual watch-men of the Lord's flock. For the unfaithful shepherds, being there likened to dumb dogs that cannot bark, were not censured under the simple image of watch-dogs, but because as such they were faithless and use-less; implying that the good watch-dog is an honour-able emblem of the true pastor, watching for the souls committed to his care, and solemnly warning them of approaching danger.

But to return to Huntly Lodge: The house is approached by a bridge over the rocky Deveron be-neath the old Castle, between which and the Lodge is a long, straight avenue, with a broad green sward of grass on either side, and lined with rows of noble beeches and limes. The scene, though rather formal, is invested with an air of stateliness ; and the Duchess greatly delighted in the view from the windows, with the long stretch of bright grass ended by the bridge and the Castle, and the hills seen over them in the distance ; while the lines of beeches were a constant refreshing to her eye, with their large round tops clothed with rich brown foliage that hung long through the winter, to be followed each new summer by a green that looked fresher than the summer before.

In front of the house she had planned a flower-garden, fashioned in shape of a flower-basket, with its base towards the windows, various gay beds for its contents, and its handle represented by a wreathed border of flowers forming its outer circuit. Outside of all, two fine araucarias, tall and unscathed by frost, made a pleasing contrast to the soft and fragile flowers, as if the trees had been transplanted from an older world before nature was waved into beauty and soft-ness ; with their straight unbending stems, and their formal boughs artificially jointed like the metallic branches of a candelabrum, and their stiff, everlast-ing leaves, as of cast-iron painted green, that bade defiance alike to the hand of man to touch their sharpened points, and to the hand of time to loosen one of them from its stem.

The garden, which was to her a constant source of

interest and enjoyment, was close to the Lodge, from which however it lay quite concealed. Its own situation was elevated and free, with terraced walks toward the top, and sloping down toward the south in a succession of gardens to the open sheep-park below, which stretched onward to the river. In the midst of the old garden stood a clump of six large silver firs, some of them broken and covered with ivy, that had been planted by the Duchess Katharine for her six children. In the lowest garden, where there was a fine collection of roses which she cultivated with much care, the Duchess had a favourite resort in a beautiful summer-house, overlooking the sheep-walk and the river and the woods beyond.

The Duchess took great pleasure in having her garden and grounds kept in the most perfect order, thereby also giving employment to a number of old people who were able for no other work. But there is a temptation in every natural taste, and our heavenly Father provides some chastening to correct it. With Lord Brodie it was by the soldiers quartering on his young plantations ; with the Duchess of Gordon it was by the death of a beautiful boy of three years old, the son of her chaplain, who fell through the ice in a basin for aquatic plants in one of the flower-gardens. This sad occurrence, which took place some years after her return to the Lodge, she thus relates : " You have perhaps heard of the event which the Lord has caused to warn us during the past week; if you have not heard the particulars I will tell you. Mrs. Hull's three younger children, with the maid, went to walk in the flower-garden; for the present maid did not know how very strongly I enjoined that they should never go there without one of themselves. With the little girl in her arms she passed near the basin, and Charlie followed her, saying, 'Johnnie won't come.' She put down the infant and left her in charge of Charlie, while she ran back and saw Johnnie in the pond. She plunged in after him, and went over her head in the water, which with fright and ice made it many minutes before she could raise him. Mrs. Hull had gone to see the poor old woman who is dying in the poultry-house, and as she returned she met one of the gardeners with the child in his arms; she thinks he moved after she took him, but he never gasped or sighed. You may believe everything was done that could be thought of; Dr. Wilson was soon at the cottage, and for two hours tried every usual means of restoration, but in vain. It is a comfort to Mr. Hull, that the last time he heard the child's voice he was singing,—

' Jesus Christ, my Lord and Saviour,
　　Once became a child like me;
　Oh that, in my whole behaviour,
　　He my pattern still might be.' "

The Duchess had the pond immediately converted into a rockery for Alpine plants, both to remove the sad association and to prevent all future danger. The affliction helped to transplant her affections from every paradise below to the garden of God above ; and to set them here on earth on the trees of righteousness, the planting of the Lord, on the fir-tree that supplants the thorn, and the myrtle-tree the briar. In latter years, far beyond all her hopes, she was privileged to see her very grounds and parks converted into gardens and nurseries for heaven, by the sowing of the "good seed" in the hearts of assembled thousands, hungering for the word of life. Every other enjoyment to which they had ministered she counted nothing in comparison ; then the blessing of the Lord enriched her, and he added no sorrow with it ; then in those pleasure-grounds her spirit heard the Bridegroom calling :

> " Rise up, my love, my fair one, and come away,
> For lo ! the winter is past, the rain is over and gone ;
> The flowers appear on the earth ;
> The time of the singing of birds is come,
> And the voice of the turtle is heard in our land ;
> The fig-tree putteth forth her green figs,
> And the vines with the tender grape give a good smell.
> Arise, my love, my fair one, and come away."

Having commenced this section with the return of her Grace to Huntly Lodge, we shall conclude it with her first revisiting of Gordon Castle the following year : " *Huntly Lodge, 18th January* 1838.—As on my first coming here I felt little because I sought strength, so with my first visit to Gordon Castle; and in the state of the infant-schools an earnest of blessed fruit, which I have been permitted to see gathered by the Lord of the harvest, has made me so happy that I must expect a reaction when the effervescence is over; and I am sure I need very soon to take a day of solemn business.

"The little lamb, who is gone to the bosom of the Good Shepherd, was buried the very day I passed through Fochabers, and visited the infant-school for the first time since my return. He replied some time ago to Mr. Bigsby, who asked him where he learned to love Jesus,—'I was learned at the infant-school, but God put it in my heart.' His sufferings were unusually great from decline after measles; but while life remained, he always turned his eyes towards the namer of the beloved name of Jesus; and his little hands were folded in prayer, while four people were necessary to hold his convulsed body. His mother heard him groaning, as she thought, one night before he was speechless, which he was for ten days; and on approaching his bed, heard him saying over, 'My Jesus! my Jesus!' She asked if he wanted anything: 'Oh no;' but often he asked for light in the night to have the Bible read when he could not see. There is another little wee boy in the school very remarkable,

but I shall not have room to tell you more of him than
one text he gave me : 'In all thy ways acknowledge
God, and he shall direct thy paths.'"

HUNTLY LODGE: ITS DAILY LIFE.

When the Duchess returned as a widow to Huntly
Lodge, in 1837, to reside during the remainder of her
life, her religious course and the whole arrangement
of her household were placed for the first time entirely
under her own control, and they took at once that
form which they retained for nearly thirty years afterwards; the fruit alike of her decision in choosing her
path, and of her perseverance through grace in walking in it onward to the end.

After her decease the charge of Plymouthism was
brought against her Grace's memory. But "there
must be order in the Church" was the expression of
her own sentiments on that head; and while she had
valued friends abroad belonging to that communion,
there was not one of her associates in Scotland over
whom the Plymouth doctrines had any influence.
With the excellent "Brethren" the good Duchess had
nothing in common, save our common Christianity.
Her brotherhood was not like theirs, first severing other
Churches and then their own. Their frequent enuncia-
tion, "He is a good man, but I could not break bread

with him," was contrary to every thought and feeling of
her heart ; for there was no good man throughout the
world, with whom she would not have been too happy
to sit at the table of the Lord, only counting herself unworthy of the privilege. So with their other
peculiarities. In her clear and strong views of the
imputed righteousness of Christ, she differed from such
of them as hold it loosely or deny it ; in her fervent
admiration of nature she differed from others ; in her
firm belief in the perpetual obligation of the Sabbath,
in her appreciation of the inestimable privilege of infant baptism, and in her high value for the Christian
ministry, she differed from them all.

Her daily life at Huntly Lodge was a testimony
against those doctrines which level all earthly distinc-
tions ; a constant witness to the scriptural institution
and the attractive beauty of a regulated order in the
world. From the door-step of the mansion of another
devout and noble lady in Scotland, you might trace a
quiet handwriting on the wall : " I'd rather far be one
of nature's own nobility." The preference was doubtless wise. But the men ennobled by nature form the
rarest of all the orders of nobility ; and the high
distinction cannot be got by sighing for it, any more
than a marquisate or a dukedom. The Duchess of
Gordon did not lack some features of character quali-
fying her to rank among the nobles of nature, and

grace had given her a high position among the nobles of Israel; yet she did not therefore trample under foot the coronet of Gordon, but strove to make it shine with a purer and brighter lustre. For centuries it had shone before the eyes of men in indomitable energy, in heroic courage, in military skill, in the mastering spirit of rule, in princely splendour, in distinguished talent, in brilliant wit, in largeness of heart, and noble generosity. But its lustre was of earth, and not of heaven; and its blemishes, moral and religious, were not few nor small. The last Duchess of Gordon sought now to make that ancient coronet shine with the beauty of divine grace; and the Lord gave her the desire of her heart.

After her widowhood it became a serious question with her how far she should continue to maintain the style and living of a duchess. To some of her friends it seemed that her own taste would have led her to prefer the retired life of a simple gentlewoman, without the establishment associated with her rank. But the preference of the Duchess was certainly rather for a measure of the state to which she had been so long accustomed, and her natural tendency was more towards maintaining than renouncing it; without, however, interfering either with her humility toward God, or her self-depreciation as compared with others ever so humble. At the same time, she would have made the sacrifice at once had she seen it to be duty ; and on being left a widow she seriously weighed the question of letting Huntly Lodge, and retiring into a humbler life. To live on a thousand a year instead of ten would have saved her many temptations, spared her much trouble, and given her a magnificent opportunity of directly furthering the cause of the gospel, relieving much distress, and promoting many schemes for the good of mankind. But to use her own words, she saw that "position is stewardship ;" and she wisely resolved not to cast it away, but to devote it to the Lord and his service. The precept, " Let every man abide in the same calling wherein he was called," she took as the guide of her path ; and having been numbered by the Lord in the rank of the " not many noble that are called," she determined therein to abide with God.

Before going abroad after the Duke's death, she had written in prospect of her return : " The daily occurrences, which rub so severely on the tender wound, will have brought about changes so that at least the sharp edges will be somewhat smoothed ; and I shall be able to go to Scotland and commence a new course of service, which I trust it may please my Divine Master to bless. The circumstances in which I have been placed in England, not only by my rank but by the friendship and esteem of my Queen

(Adelaide), forbid me to place myself now in such a
position as might mar my future usefulness, if it be
the will of God to give me grace, wisdom, strength,
and opportunity.   Therefore, hearing the effect that
following my own inclination to retire to the west of
Scotland would have on my worldly friends, and considering that many sincere ones have urged me not to
go to Scotland till I can at least visit my own house,
I have resolved on going abroad.   I believe the Lord
in his providence would have me know what it is to
be a stranger and a pilgrim ; and I trust when I get
to my own home, if he sees fit I should, I shall know
better how to perform his will."

It is impossible to calculate the good she was
enabled to accomplish by thus retaining and adorning
the position that belonged to her.   The light that
shines through the cottage window in the lowly
valley will cheer and •guide the midnight wanderer,
who chances to pass within its narrow range ; but the
lamp on the lofty light-house is seen far and near,
and directs thousands to the sheltering harbour.   Her
burning lamp was placed on such an elevation ; her
pure and loving and heavenly life told the world
whence its light was kindled, and guided some of its
children to the hope within the veil, where they also
might cast their anchor and be for ever safe ; while
her steadfast and holy walk was a lofty pattern in the

Church, an epistle known and read of all men, which
provoked many in their own humbler spheres to walk
as she did on an elevation so peculiarly trying. Compared with this wide influence, the benefit must have
been little that would have been produced by the
additional means to be placed at her disposal by
descending into a lower path in life.

While retaining the accompaniments of her rank,
she kept also the society of all her own or her husband's friends, who were willing to associate with her
without any compromise of her own principles. The
sentiments of many of them were different from her
own touching the one great need of man; yet they
were welcome guests at her house, but without the
alteration of a jot or tittle of her own arrangements
on their account. Whether so much society and so
varied was desirable or not, we offer no opinion. But
from the time of her marriage she had been always
accustomed to a large circle; by her natural choice she
enjoyed it, and she earnestly sought to have all things
sanctified to herself and to her guests; while a heart
less open to all mankind would also have been more
reserved to the wide circle of Christ's followers. But
her "desire was toward the excellent in the earth, in
whom was all her delight;" and without bringing the
rude and uneducated to her table, as has been foolishly
asserted, many were invited to her house with whom

her only tie was an interest in the common salvation; and that long before the wide religious efforts of the last few years, and while she was still a member of the English Church.

The house, while wanting nothing that became her position, was marked by simplicity, regulated with strict economy, and conducted with remarkable quietness. The most beautiful order was the constant aspect of the whole establishment, pervading all its departments, and sweetening all the relations of the servants towards each other:

"Hers was a gracious and a gentle house :
A cool repose lay grateful through the place ;
And pleasant duties,—touched by hidden springs,
Oil'd with intelligence—moved smoothly round."

Everything throughout the day was conducted with the exactness of clock-work, and the Duchess was as obedient to the times she had arranged as any of her guests or attendants. Her own hours of rising were very early ; her fire was lighted at six, and she rose not long after, except in the weaker health of later years, when she meditated in bed before rising ; the family met at nine for breakfast, and separated soon after ten at night. Both morning and evening, exactly at half-past nine, they assembled for prayers ; or, in the more definite Scottish designation, for "family worship," including praise, the reading of the

Word of God, and prayer. The place of meeting
was the Library, which the servants often called the
Chapel, from the use to which it was chiefly appro-
priated.   There were gathered first the large circle of
domestics, with the men employed in the garden and
the stables, and the servants belonging to the various
guests. Then with a quiet and respectful dignity, and
in words and tone that never varied by one syllable
or accent, morning and evening, during the twenty-
seven years of her Grace's widowhood and his own
stewardship, the butler announced, "They're all assembled." The family and guests then repaired to
the Library, the Duchess taking the minister's arm, if
there happened to be one present.   All stood while a
brief blessing was asked ; then a psalm, or more rarely
a hymn, was read; and led by the solemn tones of the
organ, the sweet song of morning and evening praise
ascended on high. A portion of the Scriptures was
next read, and if the worship was conducted by one
qualified for it, the passage was explained more or
less fully.   Then followed prayer, in which her Grace
expected that the Queen should never be forgotten ;
and while many have suffered much by her removal
from earth, Her Majesty has lost the benefit of her
daily remembrance ; but she enjoys the gain of all her
prayers for so many years in secret and in the family
still remembered by the Lord Most High.

After breakfast every morning, for many years, the
Duchess visited her maid Cossens, now old, invalid,
and bedridden. Having served faithfully for fifteen
years, she lived for nearly thirty more in Gordon
Castle and Huntly Lodge, in a room of her own,
and waited upon with every attention. The Duchess
herself, in a beautiful interchange of their former
relations as mistress and maid, ministered continually
to her wants, whether for the body or the soul, with
most considerate kindness ; bringing also her more
intimate friends to visit her, as well as ministers, who
were guests in the house, to read and pray with her.

At noon, in her own beautiful room, the Duchess
had a daily reading of the Bible, with conversation
and prayer. When the family were alone, it was with
Miss Sinclair or Miss Sandilands, and some other young
ladies usually living at the Lodge ; when she had
visitors, it included the more intimate of her friends,
who were always such as could enjoy the privilege.
Each took part in the reading, which was intermingled
with conversation and followed by prayer. Conversa-
tional readings of this kind are not easily conducted
well, being apt to run into fanciful or petty questions
and remarks, or into a minute hair-splitting of Scripture, and making an idol of the letter apart from the
spirit of the Word. But at Huntly Lodge there were
two effectual preventives against these evils. The first

was in the strong good sense of the Duchess, which
had no sympathy with fancies, and no relish for trifles.
The second, and the more powerful, was in her intense
hunger for spiritual food ; for the pleasure of uttering
her own remark, or listening to another's, was nothing
in comparison with her delight in obtaining the least
morsel of bread for her soul. She used to say of such
meetings elsewhere, "I enjoy most what others relish
least, when a spiritually-minded man speaks at length,
and simply for edification." The presence of a minister
was, therefore, always welcomed and coveted at her
noon-day readings ; which were, however, most remarkable for the proof they gave of her own intense and
constant longing for the Lord and his word. The
character of the Duchess was in that respect a most
interesting study of itself. To some who knew her
longest, it still remains a wonder and a mystery. She
entered into the enjoyment of life fully as much as is
done by most ; she possessed a quiet and happy assurance of the life to come ; and her disposition was
singularly placid, cheerful, and contented. But she
longed for the word of God and prayer, as another
would do in the deepest distress of spirit ; she both
coveted these earnestly at any time, and when once
engaged appeared never to weary of their continuance.
There seemed to be a well-spring of joy within, flowing
up in a continual cheerfulness, and at the same time

a deep and intense thirst which no abundance of water
could satisfy. While these two are indeed in no conflict with each other, but in perfect harmony, yet we
marvel at the combination exhibited so beautifully,
and admire the grace so fully brought out in one
"of like passions with ourselves."

The afternoons or evenings were occupied with reading the most interesting publications of the day, both
religious and literary, with the exception of novels
and everything of a kindred character. The following letter refers, among other things, to the course of
daily life now commenced at Huntly Lodge: "*Dec.
8th.*—I begin to think it is not profitable to speak of
our feelings and ideas to any mortal ear, for the act
of doing so nourishes self-love ; and I have often felt
myself satisfied, after having made that sort of confession, in a way which I am now convinced was not
the work of the Spirit of holiness and humility.
Truly the heart *is* deceitful above all things, and
desperately wicked ; but he who knows it and searches
it can cleanse it, and not only he can, but will, for he
has promised. Various are his ways of performing his
promises, and hard is the struggle he will occasion
his children before he will give them that which is
their own, purchased for them by the blood and
righteousness of his dear Son. Oh, it is a good thing
to wrestle with God, and I think it must be done not

only when actually on our knees, but every moment.
Surely there is no moment in which we need not to
say, "I will not let thee go.' I think I would not
even say with Jacob, 'Except thou bless me ;' but
'Stay and bless me,' with a sense of thy presence, thy
love, and thy strength. I will not say any more, for
the devil is saying to me, 'This is well said.'

"At 12, Annie and I read with Commentaries. We
have begun the Gospel of Matthew, with Quesnel and
Boys ; and seeking wisdom to know what we should
choose, we prepare a little commentary to read to the
servants at night. When we have read we intend
going out. From 3 to 4, in general, we have to ourselves ; at 4, she reads Stevenson to me, but I have a
little quiet before going to Cossens at 5 ; at ½ past 6,
dinner; after it a chapter in Proverbs. At 8, I read
Erskine Murray on the Pyrenees, till 9 ; 9½, prayers.

"You ask for my further recollections of Mr.
M'Cheyne. It was rather by inference than from
what he said that the ideas on baptism took hold on
me ; therefore if wrong they are not his. Our Lord's
baptism being a type of the baptism in his own blood
by which he passed under all the waves of his Father's
wrath, so his rising up out of Jordan is a type of the
resurrection from the dead, whereby he was declared
to be the Son of God with power, and the heavens
acknowledged the type by the voice, 'This is my

beloved Son.' Now, as Christ desired to be baptized, because he said, 'Thus it becometh us to fulfil all righteousness,' so the baptism of each individual is an acknowledgment that He has fulfilled all that could be required by the justice of God ; and by imputation, at baptism we make the acknowledgment that the work is finished. I cannot make the idea clear to myself to-day ; I beg pardon for spoiling so much paper."

In the music in the drawing-room, after dinner or tea, she often herself took part, and with such spirit and taste as to delight even those least sensible to its charms. One evening after her return to the Lodge, and within two or three years of the Duke's death, there was a proposal for music, to which none seemed ready to respond, when she suddenly rose to the piano, and played one of her old Scotch tunes with the ex-quisite skill of a right hand that had not forgot its cunning. But as she played to the intense delight of the listeners, the tears were rolling down her cheeks, and when she had done, she apologized to her guests by explaining that it was the Duke's favourite tune, and that this was the first time she had attempted it since his death.

The relief of the poor always occupied a large place in the thoughts of the Duchess. She was very patient in inquiring into cases of distress brought before her, and very generous in relieving them when satisfied of their truth ; besides occasionally sending sums of money through the post, without her name, where she knew it was needed. Her regular disbursement for the poor in meat, clothing, and money, was very large ; and she did not forget the Lord's command to " make friends of the mammon of unrighteousness," but took care to provide spiritual counsel for those who shared her temporal bounty. After settling at Huntly Lodge, and while many workmen were still engaged in setting things in order within and without the house, one of her first cares was to find a godly chaplain, both for the sake of her own household, and for the benefit of the people around. On this subject she wrote to one of her earliest friends, to whose kindness we owe the most valuable materials in these Memoirs. The list of two hundred poor families, whose wants she regularly relieved, had in later years increased to three hundred :

"HUNTLY LODGE, 3d *April* 1838.

" MY DEAREST LADY HOME,—I hardly thought that a letter from you could have disappointed me so much as that received yesterday. But it is the Lord's own work for which I desire a workman worthy of having souls for his hire, and our Master knows best what will suit his purpose. I cannot doubt that He has a purpose of mercy for this place, since he has put it into the hearts of so many of his dear children to pray for us. Perhaps this solemn time at Glasgow will enable some to see his will more clearly. Might not some zealous and wise-hearted godly man be prevailed on to come for a few months, while there are so many earthly workmen about this place, and before the term when some of my old people are to leave me? I have in the time of the severe winter been so often deceived by statements of distress from the least deserving of assistance, that it is absolutely necessary I should have some one statedly to search into the true state of the cases; and besides extraordinary calls, there are upwards of two hundred poor families on my list, who, though belonging to different congregations, would yet afford no small field for an able worker. Of course, one who meant to remain would do the work more efficiently; but still I would thankfully accept temporary assistance, provided I could obtain it directly,—say within three weeks. May the Lord help us! He has commanded us to pray for more labourers, and we know that he heareth and answereth prayer according to his will; nay, more, Jesus ever liveth to make intercession, and I believe that these very difficulties are raised in tenderness to me, who have never before felt the value of souls, and should perhaps not now have felt for their necessities had not the apparent opposition roused my stony heart.

" There seems nothing to prevent me receiving the Duke of Richmond, when he comes to take actual possession of the estates in May; and this I am anxious to do, as I was absent in November when he wished to come to me. I did not answer your dear, kind letter which came in Helen's packet, for I have had *surcroit d'embarras* of writing lately; and though I do so need advice and wisdom in my own matters, the most extraordinary people think proper to consult me about the most extraordinary things, and I cannot lose the opportunity of giving the only Christian advice they may be in the way of receiving. May the Lord help me ; oh, how constantly do I need help !

" Now, my dearest Anna, you must not for one moment think of sending me Mr. B. . . . *I should not expect a blessing with him.* It was quite necessary you should have a tutor for your boys, and his work is pointed out and settled, and so it must be. We must not change, for He whom we serve changeth not, and in his service you know he has some apostles, some pastors, some teachers, each in their several vocations. This is what I feel with regard to myself; He will not strengthen us for a work, which is not that to which he has appointed us."

The circumstance to which her Grace refers, of the most extraordinary people consulting her on the most extraordinary subjects, arose from her singular kindliness of disposition and largeness of heart, and was responded to on her part with unwearied patience and good-nature, along with watchfulness to scatter the seed of life. With correspondents in every sphere of life, the same kindly and Christian spirit pervaded all her communications. Whether writing to friend or equal, or to her land-steward or housekeeper when from home, she would introduce anything that seemed fitted either to profit or to interest.

HUNTLY LODGE : ITS SABBATHS.

Among the seven days of the week, the Sabbath ever held its own high distinction at Huntly Lodge. It was a day of holy rest to the servants; all work that admitted of it was gone over on the Saturday evening; and no fire was lighted in the drawing-room, both to save unnecessary work, and to present no inducement for visitors to meet together for idle conversation. During the hours of Divine service the doors of the house were locked, and the servants were all at church with the exception of one, or in winter two. But there was no slave-like bondage on the holy day; no want of sunny cheerfulness; no restraint from admiring and rejoicing in all the works of the Lord.

To the Duchess herself it was the day looked forward to with hope, and the day remembered with delight through all the week. No godly Highland woman, to whom the house of God was the one channel of instruction, ever longed more for the courts of the Lord or delighted more in divine ordinances than the Duchess of Gordon. A false or an uncertain sound from the pulpit struck a deep wound into her spirit, and the dry form of godliness without the power was a grievous disappointment ; but when there was any unction at all from the Holy One, in the word or prayer, the house of the Lord brought unwearied delight. Morning and evening, in strength and weakness, in rain, frost, snow, the Duchess was at the house of God, and always early, so that her servants might also be in time. Others may have had more grace, the Lord only knoweth, but few have ever loved more all the means of grace. If there was any atmosphere of spiritual life in the ordinances, private or public, in the word, sacrament, or prayer, no prolongation of the services, and no multiplication of them, seemed either to fatigue the body or exhaust the mind. Her note-taking during sermon did not interrupt her mental exercise at the time, and the copying out of the sermons afterwards helped to diffuse the Sabbath blessing over the week.

At Huntly Lodge there were no letters posted or

received on the Sabbath; and no arrivals or departures of guests that day. One morning, when sitting
down at the breakfast table, a carriage-and-four had
come round from the stables. Startled with the unusual sound, the Duchess exclaimed, " What is that ?"
when a young English nobleman, who had been staying in the house, entered the room to bid her Grace
good-bye. " Oh no," she said, " not on the Sabbath ;"
and taking him affectionately to another room, she
easily persuaded him to remain till the following
morning.

When from home she carried the Sabbath most
carefully with her. In visiting her friends, in the
Duke's lifetime as well as afterwards, she made a
point of retiring on the Saturday night in such time
as to prevent the least encroachment on the Sabbath
on her account. On the Continent she invariably
discouraged any social meetings, even with the presence of a pious clergyman, where she feared that the
tone of conversation might not fully accord with the
sacredness of the day. If any views were advanced
on the subject by religious foreigners, that seemed to
be loose, she would argue most earnestly against them,
and in favour of the strictest observance of the Sabbath, as a day divinely set apart for spiritual employment from morning to night.

Another subject of a character partly kindred to

the Sabbath is referred to in several of her letters : the setting of a day apart for prayer, which she was in the habit of doing, both when any very special occasion called for it and on certain days of the year ; keeping her room all the morning, eating sparingly, and then joining the family at dinner-time. The days to which she refers in the following extract were her own and the Duke's birth-days, their marriage-day, and the day of his death : " Your word this morning, ' Remember the 22d,' was seasonable, for I never can, so cold-hearted am I. I seldom remember any days but four in the year, and those concern myself : the 11th December, the 2d February, the 28th May, and the 20th June. How different from you, who have as warm a recollection of what concerns me, as of what concerns yourself. I do not, however, forget you any day ; and my prayer, individualizing you as well as myself, is that we may ' do the will of God on earth, as it is done in heaven :' the entire will, as appointed, by Providence, with alacrity, with ardent love, with the whole mind of Christ, with heavenly-mindedness, as it is done in heaven. All this I desire for you more and more, that all our conversation may be in heaven, and that though in the world we may not be of the world."

One of these seasons of prayer is thus recorded : " The day was a very comfortable one, and has had very comfortable results ; the Lord delivered me from wandering thoughts, more than for a long time. Some former days of humiliation were attempted as a task, instead of as the privilege of a child to come near to a reconciled Father. And though I have not now the sense of sin or warmth of love I desire, yet I know that in Christ they are both to be found ; and I doubt not the blessed Spirit in his own good time will give me what I need. I found I had little enough time from 8 till half-past 5 to say all I had to say, and find out what I wanted, even though I had thought of it long before. The chapel at Fochabers was a principal concern, and the mountain has become a molehill."

The Duchess wrote a little tract on the Sabbath, with the view of directing some of her friends in the higher positions of life to just views on the subject, and had it printed for private circulation. We extract a few sentences : "The tables of the moral law were given to Israel ; but that law is a transcript of the mind of God, and there is nothing in it peculiar to time, place, climate, or people. The promises of blessing to the keeping of the Sabbath are not applicable to the Jews only ; but, as in all the other promises to the children of Abraham, the blessing is given to all who are his children by faith in Christ Jesus (Gal. iii. 29).

" The Sabbath was made for man, that man might learn to know Him, whom to know is life eternal; it was made that the bodies of men might be refreshed as well as their souls; and that their minds and intellects might have a time of repose from the agitations, and cares, and calculations, and contradictions of the world. It was made for man, not to exclude works of necessity and mercy, but that man should delight himself in God. 'If thou turn away thy foot from the Sabbath, from doing thy pleasure on my holy day, and call the Sabbath a delight, holy of the Lord, honourable; and shalt honour Him, not doing thine own ways, nor finding thine own pleasure, nor speaking thine own words, then shalt thou delight thyself in the Lord.' What a blessing! what a privilege! to delight in the Lord, to enjoy God, to enjoy his presence, his promises; all the blessings of the new Covenant, all that is treasured up in Christ in whom all fulness dwells.

" Can anything be better fitted to promote the end of man's creation than the observance of the Sabbath? 'Man's chief end is to glorify God and enjoy him for ever.' Is it not the very purpose of the day, that we may give glory to God, by acknowledging his sovereign power, his omniscient wisdom, his infinite love, his never-failing compassion, his long-suffering patience, his adorable holiness and justice? Above all, acknowledging that on the day we now call the Sabbath, the Lord's day, Christ rose from the dead, thus being

declared the Son of God with power; who had satisfied all the demands of the law, and endured all its
penalties in the place of sinners, the Just One for
the unjust, that he may bring us to God; and
who now, as the great and glorious Mediator, ever
liveth to make intercession and to give gifts unto
men.   He honoured the day by appearing among
his disciples and giving them his peace.   'Peace
be unto you,' were the words of Him who spake
the worlds into existence : 'My peace I give unto
you; not as the world giveth give I unto you.'
The world's gifts are but a vapour; but when Christ
giveth his peace, he giveth himself as 'made unto
us wisdom, righteousness, sanctification, and redemption;' he giveth his Holy Spirit that we may know
and enjoy him.

"Blessed be God, all this is, not exclusively, but
specially the privilege of the Lord's day, his own day,
which an old author calls 'the girdle of ordinances ;'
that which binds together all God's commandments
relative to his service, the day which he has made for
himself, that his people in whom are his delights may
delight themselves in Him."

Of the entire Sabbath from morning till night, and
of every new Sabbath as it succeeded the last, she
could most sincerely say that it was her spiritual joy,

and that without its light the whole week would have
been dark :

> " O day most calm, most bright,
>   The fruit of this, the next world's bud ;
>   The endorsement of supreme delight,
>   Writ by a friend, and with his blood ;
>   The couch of time, care's balm and bay ;
>   The week were dark but for thy light,
>   Thy torch doth lead the way."

Of few, indeed, could it be affirmed more appropriately
than of her, that the threaded Sabbaths of her life
"formed bracelets of beauty for the Bride of the
Lamb :"

> " The Sundays of man's life,
>   Threaded together on time's string,
>   Make bracelets to adorn the wife
>   Of the eternal, glorious King ;
>   On Sunday heaven's gate stands ope ;
>   Blessings are plentiful and ripe,
>   More plentiful than hope."—HERBERT.

For her part, she abounded in hope of its plenteous
blessings, and obtained the fulfilment of her longing
desires. Her cherished Sabbaths on earth gave vigour
of spiritual health and fulness of spiritual life here ;
and prepared her for the Sabbath which she now
enjoys for ever above, in the presence of " Him whom
having not seen she loved, and in whom, while yet
she saw him not, she rejoiced with joy unspeakable
and full of glory."

LETTERS—MEETING OF MINISTERS—GORDON SCHOOLS.

1837-1841.

The following section consists chiefly of portions of letters written by the Duchess during the first years of her residence at Huntly Lodge. The first extracts are dated at Edinburgh, which she visited for a few weeks in the autumn of 1837, after living a short time at Huntly on her return from abroad. She took this step on account of a lady in bad health, which the Duchess believed to be chiefly caused by spiritual darkness. It pleased the Lord to send the light of salvation into her soul during their stay; and the Duchess wrote several letters filled with gratitude for having been made the means of benefit to her friend.

"*Edinburgh, Oct.* 1837.—I never did before feel the meaning of the word 'marvellous.' To think that my Lord should so magnify his word to myself, and in reality, as to send it through such a poor earthen vessel as I am; to bring peace almost in an instant to the troubled soul, and to give me the delightful · work of comforting and establishing, I trust, one of his lambs. I never saw such a change as on Mrs. G.; she now sees Jesus as most precious, and lovely, and loving to herself. . . . The preaching seemed on purpose for her, and what to us was most searching and rousing, was to her really life from the dead: the subject, the thief on the cross, praying the Saviour to remember him, in all his iniquity to remember him, so completely putting human merit out of the question. I cannot tell you how happy I was last night when we settled to stay; but I know nobody in town, and don't know how to get at Mr. M.

"I think my stay at Huntly Lodge has done me good; my bonds seem loosed; daily I have seen more of Jesus, and in his light more of my own sinfulness; but oh, the Lord's dealings with me have been so wonderful! May that dreadful provoking ingratitude be cut away, if it should cost me far more than a right eye or a right hand. The Lord can support, and will not lay on me more than I can bear, but hitherto he does all by love. Oh! no words can tell his love and goodness, and patience, and long-suffering, and tenderness. I thank you much for the verse, Deut. xii. 7. The mirth is that which I feel to strengthen me; the prospect of the inheritance and rest, and the recollection that it is not now possessed. Annie (Sinclair) and I have finished Esther at 12 o'clock, and are now going to begin Job. May we through the Spirit sanctify ourselves to the work as Job did his sons."

The next extract relates to a visit paid to her at the Lodge by the Rev. Dr. Muir of Glasgow: "*Huntly Lodge, May* 1838.—I wish you had been with us these last ten days; truly I did not believe I could have enjoyed anything so much and so uninterrupt-edly. I expected Dr. Muir to come in the fulness of the blessing of the gospel of peace. I opened my mouth wide, and it has been filled, not for my sake but for Christ's; and yet for my sake also, and for that of all the souls that have been brought within the glad and glorious sound of the gospel of grace and truth as it is in Christ Jesus, sent through his faithful servant."

"*Huntly Lodge*, 1838.—When I said my prayers were quickened, I meant only on particular points, and surely we all do need often to be quickened; yea, daily, hourly, every minute. If the mind is occupied by anything that distresses, prayers for other things become general. If, on the other hand, the heart is full of thankfulness, then my most evil propensity is (though now the Lord in his mercy shows me the evil of it) to generalize all wants in abounding thanks-giving. But more gratitude is due for being reminded how little that is true gratitude, and how often it is nothing but deadness and coldness. Indeed, indeed, I feel with you this is my complaint, and requires greater effort to conquer than any other evil, and yet the Lord can, and, I believe, will do it. I was almost seeking for something from without to humble me, and can thank the Lord that he has sent it. . . . But I must not seek that, for he can humble me more effectually from within ; and by the very light of his infinite love in Christ Jesus, he can break the heart of stone, and bring us to the foot of the cross. Truly it is our own transgressions that, as a thick cloud, come between us and our God. When I am happy, I always think it is our own fault that we are ever otherwise : being heirs of such a portion as Christ has purchased. But then so much of our happiness is of earthly mould, deceitful even as our hearts."

"*Huntly Lodge*, 1838.—The Lord continues to manifest himself to me as a very present God ; and to show me that it is my own fault, when I do not see as much of his love as I need. Every moment I must seek him, and if so, he will assuredly be found of me ; but if he is once lost sight of, like a track we would follow on the ground, it is much more difficult to keep up with or trace the footsteps. I see much that I never saw before of the meaning of the expression 'living near to God.' Everything out of Christ is vanity and sin ; and even duty, without being done unto him, leads us into darkness."

"*March* 1839.—Oh, how comfortable to feel a Father's hand on us in every shape, and to know that Father unchangeable in his design of mercy and love ! My difficulty is to see his anger against sin, and this is very needful, for otherwise how can we say, ' Holy, holy, holy, is the Lord God Almighty' ? It seems as if

all the anger had been laid on Christ, and so in one
sense it has, for those who are his ; but we must know
ourselves to be his by our hatred and dread of sin,
not only in its consequences, but in itself. His suffi
ciency to atone for sin is not greater than the willingness of the Divine Spirit to cleanse from sin, and all
this power is ours, for 'all things are yours if ye are
Christ's.' "

"*Huntly Lodge, April* 1839.—I have been thinking
much of you at this time ; and I pray that each year
you may increase in likeness to Him, whose image is
reflected on those who by the Spirit are enabled to
look on him continually. Oh what is contained in
that 'looking unto Jesus,' besides all the ordinary
looking as a maiden unto the hand of her mistress.
If we were always looking unto and at him, we could
not live as we do ; for we should ever have light to
walk in the light. If we were for ever hiding ourselves from wrath under the robe of his righteousness,
we could never deserve wrath, for he would bear all
we had deserved, and would keep us from all evil. . . .
It is very comfortable to feel that it is all God's work
when we do anything according to his will ; and that
he has ordained it and us, that we should go and
bring forth fruit and that our fruit should remain.
Yes, remain, though we see it not now ; and the more
he makes us feel that it is not our work but his, the

more sure we may be that he will finish it to that whereunto he purposeth."

The next brief extract refers to a meeting of ministers at Huntly Lodge, which she had already commenced, and which she continued, or resumed after intermission, to the very close of her life. The ministers met together for prayer and conference by themselves, then at a more open meeting at which her Grace and some of her friends were present, and finally at family worship or in a more public meeting in the church. At the first of these meetings, the Duchess was full of interest and anxiety about the Protestant Church which she had founded at Pau, and its prosperity was made the special subject of prayer. Afterwards, the accession of our youthful Queen to the throne made her the subject of very special and repeated intercession, the Duchess pressing it very earnestly on those who conducted the devotions. The meeting referred to in the following letter took place on the coming of age of the Earl of March, now the Duke of Richmond : "*Huntly Lodge*, 31*st July* 1839.—To-morrow I hope for a very nice prayer-meeting at 7 o'clock, before breakfast. Mr. Bigsby is here, and Mr. Mackenzie; I expect Mr. David Brown of the Ord (now Dr. Brown of Aberdeen), Mr. Davidson of Drumblade, and Mr. Walker (parish minister)." The prayer at seven o'clock in the morning on this one occasion was added to the afternoon and evening prayers, because the Duchess was herself so impressed and anxious that she could not think of letting her ministerial guests depart without another meeting; and she met them at so early an hour, because they had to return to their homes during the day. In this department of Christian work the Duchess took nothing upon herself; but rejoiced to open her house to the Lord's servants, while she and her household shared in the benefit as listeners, or as fellow-worshippers.

Our next extract belongs to the following year :—
"*Huntly Lodge, Dec.* 1840.—You will be glad to hear that I think I am getting better acquainted with myself every day. I do think light has been given me lately; and why should I doubt it, for much have I prayed for it? What a blessed thing it is, that we can flee even from hateful self to Jesus! He is the only one who does not love us the less for all our unamiableness and sinfulness; but pities us the more, and gets the more glory, the lower the evil and deception from which he raises us. Certainly there is nothing like enlarged views of God for showing us how great must be the love of Christ to die for us, and of the Holy Spirit to strive with us odious creatures, especially when we have been so unwilling to see and believe what we are. How closely we need to watch both

within and without! I have just been interrupted by such a kind letter from the Queen-Dowager, who has sent some cards with texts, and her initials. By what she says, I suppose they are all in her handwriting; but she has sent them to Lady Colquhoun, so I have not seen them."

"*Huntly Lodge, March* 1841.—I am truly delighted to find that you are able to sing a new song of praise; in it, through infinite mercy, I can join you. I think I have never felt the love of God more tender, more clear, more sure through our blessed Surety, our precious Lord Jesus, than I have done lately; though amid many crosses of various kinds, and very many things to make me feel that my hands would hang down if my faithful God and Father in Christ Jesus were not my Helper, and his blessed Spirit my own Comforter. Through infinite mercy there is no wall between me and the bright light of the Lord's countenance, though I do not know that I have ever had more anxiety, or in more varied ways, than this winter."

One of the distresses to which the Duchess refers as occurring during this winter was a severe accident to her niece, Miss Sinclair, who had lived with her as a daughter since her widowhood. While standing talking to her younger brother, before retiring for the night, her muslin dress took fire; she ran out of the

room in a sheet of flame, and although it was soon
quenched by a rug thrown over her, the burning was
very severe, and its effects on the nervous system
were never quite removed. Miss S. was of one mind
and heart with the Duchess in following the Lord,
and was extremely beloved by the poor in Huntly.
She died in the Lord at her father's house in Hadding-
tonshire, a few years before the Duchess, who watched
over her last hours with a mother's affection.

Another of her trials consisted in the difficulties
that beset the Church of Scotland, to which she refers
at the close of the following letter : " 18*th Aug.* 1841.
—Though I have written eight letters to-day, yet I do
not like to put up, or rather close my blotting-book
without a word to you. I can quite return you, as my
portrait, Deut. xxxii. 10 to 16 ; and my only comfort
is in Him who, through the Holy Spirit, enables me
to believe that Jer. iii. 19 is addressed to me by him
who will do it ; and do both in us and for us above
what we can ask or think. Yes ! I can join you fully
in your prayer. I would not only see more of the
glory and majesty of God, but of his infinite holiness,
that self may be utterly subdued, and everything but
Christ abased. I do feel the *utter* impossibility of any
access to the Father but through the Son, our blessed
Mediator and Advocate. I do feel *at times* the utter
worthlessness of anything that has not the glory of

Christ for its aim and object; and I do trust, though the cross be somewhat heavy, that I shall be more and more willing to be despised, if need be, for Christ's sake."

During the years in which these letters are dated, the building of her Grace's schools was advancing. Wherever she lived, one of her first desires was to erect an infant-school; but at Huntly she added to this a school for older boys and girls, and an industrial school at which fifty girls were well educated and trained for service. These schools, which were finished in 1843 at a cost of several thousand pounds, were commenced in the summer of 1839. Accompanied by some of her friends, and by several ministers of the gospel by whom prayer was offered before and after the ceremony, and surrounded by about a thousand children who sang a hymn prepared for the occasion, the Duchess laid the foundation-stone with deep emotion, which all but overcame her when her part was done; for the schools were designed by her, as the best monument she could raise to her husband's memory. They were built at the entrance to the old Castle Park, and the approach to the Lodge was through the centre of the building, by an archway adorned with fine busts of the Duke and Duchess. They formed a subject of constant attraction and daily interest to her Grace for the last twenty years of her life ; as they occupied much of her own time and heart, they formed for her the most interesting scene to which she could conduct her visitors ; and she endeavoured, by leaving a liberal endowment, to make them a benefit to coming generations.

DEEPENING OF THE LORD'S WORK IN THE SOUL.
1844-1847.

There is an interval between the preceding letters and the following, and a marked change in their tone. In the process of years the work of the Spirit in the soul had imperceptibly declined : the conviction of sin had become blunter ; the joy of the Lord shallower ; the sense of his presence less vivid ; the pursuit of holiness less earnest ; and the victory over the world more doubtful. Her state was still higher than that of most believers, and not without fruit unto God, but in the retrospect she saw a gradual waning of inward power. Trust in a past experience began to supplant the present witness of the Spirit ; the form of godliness often lacked the power ; the light of the soul grew dim ; and a painful sense of distance followed, without any clear apprehension of the cause or of the remedy. That finest of the wheat, " no condemnation in Christ Jesus," had been eaten till the appetite was cloyed ; and the soul did not know that

its health now demanded the "bitter herbs" of conviction of sin and repentance toward God.

In the year 1844 the Lord sent conviction to her
conscience with great power, and it was accepted, and
even welcomed in all its humility and painfulness;
not, however, in the way of doubt regarding a past
work of grace, but in a deep sense of departure from
the Lord, of double-mindedness, of unfruitfulness,
of innate corruption, and of manifold transgression.
After a time this was followed by greater nearness to
the Lord, and livelier joy in his salvation than before.
The spiritual restoration lasted in the main throughout her life, for the work was deeper than ever, and
therefore more abiding; and till her dying day she
looked back on the period to which we have now
come, as one of the happiest and most helpful seasons
in all her spiritual history.   But we cannot easily
present it in the form of a narrative, on account of
her Grace having lived much in Edinburgh at this
period, and having sat under the ministry in St.
Luke's Church.   We shall therefore do little else than
transcribe portions of her own letters, at the risk of
trying the patience of the reader by the want of relief.

"*Huntly Lodge, 7th August* 1844.—I wish you
could have stayed with us at present, for certainly I
know no one who turns me inside out like Mr. ——,
and I do certainly greatly need that sort of searching.

If we compare ourselves with the word of God, oh, what grievous falling back from first simple convictions! How far we are from living unto Him who died for us, from remembering that we are bought with a price! We think we are our own, and that we may give unto the great and holy God only just that which we are willing to spare, that which costs us nothing; if we give the clay into the hand of the potter, the little precious stone is still left in the lump to mar the vessel. We do not remember that He can make us willing, so willing that with the mind of Christ we may learn to say, 'I delight to do thy will, O my God: yea, I am content to do it; thy law is written in my heart.' Is not this what he has promised: the new heart, the right spirit that shall not depart from him? Why do we not believe him, and live as if indeed we did know that we are his children, living to serve him, and to do his will on earth as the angels do in heaven? Think how they do the will of God!"

" *Huntly Lodge, October* 1844.—One ought to find help in every time of need, and so it is provided, for company is in some sort a duty; at least I cannot avoid it, and I ought to be ever ready to speak a word in season, but alas! May the Lord give us both sound wisdom and discretion; but above all, may all our thoughts and words and works be done, as Dr. Duncan translates, 'truthing it in love.' Oh, I feel how glorious is the truth of God; how holy those should be who walk in the light of Him who is the light of the world, as well as the life of man; who feel the necessity of singleness of purpose and of eye. I feel how the world blinds us to this. We think sometimes to do the work of God in our own way; but he will only honour his own way, which is truth. My self-convictions have taught me this, or perhaps I could never have suspected that others may be ignorant of it."

Two or three of the following months of winter were passed in Edinburgh, and the next letter is written after returning to the north : "*Huntly Lodge, 10th February* 1845.—I rejoice to hear that Winslow's preaching has had the same effect on you as his book had on me, that is, in convincing me that declension in religion is a much more easy thing than we are aware of, till we find it in our own experience. We do, it is true, think it easy in others, and that this and that mixture with the world will cause others to go back; but we do not see that without doing those very evident things of the world's proposing, we may be 'settling on our lees,' and have gone far down indeed before we are aware. And though the child of God will never perish, yet we can only know that we are children of God when we 'hold the beginning of our confidence firm unto the end."

" But is it becoming in a living child of God to be contented with 'the beginning of our confidence?' Oh let us never lose hold of that, let us never have any other plea before God than that 'Jesus Christ came into the world to save sinners;' but let us press forwards toward the mark for the prize of our high calling in Christ Jesus, in single-hearted desire to honour him who hath so loved us; let us take the word of God as it is written, and let us beware of fancying that such and such parts were intended for other times. They are the words of God, the inditing of the Spirit of truth according to the mind of Him who is the same yesterday, to-day, and for ever, and who is 'no respecter of persons.' How awful is the thought that it is our Lord who says, 'Every branch *in me* that beareth not fruit, shall be hewn down and cast into the fire!' 'He that abideth in me, and I in him, the same bringeth forth *much fruit.*'

" What fruit have we borne unto God? what have we done for his glory? Oh what infinite, wonderful, long-suffering love is it that asks this of our inmost souls, before it be too late ; and enables us to hear also the voice of him who so loved us as to die for us, even the voice of Jesus saying, 'Except ye repent ye shall all likewise perish.' 'There is none other name given whereby we must be saved, than the name of Jesus.' 'If we do not the things that he says, we are none of his.' Oh, it is love, infinite love, that would now shut us up to be not almost, but altogether Christ's. We cannot serve two masters; Christ must be all or nothing to us. Where are we? what have we? what have we done for Christ? If anything, to him be the glory; but have we done what we could?

"I find the signs of the times portentous on all hands, but in nothing more remarkable than in the awakening of God's people. 'Let us not sleep as do others, but let us watch and be sober.' We have been living on doctrines instead of by doctrines; they are but dry morsels without the Spirit, and the Spirit of light bringeth to the light, that our deeds may be reproved. *The Comforter* is the reprover; and he must show us our need of salvation by the knowledge of ourselves, that he may lead us to Him who is light, and the light of life, and whose blood cleanseth from all sin *only* those who walk *in the light.* The whole work is of God, but it is *in* us, as well as *for* us; and we too must work, nay, cannot but work with every faculty under our control, if we are living children of the living God. I heard nothing more of Free Church principles after you passed through Edinburgh; but we have indeed been richly fed with the word of truth, and I trust we are returned with the resolution, through divine grace,

of walking in the liberty wherewith Christ makes his
people free; a liberty bound up in his Word and by
his Spirit, and which would not for worlds transgress
any of his commands."

The following letter and several others were written
by the Duchess to the late Miss Banks, of Moray
Place, Edinburgh, whose pupils were in the habit of
sending her Grace notes of sermons and lectures after
her return to Huntly. A manuscript book of the
Duchess, commencing three days after this letter,
contains more than two hundred and fifty questions,
founded on the notes thus sent, as well as on those
previously taken by herself. She had formed a weekly
class of about twelve, composed of her female domestics; and copying out a number of the questions she
had prepared, she gave a written slip with a single
question to each, to be answered the following week.
The household greatly enjoyed this exercise for themselves; and some of them who survive her have said
that at no period of her life, before or after, had they
known the Duchess so completely happy, so unburdened, so spiritual, so full of hope and joy in the
Lord.

"*Huntly Lodge, 25th Feb.* 1845.—It is my turn to
thank you for your great kindness in sending the
notes of sermons. The lecture on Hebrews iv. 1
brings us back to the sure foundation; but with great

cause of gratitude and praise, that we have been permitted to see much more of the glory and grace of
that foundation, in proportion as we have learnt to
look into the pit whence we were digged, and to know
that nothing but the continual application of the
blood of sprinkling and of the water of sanctification
can render or keep that clay as a vessel fit for the
Master's use. I see that we must not only have the
sure and certain hope, not merely that we shall be,
but that we are saved; but also that the *present
salvation* must have as little reference to what *has
been,* as to what *is to be.* It must be I *am saved*
every moment, and therefore every instant the entire
reliance on divine grace to supply *all* our need is
required."

"*Huntly Lodge, March* 1845.—I must tell you that
your last letter and the notes have been a very great
delight and comfort to me, though it has not pleased
the Lord to permit me to approach his table at this
time, as I have been confined to my rooms till last
night. I am not very bright yet, but I think my
dear Lord has shown me his willingness to wash my
feet. I feel that I well deserve the effect of long sleep
and careless walking. I have never doubted the love
or the purposes of my Lord towards me, because I
have not, since I first knew him, ever thought that
I could do anything towards my justification, or to

merit grace. What a contradiction in terms! But I now feel that I am a reasonable and accountable being, which I seemed to have lost sight of, and that if I am a living child of the living God, I must live for, and with, and unto Him who is life and light and truth. I have no life, no energy to do anything, and he must give it; but after so long neglect, I cannot expect it without earnest striving; nor for my striving, but because I am his child, and he would try my love."

"*Huntly Lodge, April* 1845.—The notes are very satisfactory; they have fallen to my share, as I have taken the Exposition on Hebrews for household use; but all are most truly appreciated. I could say much to you on our present position, because I think you could understand my feelings better than most of my friends; at the same time I confess I am not satisfied with my position. However, the Lord has promised, that those who trust in him shall be led by a way that they know not, even though they be in darkness and have no light. It is indeed a comfort to feel that our Great High Priest has compassion on the ignorant, and on them that are out of the way. He is the Great Physician, and so long as we are sick of the hereditary and most inveterate disease of our first parents, we need the medicine of his most precious blood every moment; and it is ready, and he is ready to apply it by his own blessed Spirit, the Reprover, the Sanctifier, and the Comforter."

"*Huntly Lodge, June* 1845.—I have had a good many letters on business to write, which has made letter-writing more disagreeable to me than ever. I strive, though with a sadly volatile spirit, to hide me in the secret of the presence of my Lord, who is able to help me and does help me; and would help me far more if I were as diligent in striving as I should be, if I could *feel* his love half as much as I know it. But he can also give the heart to feel; all, all must be his gift. The praise of man and love of approbation I think indeed the greatest of all snares, but he can break the meshes of that net as of every other. Dr. Duncan has been telling you just what we heard at St. Luke's, of the danger of making gods for ourselves. There is another thing we are apt to think we know, till the Spirit teaches us the difference between the truth and our conception of it, that 'God is no respecter of persons.'"

"*Huntly Lodge, July* 1845.—How dreadfully have I allowed sloth to get the better of me; how richly I deserve to go softly all my days! But then, on the other hand, the intense sense of my own vileness seems to give me a firmer hold of my precious Saviour, and he is able to keep that which I have committed unto him. But oh, that I could do something for him!

Perhaps all he wants of me now is to feel 'not my will, but thine, O Lord, be done.' . . . The friends whom we expected from England came yesterday, but I wonder if I shall ever again have that pleasure in rejoicing Christians that I used to have ; for I now fear, that when I rejoiced I did not know anything of the holiness of God ; and oh, what provocations against light and love ! Yet poor Mrs. H., who mourns over her own changes, when reminded of the unchangeableness of our God, makes me feel that, looking to self may be like burying one's face in a pillow, and forgeting that the sun shines."

Yet the Duchess both found great pleasure again in rejoicing Christians, and herself rejoiced in the Lord Jesus during all the years of her life to come. She had been awakened afresh by the Spirit, searched, rebuked, and chastened ; and was in due time so brought back to her first love, as never greatly to lose it till she was taken to see Him whom she had loved while yet unseen.

" *Fairlie, Sept.* 1845.—We have been considering 1 John i. 7, 'If we walk in the light as he is in the light, we have fellowship one with another ;' and taking that fellowship to mean the fellowship of Christ's members one with another. It is a sort of evidence of that fellowship very comfortable to the mind, when we find that the light is revealing the same thing to others, namely, those most abominable 'meannesses' and '*petitesses*,' of which we are more ashamed than of 'mighty' sins. And so perhaps we ought to be, for they show more of the deep, inward corruption of the whole man, and may lead us first to say with Hazael, 'Is thy servant a dog?' and then with the woman of Canaan, 'But, Lord, the dogs eat of the crumbs that fall from the master's table.' Truly we are 'dogs;' and if the whole nature be not a new creation we cannot enter, nay, we cannot see the kingdom of heaven.

"When I think of lost time and opportunities, and all that has been done in 'calling evil good and good evil,' how much has been 'let slip;' how much has been 'perverted;' and how truly it hath profited me nothing, even as regards this world (James i. 8), I am indeed ashamed and confounded. Alas! there is not yet the true test, the love of souls (1 John i. 8). If it were not for the tenth verse, and that Jesus came to seek and to save that which was lost, and that it is his will and the Father's will that none that come unto him should be cast out, I should be . . . I fear, hardened beyond redemption. But Jesus can and will save to the uttermost all that come unto God by him, and he has promised to give all, and above all that I can need.

"You have many to pray for, but none more need

the prayers of those who know something of their utter need. May you and I know from day to day, that in Christ Jesus the Spirit does draw with the cords of love and with the bands of a man, those whom the Father hath chosen and given unto the Son."

"*Edinburgh, Oct.* 1845.--We had a delightful lecture last Thursday evening on part of the 31st Psalm. The exposition of ver. 5, ' Into thy hands I commit my spirit," was to show the entire giving up, on the one hand, which is required ; and on the other (as the Lord gave himself, his spirit, into the Father's hand ; and Stephen said, Lord Jesus, into *thy* hands I commit my spirit), the oneness of the Godhead ; and also that all who are in Christ Jesus are bound in the bundle of life with him, and were with him and by him committed unto the Father, when he said on the cross, 'Father, into thy hand I commit my spirit.' Oh, give yourselves into his glorious hands ; they will bless and not crush you. How unbelieving we are to withhold *any* thing, when he asks for that vilest of all things,—our hearts."

The next letter is longer, written with the joy of salvation in her own soul, and with the desire of opening great first principles to her friend : " *Nov.* 1845.—I trust you are enabled to say, ' It is well : it is the Lord.' As regards your dear sister, it is very trying, and in all our afflictions He is afflicted ; but as regards yourself, I think it is a great blessing. You have had so much to do for others for some years past, that you have had comparatively but little time to think of your own soul, and I am sure there is not a truer word in the Word of truth, than that 'through much tribulation we must enter (pass to) the kingdom of heaven.' I believe that true peace is never known till every refuge, every earthly comfort, has been found to be vanity ; and then when the God of all grace and consolation reveals himself, he is altogether lovely. When the Holy Spirit brings the soul to see that it is under condemnation of the holy law for sins more numerous than the hairs of the head, and that the justice of God must condemn the smallest breach of that most holy transcript of the character of the Holy One, what marvellous, infinite goodness, love, and mercy, are seen in Him who is both the Creator and the Redeemer, the man Christ Jesus, God with us, God for us, our Surety.

"We cannot love him till we know our need of such a Saviour ; and that we cannot know till we see that we are lost, till we feel with the apostle, 'I through the law am dead to the law, that I might live unto God.' Oh, when the sinner is brought to give up all for the Saviour, and to come without money and without price, naked and miserable, and poor and famishing; there is not a tender name by which the Lord will not command that soul to call him,—Father, Husband, Friend, Brother, Saviour, Redeemer, Sanctifier, Surety. Words cannot be found to tell all he is to those who have given up all other hope and refuge.

"But this must not be (as alas! it has been with me for too long a season) a thing once done, a stock of grace laid in; it must be Jehovah who is our God, I AM, the ever-present One. Let us beware lest we should be living on past experience, and forget that our life must be hid with Christ in God; the life we now live in the flesh must be by the faith of the Son of God, who loved us and gave himself for us. Can we forget, or think lightly of such a Saviour? Can we refuse to take up our cross daily and follow him? Thank him that you have time to think of him without distraction, and pray, pray earnestly that you may know what it is to count all but loss for Christ, and may be brought into the glorious liberty of the children of that God whose service is perfect freedom. You ask me to name books; I particularly recommend Owen on the *Sinfulness of Sin.* I have taken a house in Edinburgh; and when I think how gracious the Lord has been in restoring to me the joy of his salvation, notwithstanding all my backsliding and compromising for years past, I cannot but rejoice that I am permitted to hear his truth so very fully and frequently declared."

When living in Edinburgh the Duchess, with her usual interest in children, built large schools in the destitute district of Holyrood, which she liberally supported, giving at the same time a site for the present Holyrood Church. The district was at the foot of the Canongate, where her old friends Dr. Stewart and Mrs. Buchanan had lived and prayed, and she therefore took it up with the greater pleasure in the hope of reaping the fruit of their supplications. In her house in Moray Place there were many interesting meetings of the labourers engaged in the work ; and when the mission came to be formed into a church, the first list of communicants presented a singularly interesting group of old and young, gathered in from their strangely diverse wanderings to sit down in the kingdom of God.

The letters of this period are far too numerous to present to our readers, and two more must complete the chapter. The first is one of many letters to the Rev. Charles Mackintosh of Tain, now Dr. Mackintosh of Dunoon, for whom the Duchess always expresses the very highest regard ; he had been abroad with her in 1837.

"EDINBURGH, 9th May 1846.

"MY DEAR COUSIN,—This winter has been a most

blessed one, showing me more and more of the love of God to poor sinners in and through Christ Jesus, and of the character of that God whom we too often profess to honour, whilst in truth we only insult him, the thrice holy Jehovah. But his love and his mercy are infinite ; his long-suffering bringeth salvation, and his unchangeable purpose secureth it. The communion at St. Luke's, on the 26th, was a time never to be forgotten, when the overwhelming load of iniquity and multitude of sins was seen washed away by the blood that cleanseth from all sin ; and the Holy Spirit, who alone can convince of sin, of righteousness, or of judgment, brought the seal of the New Covenant to witness to the eternal truth of the word of God. I feel the difficulty of expressing myself, the fear of saying more than I feel, and yet I believe there was that revealed which led to something more than repetition of Job's words, ' I have heard of thee by the hearing of the ear, but now mine eye seeth thee, wherefore I abhor myself and repent in dust and ashes.' Truth it is, the Lord hath dealt bountifully with me, and hath made me glad through the light of his countenance. Oh may I never rest on past mercies, for he is the great I AM, and we are so poor and so feeble that we cannot keep for one instant what will supply our need in the next."

The last letter that we shall now transcribe was

addressed to Miss Sandilands, only child of the late Colonel Sandilands of Nuthill, on the occasion of his death. In the course of the year she went to live with the Duchess as her chosen friend, and remained with her to the end :

"EDINBURGH, 30*th January* 1847.

"MY MUCH-LOVED ANNIE,—When we find in every page of Scripture the loving-kindness of the Lord, when we are enabled by faith to have some glimpses of his infinite love as revealed in the cross of Christ, can we hesitate in casting all our care upon Him who careth for us ? The text on the Communion Sabbath was, 'Keep silence all flesh before the Lord, for he is risen up out of his holy temple.' This God is exalted to show mercy ; his arm is stretched out to bless and deliver. He was led as a lamb to the slaughter, and as a sheep before the shearers is dumb, so he opened not his mouth. See Him who was innocent bearing our punishment ; the great God by whom the worlds were made, God in our nature, the Son of God, the son of David, the Judge of all the earth, opening not his mouth ; silent before God the Father, when upon him was laid the iniquity of us all.

"If the mighty God could submit to be humbled and spit upon, there is surely no mercy too great for him to show. Is there any limit to the grace of God the Lord, God who spared not himself; is there any limit to the grace of the Holy Ghost, by whom Christ was offered in sacrifice? Is any love too loving; is any grace too gracious? This is the tried stone, the precious corner-stone, on whom we may lay all our trials; who delights to be trusted, who has commanded us to take up our cross, not to bear it, for he bore it for us. Oh, dearest, lay your heavy cross on Him, lay your weary frame on his compassionate heart. He, too, was weary and afflicted, and knoweth how to succour them that are tempted. More, when the sinner is silent, he is the advocate, and is able to rebuke the accuser of the brethren, and Satan is silenced. And child-like Joshua must be silent, not only when he stands in his filthy garments before the Angel of the Covenant, Jehovah; but silently consenting when those garments are taken off, when beauteous raiment is put on, and a fair mitre put upon his head, even the hope of salvation for an helmet. Cast all your care upon him, for he careth for you. I have thought of you constantly, and how much more carefully does the Refiner sit and watch! His love, his tenderness, is infinite; may it be poured out into your heart by the Holy Spirit, the Comforter.—Ever your truly affectionate

" E. GORDON."

CHAPTER VII.

STRATHBOGIE.

1839–1847.

" THUS a witness to the Churches,
  Scotland's Church hath ever been ;
Carnal men, with vain researches,
  Musing what the sign may mean.
Like her Master, poor and lowly,
  Seeking nought of price below,
All she claims, with freedom holy,
  Still about his work to go.
Strange, that in her pathway ever,
  Strifes and oppositions spring ;
Nay, she sows beside a river,
  And her shout is of a King.
Hope thou not, then, earth's alliance,
  Take thy stand beside the Cross ;
Fear, lest by unblest compliance
  Thou transmute thy gold to dross ;
Steadfast in thy meek endurance,
  Prophesy in sackcloth on ;
Hast thou not the pledged assurance,
  Kings shall one day kiss the Son ?
Haste, thy coming Lord to greet,
Cast thy crown before his feet ;
Only, may his quest for thee
Find thee, what he made thee, FREE."
                    Lays of the Kirk and Covenant.

R

OF the first sermon I was privileged to preach in
Strathbogie, while on a visit to Huntly Lodge in 1838,
my only remembrance is of a parish church oppres-
sively large, and of an old man standing all the time
with upturned ear and earnest eye at the foot of the
pulpit stairs. He waylaid me in going out; and the
style of his address attracted my attention, as much as
the sermon could have arrested him : " It's mair than
thirty years," he said, "sin' Maister Cowie dee'd, and
I ha'e heard mony a minister sin' syne ; but frae that
day to this, I ha'e never heard just the verra same
doctrin' as ye preached till us the day;" meaning that
the statement of the helpless ruin of man and the free
grace of God, of the righteousness of Jesus Christ and
the new birth by the Spirit, was cast in the same
mould as that in which he had first received the truth.
It was impossible not to be cheered by his sympathy
of heart and communion of thought; but the added
honour of comparison to his old minister was thrown

away, because I had not even heard his name before. But I soon found that both minister and man were well known to the Duchess of Gordon : the old man personally, as a living epistle of Jesus Christ read of all men ; and the old minister, by his memory still fragrant in all the country round, and by his deeds and sayings in which she took great delight.

The Rev. George Cowie of Huntly was a fearless advocate of the truth as it is in Jesus ; with a holy and intense hatred to the blighting Moderatism[1] of the district, to the " dumb dogs that could not bark." But he was a man of a large heart, sympathizing with Rowland Hill and the Haldanes, at the cost of exclusion from his own communion ; and of a truly genial spirit, becoming all things to all men to save some. One of his attached hearers was the wife of a wealthy farmer who, after weeping and praying in vain for her ungodly husband, brought her grief before her pastor, whose preaching she could by no persuasion induce him to hear. After listening to the case, which seemed quite inaccessible, he inquired, " Is there anything your goodman has a liking to ?" " He heeds for naething in this warld," was the reply, " forbye his beasts and his siller, an' it be na his fiddle." The hint was enough ; the minister soon found his way to

---

[1] The terms *Moderatism* and *Moderates,* employed in this chapter, will of course not be understood as if they were applied to the present Established Church and its ministers.

the farm-house where, after a dry reception and kindly inquiries about cattle and corn, he awoke the farmer's feelings on the subject of his favourite pastime. The fiddle was produced, and the man of earth was astonished and charmed with the sweet music it gave forth in the hands of the feared and hated man of God. The minister next induced him to promise to return his call, by the offered treat of a finer instrument in his own house. There he was delighted with the swelling tones of a large violin, and needed then but slight persuasion from his wife to accompany her and hear his friend preach. The word took effect in conviction and salvation ; and the grovelling earthworm was transformed into a free-hearted son of God, full of the lively hope of the great inheritance above.

The name of the old disciple was James Maitland, a man poor in this world but rich in grace, whom rank could not overawe nor wealth attract. The Duchess delighted in his sterling character, and often repeated his pithy sayings. Her own liberality was unbounded to the poor and to all that were in distress ; but she knew well the Scotch independence of character, and enjoyed a hearty laugh at the expense of an English lady visiting at the Lodge, who had selected her old friend James as an object of charity. The stranger had been deeply interested in the good old man, and on returning home she sent two pounds for him by one of the elders of the church. The commission puzzled the almoner not a little; but taking a brother elder along with him, he went to their friend, now aged and infirm, and found him in bed. They took courage and opened their errand, expecting an immediate, and fearing an offended, refusal of the gift. But to their great surprise the old invalid grasped the money eagerly, sprang from his bed, and called out, "She's verra generous; wait a wee, an' I'll sune let it be weel kent; aiblins the leddie means it for the Lord's puir, but I'm nane o' them." So saying, he dressed and sallied forth into the town, and did not return till he had gladdened the hearts of forty poor people with the alms.

Old Isabel was another of the Duchess's friends, brought up in the same school; aged and blind, but acute in hearing, in spirit, in intellect. "The Duchess has come to see you, Isabel." "It's nae the Duchess?" "It is indeed." "Weel, it's sae like her Maister." The definition of Effectual Calling in our Catechism was what she called her "gran' question;" and her rehearsal of it opened to the listener a new idea of the power of thought and feeling to put life into words. The words are these: "Effectual calling is the work of God's Spirit, whereby, convincing us of our sin and misery, enlightening our minds in the knowledge of Christ, and renewing our wills, he doth persuade and enable us to embrace Jesus Christ, freely

offered to us in the gospel." So extraordinary was
the effect of her repetition of these few clauses, that
it was only by recalling the whole, word by word, that
you could believe that the blind old woman had not
enlarged and explained as she went along. The over-
awing majesty of the great Spirit, the shame and
misery of the convinced sinner, the bright light dawn-
ing in Jesus Christ, the loving alteration of the will,
and the cordial and joyful embracing of the freely-
offered Saviour, all appeared like parts of a process
which her mind and heart were undergoing step by
step at the moment. And in listening to words you
had lisped from childhood, now so freshly breathed on
by the Spirit, you were awed, convinced, enlightened,
allured, and gladdened by the grace of God in Christ
Jesus, and seemed to pass anew through the whole
process of effectual calling in your own soul.

But in Strathbogie these were thinly scattered stars
shining through a wide and dismal night that covered
the land, and none of them shone within the sphere of
the Church of Scotland. We find the Duchess after her
widowhood thus lamenting her isolation at Huntly :
"It is really a trial to feel that the truth is preached in
the Dissenting chapels ; but then they are Voluntaries,
and here I am on a hill. Oh for wisdom, and above all,
grace and love." She drew specially to the pastor who
then ministered in Mr. Cowie's church, and invited him

to a weekly meeting for prayer at the Lodge with her Presbyterian chaplain, and herself an Episcopalian; the three anticipating thus the Evangelical Alliance. Of his flock she writes: "The missionary people, or Independents, are active, practical Christians, and it is really a blessing to have such people at hand."

Neither her large liberality of spirit, nor her regard for the Established Church, nor her respect for individual ministers with higher aims, could blind her for a moment to the death that reigned in the parishes around her, and to its source in the fatal blight of a Moderate ministry. A minister lacking the great essentials for his office was nothing to her; no other qualifications were of any account, or could induce her to look upon him except as a cumberer of holy ground. "Nobody need tell me about the Moderates," she said severely, "I know them well; I should never think of consulting them on any religious subject, or asking them to my house for spiritual profit. All I can do is to invite them to dinner, when the Duke of Richmond is here with the farmers at the cattle show." Continually, therefore, did she mourn over the people as sheep without shepherds, and prayed that the Lord himself would send them pastors to feed them. In the end of December 1837, soon after her return to Huntly Lodge, we find her writing these striking words: "We must pray very, very hard for more labourers in the

Lord's vineyard, and that he may send us 'pastors after his own heart.' I do not see where they are to come from at all, and therefore I think I can pray with more entire faith, and feel sure that the Lord will give them in his own time and way."

THE UNLOOKED-FOR ANSWER TO PRAYER.—1839, 1840.

The resolution of the Duchess to pray for right-hearted pastors for Strathbogie, when she did not see where they were to come from, and her " feeling sure that He would give them in his own time and way," are very remarkable when taken in connexion with the result; for within the space of two years, by events as little desired as foreseen, this praying "very, very hard" was abundantly answered. The Lord himself sent forth a band of faithful labourers into the district; and the house in which the prayer was offered was freely opened for their reception, though amidst a painful strife of conflicting emotions.

The unexpected intrusion by the Civil Courts into the spiritual jurisdiction of the Church of Scotland, which had been commenced in other districts, soon found an inviting harvest field in the intensely Moderate region of Strathbogie. The call to the presentee to the parish of Marnoch was signed by only three out of thirteen heritors; and out of a parish of nearly 3000 souls, it was signed by none but a single communicant, the keeper of the public-house where the Presbytery were wont to dine ; while six-sevenths of the members of the church entered their solemn protest against his induction.   The people's dislike arose neither from ignorance nor faction, for he had previously been assistant for three years in the parish, till he was removed at their urgent request.

A preacher, whose " life, literature, and doctrine" were examined by a Presbytery, might be correct in character, a good scholar, and a sound divine, yet not likely to prove a good parish minister ; and the call of the people, in addition to the presbyterial certificate, was recognised by the law of the land, as well as by the usage of the Church from the earliest ages. Even in the darkest times of last century, this call had never been either abolished or disused ; the Presbytery declared themselves satisfied in every case with its sufficiency, and the minister at his ordination solemnly accepted the "call" to be pastor. All this was often only a solemn show in a dead church. But with the awaking of conscience and the revival of spiritual life, it was impossible for thoughtful ministers to go through these grave transactions as meaningless forms ; to accept of the publican's single voice as a sufficient " call" from three thousand souls ; or to be coerced by any power on earth to sell their consciences, and yield themselves as instruments of such mockery in the house of God.

The Moderator of the Presbytery of Strathbogie at this time was the minister of Fochabers, the Rev. David Dewar, already known to our readers as the chaplain at Gordon Castle, to whom the Duchess bore so high a testimony for his "Nathanael-like" freedom from guile, and his singular meekness that disarmed every enemy. On a vacancy occurring in the parish church, after the Duke of Gordon's death, he was presented to the charge by the Duke of Richmond at the earnest recommendation of the Duchess. There, as elsewhere, his genuine godliness, unfeigned humility, and quiet judgment endeared him to all; and the Duke used to say that "he had no fault but one, which was, that he preferred walking to riding." Notwithstanding the flagrant inadequacy of the call, the Presbytery by a majority of seven to four resolved to proceed with the ordination, because the presentee had procured an order to that effect from the Court of Session. By Mr. Dewar's wisdom and courage they were prevented going forward till the matter was brought before the Supreme Ecclesiastical Court, by which they were enjoined to desist. When they refused to obey, they were solemnly suspended from the exercise of their holy office; and when they ordained the presentee notwithstanding, they were ultimately deposed by the General Assembly from that ministry whose most sacred functions they had so grossly abused.

During the suspension of the seven ministers from the preaching of the word and dispensation of the sacraments, the Commission of Assembly sent ministers and preachers to supply the lack in their parishes. These were first interdicted by the Civil Courts from preaching in the parish churches, churchyards, and school-houses ; and over these they at once acknowledged the right of the courts of law, and made no attempt to enter them. But they were next prohibited from preaching anywhere within the bounds of the parishes, in market-place, or barn, or open field. The deputed ministers were waited for as soon as they arrived in the district, their names were ascertained, and they were eagerly served with this prohibition to preach from the Supreme Court of the land. But their commission from the Lord was, Go ye into all the world, and preach the gospel to every creature ; and none of them were tempted to obey man rather than God, and refrain from publishing the word of life. The sainted Robert M'Cheyne, who was one of them, gave this reply to the interdict : " I can say with Paul, that I have preached the gospel from Jerusalem round about unto Illyricum, and no power on earth will keep me from preaching it in the dead parishes of Scotland."

The people disregarded it as much as the ministers. They were building an additional church in Huntly for the accommodation of the large parish ; and as the most lasting service to which the interdict could be put, they deposited it *in memoriam* beneath the foundation stone. After sermon in a barn in one of the interdicted parishes an old woman said to me, "Sir, when the Court's interdickin' sae mony things, I wish they wuld interdick the papers ;" referring to the weary reading of sermons, which they knew almost by heart, and had to endure in a continually returning circle. "Oh, no," I answered, "they could never meddle with the way that ministers preach." "I dinna ken," was her unanswerable reply, "they're middlin wi' a hantle o' things noo ; and I think they might just tak' a shave at the papers as weel."

This sketch is necessary to explain the trying circumstances in which the Duchess of Gordon was now unexpectedly placed. She was in England at the time. The desire of her heart was granted at last; the precious seed of the gospel was now to be scattered broadcast over Strathbogie ; and while she withheld her name, she sent a liberal contribution toward the travelling expenses of the ministers. But it was the still small voice, sounding like sweetest music only through the whirlwind and the earthquake ; and her heart was rent with distracting thoughts. Not belonging herself to the Church of Scotland, she had yet greatly rejoiced in its growing life and vigour ; and had cordially concurred in the measures taken for limiting patronage, which had hitherto worked admirably and gave the brightest promise for the future. But this unexpected collision with the civil powers tried her to the utmost, and she could not concur in the steps of resistance which her friends were now taking.

Knowing that I was among the ministers deputed to preach in Strathbogie, her Grace most kindly invited me to Huntly Lodge ; but when so many of the fathers and brethren were going north in the same cause of the gospel, I did not see my way to accept the invitation on the footing of personal friendship, when the Duchess was herself from home. She then invited Drs. Chalmers and Gordon, along with myself, asking us at the same time to invite any other ministers whom we chose, and placing a wing of the house at our disposal. Dr. Gordon with characteristic delicacy advised that this offer should be respectfully declined ; because it would commit a widowed Lady to a course of action to which both her own and her husband's relatives were strongly opposed, and perhaps all the more from their Conservative principles. His own political views, which were equally Conservative, only led him the more submissively to bow down to the authority of Christ, as the only King over his

own house.   The Duchess knew from the first that the
question had nothing whatever to do with the politics
of earth; but he thought, and we concurred, that in
the circumstances she was not called to commit herself in such a manner, and especially in her own
absence from Scotland.   She wrote however in reply,
entreating and insisting that her invitation might be
accepted; stating that having already made all the
arrangements for our reception, our refusal would be
extremely painful and embarrassing, and leaving us
no choice but to accept.

The following extracts are from letters to Miss
Home : "30th December 1839.—I shall send you
something to assist in paying the expenses of the
faithful ministers, who I hope will be sent among
them.   I must put aside all political feeling on the
subject, for I do believe, and have felt from the first,
that this may be the Lord's way of answering our
prayers.   Certainly the removal of the seven would
be a benefit.   Oxford tracts are gaining ground; Plymouth Brethren busy; in short, the destroyer is as
active as possible, and gives us daily more reason to
believe that he knoweth his time is short."

"—— Castle, 8th Jan. 1840.—I wish I had time
to fill the last frank that I shall probably be able to
get for you, but I have been doing the business for
which I came here, talking to Lady ——.   She is

inquiring, and seems thoroughly convinced of her own helplessness and sinfulness, but very ignorant. She is clever, and speaks well. It is singular how much I have been helped to speak both here and at H.; and yet if it were not from the consciousness that I could not have said one word in my own strength, I should think I had spoken very little to the purpose. He who has commanded us to cast bread, or seed, on the waters can cause it, like the rice, to take root and spring up, and bear fruit after many days.

" The help I have got in some of these conversations has been a very great comfort to me in the troubles which occupy my mind night and day, because it is an earnest of that help which I may hope for in time of need. I wish I could see the way as clearly as you do; as it is, I desire to remember that it is for *each day* alone that strength and guidance are promised. In the first place, I do not see as clearly as you do, that the General Assembly are right; indeed, if it were not for the men who take the side of the Commission, I cannot see that I should not think them wrong. But I cannot differ from such men, while they act in a spirit conformable with the Word of God, and cause the gospel to be faithfully preached in the wilderness. I am *quite sure* the majority of the Presbytery of Strathbogie is wrong, and therefore I have no hesitation in helping the Assembly there.

My prayer night and day is, that I may from moment
to moment be taught what is the 'will of God,' and
be made willing to do it with all my heart without
fear of man.   If I please neither party, *you* know
what a trial it will be to me who do so love to cling
to approbation ; but I know *He* is able to keep me in
the narrow way, though it be by briars and thorns,
and rods and scorpions."

The £100 referred to in the following letter as sent
to myself, as well as another contribution, she gave to
assist the Church in its struggle to maintain its position
in Strathbogie, and to defray the travelling expenses
of the ministers who were deputed to preach in the
district.   " *Rempstone, Feb.* 12.—I must write to-day
that you may get the letter before Saturday, and be
able to carry me in your heart without any incum-
brance of earthly weight, casting *all that* into the
fountain opened for sin and uncleanness.   Oh what
a depth that fountain must be, when we only see
the constant supply we need for each individual little
worm.

"I wrote to Mr. Moody the day I got your last
letter, and sent him £100.   However, I have not
time now to enter upon these subjects, and I want so
much to be carried up to the feast on Sunday that I
will not put off my letter.   If you do not know all I
want, Jesus does.   Especially I want to know his will

S

in all things, and to have courage to do it without any of that fear of man, or (which is the same thing) love of approbation, which bringeth a snare; without any high thought of self of any kind or sort; and yet with a firmness of purpose which should be able, with the strength and the armour of God, to stand against all the fiery darts of the wicked one, or against his wiles though clothed as an angel of light. Do you not want all this? All and more is asked for us by St. Paul, Eph. iii., and why should we ask for less?

"Certainly this matter and the whole circumstances of this winter have kept me nearer to the 'Counsellor' than I ever was before; and the dependence on Him makes me very happy, because I feel that if for my ultimate good he suffers me to err now, he will make 'all things work together for good,' and especially for his own glory. I feel *now* that I would count all but loss for Christ; and he will give me power and strength to do so indeed, if he sees it needful.—It was really most disgraceful of the suspended ministers refusing to see Drs. Gordon and Bruce at Aberdeen, but through an agent. May the Lord turn their hearts."

To her chaplain, the Rev. John Mackenzie, now the Rev. Dr. Mackenzie of Birmingham, she wrote :—

"*December* 26.—I feel that the case involves a question as interesting as any that has existed in the nation to which we belong.   It must not be answered lightly; may the Lord give light from above; may he direct, guide, and strengthen; he *has* promised wisdom to them that ask it.   I have desired Mr. W. to give directions that every accommodation should be given to Drs. Chalmers, Gordon, Mr. Moody, and any friend who may accompany him; and I trust we may soon see what the Lord is doing in this storm, and hear the still small voice of wisdom and love to our own souls.   I only wish I were there to receive them.   Oh may they come in the fulness of the blessing of the gospel of peace : and may they be able to order the matter for the glory of God, and the good of *His Church;* and also for our country, for the Church in our land.   I must at present, however, have it distinctly understood that I desire to receive these excellent servants of the Lord Jesus Christ as such, and as individuals whom I highly honour and esteem ; and not as taking a part politically in the question, which as a woman I do not feel called upon to do, till I have heard, or perhaps I should say, till I understand better, what it may involve.   Pray order for me such newspapers, or other papers on both sides of the question, as may enable me to see clearly. I hope to be permitted to lay the matter before the Lord without interruption to-morrow morning, for there are difficulties on every side.

" 27th.—This morning I rose early to endeavour to find what the Lord would have me to do. My only interruption till two o'clock was by letters from Huntly; one from Mr. Davidson, like himself, Christian and excellent, another from Mr. Walker. Oh, sir, we need *every moment* to ask counsel of the Lord; the strongest of his children cannot walk alone. Jesus says, My sheep hear my voice, and they *follow me;* not at a distance, as a dog might follow, but close, close; feeling, as sheep, need of the protection and guidance of their Shepherd, either hearing him, seeing him, or staying on him if they be in darkness. He will lead them into all truth, in practice as well as doctrine, though it be through much tribulation. I had no idea that the majority of the Presbytery of Strathbogie would refuse to submit to the censure of the Church to which they profess to belong. Repentance towards God *follows* a sense of his willingness to pardon, but repentance towards his Church must, I suppose, precede reconciliation. Oh, may whatever is most conducive to his glory and the good of his people be speedily manifested in our troubled land."

To the Rev. Mr. Davidson of Drumblade, now of Lady Glenorchy's, Edinburgh, she wrote : " *Jan.* 1, 1840.—I thank you very sincerely for your kind and Christian letter. The spirit in which it was written made me feel, that the view of the circumstances it detailed was not distorted by the heat of party, but placed as much as possible in the light of Divine truth. The subject is of the most intense interest to me, as well as to the whole Church of Scotland ; but there are several sides on which I have to view it, which render a clear judgment peculiarly difficult, and a clear decision on either side painful. In the first place, I believe that many of those who have acted in favour of the suspended ministers have done so from looking at the question politically, and not religiously, and have felt it their duty conscientiously to take part in favour of the Civil Courts. Among these may be counted any members of the Episcopal Church who have so acted ; and in this lies my first difficulty. Having always been an acknowledged member of that communion, am I justified in taking a decided part with that authority, which has only a right to command me as it is connected with the State, against which it is accused of acting? My second scruple lies, as a woman, in disagreeing with many whose opinions I have been taught to follow. My third difficulty obliges me to be cautious ; it rests on inability to find one to whom I could commit my authority.

"To turn, however, from all these worldly difficulties, I do feel that my heart goes entirely with yours in the earnest desire that the opportunity may not be lost of making known the truth of God in its fulness to my poor neighbours. I trust Dr. Gordon and the other ministers, who may be sent north, may be able to place the matter in a proper light. I have thought of all my dear Christian friends who used to meet together on the first of the month, and especially on the first of the year. We are bound earnestly to pray for the outpouring of the Holy Spirit, to teach us and lead us to receive all the truth, and walk by it. Oh may we walk in the Spirit, and so fulfil the law of Christ. May we be ready and willing to count *all* but loss for Christ; to set aside all fear of what man can do; and to seek in the strength of Him, who to those that hath no might increaseth power, to walk worthy of our high calling.

"I have been interrupted in writing so often, that I fear my letter is confused, and not expressive of my feelings and opinions; and I can only add that I never so highly honoured the Church of Scotland as I do at this moment; or felt so much encouraged to believe that the field of the first battle being in our wilderness is a token for good, perhaps in answer to our prayers. The Lord has promised to give his people teachers after his own heart, and he will do it. The Church of Scotland stands almost alone as a spiritual Church at this moment, with many evidences that the Lord means to work in it and by it for his glory. Surely there can be no higher privilege than to be a helper in such a cause, and I do hope that I shall have light and strength given to do the work which the Lord appoints me. If you see anything of my worthy friend Mr. Dewar, pray say everything kind from me to him."

PROGRESS OF THE GOSPEL IN STRATHBOGIE—LETTERS ON THE CHURCH.—1840.

The blessed fruit of these stirring events was the free running of the word of God in Strathbogie, such as that land had never known from the beginning, and such as is witnessed only at distant intervals in the history of the Church. The doctrines of the gospel were in a great measure new to the people, and salvation by grace was welcomed with deep inquiry and intense delight. Although the vindication of the headship of Christ over his own Church had been the immediate cause of the evangelistic deputations, it formed no part of their sermons, but only the gospel of the grace of God. But their living Head, practically confessed by them and honoured by their obedience, manifestly owned his servants in their message. Their own souls were refreshed while breaking the bread of life to hungering congregations, or as an old Highland elder expressed it at the close of one of the services: "I saw you were feeding yourself on what you were giving to us; for the Lord will not have the ox muzzled when he is treading out the corn."

The people were attracted, awakened, melted; and many who took no interest in the ecclesiastical testimony were riveted and converted by the word of salvation. "The rich folk," said a young woman from the country, "the rich folk talks about la', la'; we puir folk ken naething about the la', but we ken fine fa's the best preachers." Yet after all, the whole debate in law had practically risen out of the question, whether the "poor to whom the gospel is preached" could know good preaching from bad. The convictions were intelligent, deep, and abiding, and the fruits in many cases remain to this day. Some have entered into their rest, with their works following them; and some have been blessed to the souls of others in teaching, in the eldership, and in the ministry. One young woman, driven from home by her father because she would not cease to pray, was recalled after some months; and in due time saw her father and mother praying like herself, and living and dying in the Lord. Men's mouths were opened to speak, and their ears to hear in private as well as in public. Yet the sovereignty of the Spirit was remarkable in the midst of such a work, and his special breathing was felt on particular occasions. After the lapse of twenty-five years, various texts are quoted by the people as having been blessed to the conversion of individual souls ; and some as having come home to many, either still living or gathered to their rest. One of these was the passage commencing, "I knew a man in Christ fourteen years ago," the text on the evening of a Communion Sabbath, when Robert M'Cheyne was enabled to preach with remarkable power ; the impression on the congregation was general, and the number of inquirers large.

The Duchess remained in England through the winter, and wrote again to Mr. Davidson in May : "My thoughts are constantly turned towards my home and neighbourhood, with earnest prayers that even in this day all things may be made to work together for good. I do trust that the trials have led many hearts nearer to God. My own difficulties have been very great, but I have endeavoured to cast all my care upon Him who careth for me, and can make the weakest and most worthless of his creatures to glorify him. He has promised wisdom and strength to them who need it. I have had none but him to understand me in regard to the affairs of the Church : for those I value most in Scotland are displeased because I cannot agree with all their opinions, and seem to have given me up ; and in England I am looked upon as being one of the Scotch Church party. I must say, however, that in England I have been quite left to my own opinions; for no one pretends to understand the question, and few have patience to have it explained.

"I know, my dear sir, that you will still pray for me. In the meantime, I may learn to be less greedy of human approbation than I have been, as our Lord has said, 'How *can* ye believe, which receive honour from men?' I long to hear of the progress of the Church affairs in Strathbogie, and what is the opinion of Lord Aberdeen's bill. His speech surprised me, as I thought he understood the sentiments of the Church much better than he appears to do. Having been out of town till within a few days, I have not seen him, or indeed any Scotchman connected with Parliament. Oh that it may please the Disposer of all events to direct some measure for the restoration of peace and unity in the Church. The extreme ignorance in this part of the world, of the difficulties of the case as affects Scotland, is really surprising. Is not the blindness judicial? Alas! alas! for our ungrateful country."

Her Presbyterian chaplain having obtained another appointment, the Duchess was induced, chiefly by the difficulties of the Church of Scotland, to select an Episcopalian for the office. The first clergyman appointed did not officiate long; but his successor, the Rev. Mr. Hull, an amiable and excellent man and an evangelical preacher, remained for a number of years, till she discontinued the chaplaincy altogether. The Duchess had arranged to return to Scotland in July; but before her arrival, the resolution to have an Episcopalian chaplain drew forth a remonstrance from her zealous Presbyterian friend, Miss Home, who had been invited to meet her at Huntly Lodge on her return. In reply to that letter, the Duchess wrote from Edinburgh at great length:

"*Edinburgh, July* 1840.—MY DEAREST HELEN,— I am very anxious to answer your letter of the 2d before we meet, that we may feel that we have nothing to speak of but those things on which I believe we agree; those things which belong to our peace, the infinite goodness and love of God in Christ Jesus by the Spirit. But why need I say what we shall speak of, since the subject is infinite as its Author?

"Do you really think that I could have heard and seen all that has been brought before me publicly and privately, without considering with as much attention, devotion, and prayer, as I believe my nature is capable of, the subject on which you write? Yes, dear Helen, and I must answer you, which I will do according to your letter. In the first place, is my looking-glass quite sure that it has not been standing so much on one side, for a long time past, that objects are not reflected straight forward when they relate to certain points? for you begin by speaking of 'the Church of my fathers.' Is not that touching the very point of family pride, which both you and I know to be our snare? And yet I am sure that neither anything connected with that, nor the love of praise, nor any other of those things which too often possess my most deceitful heart, has ever cost me half the pain or the struggle that the thought of differing from you, in what you consider so important, has done. As to the pride of being confirmed by a bishop, the idea seems to me so completely novel, that if ever I said anything like it, it must have been with another meaning. Pride I have, alas! and I do indeed daily deplore it; and so foolish is it that I am quite capable of having felt what you say, or something worse; but as far as I know my own reasons, they are not what you suppose. I was brought up by Episcopalians; I believed my mother to have been one. I came to Scotland, disappointed at not being confirmed by the Bishop of London, Beilby Porteus, whom I had looked upon as an apostle. This disappointment may have been from pride, and certainly was not from any good motive, but it was not so much with reference to a bishop.

"Then you have heard what Fettercairn was when

I went home; so that I was too happy to fall back on the Episcopal Church, to which my father made no objection. I certainly knew not the difference in anything but form and order. But having been led by a way that I knew not to enter the Episcopal Church, it was in that Church that I was brought to the knowledge of the truth; that is, 'the chamber in which I was born;' and to that chamber I have been the honoured instrument, and the only one so honoured in the North, of bringing the presence of the Bridegroom in 'the word of his truth.' Though the souls are few, yet they are souls to be saved, and I could not lightly forsake the work given me to do.

" But now the circumstances of the Church have led me to inquire into the doctrines and discipline of the two Churches; and I am led solemnly and conscientiously to prefer that to which God in his providence has led me to belong, and against which I believe your prejudice would not be so strong if you had examined it as closely as I have. I believe that as with the difference of dispositions and countenances, the different manner necessary to be employed in the right education of children, so the Head of the Church, even our blessed Lord Jesus, employs different orders of discipline for different members of his body, whether as Churches or individuals. I believe that were I now to leave the Church of England, I should act contrary to the mind of the Spirit, the leadings of providence, and my own conscience.

"I am sure, after having said this, you will neither by word, deed, nor allusion, bring forward the subject; for if you insist on my being a consistent member of the Episcopalian Church in Scotland, I must forego the happiness and advantage of hearing the truth when I can from the ministers of another part of the body of Christ, whom I love in the Lord with all my heart and soul. I may be wrong; if I am, the Lord will show it in his time; for I do ask it sincerely and constantly. He has led me all my life long; he has guided me through difficulties and dangers; he has led me to a city of habitation; he has preserved my soul from death: will he not also keep my feet from falling, that I may walk before him in the land of the living? Oh, dearest Helen, if there must be difference of opinion (and there can be no unity of opinion in this world), let there be unity of spirit, love in the Lord Jesus, resting on him, striving in his strength to do his will; believing that if we do so strive, we shall know of the doctrine whether it be of God. May we meet in the Spirit, walk and talk together in the Spirit; may Christ be our bond of unity and union; and may we feel ourselves to be children of one Father, rejoicing in one Saviour, members of one Christ."

HUNTLY LODGE IN 1840—M'CHEYNE, MACDONALD, CHALMERS, BONAR.

Soon after her return, the communion was dispensed in the parish church by the parish minister, but his ministry she never countenanced in any way from the time of his suspension by the General Assembly. About the same time it was administered to the other congregation by the deputies from the General Assembly, the Rev. Messrs. Cumming of Dumbarney and M'Cheyne of Dundee. To miss their valued preaching was a trial to the Duchess, but she was firmly resolved not to partake of the Lord's Supper with them. The resolution was remarkably unlike herself. From her conversion to her death, she had always an ardent longing for the tokens of our Lord's dying love; and could not resist an opportunity of sitting down at his table in any true Church of Christ. Now, however, she would not commit herself by such a course, and went to the Episcopal Chapel. But when the services were concluded there, she came to listen to the Assembly's ministers. It was the afternoon of the day when so many were impressed under Mr. M'Cheyne's evening sermon; the Spirit of the Lord was present in the midst of the people; and her spiritual instinct quickly overcoming her ecclesiastical predilections, she sent to ask if she

might have a token, and sat down at the table of the
Lord. Next morning she received a note from her
own (Scottish Episcopalian) clergyman, strongly re-
monstrating against the schismatic step she had taken.
But she immediately wrote the decided reply, that she
had been communicating with the Church of Scotland,
and only doing again what she had occasionally done
before when occasion offered; that the Duke had been
an elder of that Church; and that, Episcopalian though
she was, she had gone to the table leaning on her husband's arm without incurring the slightest censure.

Among the ministers sent to Strathbogie, not the
least eminent was Dr. Macdonald of Urquhart. The
ministrations of that great evangelist were most
effective in Gaelic, and their chief sphere was in the
purely Highland districts of the north. His heart,
however, was as large as his lips were eloquent;
and having sympathies wide as the world, he boldly
preached a world-wide gospel everywhere, and with
great acceptance and success. Twenty years before
these events, his eye had rested on the stagnant
swamps of Strathbogie; and disregarding ecclesiastical etiquette, he had roused the jealousy of the
ministers by preaching in their parishes; and through
their complaint had been reproved for the irregularity
by the General Assembly. Into that very district
the Assembly, in its morally altered tone, now sent

him to preach, and although he was personally unknown to the Duchess, her heart was set on finding
profit from his lips.

"*Huntly Lodge,* 5*th Oct.* 1840.—Mr. Mackintosh
of Tain was detained last week, but intends being
here to-morrow, and he will find Mr. Macdonald of
Urquhart preaching in the evening. I earnestly pray
that he may have a message for *me*, and that the sword
as well as the unction of the Spirit will plant it in my
inmost heart to bring forth fruit abundantly. I charged
Mr. Davidson to tell him how very much I wished to
see him. I trust we may both be guided by that Spirit
which we desire more and more earnestly to seek.
May we hear the voice saying, ' This is the way, walk
ye in it ;' and may we remember, that as He in whose
footsteps we desire to tread, while he went about
doing good, was meek and lowly of heart, so the
peace and rest promised to the soul is with Him, the
meek and lowly of heart. I do pray about it, and
leave it in the hands of Him who will order aright.
—I found myself praying in an unqualified manner,
that nothing might prevent me going to hear Mr.
Macdonald, but recollected in time to add : If it be
for thy glory and my soul's good, and according to
thy will, O Lord, thou canst order all ; only quicken
me to feel and see all that thou wouldest have me to
do, and do as thou hast said."

T

The next visitor of note, eight days later, was Dr. Chalmers, of whom she thus writes : " I am sure you will like to hear of Dr. Chalmers's visit to Huntly. I think his report will be favourable ; mine is very comfortable. On Saturday Dr. C. came to dinner, and as there was no one but the Pelhams and Mr. Mackintosh, we had a great deal of conversation in the evening, and he conducted the worship. On Sunday morning, though rather unwell, I was prepared for a squeeze in the North Kirk, but when we came to the turnstyle the carriage stopped, and the party were assembled at the well. Dr. Chalmers came up, and advised me not to stay ; it thereupon appeared quite clear to me that I was to go to chapel in the morning, and Mr. Brodrick gave a most excellent sermon on the third Person in the Trinity : ' Have ye received the Holy Ghost since ye believed ? ' It was really sound, excellent, and practical; the divinity, the personality, the necessity, the efficacy, and the application of the Holy Spirit.

" I went to the North Kirk with Annie and Miss H., and heard the third part of Dr. Chalmers's sermon in the evening, on Isaiah xxvii. 4 ; Dr. Dewar prayed. Mr. Logan prayed in the afternoon, and Dr. Chalmers did all the service in the morning. He said he liked the open air very much ; it was the fourth time in his life he had preached out of doors. The freeness and

fulness of the gospel was his theme, and he put me in
mind of old Bridge, so you may believe I was pleased;
I like him a great deal better than last year. On
Monday he had business in Huntly, and Dr. Dewar
preached in Gaelic before the prayer-meeting.

"The Duke of Richmond and a large party came
here, but the three Doctors came up in the evening.
Dr. M'Kellar gave us a most excellent exposition on
2 Cor. v., but it was thought very long. The Doctors
slept here, and went away next day at 11. Dr. Chalmers called on Mr. Walker (parish minister), and was
well received, but the subject (of the Church) was
avoided; it seems the seven are determined to ordain
Mr. Edwards. Mr. Macdonald went away yesterday;
he preached in Mortlach on Sunday. The Duke is
still here, to remain till Saturday, and I believe to
return on Monday; the Pelhams are going to-morrow, when the Clunys, March, Lord Crofton, etc.,
come. Lord Bathurst and Colonel Macdonald are
here; Lady Rosslyn talks of coming next week; and
the Duchess of Bedford, the Abercorns, Storrat, Captain Hamilton, and old Lady Saltoun, all propose the
end of the month; I hope not all at the same time.

"I am so pleased with Durham on the Song; I think
I never saw the experience of the Christian so clearly
set out. As you are alone, I send you this account of
us, and I do indeed earnestly pray that the Comforter

may be with you in all his power, with love, grace, and peace."

In November, the Duchess writes of Mr. Andrew Bonar : " Last Monday we had a very comfortable day, after a most admirable sermon on Sunday night from Mr. Bonar. He came here at two o'clock to dinner, with Messrs. Thorburn and Davidson. They held a prayer-meeting, till we went to the kirk for the evening lecture ; and they all stayed till the middle of next day. On Wednesday, Mr. Bonar gave a lecture on the Jews. . . . I began Matthew on the 30th October." Mr. Bonar's notes, taken at the time, are full of interesting proofs of the remarkable work of the Lord in the whole district, both in the deep impression on the congregations which he visited, and in many cases which he records of individual conversion.

THE MENTAL CONFLICT.—1840-44.

In commencing these memoirs, it was no part of our design to enter thus at large into the present subject, but rather to state the well-known result, and leave it to speak for itself. We had then hoped for materials to bring out fully the mental process through which the Duchess passed at her first conversion ; and the want of these has induced us to present this subsequent conflict more in detail, in the hope that the

struggle of an earnest mind after truth may not be
without interest and profit, even to those to whom the
question will seem unattractive, or her conclusion
unfounded. "I can't understand how people should
love me," the amiable Duchess sometimes remarked,
while highly valuing the love which she wondered
at enjoying; and the prospect of having this love
estranged in the struggle now before her was severely
trying. In the contemplation of such an issue, she
wrote at this time: "I cannot pray to be hated, but I
can pray to be made willing to be so, if it be the will
of God." The thickening of the conflict is indicated in
her next letter by a brief reference to Lord Aberdeen,
who took so leading a part in the great ecclesiastical
struggle: "*Huntly Lodge, Dec.* 1840.—I was prevented writing to you by a visit from Lord Aberdeen.
We were *tête-à-tête* for almost an hour; and his asser-
tion, that legislation, education, feeling, and with
peculiar emphasis *sense*, was against the majority of
the General Assembly, made me feel that the wisdom
of this world was foolishness with God.

"The visit of Lady —— has not been satisfactory, yet I prayed constantly, and I did not feel
afraid; the Lord however can work, and none can
let. The Duchess of Richmond is to come on Monday. You like to know my own feelings: I can say
that I feel more than usual the need of the *constant*

assistance of the Holy Spirit, and I am sure that he
will help me and make me serve Christ and do his
will, as he has made me willing and desirous to count
all but loss for him. The Lord will show me when he
thinks it needful to re-employ me; in the meantime,
his Word shows me more about weakness and humility, and the character of Him who was lowly of
heart; and I feel that keeping close is my safety. If
he goes not before me I cannot go forward; and I
have never yet done anything conspicuous to the
public, but what I felt rather looking for him than
being with him. I go on with Durham, and I like
it much."

Within six weeks after the date of this letter, the
suspended ministers met at Marnoch to ordain Mr.
Edwards. Though the roads were nearly blocked up
with snow, the people gathered in earnest crowds to
the spot. Then four hundred and fifty communicants
of the parish gave in a solemn protest which they had
signed against the intrusion; took their Bibles from
their pews and withdrew in silence, many of them in
tears; and assembling amid the snow in the valley
beneath, they resolved with one consent to retire
straightway to their own homes, that they might
neither witness the desecration of their church and
of its most holy ordinances, nor be tempted to interrupt proceedings which they felt to be so scandalous.

The procedure on the part of the suspended ministers, if it created less surprise in the Duchess than it did in some of her friends, excited the same indignation and sorrow : " *Huntly Lodge, 29th Jan.* 1841.—I am grieved to the heart that my friends and neighbours are now in connexion with actual sacrilege, but must thank God that the poor Marnoch people have behaved so well."

After this time she said to a friend, "The question to my mind is this : Will a Government in this country admit of a really faithful ministry ? That to me is the grand question, and I feel most deeply anxious as to what may be the result." But the whole question at issue greatly perplexed her ; and from the protracted struggle in her mind, some idea may be gathered of the sharper and far more urgent conflict that was now passing within hundreds of quiet manses in Scotland. Personally she could stand aside for a time, as a member of another Church ; though the same cup must be drunk in the end by every endowed Church that will be faithful to her Head, until the kingdoms of this world shall become the kingdoms of the Lord. The ministers were naturally more conversant with the subject than her Grace ; and had she been in their place, and commanded to ordain an unsuitable pastor by a power that was not spiritual, she would unquestionably have been among the first to refuse. The question had thus already come home to their consciences in a practical form, and was now advancing with alarming rapidity to cast all their earthly interests into a heated furnace. The Established Church of Scotland had been their glory, as the great visible chain that bound heaven to earth in the land; and the endowed Church was the whole earthly stay of themselves and their families. The result was severe enough to many, but it was as nothing when compared to the anticipation; for even so popular a minister as M'Cheyne seriously contemplated for himself emigration to America as the necessary issue.

The predilections of the Duchess were deep-rooted against every change in the established order of the country; they were hereditary and constitutional, though scarcely more so than in many of the ministers and elders of the protesting Church. Most of her natural friends and associates were strongly opposed to the attitude the Church had been compelled to assume toward the Civil powers. But on the other hand, her religious friends in Scotland were all of one mind in holding that Cæsar had no authority over Christ's household in things purely spiritual. Among these the earliest and dearest of all, to whose words and prayers she felt indebted more than to any one else, was both decided for herself, and constantly urging the Duchess to decision. The remarkable diversity of their minds had helped to cement their friendship hitherto; but now it almost threatened to dissolve it. Miss Home, acute and clear, saw quickly with an instinctive perception nearly all that was ever to commend itself to her as important in a subject; and had too little patience with the reasoning mind of the Duchess, whose deliberation appeared to her to be indecision. But in this, as in every other case, nothing could move her one step beyond her own conviction: if her judgment was satisfied she would act, but no amount of pressure would advance her one hair's-breadth. The threatened loss of the dearest friend on earth moved her indeed to weigh the subject most carefully; but was never suffered to affect the judgment, or the conscience, or the mode of action. The excessive urgency of friendship did not hasten by one hour the decision of her own mind, but only retarded it by awakening a feeling of wrong, and therefore of resistance.

In the autumn the Duchess went to the south of France for Miss Sinclair's health, and did not return again to Scotland for two years. The indecision of her mind as to the course she might ultimately have to take made her not unwilling to be absent from the scene of conflict, and perhaps too willing practically to forget it in the midst of other thoughts and occu-

pations.   The tendency, also, of all that surrounded
her on the Continent was to lower the significance
of any question that did not immediately affect the
salvation of the individual soul, however essential its
issues might be in the great work of human redemption.   Yet the following remarks show how far she
was from being indifferent, and how decided her views
were on the great ecclesiastical merits of the controversy : "I hear nothing of the Scotch question that
leads to disputing, and have found that Dr. Gordon's
memorial, and the extract from the *Wesleyan Maga-
zine,* of which I brought a number of copies, have led
all who think on the subject at all to a right view of
the question ; at least thus far, to the conviction that
Dr. Gordon's party is acting according to the principles and standards of the Church to which it belongs,
and that those who differ from them, and remain
Presbyterians of the Church of Scotland, must either
be ignorant or worse."

Dr. Gordon, with whose views she thus expressed
her concurrence, had solemnly declared : "For a
long time the controversy was involved in all the
tortuosities of legal questions.   But now it has come
to this, that if we define the principles of the Church
as they have been recently laid down in certain
documents and speeches, we must intrude ministers
on all the parishes of Scotland, for if it can be in one

it can be in all ; that we are bound and astricted to intrude ministers without even the shadow of a call from the Christian congregations over whom they are to be placed, and with whom the pastoral connexion is to be formed. And more than that, it has come to this plainly and distinctly, that I, a minister of the Church of Scotland, who have solemnly sworn before God, and as I shall answer to him at the great day of judgment, that I believe in my heart and conscience that Christ is the great Head of the Church, and that he has appointed office-bearers in it distinct and apart from the civil magistrate, to whom he has committed the keys of his spiritual kingdom, who are to loose and to bind, to lay on and to take off spiritual and ecclesiastical censures: it has come, I say, to this, that I am called upon either to renounce these prin- ciples, or to renounce the privileges which I hold as an ordained minister of the Church of Scotland."

The Duchess passed another winter in France, and in May of the following year, 1843, the great Disrup- tion took place in the Church of Scotland, by which four hundred and seventy-four of her ministers sacri- ficed their earthly livings for the sake of Christ, and cast themselves and their families on the free bounty of that God in whom they trusted, and for whose sake they suffered. The event, which filled the com- munity with admiration and the unbelieving world with astonishment, carried sorrow and perplexity of heart to the subject of this memoir. Though herself an Episcopalian in Presbyterian Scotland, she held so strongly the union of Church and State that she could not regard any cause as sufficient to justify their severance. On the other hand, the men whose characters the Duchess admired, whose sympathy she cherished, and with whose doctrines she agreed, had all cast off the yoke for the sake of Christ their Head. They were the men with whom she desired that her soul might be gathered; her love toward them was not cooled, her esteem for them was enhanced. But though she could not approve of their course, nor cast in her lot with their community, a single hasty sentence, written from Geneva on the 27th of May, will show with how deep emotions she read and examined the accounts of the proceedings: "I cannot begin on the subject of the Scotch Church, but I do feel very much, and would give all but my conscience, if I could go along with you in everything. I do love and honour those dear men; and Charles Mackintosh, how I wish I could talk with him! I don't see Alexander Stewart's name"—of Cromarty, than whom however there was none more resolute in quitting the Establishment, rather than consent to cast his Lord's crown into the dust.

The Duchess arrived in England on the 15th of

June, and wrote to Miss Home on the 22d : "I am sorry to have been so long in Britain without calling on you to join in thanksgiving with me, and prayer that the blessing of the Lord may rest on my return to my own country, and lead me in the right way to do all the will of my Father to the glory of my Lord Jesus. I know you pray for me ; and I do pray most earnestly (if anything I do can be so spoken of) that I may be willing to count all but loss for Christ, and to cut off the right hand, or to pluck out the right eye, if they be a hindrance to the following the Lord fully in the way he has appointed for me."

A month later Miss Home wrote an earnest letter, urging her to take a decided stand in favour of the Free Church on her return to Scotland, and to show her attachment to its principles by joining in the communion, which was about to be held in several of the Edinburgh Free Churches. She sent this decided reply : "19*th July* 1843.—There are few things in this world that pain me so much as to differ from you, whom I have looked upon for so long a time as my oracle. I know your affection for me, and that all you do and say is with a view to my eternal good ; and I am sure you will pray that I may be led to act, not as *you* would have me, but as *God* would have me. If in looking with prayerful earnestness for the guidance of the Holy Spirit, I yet cannot see that your way is my way, and that I think I see most clearly and plainly that I am at this moment in the way of duty in that situation in which the Lord has placed me, and in doing the work which he has given me to do, you will at least allow that I ought not to walk where I see not that guidance for me. All my prejudices and prepossessions have been in favour of those with whom your lot is cast, and I do fervently trust that when the things of this world have passed away, and we know even as we are known, we shall be found together with the Lamb, our King, our Head, our present Hope, our eternal Redemption. But now I see not my way with you. The Lord knows that there is no worldly advantage to me, or pleasure, so far as I can perceive, in the line I must follow. The heart is deceitful above all things, and I may be deceived in this; but your letter received this morning requires a decided answer, and with pain to grieve you I give it, seeing that it is not the will of Him that doeth all things well that we should meet at present. Adieu. May the Lord by his Spirit teach us both not only to say but to act, ' Thy will be done on earth, as it is in heaven.' "

The next week she came down by sea to Scotland, where she wrote again: "*Edinburgh, 30th July* 1843.—I do so much miss your dear, kind welcome in Edinburgh, and dear Anna's (Lady Home), that I cannot go through another day without telling you so, and how truly unhappy it makes me to grieve you, for well do I know that all your anxiety is for my true welfare. May the God of all grace and consolation be with you both : may his Spirit lead us all into *all* truth through him who is the truth, the life, and the way. Yes, dearest, I fully believe we are both in Him who is the only way. I doubt not that the time will come that you will acknowledge I am not so wrong as you now think me ; you will, I am sure, acknowledge that except we walk 'in the light of the Lord' we cannot walk aright. I do most sincerely desire to walk in that light and no other, and to listen earnestly for the voice behind, saying, 'This is the way, walk ye in it.' In the meantime, I still think you are taking a partial and limited view of the glorious truth which occupies you so warmly ; and that that part of the body of our Head, Christ Jesus, to which in his providence I belong, no less acknowledges the obligation of looking on him as 'Head over all things to the Church,' than you do. At all events, as my own way is clear to me, I have no business to meddle with other people, who I believe are walking in all sincerity in the light given to them, and in the truth of God. Oh that there were more love, more tenderness of love, with us all. Indeed, indeed, dearest Helen, I feel that I love you too well, and not a whit less than I used to do. If it were not so, I should not be thinking of you night and day, and weeping when I think you are vexed about me. Never did I feel so ready to do anything and everything for you to prove my affection, except giving up my own convictions. I cannot see with your eyes, but I think *you quite* right in acting up to your light, and in walking in the path you have chosen.

"We came in the steamer with Mr. Moody, and had much conversation with him ; we heard him preach yesterday.—Cumming (her Grace's maid) came in just as I was beginning about Mr. M. ; and now I must dress, as I have a great deal to do to-day, which I shall do with a lighter heart when I have assured you of my constant and tender affection, and of my love to Anna and the boys." Want of time prevented her explaining the conversation to which she refers ; and both here, and in some future parts of this particular narrative, I am compelled reluctantly to introduce my own name, or else to leave the sketch imperfect.

Our meeting on the passage to Leith was altogether unexpected, and my information on the recent history of the Church was not so full as her own. While staying at Huntly Lodge about two years before, and preaching in many parishes around, the labour and exposure had brought on a severe affection of the throat, for which I was ordered to Madeira, whence I was only now returning after sailing round by the Brazils. Our paths had once accidentally crossed on the Rock of Gibraltar, but with that brief exception we had not met for two years; and now on our returning to Scotland everything was strangely altered. Between four and five hundred ministers had for Christ's sake given up their stipends and left their manses, that they might freely preach the everlasting gospel to their countrymen; and the Church of Scotland, as determined by large majorities in her General Assembly, was no longer the Church established in the land, while still holding fast all her ancient principles.

This severance of the Church from the State was more than the Duchess could receive. But being deeply vexed with the letters of her friends, urging her to sanction the step by immediately sitting down at our communion, she gladly embraced the unexpected opportunity for conversation on the subject, and freely opened all her mind. Distance, time, quiet, sickness, had altered or modified many of my own thoughts, since I had seen her Grace at Huntly Lodge In the silent retrospect of life, with the prospect of a possibly near eternity, much that had seemed first was now last, and the last was first; but the truth and magnitude of our Church's testimony to the Headship of Christ over his own house, even unto separation from the State, had only stood forth in greater clearness. After every deduction for the elements of earth that had mingled in the conflict, the great principles looked still greater than before, and the broad lines of procedure more brightly shone upon by the word, by grace, and by providence. There was leisure on the quiet deep to talk over all these things; but the Duchess could not see the clearness of our path, and much less of her own in the way of taking part with the Free Church. I had therefore no hesitation in confirming her own opinion as to her line of conduct, and advising her by no means to communicate with us in her present state of mind, for as a member of the Church of England she was fully entitled to stand aloof. Our conversation ended with giving her this text, by which she was greatly comforted : " He that believeth shall not make haste."

How unaltered her mind continued for some time after her return to Scotland, and how little disposed she was to depart from the neutral position she had taken, will appear from the following letter : " *Huntly Lodge*, *Nov.* 1843.—The point on which I should like to write to you is in a former letter, on the subject of openly assisting and countenancing the Free Kirk. Now, I do pray earnestly for light, and every day I see more clearly that this is not the Lord's will concerning me. I am certain you and many see that your way is plain, and you are right in following it. I am certain that such men as Dr. Gordon and Mr. Mackintosh cannot but act as the Lord would have them, looking as they do for the guidance of his Spirit in all things. But even these men are not infallible; and I see so much more of the evil consequences of the movement than of the necessity for it, and so clearly that it is not my present duty to take any part in it, that nothing is left me but to grieve that I must differ in this thing from them and you. I trust we may yet find that even with this difference we are one body in Christ, and have him alone for our Lord and Head; those who think with me, as well as those who agree with you in all things. This being the case, I can only help individuals, because I believe that their preaching will be blessed. Oh, may He give us, by his Holy Spirit, his promised Spirit, life to quicken, love to warm, light to see, and strength to do all things according to the very mind of Christ."

THE ACCEPTED CROSS.—1844-1846.

In the summer of 1844 her Grace's pressing invitation to Huntly Lodge was met on my part with an unhesitating, yet most reluctant acquiescence. Though frequently corresponding, I did not care to introduce the question of the Church, on which nothing

could be written which she had not heard a hundred
times already. But now the subject could not be
evaded; if she spoke of it, I must express my mind; if
she keep silence, I must speak. Last year it was easy
with a clear conscience, or rather conscience then
commanded, to advise her to sit still; but the twelve
months that had. now elapsed allowed more than
ample leisure for "not making haste." Personally,
indeed, she was a member of the English Church;
but as such she had countenanced and communicated
with the Church of Scotland; and now she did not
countenance or communicate with the Free Church of
Scotland, however much she honoured and loved its
individual ministers. Neither had she taken, with
some good men, the ill-advised position of neutrality
toward all Churches, nor was she ever likely to take
it. But in a word, she disowned the Disruption; she
disapproved of our having severed ourselves from the
State; and not altogether as a mere onlooker, but as
one who had been in communion with us before, and
with my own Church in particular, although not expressly as a member.

Her position was not one that she could always
maintain; but it must unavoidably result either in
greater estrangement or closer fellowship. From her
wide influence by character as well as by rank, the
importance of the course which the Duchess might

ultimately adopt could hardly be exaggerated, as regarded the cause of the gospel in her own district of country. For her now to halt longer between two opinions was to trifle with a great subject; and for her to take any more decided step without a clearer conviction was to thrust herself into a snare. For an adviser to set arguments before her was to repeat a tale already told a hundred times, while to be silent was to compromise his own conscience. What course was to be adopted in the circumstances? After sifting this inquiry to the uttermost I was baffled, and completely failed in finding any solution, or discovering one ray of light on the path of wisdom. At last I gave it up in utter helplessness to the Lord, who asked, "Am I a God at hand, and not a God afar off?" God was in the north as well as in the south; in Huntly as much as in Edinburgh. There was therefore no need to obtain counsel here and carry it to the spot, because the Counsellor himself was there; and had He not commanded, "Take ye no thought how or what ye shall speak, for I will be a mouth and wisdom unto you: the morrow shall take thought for the things of itself"? It was enough; there was no gleam of light on the future path; but fear and care had fled, and were followed by trust, joy, and hope.

Huntly Lodge I found on my arrival full of visi-

tors, from England as well as Scotland. At prayers
in the evening the Duchess expected, as usual, some
exposition of Scripture ; and on leaving the drawing-room said to me, " We are reading in Luke,
and are at the 23d chapter, but read anywhere you
like." The selection of a passage for the family
that night had cost no forethought, because after
three years' absence many suitable portions, which
would be fresh to them, had become familiar to myself ; and her Grace's remark made no impression, till
she repeated it without qualification on entering the
library door, " We are at the 23d of Luke." This
was obviously said without any thought of what the
passage might contain ; but was so altogether unusual
with her as to induce me to turn up the chapter,
under the impression that it might be well to offer
from it some remarks on the central, and always
practical subject of our Lord's death. But the first
topic in the chapter I found to be the Jews' accusation of Jesus, as denying the authority of Cæsar,
" saying that he himself was Christ a King ;" and
explained elsewhere by his kingdom not being of
this world. It was impossible to open such a passage
in such a place. The household, with the visitors
and their servants, formed a company of more than
fifty worshippers. Our hostess disagreed with the
views of our Church on the subject ; to introduce it

to her guests was at once to abuse her hospitality, and to speak to many of them as in a foreign tongue; while for the whole assembly, it was to lose a precious opportunity of speaking to the salvation of immortal souls. The subject was suitable only for the Duchess herself, and the only suitable time for it was in private, for which there would be ample opportunity in days or weeks to come. Her Grace was ever sensitively alive to the fitness of things, and greatly disliked any breach of propriety. The imputation of rashness in speech and action was a chief accusation against the ministers of our Church; she made no secret of her concurrence in that charge; and to introduce this controverted topic on the very first evening at family worship would have been the last extreme of indiscretion.

The 23d of Luke, therefore, did not occupy a moment's thought, but was set aside at once as out of the question; and some other passage was sought for, with no apprehended difficulty except in the way of selection. But during the preliminary notes of the organ first, and then in the singing of the psalm, the search was fruitless; the leaves of the book without, and the recollections of the heart within were turned over and over, but all in vain. It was one of those crises in life in which the thoughts of hours and days are compressed as if into moments. Was this to be the end of all the anxious consideration, and prayer for wisdom from above? had I thought so much and come so far, only to dash to the ground by one blow all hope of this great subject being favourably entertained in that house?—for to open it then seemed the sure way of closing it for ever, a step fatal at once to every prospect of success. Was the Lord at length provoked with the long halting between two opinions, and was Christ in his Headship now to be set before this family only as a stone of stumbling and rock of offence? "O Lord, the way of man is not in himself: O Lord, thou art stronger than I, and hast prevailed; for the foolishness of God is wiser than men, and the weakness of God is stronger than men."

The first verses of the 23d of Luke were read and explained: Christ's kingdom is in the world, yet not of the world; the Church is subject and responsible to him alone in the appointment and removal of pastors, and in the entire rule and discipline of his house; and she is unfaithful to her Head if she resigns that trust to any other, or executes it at the command of the highest power on earth. Nor was the question a light one, since on it had hinged the death of our blessed Lord himself. This truth was not the end for which He died, but it was the turning-point of his death; it was the good confession that he had witnessed before

Pilate ; and it was because he would not retract his declaration that he was a King, that he was led to crucifixion. If this truth was great enough for our Master to suffer death for declaring it, it could not be too little for us to accept as a ground of suffering, of imprisonment, or of death itself.

The message was delivered and left. The ministers of our Church were now out of that conflict. We had fought for that citadel of the truth, and had kept it at great sacrifice ; and we were now bent on bringing the living water to the flocks within its walls, and to all who were willing to drink and live. The Assembly of 1844 had been a deeply impressive one, with much quickening and searching of heart, especially in the ministry. Its hallowing influence was now spreading throughout the country ; ministers were conferring with each other, and praying together with deep emotion, and going forth to their flocks with renewed earnestness and faithfulness. Such a process was going on at Huntly, as elsewhere ; and the Church question was little thought of, and never suffered for a moment to withdraw us from our great work. After that first exception the one subject at Huntly Lodge, as elsewhere, was repentance towards God, and faith towards our Lord Jesus Christ.

Three days passed, and on the fourth the Duchess sent for me to her sitting-room, and said with great emotion : "I can't get a word with you alone, and how have you never come to see me? Since the night you came, I have not been able to get this Headship of Christ out of my mind, and I *must* get to the bottom of it ; you must tell me all about it." This was only too welcome a task, and it engrossed several long conversations. The subject had been for years before her mind ; but now the special presence of the Spirit so cleared the moral and spiritual atmosphere as to render her willing to face all the consequences of a thorough conviction. This willingness to take up the cross went far to remove the intellectual haze ; and she soon saw both the claim of Christ as Head over his Church, and the obedience of the Free Church in loyally submitting herself to her Lord and King. Another question remained for herself, with which I had nothing to do, and into which I did not care to enter,—her relation to the Church of England. Our conflict had not been on that field, and that Church must stand or fall to her own Master.

After a few more days had passed, her Grace sent for me again, and said very earnestly : "The last of my own visitors leaves to-day, and this whole house is at your disposal ; I wish you to invite any you know in the neighbourhood, who may either do good or get good by being here." She knew herself by name the

few gentlemen who had been zealous for the further-
ance of the gospel in the neighbouring parishes, and
immediately wrote to several of them, inviting them
to the Lodge with their families. This step proceeded
entirely from herself, and was far beyond what I could
have asked or suggested at the moment; for these
gentlemen had been called to take a prominent part in
the Non-Intrusion controversy in their own parishes,
and such an invitation would be held throughout the
district as unfurling the banner of the Free Church
over Huntly Lodge. But though she had not yet
satisfied herself on the whole question in all its bear-
ings, her understanding was now convinced of the
scriptural truth of our great principles, her heart was
opened to embrace them, and she rejoiced thus to
make an open confession of Christ as Head over his
own Church.

After leaving Huntly Lodge, I am not aware that
I ever introduced the subject of our Church again;
but of her own accord the Duchess proceeded to
examine further for herself, and to correspond with
other friends about it: "*Huntly Lodge, 7th March*
1845.—I cannot say I liked the paper you sent me,
and I think I could answer most of the objections.
The great fault of the Church of England is summed
up in three words, 'want of discipline.' The Liturgy
was written for real Christians, and I do confess that

others ought not to use the services. *You* will say that real Christians *ought* to object to any form of prayer; I have not come to that conclusion. Your last letter was quite a disappointment to me; not because I wanted mere praise for the step I have taken, for as yet I have not been troubled by man's opinion of the matter. My own soul occupies me more than any outward circumstances. I think through grace I am getting nearer to the light, with a more single eye to my dear Lord; I fully expect ere long to have a glimpse of the King in his beauty."

If the freedom from "trouble by man's opinions" included outward as well as inward quiet, she could not have written this some months later, when she wrote to another friend: "*June* 1845.—I believe you judge very truly, that the honour from man I have so long enjoyed and cherished will be much withdrawn. I would bless the Lord for everything that can send me to him alone for strength." But she had been counting the cost, and she met it now without fear or shrinking. The penalty of confessing Christ was no longer to be summoned before the judges and to be fined, like her ancestor Lady Mary Brodie; but it was to stand on a pinnacle alone, bearing his reproach. To give a single instance: she had a visit from Lord Aberdeen who, after the controversy had terminated in the Disruption, was most liberal in his own district in granting sites and otherwise, but was naturally vexed at the new position taken by the Duchess. He reasoned with her earnestly on the line of conduct she had adopted; and when his arguments failed, he remonstrated with a warmth unlike the usual amiableness of his disposition and the extreme courtesy of his manners. But the able statesman mistook his gentle hostess, when he hoped to turn her from her course by strong representations, unsupported by convincing arguments. The Duchess felt the interview more keenly than almost any incident that we have ever seen cross her path. But like the taunt of Methodism in earlier years, it only tended to root her more deeply in her own convictions, and to make her advance more boldly in the way that she had chosen.

While staying at Windsor with Her Majesty, whom she was frequently called to visit both there and at Balmoral, the Duchess had an interview of a different character with her old friend the King of the Belgians. He had looked quietly on the conflict as a remote spectator; and his own feelings being engaged on neither side, he spoke of it with pleasantry and great good-nature. "So, my dear Duchess," said he, "I hear you have joined the Church militant?" "No, Sire," she replied, "but I have a great regard for it;" for while she now fully recognised the rightness and

Christian necessity of our position toward the State, she was still herself a member of the Church of England.

The following letter was written to one of her oldest friends, a member of the Scotch Episcopal Church : " *Sept.* 1845.—You cannot doubt that I feel most deeply your present difficulties ; the more so as anxiety about your sister, and all you have to do, must rather unhinge the mind from that connected view of the subject of the Scotch Episcopal Church, which would make it perfectly clear. When we are troubled and anxious, the externals of religion lose their importance so much, that we find it a trial of patience to argue about them ; but on the other hand, we are more than ever surprised that those we love and esteem should put the means for the end. I do think it is most dangerous and deceptive, and dishonouring to the character of the holy God, to limit him to any means which are not expressly stated in his Word ; and *there* I am sure there is no authority for, but on the contrary many warnings against putting the Church and the ordinances in the place of the work of the Divine Redeemer, the grace of the Holy Spirit, and the faith which worketh by love unto repentance. We are weak just because we do not live as near to God as he has invited and commanded us to do ; in all humility obeying every ordinance of

man for the Lord's sake, but calling no man master
(for our Lord has said so) in those things in which he
has promised his Spirit to teach, and given his word
to reveal."

The Duchess of Gordon had now great difficulties
on some parts of the service of the Church of England, and she no longer relished its form of prayers;
but it was on neither of these grounds that her mind
was specially exercised, or that she came to her final
conclusion. The vital Church question with her was
the Headship of Christ over his own house; and the
three words "want of discipline" formed the chief
substance of her difficulty, and the main subject of
her inquiry, reading, and prayer. To another friend,
the daughter of an English clergyman, she wrote :
" *Edinburgh, Nov.* 1845.—Many thanks for your book.
I have sought out those passages that might show me
something relating to the Royal Supremacy, but I can
find nothing to modify it, as I expected, since the
settlement of the Protestant succession."

Holding to the end of her life the desirableness of
union between Church and State, and the duty of such
union where it can be effected without sacrifice of
principle, she came to the distinct conclusion that by
its terms of union the Church of England had sur-
rendered its power of discipline; on that ground she
left it, and during this winter in Edinburgh she

became a member of the Free Church of Scotland.
Having done so, she identified herself with all its
religious and missionary interests at home and abroad ;
and, as one instance of her liberal support of its insti-
tutions, she subscribed £1000 to the New College.
Doubtless her love for the people of Scotland made
her the more willing to become a Presbyterian, and
helped to open her eyes to the great mistake of the
aristocracy in severing themselves from the Presby-
terianism of the country.   But the severity of the
trial through which she had come may be gathered
from a remark she afterwards made at her own table :
" Had it been said to me at one time that I should
become a Presbyterian and a Dissenter, I should have
replied, ' Is thy servant a dog, to do this thing ?' "

The trials that encompassed her through taking this
step are referred to in a letter, written in the summer
of 1846, to a valued friend who had passed through
the same ecclesiastical experience as herself :—" Pray,
think of me before the Lord.   My God has indeed
been gracious in giving me to taste of the joy of his
salvation, to prepare me for peculiar trials and difficulties which have come upon me like the waves of
the sea, one after another.   I think that it is like the
outer storm now raging around me, to lift my heart to
Him who guides the storm, and who out of confusion
brings perfect beauty.   I am sure there will be a way

of escape that I may be able to bear it. Pray for me, that I may be willing to count all things but loss for the glory of God in Christ Jesus, and that, while witnessing to the great things he has done for my soul, I may also be a witness for the glory of Christ our King, and the power of the Holy Spirit to guide and teach as man's word can never teach."

The following letter of the same summer to another friend is of a practical character; but we copy it the more willingly on that account, because the final step she had now taken was reached through a process all along of more thorough severing from the world, and more perfect readiness to take up the cross and follow Christ. In the reference to Christ's confession before Pontius Pilate she was recalling in her own mind that night, when the truth of Christ's Headship had laid fast hold on her conscience, and along with it the necessity and privilege of giving up all for his sake.

"*Huntly Lodge, 1st July* 1846.—We have been apt to think (at least I have), brought up among Christians and in a Christian country, with the Word of God in our hands and the Spirit of God as near, that the offence of the cross had ceased. But the Word of God is the same as when it was written, as unchangeable as the living God whose will it reveals. I believe there is nothing that Satan loves so well, and which adds so greatly to the number of those who shall partake of his punishment, as an easy religion; resting on forms, doing as much as is convenient, or rather as little as conscience will allow for God and his glory, bearing no testimony, taking up no cross. It is true the testimony may not be in words, but by a walk and conduct becoming the gospel, as Christ walked, leaving us an example ; who pleased not himself, but before Pontius Pilate witnessed a good confession, even that he was a King, and must be honoured and obeyed as the only King and Head of his people in all things concerning his kingdom. 'Thus it is written,' was his own rule, and 'thus it is written' must be our rule, and *no other*. Oh, let us above all things beware of taking for doctrine the commandments of men. . . . The great secret of safety is the sense of our utter weakness, which obliges us to look continually to Him who is able to help and who giveth more grace. There can be no compromise with the world; that is a most fruitless and vain struggle, for God will not have a divided heart ; but how rich is the reward he has in store for those who diligently seek him according to his own command, and in his own strength. May the Lord be about your path and all your ways continually, to keep you from every evil.

The Duchess held firmly to the last her own principles, the fruit of long inquiry and deep conviction ; but she retained also to the end of her life the same catholic spirit that characterized her Christian course throughout. Some cherish a catholic spirit with unfixed ecclesiastical principles ; while others so hold their principles as greatly to lessen their Christian love. To keep fast hold of truth and love requires much grace, and may be regarded as a rare attainment in the Church ; and we have never seen the union equally exemplified in any other, as in the Duchess of Gordon. Though she had left the Church of England, she loved and honoured it to the end, while abiding in the fellowship of her own Church both in Scotland and in England.

Her thoughts in this respect are expressed in the following letter on the subject of her Episcopalian chaplain at Huntly ; for though that office was given to a Presbyterian for a year or two after her widowhood, it had been filled by an Episcopalian ever since : "1st Feb. 1847.—As you ask me solemnly about your friends, I may just state that the whole matter is in the Lord's hands ; they have not the smallest intention of moving, and I see no reason for it. When an Episcopalian, I had formerly a Presbyterian chaplain, and the case is only reversed. Wherever the truth is preached I honour it ; and although I believe godly discipline to be essential to the maintenance of divine truth, and an ordinance of God, yet

I cannot say that doctrine and practice according to godliness may not be preached effectually with the Lord's blessing for the salvation of souls, where the discipline is maintained more by principle than by church government. But, oh, I believe that whoever can hear the preaching of that 'doctrine which is according to godliness,' and does not make use of the privilege, will assuredly suffer by the leanness, if not the loss of the soul. I have not time for entering into my reasons for separating from the Church of England, but they were purely conscientious ; and I believe I could never be a blessing to the little body of English Episcopalians, if acting against my conscience. They want God's blessing, not man's help : the latter without the former is a curse. 'Put not your trust in any child of man.' But I am not against those dear friends, and can feel myself more at liberty to help them now than before, because I am now acting openly in all things. May the Lord Jesus enable you to look to him, and to feel and say with Luther, 'Lord, I am thy sin ; thou art my righteousness.'"

THE QUIET REST.—1847.

The mind of the Duchess of Gordon had at last entered into rest on a subject that had occupied her for so many years, ever since the suspension of the seven ministers in Strathbogie in 1839. She was now to return to Huntly with a heart at peace with itself, and rejoicing in the Lord with a renewal of early love ; and she wrote to her friend Miss Home, who had carried on so constant a correspondence with her on the subject during those eight years : " *May* 1847.—I have been thinking of your going to Huntly, and that it is best to be quite honest with you about it. When I was thanking the Lord for again making us of one mind, I thought how pleasant it would be to be together there ; but I have since considered that my feelings and yours are not the only ones to be consulted. I think it would be better at first on my return home to endeavour in the strength of the Lord to go without outward help, straight forward as he shall lead ; when I have been a month or two at home, perhaps I may be indulged with the comfort of having you. I think the Lord is showing me more of his love, and how I may lay hold on his strength ; but I do find it difficult to lay hold of his wisdom, for I have not even wisdom enough to know whether I do it or no. I think he is leading me ; he has been very, very gracious, and surely the lower we are in the pit of self-abasement, the more clearly do we see the glory of the Sun of Righteousness. Truly our God is faithful and gracious and glorious ; truly our God is Jehovah ; truly our God is Jesus.

What a God! glorious in holiness; may we know him more, and serve him better."

The Free Church with which she worshipped was about to commemorate the Lord's death on the Sabbath, and although she had already joined that communion in Edinburgh she was now to communicate with them for the first time in Huntly; and in so doing was to partake of the Supper for the first time along with the people, as a member of their own Church. Many godly strangers had gathered in the end of the week for the solemn feast, some from a distance of twenty, others of fifty miles; and the place of meeting was found to be too small for the expected worshippers. Ere the sun had set on the Saturday evening, she heard of their difficulty; and conceiving that the old Castle might supply the want, she immediately ordered the grass to be cut within the open bounds of the ruins, and the broad green area of what had once been the Castle court to be placed at the service of the congregation. The space would have held several thousands with comfort. The site of the old stronghold on a rising ground was dry and airy; the walls of the Castle, like " the shadow of a great rock," afforded shelter on the south from the rays of the midsummer sun; and a circuit of lofty trees formed a screen from the wind on every side. The Duchess ordered two or three military tents of the

Duke's to be sought out for the ministers and for the communion elements, as well as for herself and those for whom the open air was too trying; and a naval Captain, with other visitors at the Lodge, assisted in setting them up. The ancient fortress was turned into a temple; and the soldiers' tents, planted on the turf for peace and not for war, with their white canvas and scarlet mountings, added a picturesque ornament to the scene.

There, next morning, a large congregation assembled under the blue vault of heaven, and a noble church it was; for

> "Then did we worship in that fane
> By God to mankind given;
> Whose lamp is the meridian sun,
> And all the stars of heaven;
>
> "Whose roof is the cerulean sky;
> Whose floor the earth so fair;
> Whose walls are vast immensity:
> All nature worships there."

The long communion table covered with white, and surrounded with benches for the communicants, occupied the centre; and round it during the action-sermon the crowd were closely seated on the grass, becoming less dense in the outer circles. Some young men stood outside, but drew gradually nearer as the service proceeded, and their hearts softened. One country young woman with rosy cheeks and gay attire had taken an elevated seat on a heap of the

old ruins, evidently meaning to be merely a spectator
of the scene. But by and by her wandering gaze
became fixed, her lofty neck bent slowly down, and
ere the services of the day were closed she had hid her
head in her bosom to conceal the fast flowing tears.

One of the Passover psalms was sung ; and as the
grave sweet melody from a thousand lips echoed
within the Castle walls, we could not but contrast
our circumstances and our employment with the
scenes of other days ; with the wild revelry of the
" gay Gordons " in the olden time ; and with the dark
superstition that reigned under the Popish Earls of
Huntly. But most of all our thoughts reverted to
the donjon-keep, within a few paces of the tents, with
its dark round pit sunk fathoms deep beneath the
ground ; where no ray of heaven's light ever pene-
trated, and whence no effort of the captive could be
of the least avail for his escape. We thought on the
hopeless sighing of many a bondsman there, for whom
there was no deliverer ; while for us the Lord had
looked down from the height of his sanctuary to hear
the groaning of the prisoners, to loose those that were
appointed to death ; had brought us up out of the
horrible pit, out of the miry clay, and set our feet
upon a rock ; and had put a new song into our
mouth, even praise unto our God.

The old wives in their snow-white caps now rose

from their seats on the grass to take their places at the table, their widowed Lady amongst them, and the men following with backward and reverent air. The rest of the people, who were not partaking of the Supper, likewise rose; not departing, but standing compact 'like a living wall around the communicants in deepest reverence. As the bread and the wine were blessed and divided among the guests, the lofty heavens appeared to open clear to where the great High Priest standeth at the Father's right hand; and the blessing seemed to descend even sensibly upon the worshippers below:

> "There they sit, the men bareheaded,
> By their wives in reverence meek:
> Then the voice of pleading prayer,
> Cleaving slow the still blue air,
> All the people's need laid bare.
> Noiseless round that fair white table
> Hoary-headed elders moving
> Bear the hallowed wine and bread.
> Tender hearts, their first communion,
> Many a one was in that crowd,
> While far up, on yon blue summit,
> Paused the silver cloud."—*Kilmahoe.*

Seldom before or since did the good Duchess so enjoy any communion. As the blue sky in the heavens above met and kissed the green earth beneath, so the unseen above the heavens was revealed by the Spirit to the opened hearts of many; and together with her they were enabled and constrained to say, "God hath shined in our hearts, to give the light of the knowledge of the glory of God in the face of Jesus Christ. He hath spread a table for me in the presence of mine enemies, he anointeth my head with oil, and my cup runneth over."

We have given the scene from memory; but having since unexpectedly found it described by her Grace at the time, we must present it in her own words, though at the cost of rendering ours tame and superfluous: "*Huntly Lodge, Aug.* 5, 1847.—Now to tell of a time I hope never to forget. Friday was the fast-day; Professor M'Laggan preached in the morning, and Mr. Moody Stuart in the evening. For Sabbath Dr. Russell, who arrived on Friday afternoon, assisted to arrange a pulpit and two tents in the court of the old Castle, one for the elements, the other for our party. Oh! it was indeed a communion; the Lord was there evidently set forth before us, and not only set forth but present. God the Sovereign and Judge, God the Creator, without whom nothing was made that is made, is God the Saviour, Immanuel, the Lamb slain from the foundation of the world. There seemed truly nothing of man's making between us and the living God; a realization of being God's creatures, God's redeemed children, formed for himself, for his own glory. Mr. Dewar preached the action-sermon, after which Mr. M. S. fenced the tables, and addressed us, and served the first table. He told me he never had so realized the oneness of Jehovah in Three Persons. If we had seen the Heavenly Dove overshadowing us, and heard the voice saying, ‘This is my beloved Son, hear ye him,’ we should have been doubtless overwhelmed; but could hardly have had a more real sense of the presence of Him who made the heavens and the earth, the trees, the grass, and the new creature in Christ Jesus. Mr. Dewar served two tables and gave the concluding address; and Mr. Moody again preached in the evening on Isa. i. 18 : ‘Though your sins be as scarlet, they shall be as white as snow.’ Many were much affected, and the place was so beautiful! I hope the weather will permit our having the tents pitched again.”

Before we left the hallowed spot, the descending sun glanced on tower and battlement of the ancient Castle, which shone now to us like the walls and bulwarks of Zion. His rays brought up to the memory of others the words on the lintel that were shone upon so seasonably, in an hour of darkness, exactly twenty years before. For the Duchess herself those letters were graven on the tablet of her heart, and remained there as fresh as they do this day chiselled on the stone. In the long and varied interval, she had passed through anticipated scenes of greatness and unlooked-for days of sorrow :

"Both crowns and coronets were rent the while."

The ducal coronet had been placed on her husband's head, and now lay entombed along with him, to be worn by no succeeding heir. She had stood beside Queen Adelaide at the coronation of William IV., and his crown had been transferred to the brows of our youthful maiden Queen. She had wept as a widow for the husband of her youth, and her heavenly Father had wiped the tear from her eye; her spiritual light had been eclipsed for a season, and had shone forth brighter than before, never to be darkened again; her providential path in the Church had for a time been dark and perplexed, and now her way had been made plain, no more to become doubtful or uneasy. And now after proving the word of the Lord for so long a time, through judgment and through mercy, she could set her seal to His unfailing love and truth, and renew her grateful Amen to the treasured promise:

TO · THAES · THAT · LOVE · GOD · AL · THINGIS ·
VIRKIS · TO · THE · BEST ·

CHAPTER VIII.

THE CONTINENT.

1841–1857.

O'er many a weary mile,
And lonesome way, my child must roam,
   Far from the welcome smile
Of her own happy home,
      Through many a scene
      Of brighter green ;
Yet oft she'll wish she had the swallow's wing,
Back to the one loved spot her longing soul to bring.

      It is not that my child doth dwell
In high and spacious halls,
      For home is loved as well,
   Though mean and narrow be its walls :
      Sweet to the poor,
      Their lowly door,
And glad are they to reach the wicket-gate,
As proudest lord returning to his halls of state.

      There is but one sure HOME,
Where peace is ever found ;
      Whose links where'er you roam
Can never be unbound :
      It is the rest
      Of spirits blest,
When from the world they turn in HIM to dwell,
Whose holy peace alone its bitter strife can quell.

                         Lays of the Better Land.

DURING her widowhood the Duchess paid various visits to the Continent, for her own health, or for the health of her young friends who lived with her; partly also perhaps, from the habits of travelling acquired during the Duke's life; and once specially for the purpose of paying a visit to the Archduchess of Hungary.

In the end of 1841 she went to Pau for the health of her niece, Miss Sinclair; and she thus notices a poor woman, in whom she had been interested during her previous visit four years earlier : "I have received a most satisfactory account of poor Ninette. The doctor desired that she should be asked if she wished to see a priest; she replied, 'Oh, no! I want no priest; I am a Protestant, relying on the blood of Jesus Christ for forgiveness of my sins, and for acceptance before my God through His intercession.' She died happy."

"*Pau, 14th January* 1842.—I do trust that this is

to be a time of much blessing to my soul; and the little differences, which prevent amalgamation between many whom I believe to be God's children keep me closer to him, as I must take my own line and walk in the path which I believe to be pointed out of the Lord. In the meantime I have an occupation which leaves me in no doubt; and in needing and receiving help according to my need, I am encouraged to believe that I shall receive it for all other things. There is a poor young widow here with two little children; the doctor is surprised that she reached Pau in life. It is only within the last week she has consented to see me, instead of a clergyman; she likes me to be much with her, and, whenever she can bear it, allows me to read the Bible and pray. I feel greatly the responsibility, but I do also feel the unspeakable comfort of being employed in the Lord's service, and I hope that even at the eleventh hour she will be or has been called. She belongs to a family greatly opposed to the truth, and has been afraid to show that she wanted and hoped to receive strength from above; yet I cannot see any of that conviction of sin which makes a Saviour precious.—Annie's little schools are her pleasure; she has the children who came a few years ago, and two others they brought, with a little dwarf. On other two days, she has the Protestant school girls for religious instruction. Some of the children, and some of the parents also give satisfaction."

The Duchess mentions afterwards that she had a Sabbath evening service for her French servants, in which she appears to have taken great pains to instruct them; she was also engaged in translating the Shorter Catechism into French, although she feared it might not be simple enough for the people. The next letter is only a week later:—"*Pau, 21st January* 1842.—I believe that it was truly the Lord's will that I should come here. He has given me much work to do, and by means of Annie's health he hedges up my way so that I have little distraction in the path of duty. I have made two acquaintances, one of whom while she lived employed me entirely. I was privileged to be a comfort to her the last week of her life, and to speak to her of that Saviour who is able to save to the uttermost. The other is the wife of the banker at Madrid; she has lost her eldest boy, and is almost in despair. I trust it will please God to send the Comforter to lead her into all truth, and then she will find it good for her to be afflicted."

At Pau she made great efforts, and gave largely of her means in founding a church for the sake of a gospel ministry; and it continued for years after her return to be a subject of unceasing interest and earnest prayer.

The most interesting incident of the winter was the conversion of Manuel Fuster, a Spanish refugee, and a man of some education, having been designed by his parents for the priesthood. He was so destitute that her Grace's butler had charitably employed him to cut firewood for the house, and his clothing was so reduced to rags that she ordered some decent raiment to be given him, that he might work within the premises. As the Duchess passed out through the court in which he cut his billets, he was overwhelmed with gratitude on first seeing her, and fell down on his knees to thank her. She warned him that such homage was due only to the Most High, and spoke to him about his soul's salvation as she passed along day by day. She then gave him a French Bible, and when she went south for her summer tour left him reading the Scriptures daily with great diligence. On her return next winter to Pau, her maids saw Fuster breaking stones by the roadside, and on entering into conversation found him quite a changed man. In his zeal for the souls of his fellow-labourers he had lent one of them his French Bible, and was now in great distress because it had not been returned. But his sorrow was turned into double joy when the Duchess gave him a Spanish Bible instead; the word of God in his own native tongue was a blessing indeed, whereof his heart was glad. His spiritual progress was rapid, and his character thoroughly consistent. He was afterwards employed as a colporteur in France, where the people of a small village looked on him as their father in Christ ; then in Algiers, and now in Marseilles. His son, a youth of good promise, was educated by the Duchess for the Swiss ministry, and gave her great satisfaction ; but death deprived him of his benefactress before her kind purposes were quite fulfilled.

The next letters were written in the course of a tour which she made in summer. She greatly enjoyed both the beauty of natural scenery, and the architectural attraction of fine cities ; but wherever she went the Lord Jesus Christ was the chief desire and delight of her heart, and wherever she lived she left behind her the sweet savour of his name : "*Gibraltar,* 11*th May* 1842.—We find more and more reason to bless the Lord, that he has shown us his glorious gospel in its truth and fulness. Oh, how dreadful is the state of Spain, though perhaps not really worse than France. We had some very interesting conversations on board the steamer ; and I trust that they were in answer to the prayer that the Lord would let us say something for Christ, and that the words spoken being his own will be blessed. The steward frequently put himself in our way, especially one evening on deck when dark, and seemed very much pleased with a little Testament I gave him. I hope it will please God to enable us to be of some use here also, and to keep very close to Jesus, praying to be delivered from all evil, on the plea that his is the power, the kingdom, and the glory. As I am so far from home, I should like to see a little of Spain, and am told there is no difficulty in going to Seville from Cadiz, and to Grenada from Malaga. People seem most anxious to obtain tracts, and when we or the maids have given one, we have been followed to ask for more."

"*Gibraltar, 9th June* 1842.— Your letter of the 11th of May met me on my return from Cadiz. Through the goodness of our God, everything has prospered, and though I feel my difficulties greater and use-fulness less than in France, still I think the Lord's blessing has been with our journey ; and that it was his will, not only as the God of providence but as the God of grace, that I should come here. The cathedral and alcaza at Seville, the cellars at Xeres, and St. Michael's Church, and the city of Cadiz, so well built for coolness and so clean, are all worth seeing. Our reception at Xeres by the patriarchal family of the Gordons of Wardhouse was very gratifying. My plan is, if the Lord will, to go to Malaga on the 20th ; and I am very anxious to get back to France, and be among the mountains before the hot weather has

quite melted us. I bear the heat as well as possible
hitherto, but the mosquitos put me in mind of Beel-
zebub (the Lord of flies), and I feel that I need to
pray for patience. How frail we are, yet how strong
in the Lord. I have been studying Owen on the
130th Psalm; what courage the word of God can
give for his service, if we will but believe that word."

It is to a member of "the patriarchal family of the
Gordons of Wardhouse," referred to in the preceding
letter as long established in Spain, that we have been
indebted for many of the Duchess's letters in these
memoirs. The following was written from one of the
Pyrenean baths to Miss Home, who had accompanied
the Duchess in her former visit to France : "*St.
Sauveur, Sept. 7th*, 1842.—Everything here puts me
in mind of you; the Doctor, the *baigneuses*, the
porters, all inquire after you. Madame R. has lost
her son ; I hope to see her sometimes, and may grace
be given me to speak a word in season. Do you
remember a blind woman ? *She* speaks nicely and
seems interesting. We have found a very nice minister here. I enjoy this beautiful place extremely ; it
is even more beautiful than I remembered it. The
weather Monday and yesterday was magnificent, and
I was persuaded to order guides to be ready at
Baréges to carry us up the Pic du Midi. In the
morning Annie was unable to go ; but as the guides

and horses were gone I started with the maids and
men, and certainly a more glorious scene I never
beheld.   How *little* I felt! how great the Creator!
And he by whom all things were made is my own
Lord and Saviour, who died for me, and washed me
from my sins in his own blood, and has a fountain
open that I need every moment.   Alas! even though
his blessed Spirit is no less willing than the Father
and the Son to make me holy and happy, oh that
I could feel something of the love that Christ has for
his people; that I could feel a true influential love
for souls, and really go about doing good.

"The Pic du Midi de Bigorre is the third highest of
the Pyrenees.   I was nine and a half hours *en chaise
à porteurs;* many of the men the same as of old.
Such precipices, and such a sea of *pics* and hills could
not be imagined, unless seen; on the north side all
France is under your feet, and nothing but the atmosphere prevents you seeing it.   I think we shall stay
here for three weeks or a month longer."

Soon after this the Duchess felt deeply the tidings
of the death of the Countess of Denbigh, an old and
intimate friend, and held in the highest esteem.
"*Pau,* 13*th January* 1843.—The loss of my dear
friend makes me cling closer to those who are yet
spared to me, and I feel a desire to ask them if they
are ready, should they be called as suddenly as my

dear Lady Denbigh. Oh! it is a breach which must be felt like few others. To Lord Denbigh and his eleven children nothing in one sense can supply it; in another, it will be more than supplied if, looking within the veil whither she has entered to be for ever with the Lord, they trust to him alone for guidance. If such be the result, they will feel that it is well not only for her but for themselves. I cannot now write ordinary letters of New-Year felicitations; but I can congratulate those whom I believe to be one year nearer that freedom from sin and sorrow, which shall be the everlasting portion of those who are the Lord's people."

WURTEMBERG—ARCHDUCHESS OF HUNGARY.—1846.

The next visit to the Continent was an extremely interesting one to the Duchess, although from the peculiarity of its character we can present only a very brief notice of it. The Archduchess-Palatine of Hungary, Maria Dorothea, was well known to the Rev. Dr. Keith, who made arrangements with the view of forming an acquaintance between her and the Duchess of Gordon. She was herself a Protestant, being of the royal family of Würtemberg; her husband, the Archduke, was a Roman Catholic, but extremely kind and considerate to her, and she was allowed to instruct her children in the Scriptures. Her connexion with the Austrian Court made her position extremely trying, but she walked steadfastly in the narrow way, and clung to the Saviour whom she loved. When on a visit to her mother, the Duchess Henrietta of Würtemberg, at Kirchheim, the Duchess of Gordon with her nieces Miss Sinclair and Miss Calcraft, and Dr. Keith, stayed with her for eight days, during which the two sisters in Christ had much personal intercourse. They subsequently interchanged letters from time to time, and the Archduchess often expressed the satisfaction which this friendship afforded her, for to her the opportunity of Christian fellowship must have been rare. The letters from the Duchess to her correspondents at home were of necessity extremely cautious and reserved.

"Zurich, *Sept.* 5, 1846.

"My dear Augusta,—We left Dr. Keith at Stutgart, after having visited Kirchheim. I found iniquities prevail against me; my hands hung down; but through the infinite goodness of our God I have discovered, that it was just because I was not sufficiently thankful for unnumbered mercies. What base ingratitude! Instead of taking hold on the strength of Him who is the strength of his people, and of all the blessings and encouragements of the most faithful God, to go mourning in idleness; instead of obeying

the command 'Go forward,' waiting till the Lord
should do that which he commands and therefore
enables us to do, for 'God's biddings are enablings,'
because we cannot do all we would, we sit still and
do nothing. Oh, that is not the way of the living
child of the living God. May he give life, his own
holy life : and while convinced of the utter worthlessness and absence of all good in self, let us not
deny his grace and strength and power, for the joy
of the Lord is our strength, and we are called to
rejoice in his love and his salvation. We found the
Duchess Henrietta of Würtemberg a truly Christian
lady, and her admirable daughter all that we expected.
We cannot see her without feeling that she is a Christian indeed; all her proceedings are just 'What wouldst
thou have me to do?' but requiring the wisdom of the
serpent, as well as the harmlessness of the dove. There
is hope even of greater things than we had before
heard. I was induced to give up extending my
journey eastward, and turn my steps towards Stras-
bourg and Switzerland, as I found by so doing I
could be of a little use in gaining information for the
Archduchess. I now see how much the Lord has been
with us in mercy, and trust that yet more blessing
from the Fountain of Life will spring up of this
little tour."

This letter, as well as some portions of the pre-

vious correspondence, was written to the Honourable
Augusta Mackenzie of Seaforth, who was not an early,
but a highly valued friend of the Duchess of Gordon.
She gave her heart, her means, and her labour with
singular energy and devotedness to the Lord; quite
as entirely as the Duchess did. But with more acute-
ness of intellect and greater vivacity of temperament,
with lively wit and intense affections, she lacked the
quiet and slightly too great repose of the Duchess;
and at a much earlier age she sank exhausted by the
combination of outward effort for the good of the neglected in prisons and elsewhere, with constant spiritual
exercise in her own soul. So far as man can judge,
she was numbered here with the chosen virgins over
whom the voice from heaven saith, "These are they
which follow the Lamb whithersoever he goeth;" and
not many noble on earth, nor many hard-working
poor are now enjoying "the rest that remaineth"
above, more than the honoured Augusta Mackenzie.

The next letter is from Switzerland : "*Thun, Sept.
19th*, 1846.—We have much cause for praise, and
much for prayer. We have made a tour in scenery
which is of surpassing beauty. When will these most
lovely works of the Creator cease to be polluted by
idolatry? How marvellous does it seem that his
creatures should be so unwilling to acknowledge him
as he has revealed himself! All thine (inanimate)

works praise thee, O God! But while his people may truly rejoice in him, they have cause to sigh and cry for the abominations done in the land."

CANNES--1847, 1848—1855, 1857.

In the autumn of 1847 the Duchess, having suffered from repeated attacks of bronchitis, was advised to winter in the south of Europe. She left home, accompanied by Miss Sandilands and Miss Campbell, with the intention of spending the winter at Nice; but hearing that she was more likely to be useful at Cannes, she was dissuaded from crossing the frontier into Italy. " *Cannes, Dec.* 1847.—Constant occupation, and many many new opportunities of meeting with the Lord's people, and speaking of the glad tidings of great joy, have caused the delay in writing. I now know what fine climate is, and the country and views are beautiful; but above all, there is a field of usefulness that we could not have at Nice, and an open door for the gospel. Altogether, no tongue can tell the goodness of the Lord to us. He is letting me get glimpses both of his love and of his glory in the face of Jesus Christ, such as I never had before; and all this with such peace in outward circumstances! Is it not marvellous? You need not be alarmed about my 'exposition' on Saturday;

I feel too deeply my own incapacity to attempt anything beyond what I should say to an infant-school
at home. The people who come to it are either the
families of the servants I employ, or of the children
taught by Annie Sandilands. We live as quietly as
possible ; Lord Brougham sends me the newspaper
and bouquets of flowers ; other friends lend Caroline
their ponies, and do all kind things. Some young
English girls come here once a week to a Bible class,
and we have meetings every other evening at the
chapel at home."

"*Nice, May 9th*, 1848.—We left Cannes yesterday.
I never had such a parting in my life, and I may also
say I never had such a time of almost uninterrupted
peace ; 'kept by the mighty power of God' near to
himself, and in some little degree employed in his
service. Alas ! I feel like you, a most unprofitable
servant ; but then I know that He, who gave me the
desire to seek his glory and to live in his fear, looks
at his poor children not in themselves, but in his
Well-beloved in whom they are well beloved, and with
whom they are well pleased. The last fortnight there
were several more poor people inquiring ; and so far
the Revolution has given a feeling of liberty, which
the Lord may use to make some free indeed. I trust
that he has a little flock at Cannes. Our children
were just broken-hearted, and after we were gone

were roaring so that nothing could pacify them, but Monsieur Bettets taking them all into the drawing-room and praying with them. Those chiefly affected were little Italians, and indeed they seem to have much warmer feelings. There were some also of the Provençals quite overcome, but all of these looking to a reunion in our Father's house."

The last visit of the Duchess to Cannes was in 1855, passing through Brussels on the way. "I had a most pleasant visit to Brussels ; nothing could be more kind than the reception given me by the King and by the Duchess of Brabant." From Cannes she narrates to a young friend the dying triumph of struggling faith in one of those converts to Christ from Popery, who had interested her much on her first visit.

"CANNES, 27th Dec. 1855.

"MY DEAREST SUSAN,—We have had here a very remarkable example of the faithfulness of God. A poor woman, a mattress-maker by trade, whom I knew well when I was here before, was seized with cholera, ending in low fever. After a great deal of teazing by a succession of 'devout women,' which distressed her greatly, she asked to see the priest ; but when he came she said distinctly, 'Monsieur le Curé, je vous remercie beaucoup, mais je vous prie de ne pas revenir, je n'ai pas besoin de vous.' The curé, who throughout behaved with kindness and moderation, was rather displeased at having been sent for to be told not to come. She then told her relations distinctly that she would not have the priest, that she would only see Mademoiselle Charbonncy and Miss Sandilands, and that she would be buried by her pastor, Monsieur Boucher. From that moment her peace was uninterrupted. I called on her the next day; she was very happy to see me; she suffered dreadfully, but was very uncomplaining. On Thursday evening she fell asleep while we were there, and when she awoke we were all round her bed. I never can forget the joy of her countenance; it was a foretaste of heaven, a proof that the Lord's prayer was not in vain, that his people might be all one. Some one proposed to sing a hymn, and she joined in the chorus, with her feeble but distinct voice :

> ' Alleluia !
> Gloire a Toi, Jéhovah !' "

Her last letters from Cannes, addressed to Mrs. Hay of Fairlie, relate to the illness of her old friend Miss Home, whom however she was permitted to see again on her return to Scotland :

"CANNES, 18*th Feb.* 1857.

" MY DEAREST MRS. HAY,—I cannot persuade myself that I am not to see my dearest Helen again, but I know the Lord will do what is best for her and for those she loves. I would not withhold her from the sight of Jesus. It is a glorious thought, that her eyes will see and bear the light of the glory of God in the face of Jesus Christ; but it is hard to think of losing one who has loved me so long and so well, and who has been so faithful to me according to her light, even when I thought her wrong in her views, which did happen sometimes. Tell her with my kindest love, that Jesus is precious; she cannot hear it too often, well as she knows it. *March* 1857.—Your last letter, giving the hope that I shall again see dearest Helen on this earth, was most delightful to me. Truly the Lord is gracious."

INCIDENTS AT HOME.—1855-1858.

Between the year 1847 when the Duchess went first to Cannes, and the year 1857 when she returned from her last visit to the south of France, there was little remarkable in her life at home; and not very much in her large correspondence to bring out lines of thought which have not been already set before our readers. The Huntly Lodge narrative has been brought down already to 1847; and the twelve ensuing years, in so far as they were spent in Scotland, present slight variety in their quiet consistent course of personal growth in grace, and Christian usefulness in her sphere and neighbourhood. A narrative of this period might perhaps be drawn out more easily by a stranger. But being familiar with its daily unostentatious and simple details, we find ourselves incompetent to the task otherwise than by a mere accumulation of letters; and if we had room to multiply letters, the most important of those we have omitted belong not to this but to the immediately preceding period, which was perhaps the most spiritually active and fruitful portion of the Duchess's life, but has on this account already occupied a large space in these memoirs.

There being thus little outstanding material for a separate narrative of these years, we shall simply append to the present chapter a few extracts regarding Scotland : "*Huntly Lodge, 7th February* 1849. —The sermons of Charles Stuart (of Scone, her Grace's cousin) on Sabbath were most excellent. If he had done nothing else, I should owe him an unpayable debt of gratitude; for his view of the text 'under the curse,' Gal. iii. 10, in the morning, and of the whole of the 13th verse in the evening, was the most useful that I ever met with."

Soon after this her Grace had a settled pastor after her own choice in Mr. Rainy, now Dr. Rainy of the New College Edinburgh, who left Huntly to her great regret after a brief ministry of four years. "*Huntly Lodge, 3d Feb.* 1853.—I wish much you had heard our three last sermons from Mr. Rainy ; I never heard any more useful, striking, and impressive. I was particularly struck by the way he brought out the necessity of taking up the cross in these days ; in a real giving up of self, self-love, self-righteousness, self-pleasing."

Two months later we find her lamenting the death of the Duchess of Bedford, the only surviving sister of the Duke of Gordon, whose removal broke the last link with her husband's family circle: "*Huntly Lodge, 15th March* 1853.—You will see by the papers that my sister-in-law, the Duchess of Bedford, died at Nice. I feel her loss very much ; she was always as a sister toward me ; and the severance of the last tie which bound me to the generation that has passed away, and to which I belong, leaves a very solemn impression on my mind, which I trust will not be without effect. I had the comfort of being with her when in England last summer, and of having a good deal of serious conversation with her ; she was much occupied about her soul ; and I take comfort regarding her, from the accounts I receive of her latter end, that she was really through grace resting on the Saviour." A few years later she had a fresh sorrow in the death of her nephew, the Duke of Richmond : " My mind has been much absorbed by mournful circumstances. The death of the Duke of Richmond, and the feelings of regret and respect shown by all in this country, reminded me so much of my own great sorrow, and the feelings expressed throughout this country twenty-four years ago."

The last event that we have now to notice occurred the year after her return from Cannes; the death of her oldest, dearest, and most faithful friend, Miss Helen Home: "*April* 1858.—I am sure you will feel for me in the loss of my beloved and oldest friend, Miss Home. It is very selfish, and perhaps wrong to feel so deeply, when her great gain is so certain. But her very blindness and feebleness gave her more time to pray for me and others, and perhaps I leant too much upon her prayers.— *8th April.*—This is the day of Helen's funeral, and I have been trying to get some profit from the event, so much on my mind. I see infinite love and grace, but oh! I feel it hard to think she is no longer praying for me, though her prayers could only be accepted through Him who ever liveth to make intercession. He ever liveth, the living One and the life-giving One; he will hear I trust for us, as he is now realizing for her, the last expression of her feelings :

> More of thy Spirit, Lord, impart;
> More of thine image let me bear;
> Erect thy throne within my heart,
> And reign without a rival there."

CHAPTER IX.

THE CASTLE PARK.

1860–1863.

"I say to thee, do thou repeat
  To the first man thou mayest meet
  In lane, highway, or in the street;

"That he and we and all men move
  Under a canopy of LOVE,
  As broad as the blue sky above;

"That weary deserts we may tread,
  A dreary labyrinth may thread,
  Through dark ways underground be led;

"Yet, if we will One Guide obey,
  The dreariest path, the darkest way,
  Shall issue out in heavenly day.

"And ere thou leave him say thou this,
  Yet one word more: They only miss
  The gaining of that final bliss,

"Who will not count it true that LOVE,
  Blessing not cursing, rules above,
  And that in it we live and move."
TRENCH.

THE revivals in America and in Ireland were followed in the year 1859 by remarkable and extensive awakenings in the north of Scotland. For more than thirty years the Duchess of Gordon had passed through a varied and deep religious experience, adorned by a most consistent and attractive Christian life; and she had a mind capable of discriminating doctrinal truth, and delighted in this spiritual exercise. But there was nothing more remarkable throughout her course than her perception of the presence of the Spirit; whether in comfort or reproof, in personal teaching for herself, or in the Lord giving the word and making the company great of those who publish it. She was herself the work of the Spirit of God, and she quickly discerned the working of the Spirit around her.

In some periods of its history, there seems to be a strange division in the Church of Christ as regards the scattering of the word of life. The wisest and the

best appear often to have little aptitude, and sometimes little taste for the work ; while men of more de-
fective views, or less evenly balanced mind, are sent
to reap a great harvest. But the Duchess combined
heavenly wisdom and a beautifully fashioned character with prompt consent to become a fool for Christ
that she might win souls. She deeply and constantly
lamented how little, in her own estimation, she did
directly for the salvation of others, because from her
position those with whom she spoke were either apt
to be timid and reserved, or else to profess more than
the truth for some worldly end. This earnest and
ungratified desire to win souls made her eager to
embrace every opportunity in which her influence
might be of service in the cause of Christ.

How much her own mind entered into the loving
persuasions, which always characterize a time of
awakening, may be gathered from her manner of
writing to the daughter of a noble Lord, bound to
her by ties of old family friendship :

"MY DEAREST——: I trust you may have found
some word in the tract I sent you, which is comforting.
God is love, and has *so* loved the world that he could
do no more than he has done. He is quite willing you
should come to Jesus for all the fulness of his grace
and salvation, and the power of his Holy Spirit ; if
he were not willing he would not suffer me to tell you

so, for he cannot lie. Let me entreat you to roll your care on Him who careth for you; roll it, if you have not strength or energy to cast it, on Jesus our blessed Lord and Saviour, our most merciful High Priest, who was tempted in all points like as we are, yet without sin. His name is Love, for God is love. O put away thoughts of yourself, and only think how he loves, and what he has done and what he is doing. He freely offers you, without price or work, all the blessings he has to bestow. He would not put it into my heart to say so, or enable you to read his words of love and mercy, if it were not true that the full and free offers of his love and compassion are for you. Do look away from self, 'look off unto Jesus;' remember that he died for the ungodly and sinners, and saves to the uttermost; not to help our efforts, but to enable us to make them at all, 'for without me ye can do nothing.' "

In those times of awakening the Duchess threw open her house to the Lord's servants, Mr. Grant of Arndilly, Mr. Brownlow North, and Mr. Reginald Radcliffe whose efforts at Huntly were specially blessed. Mr. Macdowall Grant, whose forefathers were neighbours and friends of the Dukes of Gordon in times when the pleasures of this world were the great object in life, was giving himself with all his heart to the Lord's work in his own district, and was invited by the

Duchess to aid it at Huntly Lodge. "Lord, I have given this house to thee," was the speech of her heart as well as of her lips; and she asked those to visit her to whom she hoped a blessing might be given though his faithful conversations. Her hope was not disappointed, for the Lord gave her the exceeding joy of having souls born in her house among the guests whom she had invited for that end.

In the beginning of May 1858 the Duchess wrote: "We are to have prayer-meetings at the Cottage to-morrow for prayer for the outpouring of the Spirit. We had three last week, besides the Wednesday prayer-meeting at the church." A year after she wrote in reference to evangelistic efforts, most liberally aided by her, at the feeing-markets which had been formerly scenes of dissipation and quarrelling: "There were eight thousand tracts given away at the feeing-market yesterday; Mr. Williamson preached in the square, Mr. Mailler (United Presbyterian) gave the first address, and Mr. Troup (Independent) concluded with prayer." Six months later she wrote again: "18th Nov. 1859.—We had a glorious day yesterday; the Lord was truly with his poor people in the midst of the crowd at the feeing-market. . . . Oh that the Spirit of the Lord would come in power to Huntly! We do want greatly to realize the things we believe, to make them our own, and to witness the mighty operation of the love of God in overcoming all his enemies. If the truth of the eternal ruin of every unrenewed soul were really believed, there could not but be feeling ; how much more if there were faith in the unspeakable love of God in Christ Jesus." Many souls were awakened under these efforts, the Lord's people gave themselves to assist in the work, and company after company of anxious souls came to them and to the ministers and catechists for counsel. Of Insch the Duchess wrote : " 17*th Nov.* 1860.—The market at Insch was something wonderful, so different from former years. The eagerness to hear of Jesus was most earnest, the solemnity great, with the warm pressure of the hand of all around. The hall taken to speak to anxious ones was filled all day. The greatest wonder is that they did not see one intoxicated person, nor hear one bad word."

In January 1859 there was a meeting of ministers at Huntly Lodge of a very searching and quickening character; the ministers who were present being deeply impressed, and resolving to aim at a closer walk with God for themselves, and to strive for an awakening in their congregations. They held similar meetings at the Lodge frequently during the year, and in every one of their congregations some shower of blessing fell. Of her own neighbourhood the Duchess wrote : " *The Lodge, Huntly, March* 26,

1859.—It is singular to mark the various and yet similar dealings of the Holy Spirit with different cases. We have had some exactly similar to what you describe; and the work is going on, giving great joy and hope to all who desire the glory of God, especially to those who come immediately in contact with those who have, we trust, been effectually called. What strikes me much more forcibly than anything of the kind ever did before, is that the young converts are really *new creatures.* The giddy and vain have become thoughtful, happy, unselfish; the naughty and sulky have become so happy and obedient. Old men and women, and many young men, continue to attend the prayer-meetings. There is a great movement in Drumblade parish; hardly a cottage of any size that has not a prayer-meeting in the week for fifteen or sixteen among themselves. We have also cause in this place and connected with this house to thank him daily. Gifts have indeed been given to our Immanuel for the rebellious. Almost every day we hear of a new case of deep conviction and conversion among my people, or the young at the schools, or others. A young man, who has been long halting, was overheard disputing in the byre with an old self-righteous man, and saying, 'Na, na, that'll no do; if ye dinna get Christ *first* ye can do naething.'"

In January 1860 there was a much larger conferencé than that of the preceding year, and drawn from a far wider circle, when twenty-four ministers slept at the Lodge, some also staying at the manse, and those from the immediate neighbourhood returning home. At a public meeting in the church in the evening, they gave deeply interesting and most remarkable accounts of the work of the Lord that had taken place in their various districts. Throughout the winter and spring, the word of the Lord spread with amazing power through Aberdeenshire and the surrounding counties ; the fishing towns on the coast, the inland villages, the upland hamlets and farms, were visited with showers from the Lord of Hosts, "that waited not for man, nor tarried for the sons of men." Everywhere throughout the country the children of God were quickened. There were new-born souls rejoicing in the great salvation, anxious and awakened souls asking what they should do to be saved, and souls still dead in sins that were willing and even desirous to be addressed on the things that belonged to their peace.

The proposal was suggested if the Duchess might not throw open one of her parks for a great assembly for prayer and the preaching of the Word for two or three successive days. The circumstances were altogether peculiar. The people had never been in such a condition before, and might never be again ; hundreds were longing for an opportunity to praise the Lord for his mercy towards them, and thousands were more or less earnestly hungering for the bread of life. But the Duchess was by education and habit averse to novelty, and all her feelings were against publicity for herself. There was no light cross involved in such a step, with the scoff of the world, and the opposition of some valued friends. But her eye was single, she believed it to be the will of God, and gave herself to it with her whole heart and soul, and the Lord added his blessing abundantly.

The suggestion was made by Mr. Duncan Matheson, who had been her Grace's missionary in the district for many years; it was earnestly adopted by Mr. Williamson, on whom the chief burden would necessarily rest; and I must also accept the responsibility of a cordial concurrence. The Duchess herself wrote invitations, and sent them far and near to ministers and laymen of all denominations in England and Scotland to come to assist in this great work for the Lord. The time fixed for the meetings was on Wednesday and Thursday of the third week in July; and the site was the CASTLE PARK, which lay immediately after the entrance to the Huntly grounds through the archway in the centre of the schools. Both Huntly Lodge from top to bottom, and the adjoining houses, were thrown open for the crowded guests of the

Duchess ; and the good people of the town, moved by her example, exercised a large hospitality. The schools were filled with vast stores of provisions at the expense of the. Duchess, for ministers and their families, and for all whom they chose to invite ; while there were tents erected in an adjoining field for the sale of tea and coffee to the public. Everything great or little was arranged in the same beautiful order which always characterized Huntly Lodge.

But a dark cloud seemed to hang over the long-expected spiritual feast. All depended on the weather, for it was impossible to meet under rain. Whatever numbers might assemble, and however efficient the speakers, all would be scattered in disappointment to their own homes if the weather should prove inclement. The rain had been falling for weeks, to the great discouragement of all concerned ; and now on the 25th of July there was no brighter prospect. It seemed as if the Prince of the power of the air was bent on raising an outward obstacle to the inward work of grace ; and as if after all the preparations, the historic record might run, " but Satan hindered." But prayer was made unto God without ceasing ; the rain ceased before the people began to muster ; and though the clouds hung low all the first day, as if they must break at every moment, not another drop fell. The second and great day of the feast was bright and cloudless, and the rain recommenced only after the forenoon train of the day following had borne away the last of those who had lingered to the close of the blessed assembly. The crowds came, waited, and returned in the most perfect order; the fears of the timid even for the injury of the place were wholly disappointed; not a plant on the grounds was injured.

Her Grace had written to Herbert Mayo, Esq. :—

"Huntly Lodge, 16th *July* 1860.

"My dear Mr. Mayo,—I must give up all idea of going to Switzerland this year; there is too much going on here to admit of my doing so. The Lord needs likewise all the help my purse can give (and it is his own) for the young men who evangelize for his glory and the good of souls. I am very thankful to be able to tell you that the work in this country is prospering; Mr. Williamson is greatly owned of the Lord, especially in his evangelizing tours. He is going to-morrow with Duncan Matheson to itinerate for five days, and next week he has summoned a great gathering for open-air preaching, which will be held in the Castle Park. It is singular how well suited it is, having two or three places like amphitheatres on which the hearers can sit. Of course we are at present much occupied with the arrangements, but I trust that the Lord himself will be manifestly present

at the gospel feast, and that there will be more Marys
than Marthas at that time. The news from the coast
is most cheering; the change in whole villages wonderful; why may we not hope for the same here? Oh
pray for us; get all praying people to wrestle for a
blessing on Huntly and the district; and pray that
the Spirit may speak with mighty power in and by
his ministering servants on the 25th and 26th. There
will be many lay preachers, although Mr. Macdowall
Grant is quite laid up. Mr. North also is unable to
speak much, but he means to be here, and he may
perhaps meet some inquirers; Mr. Radcliffe has promised, *D. V.*, to come; Captain Trotter and his family
are to be here. I expect Mr. Moody Stuart and Mr.
Drummond and other ministers from Edinburgh, as
well as from other places, of all evangelical denominations who love the work. It is very remarkable how
the Lord is working everywhere; souls are prepared
to listen to the gospel, some of the most notorious
characters are convinced of the truth of the Word,
and are the means of convincing professors that they
do not act up to the standards of their Church.
Everywhere there is a readiness to hear, and for my
part I cannot doubt that the signs of the times are
such as to lead to the necessity of very close watching,
not only of one's own soul, but of the Lord's doings.
This is enjoined at all times on the people of God,

but now quite indispensable. So many, too, of the
people are evidently taught of God, and their prayers
carry up the heart of believers as the heart of one
man. The change in the fishing villages seems to
extend all round Scotland; in the neighbourhood of
Edinburgh, as well as in the North and East."

To a friend in Glasgow she wrote :—

"HUNTLY LODGE, 14th July.

"MY DEAR MRS. M'COLL,—We are very busy now
arranging about 'the gathering;' I went yesterday to
plant the tents, at least to fix the places. Truly the
field seems made on purpose for preaching stations ;
and if it shall please the Lord to bring many souls to
himself by the word spoken, we shall be sure that he
ordained the place and fitted it for his own glory,
even though partly by the hand of man, for it was
once the Castle Garden. The railway people are very
obliging. Children are to be sent from Aberdeen by
special train at tenpence a head, and a teacher gratis
for every twenty. I have invited the Fochabers
(Gordon Castle) children, about six hundred, to whom
I shall give tea and buns. There will be a platform,
with a canvas shade, below the bank in the West
Park, with a tent on each side (an arrangement
slightly altered afterwards), and five other tents in
the same field, besides the Duke of Richmond's large

tent on the top of the bank; refreshment tents will be in the East Park; but oh! what we want is the Lord's blessing. There is an awakening at Fochabers; Mr. Dewar has grown young again."

Another letter to the same lady is dated after the meetings were over: "*1st Aug.* 1860.—The blessings showered on the gathering by our heavenly Father are bringing forth fruit to his glory. Pitcaple has been again revived; and most of the small places between Pitcaple and Huntly are calling for help very urgently. But the most remarkable awakening was in a farm not far from here. Mr. Williamson went there on Sunday evening; I am told that thirty out of fifty in the barn were most deeply impressed, and many went away rejoicing. He has seen nothing like this except the first day he was at Hopeman; which had been quite awful, so that he could imagine nothing like it except the judgment-day. There is no excitement, but so much depth of feeling and earnestness. He is going to-day with D. Matheson to Glass market, of which the character used to be so notorious that it was a common saying that there would not be a good harvest if blood was not spilt there. Blessed be God *that* is all over.—I love to mark our Father's care in little things. There was much rain before the 25th, and that morning it was showery till ten o'clock. My housekeeper greatly feared the things that were

2 A

to be sent to the schools would not keep, especially the milk and the meat of which an ample supply was required. But she told me with grateful amazement, that both were preserved twice as long good as they had been for some time previously. Truly there was not one thing out of place or unseemly.—We are all so delighted with General Anderson; the meetings owe him a great deal, and to Captain Trotter also. The effect of their prayers, when all the people were kneeling in the open air, was overpowering."

The heart with which the Duchess entered into those great assemblies extended to every work for the Lord in the neighbourhood. "I must tell you that the meetings at Kinoir (about three miles from Huntly) have been so well attended, that neither barns nor houses would hold the people; and so I am going to put up a wooden kirk that will hold three hundred. . . . The Kinoir Kirk was opened last Lord's day by Mr. Williamson, and was as crowded as possible; the people greatly delighted, and many much impressed.—Have you heard of the wonderful work in the fishing villages on the north coast of Banffshire? Let me entreat prayer that the flood of blessing may extend to Port Gordon and Fochabers. . . . Hector Macpherson, whom I employ as a missionary, and who has been very much owned of the Lord in some places, is gone to Buckie. Mr. Williamson says the work in Port Gordon is wonderful, the whole village greatly moved; it has been a spot of much interest to me for nearly forty years. May the Lord himself carry on the work and extend it over the whole land."

Soon after the first large assembly a party went from Huntly on a missionary tour, which resulted in a permanent mission at Tomintoul, on the Duke of Richmond's estates. "*Aug.* 6, 1860.—Our friends came back from their Highland tour, all full of thankfulness and joy. The Lord has met with them everywhere; I should rather say gone with them, and given them tokens of his presence. At Dufftown, at Glenlivat, at Tomintoul, which was most interesting, there were meetings till late at night, and early in the morning; and along the roadside in picturesque glens, old and young and middle-aged coming out to stop the carriage, because they wanted to know if they could know that they were saved. Then a long way to Kingussie, where the 'cold clay soil seemed very stiff;' but still after the meeting at night, there were a hundred ready to meet them at six in the morning. At Alvie they were more impressible, but could hardly speak English; so some Gaelic-speaking Christian men remained with them. How blessed it is to feel that his hand guides everything that his omniscient eye looks upon; that eye of love and tenderness, which yet cannot look on sin even when laid on his own beloved Son." From the following spring till her death the Duchess supported a mission-station at Tomintoul. Mr. Anderson, who was selected by her for the work, was remarkably owned by the Lord, and she rejoiced greatly in the good that was effected through his devoted labours.

Large meetings, similar to those of 1860, were held in the three following years in the Castle Park, all of them marked by the same character of order and solemnity and the gathering of many thousands. The first was characterized by many tokens of the Lord's special presence, by much freedom and power in the speakers, by refreshing and lively joy and thanksgiving in the Lord's people, by the awakening of many of the dead, and by holy liberty granted to those that were bound. The number of persons then present was estimated at 7000, and in some of the subsequent years at 10,000. Of the last of those meetings the Duchess writes : "*August* 1863.—I cannot but wonder to see these meetings increasing in numbers and interest every year ; not as a rendezvous for a pleasant day in the country, but really very solemn meetings, where the presence of the Lord is felt and the power of his Spirit manifested.—I trust that I have been somewhat awakened by the preaching of our own minister, which has been very striking indeed."

CHAPTER X.

THE END.

. 1864.

HATH a snow air
　　Passed through the room, and clothed it thus in white :
What lieth there,
　　So hushed, so still, so shrouded from the sight ?
Cease rushing tears, be still, oh sobbing breath,
Let sorrow own the majesty of DEATH.

" With reverence
　　Draw down the covering, gaze upon the face,
With solemn sense
　　That sacred is the moment and the place,
One silent prayer, one gentle touch—and lo !
There sleeps the sufferer of an hour ago.

" Never again
　　Shall woe or care fall on that placid brow,
No moan of pain
　　May ever pass those lips so tranquil now ;
Her burden at His feet lies peacefully,
And ' Death is swallowed up in victory.'

" Grief stands apart,
　　And scarce dares look upon the holy sight ;
The mourner's heart
　　Is filled with a strange wonder and delight,
As prayer enclasps her hands within her own,
And casts her down before the great white throne.

" The glimmering morn
　　Pierces the shadows of the solemn room,
Where newly born
　　To endless life lies shrouded for the tomb,
She who yet speaks, with voiceless lips and dumb,
The awful words : ' Even so, LORD JESUS, come.' "

　　　　　　　　　　　　　　　La Duchesse.

IN January 1861 the Duchess was visited with a severe and all but fatal illness, which was inscribed by the Lord's own hand with all the characters of the believer's deathbed, except that He brought her up again from the gates of the grave, and prolonged her precious life for three years more. She had been unwell in December, and for the last time in her life personally entertained the children at the schools with a Christmas-tree, making an effort for the occasion to which her strength was unequal. She wrote : " 6th *Dec.* 1860.—I think of having Christmas-trees for the schools this year, of course covered with little presents ; I suppose I must provide for 600 children. I have thought over this matter, and had my scruples about it, but they are overruled ; I desire to do it to the glory of God. Children must have amusement, and if this is accompanied with good addresses, the little presents may sweeten the advice and cause it to be remembered."

One evening in the end of January, after some days of illness, she was suddenly seized with prostration of strength, and sunk into an extremely alarming state, accompanied with much suffering. But her soul was kept in unbroken calm and peace; and she gave directions, with faultless accuracy of memory, for various remembrances to be left to her relatives and friends. She then asked Miss Sandilands to repeat the hymn:

> " One there is above all others,
> O how he loves !"

and said, after it was finished, that she had been depressed for some time with a sense of her many sins, but that the Lord was now giving her tranquil and joyful rest. Next day, with that forgetfulness of self and thoughtful remembrance of others which always characterized her, she gave directions for some letters to be written by which she hoped to promote the welfare of several persons in whom she was interested.

The manner in which her soul was comforted, on that to her ever memorable night, she often related afterwards. There was nothing of the nature of a dream or trance; but as she lay sleepless, there appeared as if really before her eyes a white scroll unrolled, glistening with unearthly brightness, and with floods of vivid light ever flowing over it. Written at the head of the scroll, in large bright letters of gold, she read this inscription : " THE LORD OUR RIGHTEOUSNESS." All her darkness was dispelled in a moment : with the glorious words, the Spirit imprinted on her heart and conscience the fresh seal of the pardon of all·her sins ; she believed and knew that the Lord Jesus Christ was of God made unto her "righteousness," and that his blood had made her whiter than snow. Her soul entered in a moment into perfect rest ; the peace of God that passeth all understanding now kept her heart and mind through Christ Jesus ; and she rejoiced in the full assurance that for her to die that night was to depart and be for ever with the Lord.

Next day, at the desire of Dr. Wilson of Huntly, Dr. Kilgour of Aberdeen was telegraphed for, and ordered her to be kept quiet, fearing aneurism of the heart, and that she might be carried off at any moment. But she listened frequently to a few verses of Scripture or a short prayer or hymn, and sent messages to various relatives and friends, assuring them of the Lord's loving-kindness to her, and that the ground of her perfect peace was the finished work of the Lord Jesus. She found unspeakable rest and satisfaction in the fact, that it was so glorifying to God to save sinners through the righteousness and sacrifice of Jesus Christ. She regretted not being allowed at this

time to see the servants individually ; and sent to tell
them not to trust in a general way in the mercy of God,
but that each of them must be found in the Lord our
righteousness if they would be saved.   To her butler,
who had served the Duke at Gordon Castle and been
with her ever since, she spoke afterwards in such a
way as to make a deep impression both of her own
peace in the prospect of death, and of the importance
of the truth she urged on himself and others.   One
night to the doctor sitting by her she repeated the
whole of the hymn :

> " Just as I am, without one plea,
> But that thy blood was shed for me,
> And that thou bidst me come to thee—
> O Lamb of God I come :"

and added at the close, that it was only according to
the truth expressed in that hymn that any sinner
could find acceptance with God.   Two days later Mr.
Williamson conversed and prayed with her, and as he
left the room she said with a most joyous face, " Jesus,
the Lord my righteousness : *O how he loves !*"

Three days more brought her to the 2d of February,
a day memorable in her calendar as the anniversary
of the Duke's birth and of Lady Emily Montagu's
death.   She entered on it under some impression, that
it was to become still more eventful as the day of her
removal into the everlasting rest above.   But there
was no excitement or agitation ; she was calm and

peaceful as on the previous days, unencumbered by cares of any kind, and free from anxiety about herself or others. Meanwhile prayer had been made without ceasing by the Church on her behalf. The meetings in the Park in the previous summer had greatly extended the already large circle of those who looked up to her with esteem and Christian affection ; the value of her life to the cause of Christ in the district was felt to be inestimably great; and life preserved for so many days on the borders of death gave encouragement as well as opportunity for prayer. Some letters were brought into her room referring to the many prayers that were offered to God on her behalf; while they were read, her face slightly changed in colour and expression ; and she afterwards said, " I felt it rather trying to hear that so much prayer is made for the sparing of my life, deeply as I appreciate the kindness and love of my friends. Not that I should speak the truth, if I said it would make me *unhappy* to live ; for I have far too many blessings, and too much to make life happy, to regret living here for a time. But you know I shall never be freed from *sin* till I depart to be with Christ, and I do desire to be delivered from it ; and it was the thought of life continued in these circumstances that made the conflict in my mind." The conflict soon passed, and left her again in the same heavenly happiness. It is difficult to express the peace, holiness, and joy that filled her soul for days and weeks after that night, when the Lord was so gloriously revealed as her righteousness. The grace of God was indeed exceeding abundant toward her through Christ Jesus, and the fruit of the Spirit was in love, joy, peace, meekness, gentleness, faith, and patience. Her recovery from an illness so severe was slow and partial; it was the commencement of a comparatively invalid state; and after a few months apartments were fitted up for her on the ground-floor, which she occupied ever after. It was during this illness that she acquired the taste for learning hymns, which proved such a source of spiritual comfort and profit in her latter days. At its commencement one was frequently read to her, which begins—

> " A mind at perfect peace with God,
>   Oh what a word is this;
> A sinner justified through blood,
>   This, this indeed is peace."

The whole hymn expressed her own feelings; but she remarked that it would not be such a favourite without the second verse—

> " By nature and by practice far,
>   How very far from God:
> Yet now by grace brought nigh to Him,
>   Through faith in Jesus' blood."

After hearing it often read, she desired to commit it to memory; and having succeeded more easily than she expected, she proceeded to learn others, having them repeated to her line by line till she knew them by heart.

The following note was pencilled in recovering :—

"Huntly Lodge.

"My dear Mr. Moody Stuart,—I make the first use of my hand in writing to express the joy of my heart at the Lord's goodness to your family. . . . The Lord has been gracious to me far above what I can tell ; truly the half of his love to a most unworthy one had not been told me. Pray for me, my dearly valued friend, that I may not as aforetime forget these gracious benefits ; but that henceforth truly, with all my heart and soul and mind and strength, I may love and serve the Lord in Christ Jesus by the power of the Holy Ghost. *Huntly Lodge, 8th May* 1861.—I am very grateful for your kind letter, and must thank you for it myself, although my hand can write but very little. When first I was ill, and for weeks, through the wonderful grace of God I could see nothing but 'the Lord my righteousness ;' and I trust your letter is helping me to regain that 'perfect peace' in which the Holy Spirit can keep the soul by taking of the things of Christ. I know, my dear friend, that you pray for me ; oh pray that the life it has pleased God to prolong may be used for his glory alone. I long greatly to see you ; I have not yet been down stairs, and scarcely off my couch; perhaps when I get possession of the rooms prepared for me below, I may gain strength and get out of doors. But in regard to that and all else, I am well pleased that 'my times are in his hand;' I have not a wish but as he willeth. Oh that I could love and serve him more, who is altogether lovely."

THE END.

The Duchess spent the winter of 1862-3 in London, and enjoyed much of the society of her many friends in their morning visits to her in Queen Anne Street. After her return to Huntly in the following summer, the chief event in her spiritual history seems to have been the impression made on her mind by a sermon of her minister, Mr. Williamson, on Philippians iii. 8, " That I may win Christ and be found in him, not having mine own righteousness." She always enjoyed his preaching, and her letters testify the very high esteem in which she held him ; but the closing words of the chapter on the Castle Park allude to the special benefit she derived from this sermon. It brightened her countenance all the Sabbath on which she heard it, and was afterwards spoken of by her as a remarkable time in her history. "I thought my life was spared," she said, " to give the opportunity of devoting for a longer period my influence and substance to the cause of

Christ, but I see now a deeper meaning in it. There
is more personal holiness to be attained, more nearness to Christ, and more joy hereafter through a
deeper work here in my heart." Two aspects of mind,
partially unlike each other, now became more evident
in her day by day : one was an increasing persuasion
that she had still a lengthened period before her in
which to serve God on earth, and the other a rapidly
growing ripeness for the heavenly glory that was now
so unexpectedly near. In the beginning of the winter
she was forming plans for the following summer, such
as visiting the scenes of her youth at Kinrara, but
making the tour quite a missionary one ; while at the
same time her affections were more and more transplanted into the better country above.

"What a privilege it is," she wrote about this time,
"to see the work of the Lord prospering, though we be
but as the hewers of wood and drawers of water to
the great work. I can do but little, but I want more
of the spirit of prayer, and then I might hope that I
was filling up the measure by a drop or two. But I
can only look to Him who has done all, and will finish
all ; to Him be all the glory. Don't you love that
hymn on the last words of Rutherford :

> " 'The sands of time are sinking,
> The dawn of heaven breaks ;
> The summer morn I've sighed for,
> The fair, sweet morn awakes ;

Dark, dark hath been the midnight,
   But dayspring is at hand ;
And glory, glory dwelleth
   In Immanuel's land.

" ' Oh I am my Beloved's
   And my Beloved's mine,
He brought me, a vile sinner,
   Into his house of wine ;
I stand upon his merits,
   I know no other stand,
Not e'en where glory dwelleth
   In Immanuel's land.' "

A little incident of this autumn will serve to bring out the Duchess's habit of intercessory prayer, in which she had remarkable power and perseverance, never forgetting any person or object that had once engaged her interest. Unable now to rise early, she was in the habit of praying, meditating, or repeating hymns during the early morning hours. One morning at this time, when her maid who had been long with her entered the room, the Duchess said : "I awoke very early this morning, and have been very happy and busily engaged. My thoughts have been much occupied with three things all so different, yet each needing God's help to-day. The first is the Queen's visit to Aberdeen to inaugurate the Prince-Consort's Memorial ; the second is Mr. M.'s prayer-meeting in London in a hall that had been a dancing-saloon in his parish ; and (referring to a young man formerly in her service, but then studying for the ministry) the third is John's College examination."

Our space will only permit us to present extracts from three letters, written during the last month of the Duchess's life. The first is to Miss Marsh :—

"HUNTLY LODGE, *Dec.* 31, 1863.

"MOST BELOVED KATIE,—I have just received *your* card of prayer and note with your own dear words. Surely the prayer will be answered, and your wishes that are so much according to the Word of God. What unspeakable blessing to know that the work of. our sanctification is in the covenant of the Holy One, and for the glory of the one God; and that He will finish that work, as in the person of Christ he finished that of our justification. Should we not then 'lie down in his strong hand : so shall the work be done.' I am so fond of that hymn, always desiring to remember that it is the perseverance of saints and not of sluggards which we look for. The text which has been given me for the New Year I send you, 1 Peter i. 13, etc.: we shall indeed seek to pray with you."

The second is to the Countess of Aberdeen :

"HUNTLY LODGE, *January 12th,* 1864.

"MY DEAR LADY ABERDEEN, . . . Mr. Müller's letter is very nice; the wisdom of one taught of God. It appears to me that the faith to act as he has done is a special gift, quite independent of saving faith, and of a sort which is seldom given to those who have other claims besides those to which they desire to devote their energies. Where God gives wealth he gives responsibilities, and those he has given are not to be put away for any object, however interesting. I could not pray in faith for a supply of money for an object to which I did not feel myself specially called in a way of duty; and even if circumstances had formed claims before, the will of God was the paramount guide. I believe it to be duty to remain in that state wherein we are called. I fear I ought not to write on a subject which I am incapable of realizing from the claims which have been accumulating for fifty years, none of which I should feel myself justified in neglecting; but I could not pray in faith as Mr. Müller does, unless I could really do as he does, consistently with other duty—give up all to the one object.

"I have very great reason to be thankful for the measure of health I enjoy, but Miss Sandilands and my people take great care of me."

The last was to her niece Lady Sophia Cecil (Lennox), who accompanied her to the Duke's funeral, and to whom her letters testify the warmest affection. It was written by the Duchess within ten days of her own death, and refers thus to the death of a relative :

" But should we not rejoice for him since he had learned the way of peace, and had fled, I trust, from his sins to an almighty Saviour? Nothing can be more clear than the word of truth, 'Whosoever believeth on him hath everlasting life,' and it gives us good hope through grace."

In the end of the year the Duchess had a great desire for the renewal of the ministerial conferences, which had been first held at Huntly Lodge soon after her widowhood, resumed again from time to time, and found so quickening in 1859. A meeting was accordingly held on the 13th of January, which was felt by all who were present to be of a very awakening and encouraging character. The Duchess was deeply interested with the rehearsal of the conversation which the ministers had held together, and remarked : " I liked the meeting, and had only one thing to find fault with : some of the gentlemen prayed for me as if I was something, and I am nothing. I must speak about that before the next meeting." She warmly invited them all to meet again on the 10th of the following month, but it was an invitation to her funeral. Between the 13th of January and the 10th of February there intervened the unexpected summons of death; withdrawing now the Duchess Elisabeth from the holy conference, as fifty years before it had withdrawn the Duchess Jane from the

gay assembly.   To saint and sinner both the Son of
Man cometh in an hour that we think not; and the
day appointed for the next conference at Huntly
Lodge was the day after her Grace's burial, when the
invited ministers were assembled with others to mourn
over her grave.

Her last illness, which was found to be gout in the
stomach, gave little time for prayer on her behalf;
and was at first so slightly alarming as to defer any
urgent call for supplication.   Indeed she was never
herself aware of her dying condition; not knowing
at first the attack to be really dangerous, and then
sinking rapidly into a state of mental unconscious-
ness, though far from one of bodily ease.   During the
three first days of illness she reverted frequently
to spiritual things; and desired, when she felt able,
to listen to a few verses of Scripture, or to a hymn,
or to join in a brief prayer.   She lamented her own
inability to think; but when the words were given
her, "I am poor and needy, yet the Lord thinketh
upon me," she replied, " Yes, that's it : ' In thy strong
arms I lay me down :' " quoting the line of a hymn
she had frequently repeated to her friends during the
preceding weeks, and of which she had said the last
time but one that she was out : "That hymn more
than any other expresses the present state of my
feelings :"

"I only enter on the rest
  Obtained by labours done;
I only claim the victory
  By Him so dearly won.

"And, Lord I seek a *holy* rest,
  A victory over sin;
I seek that Thou alone shouldst reign
  O'er all, without, within.

"In quietness then, and confidence,
  Saviour, my strength shall be;
And '*Take* me, for I cannot *come*,'
  Is still my cry to Thee.

"In Thy strong hand I lay me down,
  So shall the work be done;
For who can work so wondrously
  As an Almighty One?

"Work on, then, Lord, till on my soul
  Eternal light shall break;
And in Thy likeness perfected,
  I 'satisfied' shall wake."

Before the mind became wholly insensible to outward things, and for thirty-six hours afterwards, the last enemy seemed to the onlooker to wrestle with her in a painful struggle of bodily distress. On the evening of the 29th, making an ineffectual attempt to ask for something, Miss Sandilands at last repeated the words, "My Beloved is mine, and I am His." "Yes," she replied sweetly and calmly; but from that time made no further attempt to speak, or to respond to any spiritual sentiment. Beyond this she left no dying testimony nor any parting words. She sank finally into the repose of the last sleep at half-past seven on Sabbath evening, the 31st of January, in her seventieth year.   "All His saints are in his hand ; He must increase, but they must decrease."

No member of the Church of Christ in Scotland could have left a wider blank by removal, or be more deeply lamented by a large circle of mourners far and near, in all ranks and of all denominations. The company that assembled in the house for the funeral included a small number of her Grace's nearest relatives, and the larger circle of her household. They met for devotional exercises around the coffin, which was laid in the large sitting-room occupied by the Duchess for the last three years, where the lively associations with herself in this life enhanced their sorrow ; while the snow-whitened trees without, and the walls within draped in white as if "a snow-air had passed through the room," seemed to relieve the gloom, by their harmony with the white robes· in which she now stood before the Lamb above. The spectacle was deeply affecting as the funeral passed through Huntly. All work was suspended in the town, the shops closed, the places of business vacated, and the schools set free, one object engrossing rich and poor, young and old. At the gate of the Lodge the funeral was met by a large procession of many hundred mourners, and by nearly seven hundred children from the schools built and supported by her Grace. In the town it was lined on both sides by crowds with sorrowing hearts and weeping eyes; the spectators gazing with no vacant or curious stare at the plumed hearse, followed by the carriages of the more immediate mourners, but looking with wistful grief on the last they were to see on earth of their beloved and honoured Lady; and the mourners com forted in their own affliction by the rare sympathy of a sorrow at once so wide and so deep. Her life had been passed amongst them for half a century, with the exception of a break of nine years spent at Gordon Castle; it had been mingled to nearly all with their longest, to most with their earliest, and to many with their happiest associations; many were mourning for the loss of a personal benefactor, and all as if for the loss of a personal friend. Conveyed thirty miles by rail, the funeral passed through Elgin, in the midst of deep silence and respect and universal regard, to the burying-vault of the Dukes of Gordon in the noble Cathedral; the coffin was placed beside her husband's in the last space that remained untenanted by the deceased wearers of the ducal coronet and their children; and till time shall be no more the vault was for ever closed on the last and the best of an illustrious race, who had ennobled the title far more than it could ennoble her.

On the following day the first man that we chanced to meet, thinking that he spoke to a stranger, made these remarks in these exact words, while the tear moistened his aged eye : "This is the greatest calamity that ever befell this district ; of a' the Dukes that reigned here there was never ane like her ; there's nane in this neeghbourhood, high or low, but was under some obligation to her, for she made it her study to benefit her fellow-men ; and what crowds o' puir craturs she helped every day ! And then for the spiritual, Huntly is Huntly still in a great degree, but the gude that's been done in it is a' through her." The next but one upon the road was a soldier, who had seen hard service in the Crimean trenches amidst the flowing blood of friend and foe. His countenance was changed by the force of a sorrow only beginning to subside ; it was too evident that his tears had been both many and bitter ; and even now he could not command his strong emotion, but broke out at once : "You know that I have seen much to render my heart callous, but I never was unmanned till now ; I never knew before how tenderly I loved that honoured lady." A third man, a devoted follower of the Lord and once a faithful servant to her Grace, wrote at the same time that if it were lawful, "he could wish to die with her, and to serve her in heaven."

On the Christian character of the last Duchess of Gordon, we shall not add much to the delineation traced by her own letters. Her progress throughout was marked by the deliberation and slowness with which she took every step at first, and by the firmness with which her foot was planted on the ground that had once been gained. The fulness of righteousness in Jesus Christ imputed to every believer, the penal satisfaction to Divine justice on the cross, the Divine sovereignty and eternal election, the love of God to a perishing world, the work of the Spirit in renewing the heart, the fruit of the Spirit in holiness of life, the joyful assurance of faith and the lively hope of life everlasting, were both firmly grasped by her as doctrines of Scripture, and practically submitted to, received, and rejoiced in with her whole heart.

Side by side with her glorying in the cross of Christ as all her hope, there was a prompt, patient, and courageous taking up of the cross and bearing it after Jesus. Her Christian character was thoroughly practical from the first, and the knowledge of the Lord's will was followed step by step with walking in the Lord's way. Two deeply-rooted natural dispositions made her carrying of the cross often peculiarly painful. One of these was an intense love of order, with dislike of all change, and deep aversion to disturb the settled economy of the social world; while the firm witnessing for truth and the earnest spreading of the

gospel message often led her into steps which, to a
heedless world or a slumbering Church, savoured only
of innovation, and seemed like "turning the world
upside down." The other was great natural amiableness of disposition, in which her friends rejoiced as
one of her chief attractions; but which she spoke of
with a mixture of severity and truth as an excessive
desire to please, and often lamented as one of her
most easily besetting sins. Her position of rank and
influence with ample means at her command, placing
her in the midst of a wide circle; her talents and
accomplishments rendering her a most attractive
centre; and a marked and fascinating individuality of
character, all gave a power of pleasing many in various
ways, with a corresponding temptation to please the
world in its more plausible demands. But grace so
sanctified nature wherein it was innocent, and so
overcame it wherein it was evil, that she boldly and
steadfastly carried the cross through all gainsaying
and reproach; at the same time so walking in love,
so providing things honest in the sight of all men, so
thinking of whatsoever is lovely and of good report,
so immovable in her friendships of every kind even
when they proved unworthy of her, so kind and faithful to every dependant, and so urbane to all, that even
those whose views most differed from her own probably admired and loved her more as she was by the

grace of God, than as they would themselves have had her to be.

Her increasing fruitfulness with increasing years was marked and evident to all who knew her. Others sometimes fade in old age; grace seems in them to become less lively by abatement in the warmth of the natural affections or by the world occupying more space in the heart. But with her the growth was constant and decided, and only more abundant in the last three years of her life. Jesus Christ alone is the same yesterday, to-day, and for ever; but he hath said, Because I live, ye shall live also. He loved her, and gave himself for her, and revealed himself to her; and having loved, he loved unto the end, and through grace she abode in his love. Continuing to love Him who had first loved her, she brought forth fruit in old age to show that the Lord is upright; and to the very last hers was the path of the just, "like the light that shineth more and more unto the perfect day."

It is told of one of the Dukes of Hamilton, who died in early youth, that he called his younger brother to him the day before his death and said, "To-morrow you'll be a Duke and I'll be a King." This beloved mother and princess in Israel wears the ducal coronet no more; but her spirit mingles with the kings and priests above, where she casts her crown of glory before the Throne, saying "Thou art worthy, O Lord, to receive honour and glory and power : unto Him that loved us and washed us from our sins in his own blood, and made us kings and priests unto God, unto him be glory and dominion for ever and ever. Amen."

While we mourn her departure, let us rejoice in her everlasting rest, let us ask grace to follow in her footsteps, and let us prepare to meet our own hastening summons for the Great Day :

"Another old friend is gone,
    Another familiar face ;
Another has laid her burden down,
    And finished the weary race.

"Peace with her gentle hand,
    Has quieted one more breast ;
There's another soul in the spirit land,
    There's another spirit at rest.

"Patience : time fleets apace ;
    The Present soon grows the Past ;
Others are swifter upon the race,
    But our time will come at last.

"See that the lamp burns bright,
    For the way is dark and unknown ;
None may aid us to gain the light,
    The path must be trodden alone.

"Patience : we stand and wait,
    Till in trembling we rejoice,
And we pass the eternal gate
    At the sound of the Bridegroom's voice."

EDINBURGH : T. CONSTABLE,
PRINTER TO THE QUEEN, AND TO THE UNIVERSITY.